# PLAUSIBLY DENIABLE

**BAEN BOOKS**
**edited by Jamie Ibson**

*Plausibly Deniable*
*Depth Charge* edited with Hank Davis

To purchase any of these titles in e-book form, please go to www.baen.com.

# PLAUSIBLY DENIABLE

EDITED BY

JAMIE IBSON

BAEN

PLAUSIBLY DENIABLE

This is a work of fiction. All the characters and events portrayed in this book are fictional, and any resemblance to real people or incidents is purely coincidental.



A Baen Books Original

Baen Publishing Enterprises
P.O. Box 1403
Riverdale, NY 10471
www.baen.com

ISBN: 978-1-6680-7319-3

Cover art by Kurt Miller

First printing, March 2026

Distributed by Simon & Schuster
1230 Avenue of the Americas
New York, NY 10020

Library of Congress Cataloging-in-Publication Data

Names: Ibson, Jamie editor
Title: Plausibly deniable / edited by Jamie Ibson.
Description: Riverdale : Baen Publishing Enterprises, 2026.
Identifiers: LCCN 2025043490 (print) | LCCN 2025043491 (ebook) | ISBN 9781668073193 trade paperback | ISBN 9781964856544 ebook
Subjects: LCSH: Science fiction, American | BISAC: FICTION / Science Fiction / Action & Adventure | FICTION / Science Fiction / Collections & Anthologies | LCGFT: Science fiction
Classification: LCC PS648.S3 P58 2026 (print) | LCC PS648.S3 (ebook)
LC record available at https://lccn.loc.gov/2025043490
LC ebook record available at https://lccn.loc.gov/2025043491

Printed in the United States of America

10 9 8 7 6 5 4 3 2 1

This one's for the late great Jack Clemons.
Live big, live loud. Become ungovernable. Keep a "My Bad $20"
and a trap hoodie on standby at all times.
—Jamie Ibson

## ACKNOWLEDGEMENTS

Many thanks to all of my contributors for this anthology, my first with Baen as me being the guy herding the metaphorical cats. This was my first time editing several of the contributors here, thank you for being your awesome selves and making it easy.

Special thanks go to Sharon Cauthen, for granting me permission to reprint "Bag Man" in this anthology. I invited Jack Clemons to contribute to my first anthology, *We Dare*, back in 2019, and he turned in one helluva cyberpunk story that has stuck with me to this day. It was gritty, it was stylish, it was badass, and it went out on one helluva "oof." I bugged Jack for several years afterwards to write more, but unfortunately it didn't happen. Jack kicked in the doors to Valhalla on May 4th, 2024, and Odin's hall hasn't been the same since. Miss you, big guy.

# CONTENTS

**BLOOD AND CIRCUITS**—Jacob Holo & Edie Skye
1

**BAG MAN**—Jack Clemons
25

**BACKUP PLANS**—Jason Cordova & Melissa Olthoff
49

**ONE LAST CHANCE**—Jody Lynn Nye
77

**THE HUNTER BECOMES THE HUNTED BECOMES THE HUNTER** —Craig Martelle
101

**WHEN IT COUNTS**—Marisa Wolf
127

**OFF DUTY**—Casey Moores
153

**NO EXTRADITION**—Kacey Ezell & Nick Steverson
179

**SUPPLIES PARTY**—Michael Z. Williamson & Jessica Schlenker
213

**BUFF ORPINGTON CROSSES THE FINNISH LINE**—Buff Orpington
245

**ABOUT THE AUTHORS**
275

**ABOUT THE EDITOR**
279

# BLOOD AND CIRCUITS

## A Sol Blazers Short Story

Jacob Holo & Edie Skye

Aiko had seen this movie before.

A spaceship of Average Joes and Jills just minding their own business when suddenly a uniformed stiff with a secret military budget shows up and says, "We have a problem, and your unique set of skills just happens to be the solution."

There were a handful of sentences a woman—well, preserved consciousness spread across multiple synthetic bodies—wanted to hear in her life, and she'd spent her entire extended life (and most of her meat life) waiting to hear *that one.*

Today she'd chosen the body best suited for it: fashionable combat android, red armor accented with gold filigree, triangular head as sharp as an axe wedge, leather jacket she didn't need for warmth but deemed necessary for maximum badassery.

In short, she looked the part.

Trouble was, she couldn't figure out why the man needed *her.* It wasn't like there was a shortage of people in the solar system who'd shoot stuff for pay. But he'd requested her by name, so now she and her captain stood outside the *Neptune Dragon* while their potential employer strode to meet them.

Her initial characterization wasn't exaggerated. He was a uniformed brick right down to his hard-lined blocky face and clay-red skin, modified from human baseline. The rest of that angular body was clad in a dark green uniform with black trim, tailored so precisely it looked like he'd been born in it. A patch bearing the black silhouette of a horse rearing marked him as belonging to the Neptune Concord Space Force, while his rank insignia designated him a commander.

He looked like the kind of man who could bust heads, whether by his own hands or through a well-targeted order. The kind of man you could throw through a window, and *he'd get the problem solved.*

There was a pinch in his face as he approached them, as if to say *he* wanted to be the one breaking the window but had somehow been forced to throw her through instead.

Or maybe he'd just glimpsed her captain.

If the commander was a solid brick, Captain Nathan Kade was a weathered stone that had seen a hard season of messy storms and needed a good pressure wash. He'd prepared as best he could for the potential client, but the fact was their recent jobs had pitted them against a crazed, world-ending superweapon and an invisible monster in search of love in all the wrong places. Those sorts of adventures took their toll on a person.

Aiko didn't grow tired and rarely worried about risking life and limb. Sure, she had to avoid being shot or exploded (again), but even then the most she'd lose was her current body and a handful of unpreserved memories. In some ways, she rather regretted that she'd never look tired for her captain.

In his own rough leather jacket, with that coarse stubble, the old adventure scars, the huge pistol strapped to his muscular thigh, that tousled brown hair—Nathan made tired look good in a way that put her fully back in her meat brain.

He extended a strong hand to the approaching naval officer.

"Welcome to the *Neptune Dragon*. I'm Captain Nathaniel Kade, and this is my second-in-command, Aiko Pratti."

The man greeted both of them with a handshake as solid as the rest of him.

"Commander William Hughes," he declared in a gruff, clipped voice. "Special Operations Officer aboard NCSF *Azure Eagle*."

"A pleasure, Commander. Aiko tells me you've got a job for us."

"Yes, though I can't discuss the details out here." Hughes made a circular gesture, indicating the docking bay the *Neptune Dragon* sat in.

"Naturally." Nathan gestured toward his ship. "If you'll follow us, Commander."

Aiko had looked up both Hughes and the ship he served on before this meeting. She hadn't found much information about the man, but

*Azure Eagle* was a truly gargantuan vessel—a cruiser capable of wiping the floor with anything short of a Saturnian or Jovian warship. Commander Hughes squeezed into the small side room and dropped into his seat like he was accustomed to having more space, which was probably true.

"There's a piece of trouble the NCSF would like to see taken care off," Hughes began once Nathan and Aiko were settled across from him. "Quietly and discreetly."

"How discreetly are we talking?" Nathan asked.

"NCSF involvement must be kept a secret."

"Well." Nathan shrugged his arms. "That sort of discretion comes at a premium."

"My superiors are aware of that." Hughes produced a vlass tablet and slid it over. Nathan spun it around and read the bottom line. Suddenly he looked a lot less tired.

"That's . . . what I would call 'reasonable compensation' for discretion."

Nathan slid the vlass over to Aiko, who whistled without lips.

"Now the question becomes," her captain went on, "why can't the NCSF handle this themselves?"

"The problem involves a foreign warship."

"Ah. Then you're trying to get rid of the problem without provoking an interplanetary incident?"

"Precisely." Hughes tapped a button on his tablet, and an image of Neptune appeared, its equator girdled by the green-blue ribbon of its orbital ring. He zoomed out, and icons for the hundreds of nearby habitats flooded the screen.

"There's a situation on a habitat called the Broken Bottle."

He zoomed in on one of the sorriest excuses for a habitat Aiko had ever seen. It looked like it had once been a windowed cylinder, but now resembled debris from a drunken bar brawl. Only one end remained—a disk eighty-five kilometers across and one kilometer thick, with metal teeth forming a jagged crown on one side along the rim, completing the illusion of the bottom of a shattered bottle.

"That's some prime real-estate there," Nathan grumbled.

"We believe the Broken Bottle was nearly destroyed four millennia ago during the Scourging of Heaven. It's considered worthless, and for good reason. Not much habitable space, and no deifactories or other lost technology. It's currently leased to the Saturn Union, which subleased it to the Tarsho Syndicate."

"Should we assume they've been up to unsavory business in Neptune's backyard?" Nathan asked.

"We have our suspicions, but can't act upon them," Hughes explained. "The problem is a legal one. Technically, because of the agreement between the Neptune Concord and Saturn Union, the Broken Bottle is Union territory for the duration of the lease."

"Which means you don't have the authority to move in," Aiko said.

"Correct. Given the current political situation, the NCSF is only allowed to enter the Broken Bottle under extreme circumstances, such as violation of the terms of the lease or a disaster requiring our aid. Evidence of criminal activity would also satisfy that requirement and allow us to move in."

"So, you'd like someone unassociated with the NCSF to go in and get the evidence." Aiko sat back. "Someone like us."

"Plausible deniability is key."

"Do we know who's in charge of this little enterprise?" Nathan asked. "You said it was leased to the Tarsho Syndicate."

Hughes tabbed over to a pair of images on his vlass.

"The two key players are Captain Alfonso gen Arturikk, in command of the Saturn Union Navy destroyer *Echoes of Flame*, and Director Xavier vaan Tarsho. We understand the latter's something of a rising star within his family's syndicate."

Aiko leaned in to better study the men. Both were baseline humans with cybernetic enhancements, but where Captain Arturikk's were slick and subtle, Director Tarsho's were conspicuous and boastful, perhaps even intended to draw attention to themselves.

"And by 'rising star,' you mean . . ." Aiko prompted.

"Rumor is the last subordinate to get in Tarsho's way was found hung from a meat hook." Hughes grimaced. "Alongside the rest of the man's family."

"And that makes him a rising star?"

"In his family, apparently so."

"Lovely."

"We believe these two men," Hughes continued, "are conspiring to utilize the Broken Bottle as a staging area for illicit activity near Neptune. The nature of the activity is unknown, but *Echoes* makes regular circuits of both the leading and trailing Trojan habitats, picking up unknown cargo and transporting it to the Broken Bottle."

"The Neptune Trojans?" Nathan frowned. "What's out there that has them so interested?"

"We don't know."

"Any idea who or what they're transporting?"

"They have declined to provide manifests, citing the"—Hughes sneered—"legally-correct fact they're not setting foot on Neptunian soil."

"And you'd rather not pick a fight with a SUN warship to search them," Nathan surmised.

"Exactly."

Nathan glanced once more to the vlass, then nodded slowly. "The job seems straightforward enough. Go in, secure the evidence, get out." He looked up. "Why us?"

"You're the only freelancers in the solar system with a Jovian stealth corvette." He indicated their surroundings. "You'll be able to infiltrate the Broken Bottle undetected, even with that destroyer nearby."

"True," Aiko said, "but stealth is going to be a problem once we're inside."

"Which is one of two reasons we specifically requested you." Hughes met Aiko's cameras with a steady gaze. "We have a body you can use."

"I have plenty of spares."

"Not one with this kind of weaponry, I'd wager."

Aiko tilted her head. "Okay, you've got my attention."

"Firearms *are* the fastest way to your heart," Nathan teased, then his expression turned serious. "What's the second reason?"

"This." Hughes tabbed over to another page on his vlass. "I believe you're already acquainted with Prinn Pratti."

The woman in the picture was blue-skinned and silver-eyed with a long white braid slung over a bare, slender shoulder. Despite Nathan's joke, Aiko didn't have a heart anymore, but she still felt an emotional jolt upon seeing her.

"Of course I do," she replied after a long pause. "She's one of my copy-clan sisters. She's basically another version of me."

"She's Tarsho's girlfriend."

⟡⟡⟡

"That doesn't make sense." Aiko crossed her arms once she and Nathan were alone. "All of the Pratti branches have some predisposition for deviancy. I mean, all you have to do is look at yours truly to see that! But we're not *criminals*!"

"Seems Prinn is," Nathan said.

The Jovian Everlife was composed of copy-clans: singular minds spread to multiple bodies and regularly re-integrated to maintain the intellectual coherence of one being. That was why Aiko couldn't bring herself to believe Prinn would involve herself with a scumbag like Tarsho. She and Prinn were, in many ways, the same person.

"Maybe one of Prinn's copies went bad," Nathan suggested. "Or perhaps she made some bad choices and is in over her head."

"Maybe..." Aiko sighed without exhaling. "Whatever's going on, I need to go in there."

"You know that's what Hughes wants. Prinn's the bait for us to accept this job."

"Don't care. She's my sister. Hell, she's practically *me*! I need to do this, Nate. I need to know why she's hooked up with Tarsho."

"All right." He spoke those words with an undercurrent of sympathy borne from countless close calls together. "But can you do sneaky?"

Nathan looked her up and down. She would have been flattered if she hadn't been in her bombastic commando body. (Oh, heck, she was still flattered.)

"Depends on the body they have in store for me," she replied with a shrug.

.

"Oh, this'll *definitely* work!"

The body put her in mind of a femme fatale, and there was a gun hidden in the forearm.

Specifically, the entire right forearm unfolded into a veritable cannon that, despite a barrel that looked designed to fire ballistic shells, discharged energy beams with a dull *thwomp*. It shot *energy beams* as silently as a dead body falling on a bed, with multiple settings from stun to "Where'd he go?" She'd never heard of an energy weapon this miniaturized, and when she asked Hughes about that, all he said was it involved lost technology and had taken an obscene amount of paperwork to requisition.

That was good enough for her.

There was plenty of femme in that fatale, too. The body was sleek and lithe, adapted for all manner of infiltration with curves that could exploit . . . a multitude of meat bodies' weaknesses. She showed off those curves to her captain and even made him blush a little before returning to all business. The job was to be a dangerous one, and both of them needed to keep their heads in the game.

Several hours later, the Broken Bottle loomed ahead of the *Neptune Dragon*'s slow approach.

"We'll drop you off near the disk's center," Nathan said. "You'll need to make your way 'down' to the outer edge, where gravity is about one gee."

"No problem," Aiko replied. "Zero-g? One gee? Three? I fought in them all back in my commando days."

"How about 'sneaked'?"

"That, not so much."

The *Echoes of Flame* lingered nearby, resembling a skyscraper plucked into space and slathered with guns and armor.

There were more weapons on the habitat—SUN missile batteries, courtesy of the *Echoes of Flame*. Aiko studied them through the *Neptune Dragon*'s telescope.

"Looks nasty. I bet those missiles could pop a cruiser."

"Arturikk placed them there to protect the habitat when his ship isn't nearby," Nathan said.

"And they don't violate the lease?"

"Not unless they do something dumb like shoot down unarmed merchants."

"Still, I bet firing them would be an easy way to draw *official attention*." Aiko wagged her eyebrows. She liked having eyebrows for a change.

"Resist temptation. You're supposed to be stealthy."

"I'm only kidding."

The *Echoes of Flame* vanished from view as they slid beneath the disk's dark side, heading toward the central dock. The outer door had been bent open by some ancient calamity. Aiko maneuvered them inside and then set them down within one of the many unoccupied docks.

The ship was in freefall this close to the disk's rotating center. Aiko unbuckled frrm her seat, gave her captain a confident salute, and ventured out of the ship.

Toward the mission.

Toward her copy-clan sister.

She made her way out of the dock, through black, airless passages, traveling ever "downward" toward the rim of the rotating disk. In these shadows, she sensed why this habitat appealed to the Syndicate's purposes, whatever they were. She'd navigated barely a mile from the dock when warped debris blocked her. She squirmed in through a gap in the wall and continued her descent through the guts of the habitat. She felt like a bug crawling through the intestines of a great, dead, mechanical beast.

Her journey continued downward for forty kilometers and took the better part of two days. She descended through twisted passages and pinched ducts, through holes and around great utility canyons, always downward, the gravity ever increasing.

She began to notice signs of power, passed through an airlock, and kept going with gravity as her guide.

She had to be getting close.

A short while later, she found what she sought.

The condition within the Broken Bottle made it inviable for large-scale settling—not when there were so many functional (or close enough to it) habitats left over from the Scourging—but its stark passages still carried the growing din of activity.

She heard hatches opening and closing. The clack of weapons. The rustle of clothing. The clomp of heavy boots and... clicking of high heels?

She approached those sounds carefully, cautiously, slinking her way forward and down until she came to a series of large chambers, open and interconnected around the habitat's great structural members. The nearest chamber was quiet, so she found a loose wall panel, eased it open, and took a quick glimpse.

The Syndicate must have installed its own dock somewhere nearby along the disk's circumference. The people here were far too fancily dressed to have traversed the Broken Bottle's guts like she had. They milled about in a queue leading to a giant hatch built into the far wall. Guards uniformed in Tarsho Syndicate red-and-black stood on either side. They opened the way for the guests like fancy doormen, but their slung rifles left no doubt as to their capacity for violence. The guests passing into the second chamber regarded the guards with casual aloofness.

Aiko made her way through the walls to the chamber beyond the big hatch. She located a panel she could pry loose and began to work it free. This one was riskier; sound alone told her there were a *lot* of people nearby, but she couldn't stay hidden in the walls forever and considered the risk worth it.

She cracked the panel open a hair, and light spilled into her hiding spot. Far more than from the first chamber.

She peered through to observe an explosion of luster and fashion. The mundanity of the previous chamber here shifted to a grand expanse of lavish flourishes. Red and black banners hung from the ceiling alongside diamond chandeliers that blazed like fiery rainbows. Artwork hung from the walls, and artifacts sat atop ornate plinths. Long, intricately-carved tables were laden with sumptuous feasts and great quantities of alcohol. Over a hundred people—all as elegant and ostentatious as their surroundings—milled about the tables or in more private, cushioned alcoves that all faced a central stage.

This was no mere fancy dress party. The location was too secret, the pompousness too . . . confined. She hadn't stumbled into a display meant to flaunt wealth and power to the public. There *was* no public in attendance, just color-coded goons: red and black for the Syndicate, beige with white trim for the Union spacers.

Except for the serving staff.

Those were exclusively women, baseline humans or with very subtle divergences such as unusual hair color or pointed ears.

They weren't wearing a lot of clothing, either.

Definitely not your average dinner party.

Aiko was too far away and there were too many overlapping conversations for her to ever hope to pick out anything useful. She needed to get closer.

She might even have to *mingle.*

But how to best pull that off?

The fancy guests all looked like people who would be recognized by the goons, so pretending to be one came with buckets of risk. The serving girls, though, were treated more like part of the decor than people, their faces forgotten as soon as they delivered their trays of appetizers or drinks, and all their routes passed through a small sliding door inset into an alcove behind the tables, perhaps leading to the kitchen.

A few of the serving girls deviated to a second doorway, this one labeled as the place where certain biological necessities tied to food and drink were relieved in privacy.

Aiko didn't miss that part of being organic, but it made her next step easier. She replaced the panel, maneuvered through the guts of the walls until she reached the restroom, waited above one of the stalls until one of the serving girls entered it, then put her to sleep with a soft *thwomp* from her arm cannon.

She felt a little guilty about this as she dropped down into the stall. The young woman was surely hired to serve drinks and, potentially, to satisfy other needs. The chances she was a major player in a criminal conspiracy were slim to none.

But, Aiko reflected, she could probably use a good nap... even if it'd be a drafty one without her clothes.

The short black dress satisfied all those words: so black it seemed to soak in the light, so dress its lacy bits clung to her curves like the hands of a long-lost lover, and so short it limited *no* range of motion.

She hid the sleeping body and left the restroom.

It took exactly one poured drink for a slimy patron to slap her ass, then took every ounce of her self-control not to blast him in the face with her arm cannon. Instead she flashed a carefully cowed look and skittered off to refill another drink.

Stealth was *hard*.

She wondered what all of this was for as she moved about the chamber, and quickly she began to piece together an explanation. The guests spoke of bidding on exotic purchases. An auction, then? But an auction of what?

"From what I hear, Tarsho's outdone himself this time," said one guest. Aiko tried to linger to hear more, but he switched to bragging about a recent business deal, and she couldn't stay longer without drawing suspicion.

Still, it soon became clear that Tarsho had organized this auction, and it wasn't long before she spotted the man himself.

With Prinn Pratti on his arm.

Director Xavier vaan Tarsho reclined in one of the cushioned alcoves, arms spread across the back in the manner of one who owned the place and didn't intend anyone in the room to forget it. Now that she saw him in full, she noted his cybernetics probably weren't the result of necessity. If Commander Hughes had been a solid brick, Tarsho was a whole sturdy house, if perhaps renovated to accommodate a killer security system.

He was capable of a lot with that standard body, but the cybernetics must have made him capable of more. Prinn reclined beside him, head against his shoulder like someone who'd seen *everything* those cybernetics could do and found at least some of the less savory features worth exploring.

Aiko acknowledged there were some women—meat-based or otherwise—who would risk entanglement with powerful, dangerous men, and that went double for men with jawlines that strong, even if the jaw and teeth were metal.

She just couldn't figure out what *Prinn* saw in him.

Her copy-sister still maintained the body Aiko most associated with her—an emulation of divergent human flesh with blue skin and silver eyes, clad in a dress on the skimpier end of the fancy spectrum, her hair done up in an ostentatious style.

Aiko began to inch closer when the stage lit up.

A spotlight illuminated a lectern to the side of the main stage, and a man in Syndicate formal wear strode to take his place behind it.

"Welcome once again, our illustrious and esteemed guests."

Aiko associated most auctioneers with annoyance, but this man had a voice like velvet. The kind of voice that made people want to buy things. The kind of voice that could sell a piece of scrap from a trash bin at prices reserved for artifacts from before the Scourging.

"We've acquired an enticing variety of collectables for your perusal this month, including the treasures of which you were already informed—as well as several . . . tantalizing surprises."

He smiled conspiratorially. The guests oohed as if he'd promised them an extra special cake this evening.

Aiko doubted it was cake.

"Now, to start the evening—"

"A-*hem*."

A woman at the table next to Aiko lifted her empty glass with an imperious sneer, offended that the serving girl had the audacity to leave her glass empty. She refilled it with an extra-subservient face, and then—dammit, her bottle was empty. She needed to grab another from the kitchen.

She hurried in that direction, eyeing the stage as she cut through the crowd.

"For our canine aficionados, a Dobrian Shepherd from the finest stock of Neptune."

Well, that was surprising. It looked like a normal black and fawn guard dog.

"With, shall we say, some aftermarket modifications."

The attendant escorting the dog snapped a terse command, and the dog unfolded into a true cybernetic terror, eyes glowing, claws transforming into scythes, teeth buzzing like mirrored chainsaws.

Definitely aftermarket.

But not exactly illegal, at least on Saturn, where cybernetic enhancements were fairly common. Securing deifactured cybernetics compatible with the animal must have been quite the feat, but not unheard-of given how many unexplored corners of the solar system remained.

"We'll start the bidding at—"

The bidding started at what Nathan and his crew had been paid for their last job.

By the time she'd exited the kitchen with a new bottle, the dog had gone for *four times* that amount.

Subsequent pieces were of more ambiguous legality: a selection of animals, both divergent and cybernetically modified, alongside deifactured artifacts and weapons.

But these seemed intended as teasers to whet their guests' appetites, and soon, the audience was sufficiently primed for the main course.

The auctioneer leaned over the lectern with another of those winning grins.

"Now, for one of the most anticipated items up for bid—a piece I know several of you have been yearning to see."

The attendant returned, this time conveying... a collared woman on a leash.

The woman was extraordinarily beautiful, with a shock of fiery orange hair, tall foxlike ears, and an orange tail capped in a tuft of furry white. Her skin was creamy, her eyes reddish with dark, vertical slits. The dress she wore wasn't meant to stay on for very long.

The announcer sang the praises of both her physical attributes and her "behavioral conditioning" with an ease that skipped offensive and dove straight into revolting.

The bids began in earnest, and the amount soon eclipsed all previous auctions.

Aiko recognized the first numbered paddle, held in an arm encased in beige and white, attached to the other man she'd seen in their briefing: Captain Alfonso gen Arturikk.

Her eyes glanced to Prinn, who listened to the rising bids with indifference that would have twisted her guts had she still possessed any. Arturikk won, and the moment the "item" was escorted off the stage, the captain stood to leave.

So, too, did Tarsho and Prinn.

Aiko decided right then and there she'd end this entire sickening affair.

Somehow.

It was a stereotype, but damn, she loved a good vent.

Technically they weren't vents so much as warped gaps in the walls left by the habitat's destruction, but they served a similar purpose, which was to let her creep around the place unseen.

Tarsho and Arturikk conversed as they walked, mentioning something about business before pleasure. The six guards accompanying them said nothing.

Prinn clung to Tarsho's arm until she assumed a look of boredom and purred that she would use the time to put on something more appropriate. Aiko wasn't sure what was more appropriate than the skimpy number Prinn already wore, but she liked the opportunity this presented.

Arturikk and Tarsho split off toward a side room, accompanied by four guards. Prinn continued on with two of her own down the hall. They rounded a corner, which placed the two groups out of sight of each other. Given the acoustics in the area and the noise from the ongoing auction, they'd be out of earshot soon as well.

Good.

It was time to see what her new body could *really* do.

Prinn left the two guards outside.

Aiko positioned herself above the guards and loosened another panel. She had to work both quick and quiet. Too slow and the guards would shout off a warning, ruining the surprise visit she intended to pay her copy-sister. She could have killed the two goons, but figured stealth and discretion were still the order of the day.

Her arm blossomed like a strange, flesh-coated flower, and she fired twice.

The two bodies collapsed, and she dropped down to join them.

She'd *thought* she'd been quiet, but the door swung open, and Prinn stormed out, pistol rising.

"Freeze!" Aiko brought her arm up faster, and Prinn obeyed, pistol still aimed at the floor.

She eyed the cannon's large, black port.

"Don't try anything, sis," Aiko said. "Mine's bigger."

"'Sis'?" Prinn cocked her head. She displayed no fear despite the gun pointed at her head; Jovians took a rather relaxed view of life, death, and explosive decapitation. Having spare bodies helped with that.

Instead, her eyes flicked about, cool and analytical.

"What happened to busting baddies with the Platinum Corsairs?" Aiko asked pointedly.

Prinn flinched. "*Aiko?*"

"In the flesh. Figuratively speaking."

Prinn glanced at her legs. "That's a *lot* of figure from where I'm standing."

"I could say the same about you. Strange of me to find you in such . . . colorful company. You and Tarsho, huh?"

"I can explain."

"You'd better. Otherwise, you're about to become acquainted with this gun's more impressive features."

"Same old Aiko." Prinn seemed to relax a little. "You always were the blunt instrument of the family."

"Flattery will get you nowhere. I've already seen one woman who needs to be rescued from this hellhole."

"There's more than one. A *lot* more. I'm putting my gun away. You okay with that?"

"As long as I don't see any sudden moves."

Prinn holstered her gun. There were no sudden moves.

"Now, about that explanation," Aiko pressed.

"Mind if I drag these guards inside first? We're exposed out here."

"Go ahead."

Prinn grabbed one guard by the shirt, threw him in like he was a lumpy sack of potatoes, then chucked the second goon on top of the first. Aiko followed her in and closed the door.

"I have a feeling you're here for the same reason I am," Prinn explained. "The best way to get close to Tarsho is as one of his business partners. Or one of his girls. The latter seemed easier."

"How easy were you?"

"Please don't ask for details. Tarsho's 'lovemaking'"—Prinn provided air quotes—"has all the nuance and subtlety of a woodchipper. But he likes his girls exotic, and as a Jovian, I satisfy his kink. Long story short, I had some recent dealings with the Tarsho Syndicate, caught wind of what they've been doing out here, and decided to do something about it."

"Which is?"

"You've seen enough by now. The worst of it is human trafficking."

"Why hasn't anyone reported this?"

"The victims are all from low-tech societies. Some of the poor sods are so backwards they think fire is the new, happening thing. Best they can do is send up a smoke signal. Not quite enough to get the NCSF involved."

"You'd be surprised," Aiko replied, and Prinn eyed her up and down.

"Oh, I see. I *see.* I was wondering about the arm cannon. Not exactly standard issue for a Jovian face. Anyway, I've spent the past several months trying to bring Tarsho down but haven't landed on the right opportunity."

"That dress hasn't provided you with any opportunities?"

"Killing him won't solve the problem. Sure, it'd be satisfying as hell, but the Syndicate will just replace him, maybe with someone worse. Plus, I'll lose this body," she added as an afterthought.

"Then it does sound like we're here for the same reason," Aiko said. "Who's here with you?"

"Me, myself, and I."

"How many bodies, then?"

"Just the one."

"You've trying to take Tarsho down *alone*?"

Prinn shrugged.

"Well, you're in luck," Aiko declared, "because it turns out you *do* have backup. And, after seeing their setup from both outside and within, I have an idea."

She knew it was literally an action her captain told her not to take, but... she did enjoy improvising.

And blowing things up.

Why not dabble in both at the same time?

"Would you happen to have the codes?" Aiko asked.

"The codes?"

"To the missile batteries."

"Oh." Prinn blinked. "*Oh.* No, those are controlled by spacers from *Echoes of Flame*, not the Syndicate. But... I imagine Captain Arturikk would have a copy. He has a safe in his suite. That's the first place I'd check."

"Were you easy with him, too?"

"Please stop."

"Sorry. Where's the captain's suite?"

"Back the way we came."

"What are he and Tarsho up to right now?"

"Business before pleasure. Maybe plotting their next run through the Trojans. Who knows and who cares? Tarsho will be back once I've had time to pretty myself up, and Arturikk..." She grimaced, and Aiko thought back to the captain's purchase of the fox girl.

"Yeah." Aiko opened and quickly collapsed her gun arm. She flexed her fingers. "I think it's time for some coitus interruptus."

Prinn had selected what Jovians referred to as a "face" to avoid rousing Tarsho's suspicion, which meant that while she could perform any number of functions required to interact with meat sacks, she lacked Aiko's raw combat potential.

But she could still sneak.

Once Tarsho left Arturikk's room, the Pratti sisters moved into position. The Syndicate goons followed Tarsho while a pair of SUN spacers remained to guard the entrance to their captain's suite, while he was alone inside with the slave he'd purchased.

Now the only thing separating Aiko and Prinn from the fox girl was a straight shot through a pair of color-coded bad guys. They could have dropped straight into Arturikk's room, but Aiko figured it best to take the guards out first. They might sound an alarm or something.

Besides, it wasn't often she had a body like this. May as well put it through its paces.

She dropped from the ceiling, arm cannon open. The pair began to swing their rifles up, but she fired first with a satisfying *thwomp!* The first Union spacer bashed against the wall with the loud thump of meat on metal, then slid down.

She hadn't dialed the power level all the way up to "Where'd he go?" She'd wanted to, given present circumstances, but she wasn't sure how much real estate behind the man a blast like that would vaporize, so she'd settled for "*Thwomp* with the promise of a headache."

Prinn followed her down, and her pistol barked. The second spacer crumpled into a heap, blood soaking his shirt.

They took the guns from the guards then tried the hatch.

It wouldn't open, so Aiko set her arm to "Locksmith Mode." The blast took the door off its hinges, and they stormed in.

The fox girl's dress was still on, to her fortune.

Arturikk's pants were not, much to *everyone's* misfortune—though it did provide Aiko with a convenient target. She dialed back to stun and fired. The *thwomp* threw Arturikk back, and while the force applied to his body had been nonlethal, most of it had impacted on a rather small region between his legs. He let out a shrill squeak, clutched his nether regions, then dropped to the ground.

Aiko hit him again, just to make sure he was out cold.

"Here's the safe." Prinn indicated a small, metallic square built into the back wall.

Aiko took one long look at the numbered pad, then scoffed and grabbed the handle. She ripped the front off and retrieved the vlass from the recessed interior. Its screen displayed step-by-step instructions for arming and then firing the anti-ship missile batteries. The sentences were short and didn't include a lot of big words.

"Jackpot," Prinn declared.

"You okay over there?" Aiko asked the fox girl, who was cowering behind the bed.

She peeked the top half of her head over the sheets, ears upright, slit pupils dilated.

"You want to get out of here?"

The woman paused, anxious and unsure, but then nodded emphatically.

"Great." Aiko waved her over. "Come with us. We'll find a place for you to hide until things calm down."

The good thing about derelict habitats was they came with lots of hard-to-find cubbyholes. They found a safe nook for the woman to hide in, and then took a circuitous route to the missile batteries. SUN personnel had relocated the launchers from their destroyer to a massive, jagged shelf extending out from the Broken Bottle's edge like a mountain range on its side. They'd connected the battery site to the rest of the occupied zones with a series of pressurized tunnels, but Aiko and Prinn took a different path.

One under a black, star-dappled sky.

*They* didn't need air.

The missiles were each the size of grain silos, and the dozen or so launchers were even larger. They found an airlock near the base of the main installation and made their way inside. A Union spacer must have heard them coming and hurried over to check. He performed a double take upon glimpsing the two gorgeous, scantily-clad women.

Perhaps he thought he was dreaming.

One *thwomp* later, and he was.

They hurried past the unconscious spacer, incapacitated a few more, and located the master control console after several minutes of searching.

"We going to raise an alarm when we start?" Aiko asked.

"Probably."

"Then you handle things here. I'll watch your back."

"Okay, but what's our target?"

"What else but the *Echoes of Flame*?" Aiko grinned wolfishly. "There's more mess here than the two of us can handle, but if we at least cripple that warship, the NCSF will be able to swoop right on in."

"You sure about that?"

"They have a cruiser lurking in the area. The *Azure Eagle*. Trust me, they're paying attention." She raised her gun arm. "You deal with the missiles. I'll handle the rest."

Aiko hurried out of the control room, sealed the hatch behind her, and headed toward the pressurized tunnel. Any goons trying to reach Prinn would likely try that path first. She reached the entrance and enjoyed a few moments of silence before klaxons wailed and harsh lights strobed, bathing the area in red.

She heard the forces coming soon after, as unsubtle as the sirens, heavy boots clanking across solid ground. She cracked open her arm cannon and hunkered down behind the corner.

A hatch at the far end of the pressured tunnel opened, disgorging a . . . she wasn't sure what the group noun for that many goons should be.

*A gaggle of geese,* she thought, *a murder of crows. Ah! Got it!*

She settled on an "expendable" of henchmen.

She knew she'd aimed for non-lethality so far, but Prinn wasn't as well-equipped as her. The mass of soldiers storming her way were all in hard suits—combinations of body armor and environmental protection—and their weapons came in the dual flavors of "heavy" and "heavier."

She needed to keep her sister safe. If that meant she had to take down a whole expendable of henchmen, then so be it.

She switched her cannon from stun to "fuck 'em" and blasted a patch to the side of the tunnel's midpoint. The wall burst outward, and atmosphere vented to space. One goon tumbled out, but the rest hunkered down, magnetic boots and gauntleted fists clamping them in place. Their hard suits could handle the lack of air just fine, but they wouldn't be receiving unarmored reinforcements anytime soon.

The suction died down, wheezing its last gasps into silence, and several goons opened fire. Bullets pattered off Aiko's corner, and a lucky shot took a chunk out of her shoulder.

She swung out of cover, targeted the lead goon, and blasted him in the neck. He fell, his torso resembling a grotesque canyon as his head somersaulted back over the crowd. More armored goons poured into the tunnel until it resembled a seething mass of red and black.

Clearly, Tarsho didn't like it when people messed with his toys.

Well, that was just too bad.

Bodies littered the corridor and blood boiled into the vacuum by the time she'd finished. About halfway through her gruesome work, some of the goons decided life was more important than their paychecks. They turned and fled, but the confusion sowed by their clumsy retreat only made them easier targets. A few got away, but they weren't Aiko's problem, because the next group coming her way shot the deserters!

She crouched behind her bullet-riddled corner and waited.

Director Xavier vaan Tarsho, resplendent in his black armor, rounded the bend, flanked by two elite guards in with thick riot shields. He scowled toward her, his face visible through the tinted faceplate. Clearly, he'd Had It with his subordinates today and had elected to take matters into his own hands.

To be fair, she'd been hoping for a shot at Tarsho, though he and his two buddies were better equipped than she'd expected. Still, she had a job to do. The trio closed ranks and advanced down the ruined tunnel. She took aim at one of Tarsho's guards and fired.

The man staggered back, his riot shield dented in the center.

*Huh*, she thought, *well, I've got a solution for that.*

She cranked her cannon's output all the way up to "Where'd he go?"

He went.

She fired another beam.

That guard went, too.

She steadied her aim on Tarsho and toggled the cannon a third time, but instead of a satisfying *thwomp* reverberating through her body, something *click*ed instead. She gave the weapon a quick, urgent look and tried again.

*Click.*

Tarsho unsheathed a long vibro-blade and sprinted past what remained of his guards.

*Click, click.*

*Click-click-click.*

It dawned on her, in the brief moments before Tarsho reached her, that perhaps she should have kept better tabs on her gun's capacitors.

Tarsho swung, and his blade whisked smoothly through her unfolded forearm. Sparks flew, and the front half of the weapon dropped to the ground. Tarsho closed, knee extended, arms braced for a rising stroke that would cleave her in half if she didn't move.

She moved.

Tarsho advanced.

Aiko had seen this movie, too. She knew the unspoken rules of engagement, but Tarsho wouldn't pause to gloat or explain his plans or engage in comedic banter. He was out to kill her—*this* her, anyway—and then her sister. She flinched back, and the blade whispered past. Tarsho contracted his arms, angling for a thrust through her chest.

A thought snapped through her mind, and she rushed him.

He stabbed her through the heart.

Or where the heart belonged on a meat body. But on her, the narrow path through her torso failed to bisect any vitals. She grabbed his wrist and yanked his blade in all the way, pulling him close in the process. They stood almost eye to eye, him snarling at her from behind his tinted faceplate with that ridiculous metal jaw of his.

Aiko headbutted him, and the faceplate cracked. She smacked him again, and air whistled through a spiderweb of fissures.

Tarsho's eyes bugged out. He tried to pull the sword loose, but she held it in place. He let go of the blade and scrambled to get away, but his back foot slipped in a pool of bodily fluids. He flew off his feet and landed heavily on his back.

Aiko pulled the sword out of her chest. She loomed over Tarsho, sword now upright in her remaining hand.

Tarsho gulped, his air leaking, sweat beading on his brow.

She favored him with a cruel, toothy grin.

Aiko sealed the airlock, then hurried back to the missile batteries. The ground shook on her way back, rhythmically and repeatedly as missiles launched into space, the light of their thrusters angling toward a distant gray glint.

She quickened her pace back, and when she reached the control room, she found her sister smiling ear to ear.

"We caught them with their pants down!" Prinn declared with a triumphant fist pump. "Every missile hit its mark!"

"Funny you should mention pants."

"What?"

"Nothing. I'll explain later." Aiko surveyed the controls. There were a lot of numbers and blinky bits. "I wonder how long it'll take the *Eagle* to notice."

A new light started pulsing. Prinn leaned in, hunted around for a while, then tapped a key.

"—repeat, this is NCFS *Azure Eagle* to anyone on or near the Broken Bottle. We have observed several large explosions in your area and are moving immediately to assist. Please respond on this channel with any information you may have regarding the situation. We will prep our landing parties accordingly. Our ETA is fifty-seven minutes and counting."

Aiko sniggered.

The two Prattis were long gone, climbing up through the Broken Bottle's guts when the NCSF arrived in force. The scene those spacers found shocked them—*shocked* them to their very cores. Who could have *imagined* the Tarsho Syndicate was using the Broken Bottle for such nefarious ends? Good thing the Syndicate's SUN accomplices were so bafflingly incompetent, they somehow managed to *shoot their own destroyer*!

A few weeks later, Commander Hughes visited the *Neptune Dragon* back on Neptune's orbital ring. Prinn was still with them, now in practical clothing that nonetheless flattered her blue shapeliness.

Aiko had stitched up the bullet holes in her server dress, though she now wore it with her leather jacket. Squicky origins aside, it was a good dress, and she liked the awkward way Captain Kade tried not to look at her when she wore it.

"The damage to *Echoes of Flame* came as something of a surprise." Hughes sighed. "Do you have any idea how much paperwork I now need to fill out?"

"For the record," Nathan said, "you didn't tell us *not* to blow it up."

"I'll be sure to provide more explicit instructions for the future." The commander shrugged. "Huge explosions aside, everything seems to have worked out. The Broken Bottle lease has been terminated, Tarsho and Arturikk are in custody, their ship is an air-bleeding sieve, and *Azure Eagle* is even now returning most of the victims to their points of origin."

"'Most'?" Aiko asked.

"A few have expressed interest in naturalizing as Neptunian citizens. Additionally, the Saturn Union is so embarrassed by the whole affair, all they're asking for is the return of their crew and what's left of *Echoes*."

"You going to let them go?"

"Only if we can't pin them with specific crimes. Some of Arturikk's crew were likely in the dark about what their captain and senior staff were up to. Once we've sifted through the evidence—and squeezed suitable compensation out of the Union—we'll send those individuals back to Saturn. As for Tarsho, Arturikk, and their co-conspirators, they won't be seeing the light of day for a very, *very* long time."

"How is old Tarsho doing, anyway?" Aiko asked brightly.

"It'll be a while before he's back on solid food." Hughes narrowed his gaze. "Did you really have to leave him with all those captives?"

"It was the closest place I could find to stuff him." It hadn't been, but she wasn't about to admit that. "I did ask them not to kill him. Even said, 'pretty please.'"

"How considerate of you," Hughes replied dryly, but then he cracked a knowing grin.

"What about the rest of the Syndicate?" Prinn asked.

"They're in a panic, and rightfully so. I'm not sure what the Union will do to the organization, but I expect it won't be gentle."

"How about the buyers at the auction?"

"That's a slightly more delicate matter. Attending the auction isn't a crime in and of itself. Sure, many of the goods for sale were illegal, but the guests will simply claim ignorance."

Aiko snorted. "Yeah right."

"I might agree with you, but the burden of proof lies on us. Luckily, we have you as a witness." He indicated Prinn. "Along with the victims and any Syndicate or Union survivors who might be willing to spill their guts for leniency."

"What about me?" Aiko asked. "Can't I testify?"

"You weren't there."

"Ah. Right, right." She winked at the commander. "Plausible deniability. Got it."

"And on the topic of things that weren't there, I'll need you to return that body."

"Aww," she pouted. "Can't I keep it? Maybe as a bonus for exceeding expectations?"

"Ms. Pratti, that's a level of paperwork even I refuse to face."

"You sure?"

"Come on, Aiko," Nathan said. "Just hand it back. It wasn't ours to begin with."

"But it's a really nice body!" She ran a hand up her side, prompting a brief, buoyant jiggle. "Don't you agree?"

"I, um, well." Nathan cleared his throat while avoiding eye contact. "That's beside the point."

"Nate, you've got to admit, there's some top-notch physics going on here. It's both bouncy *and* badass. Here, check this out." She rose and propped her leg up on the chair.

"Would you just return the damn thing already? *Please?*"

# BAG MAN

## Jack Clemons

The gentle vibrations sounded like the rattle of an insect's wings. They pulled at me across the gulf of soft sleep, the constant buzz of plastic on the varnished wood of the bedside table. My eyes opened reluctantly as if fighting the reality of the vibrations. Reaching out by memory without opening my eyes, I grasped the thin plastic of the phone.

I forced one eye open to view the dimly lit screen. I didn't recognize the number, but that wasn't uncommon for me. My thumb hovered over the screen briefly as I composed myself mentally to take the call. I rolled over onto my back among the cool tangle of sheets and blankets that made up my solo sleeping arrangement. Not that I minded sleeping alone. It was one of those things I had learned about myself in the wreckage of two divorces in five years. Sleeping alone is a luxury few truly appreciate.

As I sat up in the bed I swiped the screen to answer the call.

"Hello." I said keeping my voice as neutral as possible.

"Yes, am I speaking with Mr. Drake?" the controlled female voice on the other end of the line asked.

It was a work call, but that wasn't surprising. The reason this phone sat next to my bed was so that I could be on call. I checked the time. Barely ten p.m. I hadn't been asleep for an hour. I briefly considered raising my fee.

"You are. How may I help you?"

"I was given your number by a friend at UB&W. They recommended you as a specialist in adjudication."

I reached over and palmed a control switch on the bedside table, bringing the lights up in the room slowly to not be too jarring. Upham, Burke, and Waingro wasn't the name of a mid-sized law firm but it was designed to sound like one. It was a single office in the bad part of town with a secretary and a sole proprietor.

William "BillyBoy" Goldstein was a disgraced and disbarred former corp lawyer who had been drummed out of his profession for what he called, "Getting caught doing what everyone else was better at hiding." I had never asked him for the details and he never felt like giving more than that. That being said, he was a man who lived enough in both worlds that he had seen the need for a niche role of helping facilitate the corporations when it came to legalities even they weren't willing to break. To that end he maintained a stable of various specialists. He farmed our skill set to the highest bidder and took both a healthy finder's fee and a flat 10% of our net profits.

So for miss cool and collected to be name dropping "BillyBoy" she was confirming her need for discretion and violence. Her timing of the call meant this was a matter of some urgency. I processed this as I rubbed my face in a movement that stretched back to the cavemen. Touching skin to try and trigger some deeper core in myself.

"Ahh, yes. Is there a timeframe for your matter?" I asked, swinging my legs free and onto the floor.

"I am afraid the matter is quite urgent. Are you available for a face-to-face meeting?" Her voice never wavered, strong and precise. She likely wasn't the one with the issue, I guessed. Some Corporate trouble-shooter who had probably been asleep an hour ago herself, before a more frantic call had reached her.

"I am, where at?" I stood walking towards the closet, my feet moving silently through the plush carpet. "And, of course, there is the matter of my fee for such urgent meetings."

"I will send you an address. As to the fee, we were informed as such. Ten thousand Credits have been deposited into the indicated account. We do ask that you arrive quickly, as the matter is quite timely."

"Of course." That was a hefty amount. About my maximum consulting level fee, not that I thought that was where it would end. All for me to wake up and go see someone. I had done a lot worse for a lot less. "I will be on my way shortly."

"Excellent." The call ended abruptly.

I tossed the phone back onto the bed as I opened the memory

plastic door of the closet. Dilating at the touch of my finger, the coded door revealed my wardrobe. I glanced at the suits briefly. Each one a bespoke masterpiece that cost more than I once upon a time had made in a month slinging cheap bootleg TriDees and Narco injectors. If this meeting had been scheduled during business hours, these suits would have allowed me to drift among the sea of corporate drones without a second glance. But, to me, these were merely a camouflage of a different sort. One of the first lessons I had ever been taught on my rise from Street Sicario to my current lofty position of Corporate Bag Man.

"You have to be able to move in both worlds, and their world won't come naturally. So pretend, disguise, and lie. Do it until it becomes second nature. The easier it is for them to forget what you are, the better you are at your job. Just never forget yourself."

Instead, I dressed in a loose casual manner that would see me well in almost any environment. Dark jeans, a grey mag-sealed double-breasted shirt with a mandarin collar, black running shoes that pulsed a dull red on the sole with each step, and a tan all weather jacket. Reaching down I pulled free one of the dark green hard plastic military cases that rested in the closet. I rarely kept all of my working supplies here, but I kept enough hardware on hand for personal use.

I selected a thin Smith and Wesson semiauto with a concealed holster, I slipped it inside the waistband on my jeans at the one o'clock position and attached it to my belt. A spare magazine and auto knife went into my lefthand front pocket. While it was unlikely this meeting was an ambush, you didn't make it in this line of work without a layer of paranoia helping you get dressed.

I gave myself the once-over in the mirror. No matter what I did, I would never get rid of the look of being "The Heavy." Tall and muscled but not comically so. I was glad for the long sleeves and high collar to cover the gang tattoos of a previous life and cybernetic enhancements of this one. My dark black hair cut into a severe near-military fade, my beard trimmed and squared off. The edging of gray was showing more and more, for some a matter of self-consciousness. Personally I took pride in it. Neither my father nor grandfather had lived to see gray hair.

I walked out of the spartan guest room that I slept in and was assaulted by my curator's garish, trending TriDee motifs. I didn't mind the art. I just didn't feel the need to stare at it every night before drifting off to sleep. The decorator's name was Sarah, and we had met eight months ago at a party thrown by a friend of a friend. I had seen her across the room and immediately been infatuated. She was tall and pale, her red hair cut into a side shave to show off the intricate Celtic knot work tattoo that writhed and moved with the beat of the music. I can still remember her sheer red dress that left just enough to the imagination.

That night, we fucked. Afterwards, her hands traced the scar tissue and black carbon fiber of my cybernetics. She told me she could work when and where she wanted, or not, but whatever she did had to be "spiritually fulfilling." She asked me what I did for a living, and in a haze of drugs, booze and post-coital endorphins, I told her.

There were many names for my profession. But they all boil down to the same thing. In earlier times I would be called a sell sword, ronin, soldier of fortune, or mercenary. Now the masters who hired my services preferred to dress it up in a different way: Security Executive, Conflict Adjudicator, or Contractor. The street called us Kordats, Freehires, and of course Bagmen. But it all meant the same: people of resolve for hire to the highest bidder.

Rather than making her run off, she found it fascinating. She told me later it was our auras, something about her being wind and me being fire. I didn't really understand it then, and I still don't now. But the balance was there. And for now she was in my life and we enjoy each other. I know she'll grow bored some day, and be gone. And I would be left with an apartment full of art and a head full of memories.

She was stretched out on the floor, nude, wearing a full body sensory harness on and laying on a RealDee response blanket. Judging by the sounds she was experiencing some sort of sonic trance sequence, that she had informed me was all the rage currently. I had tried it. Honestly, it had felt like dancing with a Muay Thai fighter for forty minutes while the music buzzed in my ear. It was the latest thing for the Neo-Druids in their Club/Temples, but really not my bag.

Her lithe body twisted and turned in a way that was both erotic and near religious, worshipping some goddess of fertility in a mix of synth wave and bass boosted music. The Atlanta skyline outlined her through my floor-to-ceiling windows from thirty-seven stories up. Buckhead's neon and LED lights mixed with what stars were powerful enough to beat the city haze.

I didn't interrupt her, we didn't have a "goodbyes" type of relationship. She likely wouldn't notice me being gone 'til tomorrow at some point, and I needed to be in work mode, not thinking about what we last said to each other. That had happened with wife number two. My head being on the argument had led to a pretty steep organic damage build and more time in the surgery stack. Lesson learned: keep your personal life locked away. It can and will get you killed.

So I walked out of my apartment.

The armored glass elevator plunged me down, allowing the city's lights to play over me. The night had just begun in earnest, shift change from the corporate jewel of the south and sliding into the party tourist location that had made it famous. Taverns, bars and pubs, clubs and lounges, parks, restaurants, street meat vendors, diners and dives all roused from their dormant states. Likewise, partiers, punks, tourists, thrill-seekers and mischief-makers took over Late Night Atlanta. Like the first hit off an opium pipe, the city breathed in vice and exhaled experience. It was in these streets I had grown up, where I had killed my first man, and where I had evolved into what I am now. Descending from my apartment to the streets below felt like falling from heaven.

The soft ding of the elevator pulled me away from the now subterranean view. I was still somewhat groggy. As I turned and stepped into the garage I saw my BMW sedan sitting and waiting. The elevator had informed the E-Chauffeur in my car I was coming down, causing the vehicle to activate its electronic engine and drive to the elevator. The sleek black and red paint showed off the German engineering, for the modern enthusiast who could afford it. I slid into the driver seat. The door sealed behind me as I looked into the phone for the first time since the call had ended. The address was north of the city in Kennesaw. Not overly surprising. And at this time of night I could be there in 45 minutes.

"Liz." I spoke aloud as I slid the phone into its cradle.

"Yes?" The voice was sultry and sinful. Not a factory option. But I had the default personality removed and a hacked variant placed in its vacancy. Not only was it far more secure, it matched the car better.

"Get us on 75 northbound and get me Ivan on the phone. Call until he answers."

The Beemer's electric engine hummed as the autodrive engaged.

The streets were wet from a late December rain, creating reflective surfaces in every puddle. The E-Chauffeur maintained its speed with those posted, leaving me to brood as I listened to the muted rings through the car's speakers. I had known Ivan for three years and employed him for two. He wasn't Russian, but the influx of refugees from the Sino Conflict meant that the streets were learning all sorts of new slang. He was younger than me and when I met him, he barely had any cybertech. So I paid him half in cash and half in "chair-time" at my preferred mechanic.

Now, he was running so many mods he barely qualified as human anymore. Cybernetic addiction was another thing you had to balance in this life. You could run internal comms, sensors, weapon enhancements, subcutaneous body armor, organic weapon mounts, and limb replacement. A common mistake—that much tech meant you were going to flash every sensor in a three block radius. And any decent CeeCee will fry your shit, turning off vulnerable systems one by one. Keeping your anti-intrusion software up to date could be as pricey as turning your body into a living weapon.

Personally I preferred a more subdued approach. My hardware was all non-network reflex, strength, endurance boosters, and a few other "dumb" systems that allowed me to be protected from intrusion and offer minimal footprint to sensor sweeps. Of course, there were the replacement body parts, those had been necessary as the years of damage took their toll. And that didn't even account for all the possible chemical cocktails. Living at the bleeding edge was expensive, but that's why I charged the prices I did.

The speakers pinged, drawing me out of my thoughts.

"Yooooo!" Ivan's voice was cheerful and the sound of thunderous music could be heard even through his voice filter. "You out tonight? I am at Typhoon!"

"We have work. You sober?" I asked as the car took another corner smoothly. A group of young ladies were walking down the street, flesh, holograms, and minimal clothing drawing my eye. One turned and blew the car an exaggerated kiss.

"Shit man, yeah mostly. I can drop a hypo but that will mess with my reflexes."

"I am headed to meet the client, call Zipline. Go get a work van. And some tool boxes. Meet me at Landmark. Sober up there."

"Da, what's the gig?"

"No clue. Pack for a little bit of everything. There seems to be a timing issue, so I don't want to go back to the lockers if we can help it."

"Seems nexus. You want back up for the meet?"

"No, they seem relaxed enough. Besides, the down payment is already in the bank."

"Skuller, see you at Landmark."

He hung up, and my BMW slid onto I-75 north. The 16-lane freeway cut through the entire state, offering those so inclined easy surface travel to Tennessee or Florida. It also had made Georgia a smuggling hub for over a century. Drugs, people, guns, and all manner of illicit goods made their way through the country on I-75. Atlanta didn't mind as long as the right palms were greased and enough busts were made to show the housewives that gave a fuck that the Dot-Gov types were "doing something."

My first jobs, once I had been inducted into the Cartel, had been driving loads of "product" from Jacksonville to Lexington. I knew this interstate like I knew my own hand. I could still remember my hands on the wheel, tweaking on meth, high listening to older Sicarios in the passenger seat tell me the ways of the world, as salsa-pop pumped out of the speakers. My vision blurred to the tune of the beat. It hadn't seemed like a bad way to spend one's teenage years, and that's why the Cartel recruits from high schools. By 18, I had killed men for less money than I now spent on a haircut and massage. When you grow up with nothing, you really don't have much to lose.

"Manual drive. Release governor. Sport mode active." I watched the steering wheel extend from the dash. As I touched the accelerator, I felt the gasoline engine kick on, The twin turbo V6 growled as I began pushing into the light traffic, watching the speedometer climb to 140 kph.

"Anything else Papi?" The voice sent a light shiver down my spine. You could practically feel the virtual teeth biting on your earlobe.

"Yes, playlist 4. And back it off about twenty percent there Liz."

"You're no fun." The car pouted as it dutifully activated the playlist.

I dodged around a slow-moving cargo hauler and pressed harder on the accelerator.

✧✧✧

The drive back from Kennesaw was faster than the one there. The meeting had gone predictably, now all that was left was to convince my crew. The landmark diner was one of those long standing Atlanta traditions that seemed almost ageless. A large scale diner planted in Buckhead that, during the day, catered to upscale families and corporate workers looking for a meal with a wide variety of menu options. But, much like the rest of the city, as the sun set, it took on a new tone.

The front of the restaurant remained brightly lit, attracting partiers heading out for the night, and, later, partiers recovering afterwards. But in the back... we who plied our trade in violence and vice could enjoy a more private and secure environment.

I breezed past the receptionist who was lost in the holo drama before her. I walked through the mostly empty dining room and stepped through an unmarked door near the bathrooms. Most people would assume it was storage. It was not, and the sonic wash of the noise dampener came over me like a baptism of hidden vice. The backroom had been a well-known comedy club, but the years marched on and as the need for private dining had increased, the establishment had responded. Now the darkened room was lit by contrasting blues and reds making facial recognition software iffy at best. Sonic dampeners kept conversations localized to their tables, and patrons desiring maximum anonymity could rent booths with force shields.

I glanced around those in the open and saw a number of familiar faces. Herold "Limerick" Jones was at one table, surrounded by a host of hangers-on. He was a local WaveRapper who fancied himself a player in the underworld. Our dealings had all been public and polite. Our mutual acquaintances had informed me that his lyrics weren't just for show and he was more than happy to get his hands dirty. Neither I nor my clients had any desire to hear of *my* work on a chart topping hit.

Four armored police officers sat at another table. Their gear marked them as elite APEX rapid response and crime suppression specialists. When plans went sideways, and you didn't have an exit strategy, they happened. A normal patrol officer wasn't a threat to a man like me but these cops rode Mil-spec VTOLs, and ran as much cyberware as any Street Soldat I cared to think of. I looked over their faces, since their armored helms hung from the back of their chairs in a mirror fashion. I recognized two and could tell they recognized me. We had a checkered history, as men who had seen each other through holographic gunsights tended to have. But all of us viewed it as happenstance of the profession, and this place was as sacred as any church or temple. Out on the streets, they would crucify me if they could, but a good meal is hard to come by late at night and no professional rivalry was worth endangering that.

Last, I spotted my party. Posted in the corner booth, Ivan was stretched out with half a plate of wings, and a growing pile of bones next to it. The tingles of RAM still in my brain calculated the amount of time he had been here, based on the speed at which I knew he ate and how many wings remained. Close to forty minutes, I calculated.

Ivan had been tall and lanky at 6'8" and 200 lbs. Then he'd added half again his natural body weight in augments and cyberware. Those hadn't bulked him up, so his long spindly limbs had earned him the street name of "Scarecrow." He didn't care for the nickname, his ego demanded he be Ivan the Great. But even that wasn't good enough. He was "Ivan the Greatest of All Time, Goddammit," which, of course was shortened to Ivan the Goat behind his back...

He was wearing typical Soldat combat clothing, a clashing mix of Sino aesthetic and "Formal Slavic Business Wear." His Kamayhara combat gi was an eye-catching blue, and had been covered by cyberware sponsor patches. His tight, slash-resistant pants, black, were by Adidas. Multiple refugee cultures had collided with unrestrained American capitalism and resulted in some very strange fashion trends.

Ivan looked up at me with a broad grin on his face. His companion turned to see me, with an expression more sly and reserved. Zipline was a Circuit Cowboy I had used for few jobs. His specialty was Direct Action Network Manipulation and Intrusion. His skills would have landed him a comfortably extravagant lifestyle in any corporation, however that would have required a shift in lifestyle that Zipline clearly wasn't embracing. His skinny, scar-covered body spoke of a lifestyle of alternating chemical and technological addiction. His clothes were tattered cargo shorts and a denim vest bearing currently-trending Trailer Park SlamRock patches. His hair had been replaced with the interwoven tech-dreads of processors and spare RAM, giving him onboard computing power to rival most 20th century supercomputers.

Of course, keeping that kind of tech safe in the trailer parks full of factory burnouts and junkies wasn't easy or cheap. I had seen Zipline's personal cluster of trailers before. Layered active and passive defenses ranging from less-than-lethal minefields to auto-turret-controlled shotguns loaded with monofilament razor rounds. I had been curious about why he still lived there. His freelancing clearly provided more than enough for him to move to a safer environment, but he had merely shrugged and said he didn't want to be removed from the real.

Sliding into the booth, I reached over and palmed the privacy screen, causing an opaque white field to block out the rest of the room. I glanced at their faces, hungry and almost feral. My jobs never paid small, and these boys knew that came with risks. But, on the ragged edges of society, you rarely get opportunities to break out of your station in life. And these two men knew that to do so would mean the application of violence and acceptance of risk.

"What's the *rabo*?" Ivan asked, pushing aside the pile of dead avian remains in front of him.

"Recovery of an asset," I said evenly, pulling out a disposable tablet, "and retribution on those that took it."

I quickly entered an eight-digit code, opening the tablet. Ivan picked it up and began flipping through the pages of the brief. Zipline had likely already hacked the pad, he was just polite enough not to talk about what he had found. He compulsively hacked every device he laid his eyes on, and I didn't bring my personal phone out when he was around.

"So break it down, hoss." Zipline said in his overly exaggerated southern drawl.

I cleared my throat and took a second to run over the details as they had been fed to me. The scene hadn't been an entirely unfamiliar one. A stoic patriarch, the weeping matriarch, and their cluster of supporters, the story was only new in the minutia.

"Sometime around noon today, a Bankhead drug den was robbed. They did the typical sweep job looking for drugs and cash. When they didn't find enough, they started taking people."

At that moment I selected a file and pressed play. Shaky TriDee clawed to life as a desperate cameraman caught precious frames of a masked man shoving a young girl who had been gagged and bound into a cargo van. I froze it on the best frame of the girl's face.

"Video was taken by the asset's boyfriend."

"Excuse me," Zipline said stubbing out his Pall Mall. "What does some drugged out slag have to warrant our kind of response?"

"The asset is the daughter of a very prominent figure in local politics. If he involves police in this matter it gets discovered his daughter is a burned out junkie who performs in online porn shows."

Perking up at that information, both leaned in. Scandal and corruption meant even healthier paydays. Plus, who didn't like hearing about the woes of their social betters?

"Who is he?" Ivan asked.

"No one you voted for." I countered.

"You know I can't vote," he pouted. Ivan had caught a charge early on and it was a sore spot. For a known killer, having a felony record for attempting (failing) to break in an AutoBurger kiosk during a three-day drunken binge? *Less than intimidating.*

"Anyway," I said, slightly annoyed at the deviation; they knew I wouldn't discuss client details if it could be helped, "we have been charged with getting her out of the current predicament and returning her to her family."

"So, who took her? And why?" Ivan said taking a pull off a bottle. "Also, where is she?"

"Learn to read faster," Zipline quipped. "Boss, this ain't gonna be that easy. The Towers are no fucking joke."

"Fuck man, The Towers?" Ivan moaned.

"Yes." I said icily. "The Towers. Get over it. It's why you get paid the big bucks. The good news is the hard work is done for us. The family tagged the girl with a tracker on her last trip to rehab and had the family investigator track her once the boyfriend informed them of what occurred. He traced her to the tower and has sat on them this whole time. They move her and he will inform us."

"So who has her? Why did they take her anyway?" Ivan asked. He pointedly was not reading the brief as a rebuke to Zipline's jab.

"Tower gang called 47 Ronin. And, as far as we can tell, they grabbed her and three other females, likely in hopes of selling them."

"Yeah, I know those guys." Zipline said. "They're a burned-out shitty MC. Made up primarily of Russian refugee kids who have a hard on for Jap samurai culture shit. They used to be an up and comer, 'til a few months back. Half their number either got cut down or got hard time."

That part hadn't been on the brief, but I wasn't surprised Zip had that kind of intel. Guys like him had a vast array of informants and intel sources. He was as much an information broker as he was a combat hacker.

"Shit was gnarly," he continued. "Deal gone south with some crew of dudes I had never heard of before, turned to gunplay, and it just so happened that an APEX VTOL was nearby. Gunfight became a massacre, and ever since, and ever since, the forty-seven Ronin are more like, nine. Hearing that they are robbing trap houses and dabbling in human trafficking doesn't surprise me one bit. These dudes are speed freaks with some bare bones milsurp augments."

"Know any of them personally?" I asked.

"Yeah," he answered, lighting another Pall with a propane torch.

"That going to be an issue?" I kept my voice flat and didn't move. This world was made of questions like this, determining if someone was mercenary enough to take on someone they knew personally? I could feel muscle tensing and aching for the comfort of the grip of a handgun but I forced myself to remain calm.

"Nah," Zipline said, expelling smoke across the table. "I *know* him. I don't *like* him."

"Good. Got us an in on these guys?" I said as my muscles relaxed slightly, still all the chance in the world that Zipline was setting me up to stab me in the back. But, like I had told him, the risk is why they pay me.

"Yeah, like I said. Speed freaks. I can drop a Wave asking for a load of trentameth for pick up. These guys are likely mid-meth-ride and will be up for another two days."

"Do it. There is a bonus if we get her back before anyone can find out she is gone."

"Yo," Ivan interjected. "So we go in and get the girl, what do we do about the Ronin?"

"We kill 'em all. Contract is pretty clear about that. Client wants this washed away like a bad dream." I pointed at Ivan. "Me and you go in handle them, we grab her and walk out. It's The Towers. No one is going to give a shit. Zipline runs intrusion and overwatch."

"Nexus," Ivan said, "What is the payout?"

"30k each for y'all. Expenses out of my end."

"I don't think y'all get it," Zipline interjected. "Y'all got the easy slice of pie. The Towers are a jumbled mess of private networks, honey pots, bear traps, black ice, and server bombs. Place isn't secure, it's just fucking dangerous. I could end up a Toaster Strudel if one of those ICE counters slips me up."

"Oh like, our fucking end of this is easy?" Ivan growled. "Remember the meth'd Russians?"

"Zero out. Both of you." I spoke calmly. "The money is good. If shit get *oblicuo* I might consider a combat bonus. But let's not pretend that risk is a new concept."

They both looked at me, Ivan's augmented eyes a stark contrast in matte black and metallic gold. Zipline's were still his original organic, murky green ringed with bloodshot white. The TriDees would have you believe violent men would follow their leader, because there was some deep spiritual connection that made them want to follow them into hell. The reality is we all did it for our own reasons, and my leadership was more a trait of tactical ability than any thrilling heroics.

"Alright, I am in. But if I fry processors, I expect coverage," Zipline stated sourly.

"That's covered in expenses," I said, hitting the tab out button. A weak TriDee sprang to life showing the itemized list and total. I waved a preloaded card and added a 20% tip.

"Now let's get going. I'd like to be home some time reasonable tomorrow."

The security field wavered and disappeared. I stood and started walking to the door, noting that the table of armored officers were gone, their unpaid tab lazily dancing in the air over a table covered in dirty dishes. I heard Ivan and Zipline slide out of the booth and follow me, Zipline tossing a wave to Limerick and his entourage.

Outside, I saw the cluster of cops standing near an empty clearing of the parking lot, smoking and obviously waiting on their ride. The path to our van took us past them. I silently whispered prayers to a god who, if he was real, would want nothing to do with me, that my compatriots would act like the professionals they were paid to be.

As we passed, I felt one set of eyes track on me and follow. I ran my memory trying to think where I had last seen the somewhat familiar face. As the memory came to me I heard the voice. He had all the measured authority a badge and gun gave you. Trained in the academy to command respect and obedience from the frightened and weak willed.

"Well, well, well. Mr. Drake. What brings you out and about tonight?"

"Officer Anderson," I said, turning, flicking my eyes to my two compatriots, hoping they got the message to stay calm. "Just another late dinner with friends."

"Uh-huh," he vocalized condescendingly. "Where you working tonight?"

Our last encounter had not been an overly kind one. And in the end he had been forced to concede the point that police authority only extended so far. So his needling right now was less a threat and more an statement that he knew what I was and didn't care for it.

Of course, I didn't much care for him either.

"Oh," I said opening the siding door of the van and stepping in. "No place with a high enough income bracket for you to care about."

I closed the door before he could reply and turned to Zipline. "Get us rolling."

He didn't say anything, just shifted us into gear and slowly rolled the work van out into the night.

The back of the van was a strange mix of rituals. Ivan sat with his back against the wall of the van, his feet bouncing in rhythm with whatever SlamSalsaPop song filled his ear buds. Long ago, he had confessed to me that the moments before a hit were the hardest for him, so he pretended like it wasn't happening. Zoned out with his thoughts on how he would be spending his share, it was an almost sexual look for him.

I looked decidedly less serene. Stripped to the waist my body was racked with micro tremors and was drenched in sweat. I watched as the auto injector fell from my hand soundlessly—over the pounding of my blood in my ears, I couldn't hear *anything*. The cocktail wasn't one of my making. I had learned it years ago from Sicarios trained by the Mexican government, back when they gave a shit about fighting the century old drug war. A combination of chemicals and nanos would let me operate at peak combat efficiency. I would move faster, feel less pain, react quicker, and process the world around me better. But like everything in the world there was a tax to be paid. And that meant not only a hard shock to the system as it was carried through my veins and distributed throughout my body, but also a wicked hangover in the next three days... which was about the same time I would be able to get to go to sleep.

I breathed deep in and out. Pushing air from my body and feeling the tremors slow and finally subside. I reached under the bench I sat on and pulled out a black duffle bag. I had packed and repacked it over the years. My quick and dirty work bag. If the job wasn't a specialty gig, this bag would likely get me through it. As I unzipped it saw Ivan was staring at me.

"What?" I said, overly hostile, it wasn't that I particularly gave a shit if he looked at me or not. But the drugs left me aggressive and snappy.

"*Nichego* man, that shit never looks fun," he said coolly, "or healthy."

"Berserk really isn't something done for pleasure," I said, trying my best for a flat response, not that I pulled it off.

"Yeah, I get that. But typically, you dose up two or three hours before we smash someone. You about to walk in there looking like a fucking *Ángel Muerte* junkie."

He dug into his jacket and pulled out a green tipped vaporizer. Pressing it out to me as an offering he continued. "So chill man. We are going to have to be glass smooth before this thing turns to *kinzhal*."

My initial reaction was to smash it down and inform him to get fucked—which told me he was likely correct. So I took it and drew deeply off it, letting the THC concentrate flood my lungs in a cloud of water vapor.

"Thank you," I coughed out.

"*Nyet*," he said, leaning back.

I returned myself to the task at hand, hoping that the THC could stabilize me for now. I considered the hardware and tools in the bag. Hard and soft goods massed in an organized jumble. The mixed smells of sweat, lubricant, gun powder, and pine freshness (from the tree shaped car fresheners I had thrown in the bag) assaulted my nostrils in a familiar wave.

I glanced up and consulted Ivan's hardware and considered how to best compliment it. His Remington 230 Short Barrel Auto Shotgun sat across his lap, a compact and brutal weapon that made up for its lowered capacity with sheer brutality of its 10 gauge buckshot rounds. The short shotgun was a popular home defense weapon for those worried about the threat of cybernetically augmented foes. Ivan had a fondness for the gun despite its punishing recoil. He'd also taken a pair of compact Glock handguns from the office, one tucked into his pants by his belt buckle with a cheap holster, the other stuffed into the pocket of his bomber jacket. Ivan's theory revolved around disposable firearms and gear, cyberware over hardware.

Once, we had been deep into our cups after a successful hit. Sitting on a boat in the middle of Lake Lanier, our blood-soaked clothes and hardware sinking quickly into the murky waters in our wake, he got philosophical. "*It's America man, guns are the one thing we aren't running out of anytime soon. Whole country made with the things.* This here is Cordite Country."

I disregarded the compact Beretta SMG—Ivan had indiscriminate mayhem covered. What I needed was accuracy and utility. I opened a side panel and removed a padded case. Inside rested a SIG P430, customized by the company's elite Grey division. They'd taken a basic service handgun and made it a tack driving weapon worthy of any high-end special op types.

The gun featured a low profile frame-mounted red dot sight, ported and compensated barrel, flared mag well, retextured grip and reworked trigger. All these features gave a well-trained, discerning shooter a super compact and accurate weapon in an easily concealable package. Its 11mm cartridge allowed for a number of different load options for the various threats in the world. I selected four extended 20 round magazines. Two were filled with flesh and augment shredding micro-explosive hollow points, the other two with armor-piercing rounds.

I fitted myself with a gun belt, filled the pouches with ammunition, knives, emergency medical gear, and a breaching charge, before sliding a magazine into the SIG and racking the slide. I slid it into a PHLstar holster I had mounted to the right of my belt buckle, the aggressive rearward cant of the holster allowed for a faster draw, even if it was slightly harder to conceal.

Next, I pulled on a thick black shirt. The 3mm thick shirt felt much like a 20th century wet suit and was near skintight, but its honeycombed features would act as reactive armor. It should stop most frag, spall, and lower velocity rounds. In addition, I slid in two titanium plates, one front and one back.

My light-up sneakers were stylish, but also a poor decision, tactically, so I replaced them with set of black Altama combat moccasins. Finally, I pulled on a loose fitting hoodie emblazoned with the logo for a local chain of restaurants. It may have seemed like an odd thing, but it was comfortable, hid most of the hardware, and they really *did* make a tasty burger.

"Towers are coming up," Zipline said from the driver's seat. The front passenger seat was filled with his intrusion rig. "Once I drop y'all off, I'll find a parking spot. They are in Tower 3, nineteenth floor, suite twenty-nine. Don't take any fucking risks with these guys."

I looked up from my preparations and caught Zipline's eyes in the rearview mirror.

"Cornered dogs fight harder," he stated, meeting my eyes.

He was right. This gang had once been a powerhouse, content and rich off of multiple schemes. Now, they couldn't even pull off a simple heist. They were like a rabid dog riding a meth high and if they felt pressured or threatened, they would go to guns.

"They're expecting a purchase. Once they pop the door I am hitting it with a sonic charge and following a 12-bang in. We burn them down, grab the girl, and dip. This all goes according to plan, it should be a milk run."

And with that, we were there.

With the influx of refugees from both sides of the Sino conflict, Atlanta had few options for placement. It had finally been decided they would take the former Six Flags Over Georgia theme park, and convert the 300 acres into a "Rehoming Solution." They'd redesigned it to transplant the refugees into a place they could make a new home, with low income housing and open-air markets that would foster new businesses and create a thriving community.

The concept was presented as "A bold new direction in housing for the less privileged." Politicians and corporate types were on all the right talk shows saying all the right lines. The public bought it hook, line, and sinker. Those of us who are considered undesirable laughed at the whole show. We knew what was going to happen.

The first tower had a full ribbon cutting ceremony with Vladimir Ivanovic, a 16-year-old Russian refugee, holding the scissors. Smiles all around. The kid's story was a touching one—his mother and father killed in the fighting, making his way to America with his sister and grandmother, his English was just broken enough to be endearing. He was on all the morning talk shows, became a three minute celebrity.

The third tower wasn't even open yet before Vladimir was found dead.

The story was different every time I heard it, but a dozen bullets found their way into the kid in the middle of an apartment-turned-drug-den. The news didn't cover it, because his three minutes were up. It was better if The Towers project completed without scandal, and the news knew who paid their bills.

A total of twenty towers were planned. Eight were completed, but the ninth sat half-finished in a skeletal husk. By that time all the towers had become such horror shows not even the corporations could keep the stories under wraps. Much of the money intended for the refugees had found its way into bonus checks for corporate types and campaign funds for politicians, a few paltry arrests were made, all approved by the lords on high, and the damage was done. More importantly the grant money was all gone, so The Towers were left to their own devices and became what they were destined to become all along.

Now multiple factions lived, worked, and fought over them in a tale as old as time. Gangs, prostitution, drugs, weapons, and anything else you could desire could all be found there. Police rarely went into them and the corporate owners could barely be bothered to maintain them, let alone pay for privatized security firms. So, instead, the police watched the exits, the message being clear:

"Stay where you belong."

As we walked down trash-strewn walkways, we were greeted by the few dwellers of The Towers still up at this hour. Junkies, drug dealers, and hookers looked us over and in most cases immediately directed their eyes elsewhere. While we were obviously outsiders, our cyber augments and clear gun bulges also clearly marked us as apex predators. We were allowed to pass without challenge.

Once inside Tower 3, we looked around the deserted area that was once supposed to house a bustling marketspace full of restaurants, theaters, stores, and other shops a self-contained society might need.

Now all that was left was a gun shop sitting behind armored glass, and a bar where even the heaviest soundproofing couldn't contain the pulsating, hard bass.

We made our way towards the elevator bank. Designed to raise and lower dozens of citizens at a time, they had once been glass and glow bulb lit. Now years of abuse and neglect left it with chain link and armored neon bulbs. No one joined us as we slowly rose into the air.

"Place is more and more depressing every time I come here," Ivan said looking out of the elevator across the open air chasm at the other side of the tower.

"Out of one war zone to another," I replied blandly. The plight of refugees was occasionally a drumbeat by the wealthy elite who liked to pretend they gave a shit, but the reality is they wanted someone else to do the hard humanitarian work. They never beat the drum long, just enough to get the social currency they needed from it.

A noise buzzed in my ear. A micro bead bio-communicator was slowly dissolving there.

*"It's Zipline. I am in."*

"How do we look?" I said, adjusting my gun belt.

*"Good. Tower is quiet tonight. Not too many active users. The floor above the target is pure black ice. I think someone is running an offsite server farm there."*

"Weird," Ivan said, as he checked the load in his shotgun.

"None of our business," I stated as the doors opened. "Zip, we clear?"

*"All camera are down and I will start suppressing all phone service when you hit the door."*

"Golden."

We made our way down an offshoot hallway, barely lit. Graffiti stained walls and the smells of food and humanity beat down on me, tearing at my brain. But I focused myself towards the target door. A night's work was finally coming to fruition. Soon everything would come down to my team's skills vs. the other side. My muscles trembled as adrenaline mixed with the drugs already there. My gut tingled like a virgin on prom night.

The door to Suite 29 was a hardened security door with a cheap video intercom drilled into the wall. The door itself was covered in painted kanjis and Cyrillic. I reached into my pockets and pulled out a sonic breaching charge. Pulling off a protective cover, I adhered it to the door and placed the detonator in my left hand.

"Ready?" I softly whispered.

"Ready," Ivan breathed, palming a 12 bang and hiding it behind his leg.

*"Ready,"* Zipline stated calmly.

"I have control." I nodded at Ivan who reached out and hit the buzzer.

Crackling with cheap audio feedback, a voice on the other end spoke.

*"Who the fuck are you and the fuck you want,* Gaijin?"

"Zipline sent us," Ivan said calmly. "Said y'all had grade alpha crystal."

*"Yeah we do. Y'all got cash?"* the voice buzzed.

"Duh." Ivan looked disinterested. Of course when most of your face was mostly cybernetic that was fairly easy. He lifted a wad of cash in the hand not busy holding a flashbang.

*"Hold on a fucking tick,"* the box buzzed.

"Stand by," I whispered.

Ivan tensed, getting ready to hurl the device into the room. I waited, trying not to look over threatening in case they were still watching the camera. The sound of grinding metal told the door was being unlocked, I felt the tension escape. Now was my time, the time I was made for. Gone was all doubt, all fear, now there was only the fight.

*"Execute. Execute. Execute!"* I said, and detonated the charge.

Door breaching was as ancient as warfare and engineering. Defenders always want to keep attackers out, and so as long as men had invented doors, other men had found solutions to getting *through* them. Battering rams, hammers, picks, crowbars, and bombs. Bombs were *great* for removing doors, but they were also the most dangerous to the attacker.

The sonic breacher eliminated the issues of overpressure, fragmentation, and flame that traditional 20th century door charges had. Instead they sent a rapid series of ultra-high frequency pulses through the door that shook the surface so hard it practically disintegrated.

Of course it would be beyond unpleasant if you happened to be touching that surface that was being attacked in such a fashion. The Ronin gang member who had been unlocking the door screeched as his hand was vibrated to the point that his bones and muscle up to his shoulder were liquefied in a flash.

I kicked the remains of the door and him out of the way and stepped back so Ivan could do his part.

"YEET!" Ivan screamed as he hurled the 12-bang into the room.

The hallway shook and flashed as if in the middle of a rave thrown by a Norse god, each flash bright enough to be seen through closed eyes and each bang left one feeling as if they had been slapped across their entire body. Even I, someone who had trained with them extensively, had to hold onto my focus with everything I had. I was only in the *hallway*, anyone in the room would be on the ragged edge of sanity.

As the tidal wave of sound and light ended I drew my SIG and went through the door. Behind me, I heard the boom of Ivan's riot gun as he finished the doorman. The suite had a large common room, a hallway, and smaller rooms branching off. Opposite to me, across the common room was a glass sliding door leading to a balcony. Behind the glass two men clawed at the air, disoriented by the flashbang.

I shot them through the glass.

The first, I centered my red dot sight on his chest and stroked the trigger, fast. The first micro-explosive hollow-point impacted the plate glass door and exploded. The resulting pop of the embedded charge shattered the glass, allowing the following rounds to pass nearly unmolested. As each round found their mark, they penetrated several inches and then detonated, opening up massive wound channels and driving tiny slivers of shrapnel throughout the body. The target jerked, and finally folded to the ground, an oozing wreck of a body.

My eyes tracked to the next who was starting to claw for some sort of chest mounted holster. I rotated my body like a turret, finding him through the optic. I settled the red dot on his head and stroked the flat trigger once. A spray of red and pink filled the air. Watching a human being having their strings cut was always unsettling. All functions stopped, and the body went from being alive to simply another bag of meat. Gravity took full effect and the body dropped out of my sight picture.

Taking the briefest of seconds I looked at the first man on the balcony I had shot. He was still moving slightly, and I shot him in the head. While likely overkill, I'd rather kill a man twice over, than get shot in the ass by one who was only partly on his way out.

Ivan had been right behind me after dispatching the wounded doorman, and I was damn happy for that. He had covered my blind side as I had engaged the men on the balcony, and caught one coming out of the kitchen with some sort of long gun. Ivan's shotgun had splashed the man's innards and third-rate cyberware across the wall.

My instincts screamed for me to move, and I dove behind a couch as a stream of full-auto fire tore through the space I had inhabited. The deafening roar of the weapon filled the room. Tufts of couch stuffing and faux-leather filled the air as my concealment-not-cover was clawed at by the fusillade of rifle rounds. I crawled forward, desperately trying not to be where the gunman had last seen me. Getting to the end of the couch, I could see the fire was coming from one of the bedrooms. I drove my pistol out and emptied it into the doorway, causing the shooter to retreat deeper into the room.

"You with me?" I heard Ivan roar.

I rolled over so I could access my magazine pouch and quickly reloaded my pistol. Worried we might be dealing with a barricaded enemy I selected a magazine of armor piercing.

"Yeah, I am here," I stated calmly.

"Good. Let's get this fucker. *Shchit* up!" Ivan said.

I turned to look at him. The burst of fire had clearly hit him, as his coat was in tatters and his shotgun was on the ground. He shook out his left arm, causing it at first to twist and bulge as the synthetic skin on it distorted, stretched, and finally ripped. From within, a thin ballistic shield sprang into life. Covering his vulnerable torso and head, it wouldn't be able to take many rounds, but it would be more than enough to cover him pushing the door. His right hand drew his first Glock from his waistline.

"Moving!" he spat furiously. Ivan hated getting shot.

"Move!" I stated, coming to my knees and firing at the problematic doorway.

Ivan moved forward, behind his shield. As he got closer to the door I stopped firing, stood, and followed him, slipping behind his armored bulk. I was protected but blind. Ivan stopped before crossing the threshold. I reached up and squeezed his shoulder hard with my left hand. With that, he exploded into the room, taking a hard left. I went forward to cover my sector. I heard a burst of gunfire followed by several muted pops.

I stayed focused on my sector. This had once been the master bedroom, but it was clearly now more of a work room. Cheap memory plastic tables and chairs held weapons, clothes, and . . . projects. In my sector I had no one living, but I could see movement under the crack of a door in the corner.

I risked a glance over my shoulder to check on Ivan. The gang member who had opened fire on him was slumped into the corner, half a dozen ragged holes in his chest and a smoking Kalashnikov in his lap. Ivan stomped his head in with a cybernetically enhanced kick. As the body began to spastically twitch and gurgle, Ivan turned to me and flatly stated, "Clear."

I spoke, pointing my weapon at the door. "Movement. Door."

He nodded, dropping his half empty Glock to the floor. He reached over and disconnected the spent shield, leaving it on the floor, exposing a skeletal arm of carbon fiber bone and steel cable muscle. He drew his second Glock awkwardly from his jacket pocket. I positioned myself to the side of the door.

"Kick," I ordered tersely.

Ivan obliged me with his gore covered foot, leaving an unpleasant-to-see-and-smell, dark red smear across the already stained door. As the door flew off its hinges, I glanced in. It was an adjoining bedroom. There were surplus bunk beds and a Ronin gang member stood in the far corner. He was using a frightened girl as a body shield. I looked at him through the optic of my pistol as I used the wall as cover. He had driven his machine pistol into her head and had his finger on the trigger.

"Fuck you, cocksucker! Y'all come any closer and I will blow her head off!"

His voice was panicked. His face flush with fear. Our eyes locked as the situation played. As keyed up as he was, if I took the shot, there was a very real likelihood he might squeeze the trigger and kill the girl. It was a desperate plan on his part and ultimately . . . a flawed one.

"Yeah. . . . But she isn't the one I am here for," I said, and pressed the trigger.

# BACKUP PLANS

## A Bronze Legion Short Story

Jason Cordova & Melissa Olthoff

***Primus Palais, Klysgaard, Myrkyma***

*Always have a backup plan.*

Sylvie Gallagher hadn't been in the game long, but that maxim had been driven home by her handler after she'd been recruited straight out of her Survey Corps training class into the rumored but never confirmed Intelligence Branch.

Publicly, the Survey Corps only had three branches: Exploration, Evaluation, and Expedition. Like so many other applicants, she'd wanted Exploration, wanted to see what was out there beyond the reaches of known Mars Protectorate space. Then her handler had told her *exactly* what was out there, and she'd embraced her new calling with a quickness. And if that new calling had also led her to embracing the . . . perks of life as a Tyrant's concubine deep below the poisonous surface of Myrkyma in the ridiculously opulent Primus Palais, well. There were worse things than *entertaining* a man who looked like a cross between a Greek god and a classic underwear model.

Sylvie draped herself across Enki's muscled chest, her breathing still rapid, her bare skin damp from delightful exertion. He chuckled, a deep rumble she felt as much as heard, and skimmed his fingers up and down her back. Both a soothing gesture and one that sent shivers up her spine. She wasn't sure yet if he wanted another round, but she was content to wait, very much lost in post-orgasmic bliss. A small part of her mind, the part that remembered who and *what* she really was, busily churned away.

*A concubine was* not *my first choice for infiltrating this shithole, but needs must... because I know what's coming for us. This mission is important, maybe the most important thing I've ever done. With benefits.*

A lazy smile tugged at her lips.

*And damn... I really want to experience those benefits again.*

It certainly beat slogging through the mud and worse on some backwater world for the Exploration branch. It also helped that Enki was literally the hottest man Sylvie had ever seen, actually knew what he was doing with what generations of genetic tinkering had given him, and was... if not kind, then not horrible like the rest of them.

Proof that a shitty personality wasn't hard-coded into Tyrant genetics.

Which was great, because securing that genetic code for the Mars Protectorate was her entire reason for being here. And since she'd had to resort to her backup plan, it was really nice to know the Tyrants were unholy bastards due to nurture more than nature.

Enki idly wrapped a lock of her raven-dark hair around one hand, allowing the silky strands to slip through his fingers.

"Beautiful," he said, voice a quiet murmur of admiration. He tucked clever fingers under her chin, gently angled her face up so he could admire her features, paying particular attention to her pale blue eyes. "So beautiful."

Sylvie allowed her lazy smile to grow smug, because she knew exactly how beautiful she was. And Enki liked it when she was a little arrogant. A fine line to walk, even with him, but worth the results.

It was her looks that had first drawn the attention of Intelligence. Anyone who made it past the Survey Corps selection process was already exceptional, so they knew she had the quick wits necessary for the job, but they tagged her not just because they needed someone gorgeous, but because they needed someone who matched a specific aesthetic. Their theory was that the Tyrants would naturally gravitate toward a concubine who mirrored their black hair and icy blue eyes. A theory that was immediately blown out of the water after she'd been inserted into enemy territory.

Every last Tyrant in that stupid palace had turned their arrogant noses up at what they considered a weak imitation of their pure bloodlines, leaving her if not in peace—there was no such thing in the concubine quarters—but untouched and unmolested. At first, that had suited her just fine. Right up until Holly, the Head Bitch herself, self-proclaimed queen of the concubines and giant pain in Sylvie's ass, had taken great enjoyment in schooling the newest concubine on the rules. Rules which included what happened to girls who remained untouched, *unwanted*, after their first year.

Termination—and not the kind that included a fat severance package and a friendly pat on the back.

Months passed and still no Tyrant took her to bed or even so much as glanced in her direction. Desperation had Sylvie considering early extraction and damn the mission, because she couldn't complete it if she was *dead*, when Enki had returned to Primus Palais after months spent working on one of his various projects. The Tyrant known as The Doctor had casually strolled through the concubine quarters, locked in a discussion with The Butcher, a sick fuck that Sylvie was *very* glad had never looked her way, when his icy blue gaze landed on her. And for the first time, she saw something other than disdain in a Tyrant's eyes.

In a very real way, Enki had saved her life.

But he was still a Tyrant, still barely walking on the hot side of asshole.

"Your beauty is but a pale imitation of our own, of course, like catching a muddied reflection in the still waters of a pool," he mused, brushing his thumb across her full lips. So arrogant, but almost like it was a reflex, something so deeply ingrained he never even noticed. His gaze grew intent on hers. "But I find myself captivated nonetheless. Let the rest of my brethren be enamored with the shiny baubles, let them be entertained by the lessers of your kind. You are unique, and lovely, and *mine*."

Enki dragged her into a hot, hungry kiss that left her panting for breath for *all* the right reasons. Judging by the very male satisfaction on his chiseled face, he wasn't displeased either.

Which was good, great even. Because as much as she liked him, as much as he seemed to like her—as much as a Tyrant was capable of such an emotion. If he lost interest, if she failed to keep him entertained and *captivated*...

A tiny shiver that had nothing to do with pleasure skated down her spine.

Sylvie kissed Enki with every bit of skill she possessed, distracting herself from her fear in the best way possible, and then he did a fine job of distracting her from everything else. It was late by the time he gently ejected her from his quarters. He usually kept her overnight, but his current project pulled his attention from her, and she knew better than to argue.

Staggering out of his quarters on legs that didn't want to work quite right yet, Sylvie slowly made her way back toward the concubine's shared rooms.

*I'm so damn tired.*

Not because of the late hour. Not because of her . . . vigorous activities. But because this was supposed to have been a quick, in and out mission. There were always Tyrants in the concubine quarters in various states of vulnerable, whether drunk, passed out, or otherwise occupied. Getting a blood sample should have taken her a week, two weeks tops.

*One year, three months, and two days later . . .*

When Dillon Ashby had joined the Protectorate of Mars Foreign Service, he'd never expected to be selected for Aspect Red, the secretive intelligence agency of the Protectorate. Nor had he asked for it. He was not one for adventure, no. "Staid and boring" had been the common phrasing all his instructors had used when asked about him throughout his schooling phase. His career path had been heavily directed towards finance, with his studies from primary school onwards focused on the subtle nuances of interstellar commerce. An honest career, where he would remain within Martian territory, with rare exceptions of serving as a trade delegate to foreign star nations while being wined and dined by the political elite of prospective trade partners. In other words, a bureaucratic flunky.

There'd been so many options to choose from within the Foreign Service, and Dillon had been eagerly anticipating his assignment. That, of course, was before the Aspect Red recruiter had shown up at his apartment door late one night more than six months ago. After signing a confidentiality agreement in the doorway (which he'd thought was pointless at the time because everything in the Foreign Service was covered under the Official Secrets Act) he'd been whisked off-world to a space station he hadn't known existed—and still didn't know the official designation of, though everyone there had called it The Hub—and then subjected to training unlike anything he'd ever experienced in his life.

Clearly Aspect Red thought "staid and boring" translated to "perfect deep cover intelligence agent." It was thanks to this theory that he found himself on probably the worst planet in the settled universe on a dangerous assignment, one he really wasn't enjoying.

*I should've been an accountant*, he thought as a pair of concubines walked past his post, giggling and batting their eyelashes his way. As usual, he ignored their obvious attempts to curry favor. Or worse, set him up to break one of the Rules because they were bored. He'd been on the job for barely two weeks when he'd seen what happened when some guard forgot to keep it in his pants.

Sure, the eye candy was nice, but everyone knew that too much sugar was bad for you.

The Tyrants who ruled the planet of Myrkyma were barely above the mindset of neolithic, pre-Exodus barbarians of Earth who believed in nothing more than blood and genetic purity. Because of this, the Tyrants had dozens of concubines they would regularly use, switching back and forth between the women in some mysterious and elaborate pattern he hadn't been able to discern yet.

This created a strange environment within the concubine community which confused Dillon to no end. Instead of working together to kill their oppressors, the concubines engaged in petty games of one-upmanship with each other. Backstabbing, social warfare, and even minor injuries were fairly common. Some of them not-so-minor, but that tended to piss off the Tyrants, so the bloodletting was usually kept to a minimum.

Dillon's duty as an official guard in Primus Palais, the Tyrant's headquarters deep underground, was more to protect the concubines from one another than anything else. And on occasion, clean up after something went horrifyingly wrong. Or in the case of the guard who thought he'd could get away with having relations with one of the concubines, held him down as the former colleague was neutered, branded, blinded, and then tossed up into the Overdark to die a horrible death.

Dillon had done his duty without as much as a wince. Even when the guard's manhood had been sliced off and fed to one of the dogs he hadn't paled. This had drawn the attention of a senior guard, who'd been impressed by his stoicism. He moved Dillon from exterior guard to interior the next day. That'd been two months before, and the lesson had stuck, despite some of the concubines' best efforts. The concubines, for whatever reason, found the scar on his chin to be rather dashing. He still resisted their advances, going so far as speaking to Holly, the ice blonde woman who seemed to run the concubines, when one of them had gotten a little too aggressive in her advances. The calculating women had simply laughed and mocked him, true, but the aforementioned concubine had stopped bothering him.

Nothing motivates an employee like watching what happens to someone when they break the rules. After all, "staid and boring" could also be translated to "apt pupil."

There was, of course, another problem within the Palais, one he wasn't quite sure how to handle just yet... the *other* spy.

Dillon had spotted one of the cleaning staff, an older man named Jarvey, doing something decidedly *odd* around the large compound on more than one occasion. The short, swarthy janitor wasn't particularly good at the job he'd been hired for, which had been the first clue. The man watched too much and didn't keep his head down like the others who'd lived on this poisonous world their entire lives. Plus, the little janitor was chatty under his breath, which also told Dillon which *nation* the spy was working for.

After some careful observation, he'd determined that Jarvey was working alone, but he did have a handler who he met in Klysgaard proper on a weekly basis. And while Dillon had tagged him as a spy or possible saboteur early on, he wasn't quite ready to pull the trigger on blowing his cover just yet. Or Jarvey's. Not until Dillon knew, precisely, who else was working with Jarvey, and what they were after.

Though it really wasn't much of a question. Dillon was willing to bet a year's salary—Mars Primus Foreign Service wages, not the cheap scrip they passed off as money on Myrkyma—that Jarvey was there for the same reason he was... securing the genetic template of the Tyrants.

He stifled a yawn as his eyes tracked the corridor. It took quite a bit of willpower to not check the time again. More concubines walked past, though none from his doorway. The hour was late, well past midnight, and most of the concubines were returning to their quarters at long last. The parties hosted by the various Tyrants typically ended before the witching hour, though one or two were known to continue until dawn. The Butcher, for example, was one of those Tyrants. Dillon shivered slightly as he remembered that particular man's eyes. There'd been something decidedly inhuman about them, about the way he looked at people.

His current posting was outside the private quarters of the Tyrant known as The Echo. His real name was Nabu, but nobody ever uttered it in his presence. Nabu was fond of mystery, lore, and he was more of a scholar than some of the others. Nabu was also a severe alcoholic and prone to passing out. Dillon's recent reassignment to guard his doorway during the night shift meant that his mission could be completed that much sooner. He would finally be able to get the hell out of this forsaken underground complex and touch real grass again.

Myrkyma had a poisonous atmosphere and plenty of rain, which meant that the colonists had been forced underground as the terraforming took hold. The deeper the settlement, the safer the water. Klysgaard, as the *de facto* capital of the planet and home of the Tyrants, was the deepest city on the planet—which made it the home to the absolute wealthiest.

Which he would not miss at all once he'd completed his assignment.

His eyes once again roamed the corridor of the Palais as he listened. The Echo and his four concubines had finally quieted down. The squeals and other vaguely intriguing sounds had faded more than an hour before, and now there was a heavy stillness within that pleased Dillon. His hand moved to the hidden panel on his ceremonial spear—the tip blunted and the edge dulled—and felt the imperfection in the false wood.

Inside were three small vials and a syringe for the blood draw. He would need roughly three milliliters in each to satisfy his superiors at Aspect Red. Once that was secured, they could finally begin the long and torturous process of unlocking the key to the Tyrant genome. His entire mission revolved around three practically irreplaceable vials and his ability to fill them.

He didn't know why this was such a dire and urgent need, but Dillon knew his job. The Tyrants had ruled Myrkyma for at least two hundred years, yet he'd easily built up his identity and infiltrated in months. The sudden rush was disconcerting, but manageable. He glanced up and down the corridor a second time. There was nobody in sight, save for a single concubine who was staggering down the hallway, clearly intoxicated. She was a raven-haired beauty, one of the rare concubines who faintly resembled the Tyrants, though there was something different about her eyes. She was muttering something under her breath as she did her damndest to walk in a straight-ish line. He'd seen such behavior before, though not so blatant. Whichever Tyrant this concubine was with, they would not be pleased if she were found by one of the others.

It was now or never. The concubine was clearly in no state to be able to explain why a guard stepping inside the Tyrant's chambers was strange or unusual. Not that anyone would. Nabu oftentimes used his guards as sounding boards, where they made non-committal grunts while he waxed eloquently about Tyrant lore and their particular interpretation of recent history. All boring stuff, really. Dillon had already participated once before, when Nabu had been drunk and philosophical.

He was unlikely to get another opportunity such as this, not with the way things were going. The locals had been growing more and more restless the past few weeks, and it was only a matter of days now until the entire place went up in revolutionary zeal. Taking a deep and calming breath, he activated the panel for the door into Nabu's private chambers and stepped inside.

Sylvie was tired enough and alone enough in that cold hallway she allowed herself the luxury of feeling that rarest of emotions—anger. An emotion she'd ruthlessly suppressed for so long, the acid burn of it shocked her awake.

It should've been *so* easy to get what she needed from one of the Tyrants constantly passed out in the concubine quarters, except for a chilling fact she'd discovered within her first few days of being embedded. One of the concubines got a little too enthusiastic and clawed up a Tyrant's back, actually daring to draw blood. Fortunately for the concubine's continued well-being, that particular brute enjoyed a little pain with his pleasure and rewarded her for it. Fortunately for Sylvie's continued well-being, that was the day she discovered biometric sensors were built into every conceivable exit of the palace, but not within individual Tyrant suites.

Fingers curled and nails bit into soft palms.

Getting a sample was easy. Getting out with one was nearly impossible.

Ideally, she would've gotten word back to her handler on the increased level of difficulty—on her first assignment, no less—but she was on her own until she initiated the extraction plan. Outside communication wasn't permitted to the concubines, and "borrowing" one of the Tyrant's comms was impractical at best. They were all biometrically locked to the individual, and probably monitored to one extent or another. Not worth the risk.

Her only other option involved risking the cover of the Martian ambassador, and that was only permitted under extreme and *very* specific circumstances. Circumstances which didn't include a new agent who was somewhat stumped on how to achieve her mission.

Because of those *stupid fucking* biometric sensors, Sylvie crafted over a dozen backup plans before Enki's interest had made one backup plan outshine the rest. She'd enacted it three months ago, but she had stayed long enough to ensure the plan was viable. She'd managed to get confirmation that morning, so really . . . she could execute her escape from this gilded prison as soon as the correct circumstances lined up.

And if there was a very real, very inconvenient part of her that didn't want to leave, she squashed it as ruthlessly as she usually squashed her anger.

Capturing Enki's attention had been a lucky break in more ways than one. He was The Doctor, after all, the Tyrant more involved than any other in the genetic tinkering they were doing on this hellish, forsaken planet. His quarters were part living space and part laboratory, though she was never allowed in that section. In the three months she'd delayed her departure, he'd relaxed around her enough to allow some of that work to spill over to his living space.

Including two tiny devices capable of extracting information from any biological entity, like the genome of a frog or lizard . . . or a Tyrant. They were more than capable of storing that data without retaining any of the blood or skin samples sure to trigger the biometric sensors.

The less said about how she'd smuggled those out of Enki's

quarters, the better. Just because she had a hopefully viable backup plan didn't mean she'd given up on the primary. She'd wait until just before she was ready to go, secure two extra samples for genetic diversity, and her first mission would be a success.

Even if it had taken *slightly* longer than originally intended. A pleased grin tugged at her lips. Per Intelligence pay rates, hazardous duty rates, and back pay for over a year, she'd have one hell of a fat bonus waiting for her when she returned. *I'm going* shopping... *maybe drag Astra along if she's around.*

Sylvie spotted a guard down the hall and added a bit of a sway to her admittedly already unsteady steps. Usually the guards didn't bother the concubines, and they certainly didn't let the concubines bother *them*—not after the last poor fool was punished so terribly—but better to look like a silly drunk than interesting. Muttering nonsense under her breath, she tucked one hand into the tiny pocket of her silks, wrapped her fingers around the tinier knife that she'd sharpened to a razor's edge.

*Always have a backup plan.*

She got close enough to recognize the one guard she'd wanted to avoid. The one who was clearly another spy and a poor one to boot if she'd spotted him so easily on his first day within the concubine quarters. He just had that look. Too stoic, too observant, too *something*, enough to trigger instincts.

She'd thought about eliminating him. It would be easy enough. They'd trained her where to strike, how to make it look like an accident. Then she realized she could simply report that he'd touched her. That first night after she'd identified him as a potential threat to her operation, Enki had summoned her to his quarters. The words to condemn the other spy had hovered on the tip of her tongue, his life balanced on a razor's edge. Cold practicality told her to eliminate the threat. Colder practicality told her to wait, to see if he could be useful.

And now here he was, clearly dismissing her as a potential threat or even anyone of consequence as he boldly entered The Echo's room, neither moving or acting like a guard.

Dropping the drunken act, Sylvie ghosted down the hallway and peered around the doorframe just in time to see him crouch over the snoring Tyrant, four sleeping concubines draped around him on jewel-colored cushions like pretty decorations, pull a blood sample, and tuck three vials beneath his guard uniform. As he straightened up, she pulled back, scuttled a short distance down the hallway, and resumed her swaying walk just as the other spy hurried out of the room. He shut the door behind him silently, a quiet look of accomplishment on his face as if he'd achieved some impossible mission.

*What. A. Moron.*

If she let him walk out, he'd trigger every alarm, and it was entirely likely she'd get swept up in the chaos. That was attention she could *not* afford. Not now, not when she was so close. Also, it was in the Mars Protectorate's best interest to keep the Tyrant's genetic code out of anyone else's hands, and there was no telling who this moron was working for.

Her hand tightened on her little knife. She had no choice.

Sylvie put *all* the sway in her hips and approached the guard before he could walk away with the damning evidence in his pocket. She was dressed in nearly translucent silks that highlighted her figure and showed a whole lot of skin, and she knew how to move to draw a male gaze.

For just an instant, the man's eyes dipped lower than her face before his eyes snapped back up and his expression hardened. "Not interested."

She didn't let it deter her.

"You sure, handsome?" Sylvie's smile was wicked and confident, and she tilted her face up, looking at him through siren eyes. "Come with me and I'll show you a *real* good time."

The man was clearly on edge, visibly so the longer they lingered outside The Echo's door, and he jerked his gaze away from her. "Sorry, but as I'm *sure you're aware*, it's against the rules for guards to fraternize with the Tyrants' personal concubines, and I'm getting real sick and tired of repeating that," he growled, his eyes briefly flicking back to hers in an irritated glare. "Find somebody else to scratch your itch."

Sylvie was annoyed and so very tempted to let the idiot find out about the scanners the hard way, to let the other guards handle the traitor in their midst... and if she thought she had a chance of getting out of the proverbial blast zone before he got what he deserved, she would have left him in a heartbeat. But she couldn't, so she'd just have to persuade him to join her in a dark corner in a slightly different way than she'd originally intended. She glided forward until she was nearly pressed up against his chest.

"No, you don't understand," she purred, keeping her smile in place, though it was more teeth than anything sexy. "You want to come with me, *right now*."

She tapped the little knife against his groin for emphasis. Slowly, he looked down, paled, and let her push him into the nearest closet. The instant the door was shut behind them, he had a blade nestled against her throat. Even as the cold metal pricked her skin, her blade against his groin didn't waver an inch. If anything, she dug in just a little harder. His shadowy expression flinched before that hard expression snapped into place again.

"Drop the knife or I'll cut your throat."

Shock slammed into Sylvie and destroyed any trace of smug superiority. It had been *so long* since she'd heard that accent. It had only been there for a fraction of an instant, an unintentional slip on the man's part, she was sure, but real all the same. *Damn it. I can't kill him. I have to... ugh, help him.*

She dropped her act, not the knife, and let her Mars Primus accent come out to play. "Drop *your* knife or you'll be singing soprano the rest of your miserable life."

Shock stamped his bland features as he stepped back as far as the cramped confines of the closet would allow. "You're... you're *Martian?*"

"Yes," she hissed impatiently, taking control of the conversation so she could steer it where she needed it to go. He'd just gone from a threat to be eliminated to an opportunity too good to pass up. A partner at best, an excellent distraction from her escape at the very worst. Either way, useful. Circumstances, it appeared, had just lined up. "I've been embedded by our people for over a year, I was told to expect backup, but you took your sweet time about making contact!"

The man stuttered, confused and flailing, but she kept going. It wouldn't do to allow him time to get his feet under him. Or ask inconvenient questions such as who, exactly, she worked for. It was enough that they were both from Mars Primus. For now.

"Good thing I made you first, because if you'd tried walking out that door with a blood sample, you would've set off every alarm in the place and been food for the scavengers five seconds later. They don't play around here."

The other spy was silent for a few seconds before he cursed viciously. "I'm well aware."

Sylvie held out her hand. "Give me the vials. There are protocols for safely disposing of such things here."

There weren't, but he didn't need to know that she was merely going to hide them in Holly's personal items in a place sure to be discovered during the next inspection. That bitch deserved everything that would befall her perfectly rounded ass. When Holly's position had been threatened by Laurel, a gorgeous and fiery redhead with a laugh that lit up the whole palace, she'd engineered her downfall.

Laurel had been Sylvie's friend, as much as she could have friends in this place, and she'd vowed a bit of personal revenge before she left. This would do nicely. Besides, she had a few things she needed to pick up before she left.

Sylvie ruthlessly suppressed the small pang that rippled through her at the thought of leaving Enki and held out her hand impatiently. Unsurprisingly, the man didn't immediately pass over the vials. She honestly would've been disappointed in him if he *had.*

Both of them went silent and still as footsteps walked down the hallway, a heavy tread that indicated a guard, a cleaner . . . or a Tyrant. Fortunately, the footsteps continued past their little closet without slowing, and they both breathed again. It was an excellent reminder that the late hour wasn't a guarantee they wouldn't be interrupted.

A thrill rose up in Sylvie as that long-suppressed part of her, the part that had spent years rigorously training for this, woke up. She gave him a feral little grin and gambled on telling him the truth. Well, part of the truth.

"I'm Sylvie. Thanks to spending way too much time in this shithole—one year, three months, and two days if you want the time math—I know how to get those samples out without triggering the sensors. But we'll have to work together."

The bland little man stared at her for an uncomfortable length of time before he gave her a smile that was anything *but* bland.

"Dillon." He glanced at his comm and his jaw tightened. "Fine, we'll work together. It beats working with that other spy."

Sylvie's brow furrowed. "What other spy?"

A hint of triumph lit up his face. "What, little miss super spy missed Jarvey the cleaner?"

A vague memory drifted to the surface, a short, comfortably plump man with cold, dead eyes. The kind of man who would casually stab someone in the kidney then go get himself ice cream. Sylvie had spotted him a few weeks ago, and her instincts had screamed at her to steer clear. Now she was kicking herself for not paying more attention. To cover her mistake, she tilted her chin at an arrogant angle reminiscent of a Tyrant.

"Oh, that spy." Sylvie eased the door open a fraction of an inch and ensured the hallway was clear. "Come on, we've got to make a pit stop before we can get those samples out of here."

"Lead the way," he said dryly and patted his uniform shirt. "I'll hold onto the vials. I might be new at this game, but I wasn't born yesterday."

*New enough to admit you're new, or smart enough to pretend to be?*

Sylvie decided it didn't matter, because she didn't trust him either way, and led Dillon into the heart of concubine territory. Soft shadows draped the massive common area strewn with cushions and low tables, walls hung with precious silks and priceless works of art. Shiny baubles to distract the women from the very real fact that they were in a prison . . . voluntarily or not. They picked their way across the room and to the head bitch's private room. Light shone from under the door, indicating Holly might be both awake and inside. Sylvie really hoped so.

Dillon gave her a little side eye, probably because she was grinning like a psycho, but she just winked at him, shoved the door open, and swept inside. Holly lunged up from her ridiculously oversized, plush bed just in time to catch Sylvie's fist in her face. The other woman crumpled to the floor without a sound, and Sylvie shook her hand out.

"Damn, that was satisfying." Sylvie tilted her head, and then slammed her foot into the woman's rib cage. Without proper footwear, the blow didn't land nearly as hard as she wanted, but it would hurt every time the bitch breathed, and she'd remember exactly who'd done it to her. "That was even more satisfying."

A bright, joyful laugh rang out in her memory, and Sylvie echoed it with a bloodthirsty one of her own. She drew her foot back to do it again, because *fun*, but Dillon grabbed her arm and tugged her away from the unconscious woman.

"We don't have time for this," he hissed, glancing at his comm again.

"Spoilsport."

Pouting just a little, she strode over to the dusty little bookshelf in the back corner of the opulent room. Pulling the dustiest book free, she flipped it open with appropriate dramatic flair, revealing the hollowed out compartment.

"That was one hell of a risk," Dillon said reprovingly. "What if she'd decided to read that book?"

Sylvie snorted. "Please, that bitch can't read."

She'd squirreled away two identical medical devices within, along with something entirely different. She picked up the detonator and tucked it into her cleavage.

*Always have a backup plan.*

"What was that?" Dillon demanded, suspicion heavy in his brown eyes.

"Just a little party favor we hopefully won't need." She held her hand out impatiently. "Blood samples, now."

Dillon reluctantly passed them over. While she worked to transfer the genetic information, he glanced at his comm no less than three times.

"Why do you keep checking the time?" she finally asked in exasperation.

He stared at her but remained silent. If he didn't want to talk, that was fine by her. Gritting her teeth, Sylvie planted the extra vial of blood that would damn Holly, pocketed one of the devices with its precious genetic code, and extended the second to Dillon. He made it vanish beneath his guard's uniform and strode to the door.

"Because we're almost out of it," he said grimly as he looked over his shoulder. "And we need to get you a change of clothes before we can walk out of here."

Sylvie glanced down at her revealing concubine silks and grimaced. He was right. She raised her brows and flicked her fingers at him imperiously.

"Lead the way."

✧✧✧

Dillon hustled through the concubine quarters, leading his unexpected ally to the last place anyone would expect to find one of the gorgeous jewels of the Tyrants—the cleaning crew locker room. He tossed a uniform at her.

"Hurry," he barked.

Sylvie didn't bother to change, she simply pulled the bulky gray jumpsuit over her slinky little non-outfit, swept her raven locks back into a practical ponytail, and shifted her body language from sly seductress to overworked cleaner.

It was impressive.

He hurriedly pulled on a jumpsuit over his guard uniform and tucked his decorative spear inside a broom closet. The door of the locker room suddenly banged open, and a weary group of cleaners shuffled inside just as Sylvie tugged a brimmed cap low over her face, hiding her delicate features. Moving as one, they hustled past the newly arrived cleaners, but Dillon couldn't help but stiffen at a glimpse of cold, dead eyes watching them leave. He didn't relax until the door swung shut behind them, and even then only slightly.

They still had to make it outside the Palais. For the first time, he wondered if Sylvie was playing him. His gaze slid toward her, but no, she had one of the devices too, and her footsteps didn't falter as they marched through mostly empty halls, drawing ever closer to the exit, to escape.

And then a strident alarm split the air.

That was either a very good thing for them, or incredibly bad. A measure of tension leached from Dillon's spine when gunfire and the dull roar of an enraged mob reached his ears, though Sylvie understandably tensed.

"What the hell is that?" she hissed, confident stride faltering for the first time.

"Sounds like the locals finally got sick of the Tyrants." Dillon glanced at his comm, urged her to walk faster as more uniformed workers flooded the previously quiet halls. "And an opportunity for us. Come on!"

Inexplicably, Sylvie actually glanced over her shoulder, something unreadable flickering across her face. Reluctance? But then her expression hardened and she lengthened her stride. The guards at the door had already been overwhelmed by the panicking workers, an unstoppable flood of humanity determined to escape as the cacophony of battle raged ever closer. Dillon kept one hand tight around Sylvie's upper arm, determined not to lose her to the crowd for several reasons, and then they were outside and past the biometric sensors.

Sylvie blew out a relieved breath. "Glad that worked."

Dillon shot her an outraged stare. "You said it would work!"

"It's not like I had a chance to *test* it," she snapped before a large man nearly ran her over in his desperation to get away. Dillon pulled her out of the way and began bulling his way through the crowd, breaking a path for Sylvie.

It was slow-going pushing through the crowds of workers trying to leave the grounds of Primus Palais, but Dillon had the advantage of being slightly taller than most of those who worked there. Not much, but just enough for him to spot the openings in the mass of humanity as they pushed towards the gates. More than once he was able to redirect them around some fighting or, in one particularly brutal case, a dead Tyrant being ripped apart by the bare hands of those who had previously called him master hours earlier.

Looking forward, he completely missed the small group behind them who'd been following the path he was clearing. It wasn't until a familiar rotund shape brushed against Sylvie, knocking her slightly off-balance, that he noticed. The janitor mumbled something under his breath as he passed, and Dillon's ears perked up at this. He locked eyes with the enemy spy, and the short, rotund man ran off as fast as his short legs could carry him.

Sylvie slapped her hand against her side, gasping in shock. Her jumpsuit had been expertly sliced open, though it didn't look as if blood had been spilled.

"That little shit! He stole it!" Her outraged stare snapped to the fleeing janitor. "He stole my device!"

"What? He's got the other one?" Dillon swore viciously and started to pursue Jarvey, but Sylvie grabbed his arm. He spun around, flustered. She clearly didn't understand what he was trying to do. "We have to stop him!"

"Who cares? You have the first one, right?"

"You don't get it. He's working for the Khanate!" Dillon frantically explained.

During the Exodus to Mars Primus, a group calling itself the

Khanate had taken over Earth through various military strikes. Nobody had been able to stop them, since most of the people who would normally have stood in their path had already moved to other colony worlds amongst the stars. The Khanate had since isolated themselves, save for the few colony worlds who traded with them, and were an enemy to everyone who stood in their way.

The Khanate in possession of Tyrant genome? The universe would be doused in the flames of war within thirty years, max. Nobody would emerge from *that* conflict unscathed, no matter how far away they believed themselves to be.

Sylvie's face paled at the news and with that, the last little bit of uncertainty he had about the woman drained away. She truly was on the side of the angels, like him.

"How do you know?"

"He speaks Hmong at the other concubines," Dillon stated, thinking back. "He just apologized in Hmong when he brushed you and picked your pocket. When he's trying to insult them, he speaks it without them realizing it. He does it in a low voice. I don't think he's even aware he's doing it. They think it's cute because he does it all sing-song and it sounds pretty, the stupid twits. Only place Hmong is even spoken anymore is—"

"—back on Earth," Sylvie finished, then cursed softly.

There was only one way off this hellhole, and a singular location where shuttles were allowed to take off and land. A design by the Tyrants to control the populace, but now a handy way to know precisely how the Khanate agent planned on extracting himself off-world. The biggest problem was that with the lifts jammed with people trying to flee the rebellion, they would be forced to climb the stairs to catch him.

Of course, the enemy spy would have to climb them as well. Dillon liked their odds very much. The enemy spy probably looked at cardio the same way Dillon looked at asparagus.

"Stairwell!" he declared and pulled her along. "There's no way the lifts are going to be working. He's going to head for the stairs and try to make it to the top level!"

"I don't know where the nearest access door is," Sylvie admitted. He couldn't blame her for that. Concubines were never allowed out of Primus Palais.

"I do. Let's go!"

The rioting was growing heavier by the minute. It seemed to Dillon that someone had opened the floodgates of armageddon, there were so many people dragging corpses of Tyrants and their bastards through the streets. If he'd have known it would have been this easy to grab the vials of their blood, he would have simply waited. This would have been *much* simpler.

*The plan has changed. Gotta stop the Khanate agent from escaping,* he thought as they ascended the first flight of stairs. With each level above the Primus Palais being eighty more feet, his legs would start to feel the burn of the constant pounding very shortly. He could hear Sylvie struggling to keep up. It didn't matter if she did or not. The Khanate could not get its hands on that container.

It was slow going, but they were starting to gain. The Khanate agent had clearly been skipping cardio days. Dillon's grin was practically feral as they continued to close the distance with each step climbed, every landing passed. They were only a few steps behind him, with every level becoming a test of endurance as they continued upwards. Sylvie was keeping up, but only just. Not that he blamed her. The concubines had been sequestered away and not required to maintain anything but their beauty. The guards, meanwhile, began every day with a brisk five-mile run, and then worked on various calisthenics before breaking off to their assigned guard posts. There was no point in having slovenly guards, he recalled Nabu saying on more than one occasion, though he never could remember seeing the Tyrant outdoors and jogging himself.

"Faster!"

*One year, three months, two days, and a million fucking stairs later . . .*

"Can't you go any faster?" Dillon demanded obnoxiously as he huffed his way up the stairs in front of her. "Or has a year in the lap of luxury caught up to you, made you put on a few pounds?"

Sylvie barely restrained herself from murdering him. It would make her feel better. Never had the annoying man been closer to dying than at that exact moment. Her fingers actually brushed against the hilt of her little knife, but she reluctantly let go. If only because he was too far ahead of her to stab.

The worst part? He'd probably remain blissfully unaware of his narrow escape for the rest of his long, hopefully *celibate* life.

Since she couldn't choose violence, Sylvie resorted to words.

"I'll have you... know, we were required... to work out every... day, you prick." Sylvie snapped a fierce glare up at him. "But that... didn't include... a stair-climber!"

The echo of running footsteps continued to drift down the stairwell, proof that they weren't torturing themselves with endless stairs for nothing. For such a plump little man, the enemy spy was doing a damned good job of staying ahead of them. Sylvie did her best to ignore the burning in her thighs, the raggedness of her breath, and the stitch that had burrowed into her side like the tip of a blade, and pushed herself up another flight of stairs as fast as she could go.

Not because Dillon had demanded it, but because the annoying man was right. They couldn't afford for the Tyrant genetic code to fall into the Khanate's hands. That would be disastrous for *everybody*, would elevate Earth to a galactic-wide existential threat, and the Mars Protectorate couldn't afford to have their attention divided. Not if they were going to survive what was coming.

The *bang* of a metal door slamming against concrete wall sent a sharp spike of alarm through her heart. The enemy agent had reached the upper level.

Dillon practically flew up the remaining stairs, and Sylvie did her best to keep him in sight. Panting and on the verge of actually throwing up, she staggered out of the stairwell and into chaos.

Throngs of people filled the streets, some rioting, others fleeing, and still more trying to return order. Too few to actually achieve it, just enough to make things so much harder for everyone else. Flames flickered in the distance, and chants of "Down with the Tyrants" roared from so many throats it was almost a wave of sound. Fear licked up her spine when one enraged man took a closer look at her, but he was tackled by a guard before he could do more than twitch in her direction.

Sylvie tugged her brimmed cap a little lower to hide her distinctive eyes. There was less than zero advantage to resembling a Tyrant in this situation. Black hair was common enough, but not black hair with icy blue eyes.

Slowly, painfully, they worked their way through the crowd, just two more in a steady stream of people trying to get to the landing platform and escape a city gone mad. Dillon kept rising up on his tiptoes, frantically searching the crowd for any glimpse of the enemy agent.

Up ahead, Sylvie could see the landing zone, the boarding platforms that promised safety . . . and the wall of long-term storage lockers. Relief shot through her even as she laughed breathlessly.

"Why do they even have those?" she asked, gesturing at a storage locker precisely 101 meters from the launch site as they shoved past a struggling knot of guards and civilians.

"Who cares?" Dillon shot an incredulous look over his shoulder. "We need to catch up to Jarvey before he escapes!"

Sylvie was careful to keep her smirk on the inside, where he couldn't see it. She brushed her hands against her chest, then unzipped the gray jumpsuit just enough for her to grab what she needed.

*Backup plans within backup plans.*

She followed Dillon closer to the boarding platforms practically seething with people, but his rapid stride abruptly slowed, stuttered to a halt.

"Found him."

Frustration simmered even though Dillon had spotted his quarry. The Khanate agent had made it to the relative safety of the landing zone. He was still a bit distant from the boarding platforms, but he was close enough to the guards that anything Dillon did now would surely draw their unwanted attention. They were *so close.*

The Khanate agent must have known this because he stopped and turned around. There was a triumphant grin on his face. The squat man held up the small device he'd swiped off of Sylvie and waggled it between his fingers. The Khanate spy then gave him a universal rude gesture with his middle finger.

Dillon paused, uncertain. He couldn't grab him now, and calling any attention to them would draw the ire of the guards. Granted, they seemed to have their hands full with rioters and innocents trying to get the hell off the planet while they still could, but it wouldn't take much for them to spot him and start asking very uncomfortable questions. Worse still, they might interrogate Sylvie and find out what her job had been in the Palais.

Turning, he was about to ask Sylvie what their next step would be but stopped. She held a small device, barely the size of her pinky finger, in her hand. It was what she'd hid from him earlier, when they'd transferred the stolen blood samples. Dillon looked at it, not comprehending as she stared at the Khanate agent. The indecision on her face was telling, but he simply did not understand what the look was for.

"EMP trigger," she explained quickly, before she hesitated and gripped his arm gently. "But if I pop it, we'll probably lose our sample as well."

He couldn't make it to stop the agent, not without someone stopping him. Or worse, the Khanate spy making a scene to draw more attention to them. Was he willing to risk losing everything they had both worked for? A good agent would risk much to protect the best interests of their nation. A great one would risk everything to save it. He knew what they had to do, even if saying the words hurt him in his very soul.

"We... we can't ever let the Khanate get their hands on the genetic code."

That was good enough for Sylvie.

The Khanate agent was practically standing next to the locker where the package had been placed a year before by the agent from the Martian Embassy. However, *they* might be just outside the range of the EMP blast... and Dillon still had his device, still had the Tyrant genetic code. Sylvie couldn't risk it, there was too much at stake. And she didn't think she was quite good enough to steal the device away from Dillon.

Just because they were from the same planet didn't mean they were on the same side.

She just needed them to be a little closer so she could be absolutely *certain* their storage device was destroyed right along with the Khanate's device.

Good thing her backup plan wouldn't be affected in the least.

Sylvie allowed a frantic woman to shove her, dragging Dillon well within range of the EMP device with an artful stumble. The Khanate agent hadn't moved an inch from his spot near two guards. He was staring at them, a smug expression on his face. He thought he'd won, secure in the false belief neither of them could touch him now. Not with landing pad security crawling all over the place, directing people struggling to escape the violent uprising. Any physical attack to him would cause a world of hurt to come crashing down on them.

That kind of arrogance would've been much more at home on the face of a Tyrant.

Sylvie allowed a cold, wintry smile to pull at her lips and held up the detonator. "Explain this to your bosses, you little shit."

She had an instant to see the alarm on his face before she popped the trigger.

Traditionally, an EMP would need time to warm up as it triggered the electromagnetic pulse, with each "blast" coming intermittently until the device was fully powered. However, if certain shortcuts were made to the device—shortcuts like a secured power source where it could run on standby for an indefinite amount of time—there was almost no delay. Even better, there weren't any tiny little waves, just a singular, powerful pulse.

*Boom, bitch.*

The Khanate agent's face froze as the small device in his pocket fizzled and began to smoke. Dozens of other people cried out in surprise as their personal devices failed as well, a very unfortunate effect of the EMP trap going off. Sylvie felt a little guilt at the sight of a child crying at her ruined toy, but only a little. She was too busy gloating as the stunned agent fell to his knees.

He twitched once, twice—and then his head exploded.

*What. The. Fuck.*

Cries and screams of alarm echoed, and more than one person fled from what seemed like an attack as a shower of gore doused those unfortunate enough to be within the splash zone. The crowd hovered on the edge of a full stampede, and Dillon tugged Sylvie over to the side so they wouldn't get trampled. Smoke drifted out from under his guard uniform, and he yanked out the useless medical device and flung it away with a muttered curse.

Both of their attention turned back to the mess which had been a human being only moments before.

A bloodthirsty little chuckle crawled out of Sylvie's throat as understanding hit.

Of course the Khanate had shorted their agent on protective measures. People like the enemy agent were a dime a dozen back on Earth. It was simple to grab one off the streets and implant electronics in their brains. If they failed, it was no great loss in their eyes. The Khanate were almost as bad as the Tyrants when it came to valuing human life. Worse, in some ways.

Just one more reason she was glad to be of Mars Primus.

"Wha… what the hell happened?" Dillon asked, his eyes locked on the enemy agent's body.

The Khanate agent had finally stopped twitching, which was a good thing, but there was an inordinate number of grey metallic flecks of *something* mixed in with the brain matter, bone, and tainted blood pooling around him. She was no medical expert, but even she knew that this was a BAD THING.

"Neural implants of some kind," she said shortly, barely managing to hold back the "obviously." It was heavily implied, and Dillon—apparently smarter than he'd been letting on—clearly heard it, judging by the expression on his face. She ignored it. It would be a fantastic learning experience for the intelligence agent.

Nobody had ever said anything about it being gentle, however.

"That's… rather nasty," he said as people backed away from the mess.

Sylvie shrugged one shoulder. "Nasty, kind of awesome, same same."

"What is wrong with you?" Dillon demanded under his breath as they sidled away from the scene.

"So much, my friend, so much." Another person jostled her, this one carrying what looked like a makeshift spear, and she ducked her head low again. "But maybe we should leave now."

A trio of men ran past, two with torches and another with what was definitely a Tyrant's head on a wooden stake. Dismay stabbed into Sylvie's heart, but it wasn't Enki, so she turned away from the grisly sight.

"Too bad the blood is already coagulated," Dillon said quietly. He stared at them for a long moment before shaking his head. "Now is good."

Working together, it didn't take them long to bull their way through the increasingly frantic crowds and into the controlled chaos of the landing platform zone, where the guards had maintained a tenuous control.

"Not going to need this anymore," Dillon muttered, pulling off the prosthetic scar on his chin. He then removed a bit off his nose as well, and peeled off the bulky jumpsuit.

"Huh. I like the scar. Made you look rather dashing." Sylvie shook her head in mock disappointment before her lips curved into a wicked smile. "Well, I'd love to stand around and chat, but I've got to go."

"I have a plan to get back to Mars Primus," he said, gesturing for her to follow. "You can come with me."

"Sorry, I've got my own plan."

"Oh," he said quietly, visibly disappointed.

The need to escape burned in Sylvie's core, but she couldn't afford to make an enemy of him. Not when she didn't know what, or *who*, he worked for. She softened her smile into something close to genuine.

"We accomplished something important, at least. We didn't let the Tyrant genetic code fall into enemy hands." She rested a gentle hand on his slumped shoulder and lied with a straight face. "And I couldn't have done it without your help."

"Oh." This time Dillon's voice was chipper, and his spine straightened.

His expression was still slightly pained, but his soft brown eyes cleared, sharpened. Sylvie had the distinct impression she was getting a glimpse of the real man hiding behind the blandness of a spy. Clever and quick, yes, but still young and hopeful and so painfully earnest. He really *was* new at this game. Like her, but without the year-long mission to take some of the shine off him.

"See you around?" he asked, voice deepening a touch.

*Gods, I hope not.*

"Depends," she murmured.

"On?"

"How hard you look." Sylvie grinned, waggling her fingers in farewell. "Toodles."

There was always a price in this business and unfortunately for Dillon, he had paid it tenfold. The device was toast, ruined and smoking on the ground, nothing within worth saving. The EMP had completely trashed it. He glanced back over his shoulder and remembered the long, harrowing run up the various flights of stairs. Theoretically he *could* go down and take a new sample of Tyrant blood... if the bodies hadn't been too mutilated. Or the blood didn't coagulate rapidly, like his boss posited. Or...

Or what?

There would be no sample this day. Not ever, from the look of things. Still, the mission couldn't be considered a total wash. He watched Sylvie saunter off, disappearing into the crowd of people before smiling slightly, enjoying the view. She really was something else. He made a mental note to speak to his bosses about not informing him when he was being sent in to back up another agent. He'd almost killed her, and she him, and then they both really would have been up shit creek without a paddle.

Deftly maneuvering through the throng of emergency responders and onlookers who were way too interested in seeing the headless corpse, he finally made it to the boarding platform for his transport. Nobody bothered him nor tried to stop him. Why would they? He was clearly just another person evacuating from a planet torn with strife and rebellion, guard uniform notwithstanding. A nonentity, nobody in a mass of nobodies.

Exhausted, legs cramping and his calves feeling as though they had been rubbed with alcohol and set on fire thanks to the stairs from Hell, he boarded the shuttle destined for Mars Primus with his pre-purchased ticket after scanning his left thumbprint at the platform. Again, nobody thought twice of it. Why would they? People prepay for tickets all the time, even two weeks in advance like he had. There was nothing untoward about it.

Once onboard, he caught sight of a small teenager seated with four Martian legionnaires on the transport, headed off-world as well, a panicky look upon the kid's face. He immediately dismissed them from mind as he spotted a particularly attractive young redhead in the seat next to his and, from the looks of things, traveling alone. He took his assigned seat next to her and leaned back in his chair, taking care not to jostle her.

Dillon took a single breath, then exhaled slowly. A second breath. Shaking off the last vestiges of who he'd been while stuck within the Prime Palais was difficult, but he managed after a few more calming breaths. After months he was finally able to relax, to remember who he was. The Tyrant guard was gone, the molted corpse of who he'd been pretending to be nothing more than a forgotten husk. Dillon Ashby, Protectorate of Mars citizen and Aspect Red agent, was fully back. He was in his own mind again, his own being.

It was a glorious feeling.

Careful backtracking by concerned parties might have called it fortuitous that he'd had a ticket already purchased to depart on the same day that the riots broke out on the planet, and that the day of his theft coincided nicely with the overthrowing the Tyrant government. It was even more fortunate that the riots had broken out precisely when they had, and were able to cover his escape. Granted, he'd expected the sudden uprising to fail, but an unmitigated success like this was extraordinary. It'd taken him months to set everything up.

Some would call it luck. Aspect Red would have called it your average Tuesday because, in the intelligence business, things never went precisely according to plan. And their agents planned accordingly.

*Always have a backup plan*, was his last conscious thought before he drifted off to sleep.

Sylvie boarded the luxurious private spacecraft to rendezvous with her handler. The first-class recliner enveloped her in a cushiony cloud of comfort, and she accepted a glass of something sweet and sparkling from the smiling attendant. Sadly non-alcoholic, but while this was definitely the time to celebrate, it wasn't the time to get drunk.

Slowly, the last of the tension leached from her spine, leaving only triumph behind. While the EMP had been placed to disable the energy weapons of any palace guards who'd managed to pursue her that far, it had certainly been exactly what she'd needed at the end to ensure mission success.

Neither the Khanate agent *nor* Dillon had walked away with the Tyrant's genetic code. And so long as whoever Dillon worked for believed his report that *all* the samples had been lost, then everything had gone perfectly.

A little harrowing near the end, maybe, but what was life without a little spice? Clearly, Dillon hadn't suspected a thing, too caught up in the explode-y head situation to notice her lack of dismay over losing both devices, too new to wonder *why* she hadn't been nearly as upset as she should've been.

Best of all, her mission had been a success not because of *Dillon*, but because of one Tyrant in particular. The same Tyrant who'd saved her life . . . the same one a small part of her hoped survived the uprising currently tearing apart his world.

*Thanks, Enki. I couldn't have done it without you.*

Sylvie gently rested a hand on the barely noticeable swell of her belly, a fond smile on her face.

*Always have a backup plan.*

# ONE LAST CHANCE

## Jody Lynn Nye

The other three marshals on the communication feed from HQ Control snickered in the background, but Sandra Norstrom paid no attention to them. She stared at the comm scope, her heart pounding with fury. There was his *stupid* face, grinning as if he could see the news drones floating by him. Maybe he did. On the screen, he flipped effortlessly over the fences surrounding the spaceport, not really hurrying. Where were the guards? Where were the autoguns that should have been aimed at the site to take out intruders?

Oh, but here came the soldiers. *Finally*, they came rolling in, wearing their proud blue uniforms, on Orania Space Force ground vehicles, guns blazing at the man now scaling up the side of the small warship. *Finally*, here came the light flyers, dive-bombing the long, wedge-shaped ship, trying to hit the intruder without damaging the spacecraft.

She could see his frame clearly now. He'd lost a little weight since the last time she had seen him. The suit he wore was skintight, reflecting in the sun, meaning that it was impervious to the red lasers that pinged him. The soldiers would have realized that by now, and been unlimbering slugthrowers. She knew the reluctance to use solid ammunition around starships; replacing damaged shields cost more than any of them earned in a year. Damn him, why did he have to be so athletic, so confident? He had only a small pack with him, swinging on a long strap over his shoulder. Not even a weapon!

Sandra snarled and slammed a fist down on the control console. That meant he knew that the ship had been fully provisioned, or he had loaded it himself, and the obvious run for the hatch was for the cameras. She didn't think she could hate anyone more than she did Lionel LeSueur than she had before, but perhaps she had underestimated herself. Damn him to hell. The other marshals saw him as a traitor and an enemy to be taken out with extreme prejudice, but they didn't have the history with him that she had had.

Lionel's gloved hand covered the lock panel, and the hatch slid aside. How had he gotten the code? Yet another crime! He slipped into the dark air lock. The hatch closed behind him as a hail of bullets peppered it. The slugs pinged off it uselessly. Over the noise, the broadcaster's voice shouted in excitement.

"... The terrorist, Lionel LeSueur, has broken into a light speed clipper, the *Orania Ascendant*. As I am sure you viewers know, it is fully armed and prepared for interstellar battle...."

"What are you waiting for?" Colonel O'Day shouted over the audio pickup, her hazel eyes ablaze. "You know where he is. Go get him!"

But Sandra had already strapped in and programmed the coordinates for the base into IG-487's navigational computer. On her heads-up display, the other three marshals shot toward the target as if they were on fire. Sandra was marginally in the lead. She knew there would be consequences for the base staff that had failed to secure a warship, knowing that a terrorist was out there. For her too if he escaped, being a terrorist to whom she had once been engaged.

Sandra had been in the Space Force pilot class one year ahead of Lionel LeSueur, but they had been assigned to the same base of operations after graduation. They had bonded in misery over not getting into the FTL class in their first rotation on base. It had been Lionel who suggested that they learn the controls on the simulators ahead of their assignment. That experience in the sims propelled them both to the top of the roster. The unit commander almost smiled at them during examinations. Almost. Colonel Mazer was a hard-ass. Sandra respected her and did her best to live up to Mazer's expectations. But most of her efforts were because she had become smitten with Lionel.

He had a facility for memorization that went far beyond the normal. Machines seemed to like him, as foolish as that sounded. She envied him that skill, and worked twice as hard to keep up with him. It didn't really work; you couldn't fake that kind of affinity. He was a star. Everyone knew it. The brass began to notice him. He got called into conferences, taken aside for opportunities that Sandra wasn't being given, nor were any of the others in their unit. He never discussed what had happened in those conferences or opportunities. After he had told her no more than once, Sandra had stopped asking. A few of their fellow cadets avoided him like the plague, but Sandra couldn't. He had the kind of charm that few could resist, not without effort. Not that she tried.

She had been seeing another pilot, Natili, before Lionel came along. Natili was everything she wanted in a partner, or so she thought. She was beautiful, with long, shining black hair and warm brown eyes, smart, athletic, devoted to the Space Force and to Sandra, but she was the one who broke it off.

"It's inevitable," she told Sandra. "Face it. The two of you go down like fire."

Sandra was ashamed to admit it, but she had to be fair to Natili. She could hardly keep that man out of her thoughts. The lines of his face, always ready to laugh. The mischief in those bright green eyes. The shock of hair, curly even when cut to battalion standards, which he dyed in colors that lay just inside regulations. And his long, lean body—well, they were perfect for one another. He always said he loved the curve of her shoulders, and praised the waves of her copper-red hair. He could always make her purr.

They started meeting for coffee with the group, and never noticed when the others drifted off to leave them alone together. Coffee breaks turned into hours, any leave time they had in between shifts, weekend liberties, and so on. They sneaked off together, even making use of idled fighter craft or cargo transport vessels to hover behind asteroids for moments of stolen intimacy, giggling like teenagers. Lionel's charm kept them from being officially disciplined. It was almost as though the brass liked having his attentions focused on one fellow cadet instead of spreading his distracting atttentions across the whole of the class.

It didn't take long before they had moved in together in his BOQ. All her civilian clothes were left behind in hers. All her uniforms now hung in his closet. As long as she was at her assigned bunk for inspections, no one cared. He was even good in bed. She was so smitten that that wouldn't have mattered, but it was delicious icing on the cake.

The one thing that marred the perfection was his political views. Those had started to emerge a short time after he had passed his FTL certification.

The first remark still stuck in her mind. They had been hanging out with a group on the edge of the plascrete runway, watching patrol ships land and take off like eagles snatching fish out of a river.

"Lars Beckley is a coward," he had said, offhand, as though he was commenting on the weather. "We're screwed if he doesn't attack the Sulawid system, like tomorrow. We can't afford to wait. Their force is growing every day. We don't stand a chance!"

Whatever her feelings about the Premier of the Grand Council of Orania System, Sandra, and everyone else she knew, usually kept those thoughts in the privacy of their own minds. Cameras were everywhere. If Lionel was overheard, he could get hauled in for "an interview." Beckley liked to use the system against potential enemies. Sometimes they were reviled over his frequent broadcasts, but just as often, these dissenters just vanished. Sandra feared for Lionel. Not without reason. He kept coming home again. Sandra put that down to his ability to worm his way out of sticky situations. But he kept talking, and the authorities were listening.

In broadcasts with reporters over the communication channels, public and military, Beckley had kept insisting that Orania wasn't ready to go to war with Sulawid. That wasn't what fleet strength suggested. Their binary neighbor was just too powerful. The reprisals would destroy them. The longer they could put off war, the better. The premier was always sending placatory gifts and messages to the Potentate who ruled the largest nation on Sulawid Prime. While Sandra agreed that Beckley was spineless, she had read all the reports of Sulawid's much larger fleet. From the surveillance footage released hourly, a massive fleet was being assembled in Trojan orbit above the capital city. She feared that Sulawid had no intention of making peace with their smaller and weaker neighbor. The best thing Orania could do was bolster their defenses and hope that diplomacy would solve the disagreements between them. But Lionel disagreed.

"Hit them first!" her lover had insisted. "Hit them where it counts, destroy their superior firepower *now*, and we'll be equal. It wouldn't take much." He snorted. "If Beckley doesn't go to war with them, I will."

Their friends dismissed his remarks as arrogant bluster. He was the best FTL pilot in the fleet, and everyone knew it, but he didn't have a fleet of his own to take action, or anything like it. No one was surprised his position made his head swell with self-importance. Sandra shoved him sideways, and he grinned at her with the insouciance that always made her body tingle. The others laughed.

But the rhetoric didn't stop there. Two months later, he kissed her goodbye at the doorway of their shared quarters, saying that he was visiting his sister in the next town over. A few hours afterward, Natili came to visit her, and showed her a link to a news feed of a protest outside the Central Government House on her personal entertainment device. Sandra stared at it in horror. At the center of it, Lionel, in civilian clothes, was shouting anti-government rhetoric into an audio pickup device that fed public address systems on every light pole for five kilometers' radius. After the city police broke up the protest, Lionel was seen being bundled into a patrol car.

"I have to help him," Sandra had said, standing up and blindly feeling for her ID pouch.

Natili held her back, pulling her away from the door. Her large eyes were worried.

"Don't go. They'll just take your details, too. What about your own life? Your career?"

Sandra had had no answer to that. She just wanted to go to him. Her head spun so much that she couldn't see anything clearly. What was Lionel doing? And why had he lied to her?

Her friend sat with her on the edge of the hard military-issue couch for the next several hours, until Lionel swaggered in. He looked pleased with himself, not like someone who might have undergone several hours of interrogation and threats. Natili slipped out as surreptitiously as she could, while Sandra lit into her boyfriend. Who did he think he was, drawing attention to himself like that when he was a serving officer at the highest level? But no amount of haranguing or pleading made a difference, or even changed the self-satisfied smirk on his face.

"You know I'm right," he said at last. "If Orania won't destroy Sulawid, then I'll do it myself." Then, he had stripped out of his clothes and headed for the shower. She followed him, protesting, begging him not to be a fool. He ignored her and locked the door between them.

Drained, Sandra gathered up all of her possessions and went back to her personal quarters, feeling as if she was witnessing the birth of a traitor.

When he disappeared from the base eight days later, she was sad, but not surprised. The brass hauled her in and questioned her for a couple of days, but she had no information to give them. Defeated, she sat slumped over her elbows on the metal table in the interrogation room, not caring how many people were on the other side of the two-way mirror or listening remotely from offices all over Orania Prime.

When she was released, her CO regarded her with tight lips and cold gaze, giving her the worst duty and the least flight time. Sandra's career was effectively over, despite never having a clue herself that Lionel would betray the world. It did her zero good to protest to anyone—officers, former friends, the judge advocates general—that she had nothing to do with his behavior or his disappearance. She had been joined at the hip with him for months. That made her guilty in everyone else's eyes. The brass didn't believe that she had no idea where he was. People on base treated her like a pariah. She felt eyes burning into her back wherever she went.

Not that Lionel had fallen silent after vanishing. He sent manifestos to the press, demanding that Premier Beckley organize a full-out attack on Sulawid or step down in favor of someone who cared about Orania's safety.

"We have the firepower to succeed against Sulawid! We have the munitions! Why is Beckley doing nothing?" The words rang in Sandra's ears. "We're an easy target. You can't get closer than a binary system. We have to show strength, or we'll be absorbed. Orania and Sulawid should be equal siblings! If only one power should survive, it must be ours. Orania Ascendant!"

That slogan began to appear in other places. It irritated her to see it written on the lavatory mirror in the office building, or on the undercarriage of fighter craft. Oranians, even those in the service, started to talk in hushed voices. Some people agreed with him, but were shouted down by larger numbers. Still, whether they agreed with him, or feared what he might be doing, his words were on everyone's lips. Sandra heard Lionel's name mentioned by a group of pilots on the tarmac when she went to collect her gear for the last time. One of them nudged the others when they saw her approach, and they stopped talking. She felt her cheeks burn with shame. The whole sector was set to kill him on sight. And she was damned by her association with him. *Former* association didn't make a single damned bit of difference to them.

Scrutiny did get redirected to the war effort, and the mealymouthed defense that the government was putting forward got a lot of criticism. Beckley was forced to appear again and again on worldwide media to promise that peace talks were underway with Sulawid. Sandra had to admit Beckley *sounded* weak and indecisive. At heart, he was a pacifist, and had been elected on that basis. But that was no reason for Lionel to endanger the entire star system. He was going to get millions of people killed.

With the weight of Lionel's actions hanging around her neck, she found it hard to get another assignment. For a while, she feared she would have to resign from the service and go into the private sector. Luckily for her, Colonel O'Day in the Space Force Marshal Corps had never fallen for Lionel's charm, and saw that Sandra was being made a scapegoat for the one that the authorities could not catch. She had offered a place in the Corps, and Sandra had jumped at it. She was going to find Lionel and make him pay for ruining her life.

She became obsessed with locating him. O'Day let her follow any lead, however tenuous, and Sandra took after them like a bloodhound. Missing shipment of starship engine parts? He had to be behind it. A ship returning late to its berth for no reason? Had the crew been waylaid by him? One clue after another had petered out, leaving her frustrated. His facile intelligence made fools of the corps again and again. They had so far been unable to detect who, if anyone, that he was working with. Sandra followed up every investigation, poring over details. Her fellow marshals passed info her way if a break-in or missing supplies looked like it could be connected to Lionel and *Orania Ascendant*. So far, nothing she turned up led anywhere. It was as if he was a ghost. His broadcasts were routed through millions of small connections, computers that were on dead satellites, uncrewed cargo vessels, even children's toys. Shipments went astray. Munitions vanished from storehouses, no matter how much security ringed them, though there was nothing to tie the thefts directly to him. Graffiti haranguing Beckley appeared on larger and larger canvases, including government buildings, and no one could do a thing about it.

And now, this. He would not get away from her this time.

She had been half a continent away, having investigated a break-in at a supply depot on Shoreline Base. The vast pink-sided warehouse showed no real signs of forced entry, which meant an inside job of some kind. It didn't take long to crack the case. The missing items turned out to be concentrated food supplements. Nothing to connect to Lionel. She found the trio of perpetrators because tracers set in the bottom of each crate broadcast the location to any law enforcement detectors. The thieves were nothing but opportunists who worked for the secure transport company that supplied the base. They were waiting for their contact to sell the goods when she descended on them. None of them put up any kind of a fight. She turned them over to local justice just before the news feed began.

Streaking over the blur of landscape in her Marshal Corps craft, Sandra studied the telemetry reports from the scene of the crime. Her blue-toned ship, shaped like an upturned crescent, smooth-sided, with a quartet of stubby fins on its belly for landing, boasted almost sublight speeds even in atmosphere. Why had Lionel chosen that craft? Had he been lurking around it for long?

"No, it was just serviced," said Colonel Shulman, the commander of the base, in answer to her question. The dark-skinned woman pursed her full lips in annoyance on the side viewer. "We were about to put a unit of cadets on it to train them in short-orbit maneuvers."

"What about tracers?" Sandra asked. "Every ship not in service has security monitors in a dozen places." The other woman's face fell.

"They were on the ground in the dust. LeSueur must have ejected them on takeoff."

"How is that even possible?" asked Marshal Anders, one of the other law enforcement officers speeding toward the scene. Vickers and Lowell were also on the feed.

"It's not," Sandra said, with a sigh. "They're a plant. He must have transported them over the fence even before he got onto the field. I bet if you study the footage, there's a drone somewhere, within the last dark shift. Machines talk to him. I don't know how he does it."

A long pause, during which Shulman disappeared, leaving the base logo on her screen. When she appeared, she looked peeved.

"You're right. How did you even *know* that?" Her tone was suspicious.

"Smoke and mirrors is his specialty," Sandra said curtly. She didn't have time to be dragged into the situation as a co-conspirator or accomplice. She glared until Shulman quailed before her hard blue gaze. "Like I said, machines talk to him. You're not going to find a trace in the coding of any mechanism. His instructions disappear as soon as the task is accomplished. I've seen it myself, and I don't know how he does it."

"All we can do now is follow the contrail," Marshal Vickers put in. Her thin, bony face wore a sour expression. She had never really trusted Sandra since Lionel started his campaign. Truth to tell, none of them did.

Sandra watched as the other three craft converged with hers on the space over the launch point. No point in holding out hope of an easy capture. The airfield crawled with security officers and sheepish-looking spacers in cadet uniforms. Sweeper droids, looking like gigantic ladybugs, circled the burn pattern on the tarmac. She knew there was nothing to find there. Lionel was already out in space, laughing at them. His video had been broadcast all around the world and out to the space stations and colonies in the system. The secret was out, and nothing could be done about it. Sandra forcibly shoved the memory aside and concentrated on the facts.

"Colonel Shulman, can you compile the surveillance camera files from the last month surrounding that ship?" she asked.

"Why? It's been in use, up until it went in for maintenance. It's only been out on the tarmac for eleven days. You can see all the video from every camera."

"All right," Sandra said, thinking quickly. She had already turned her ship upward along the flight path that the stolen ship had taken. "Then, I'd like to see the footage for that timeframe, but give me the maintenance logs, too?"

Shulman looked skeptical, but shook her head. "All right. I'll have them beamed to you right away."

"Thank you, captain. This isn't your fault." Nor mine, she thought.

"I don't care whose fault it is! Just get my ship back!"

"Yes, ma'am," Sandra said. She cut the connection and opened the star charts across her entire display.

The four ships rose out of atmosphere, surveying the particle trails that the *Orania Ascendant* left. The broad expanse of the blue-green planet below them was in full daylight, obscuring the faint traces from the human eye. Fortunately, the OSF ships' sensors could see a single molecule in the blackness of space. Sandra plotted the trajectory against the star charts. Sensors on full, she surveyed the arc of space all around her vessel, sharing the data with the others until they had a full array. No sign of the *Ascendant*, but the trail continued out from the surface of Orania. She had the time to look over the maintenance logs and the video from the launch pad. The drones were there, as she had suspected, in broad daylight three days before. Lionel wasn't even trying to hide his antics. Someone should have noticed those before, damn him! When she got back, she was going to tear someone, or a whole flock of someones, new assholes.

Two hundred thousand klicks farther on, they found traces of a burst of energy consistent with ship's engines going into light drive. The *Ascendant* had accelerated from sublight, aiming up and out of the solar system.

"He's going to Sulawid! Right now!" Anders snarled. Red arrows appeared on their shared feed, pointing upward and outward. The automatic plotter brought up the chart that showed the location of the prime planet in the opposite star's orbit. "He's going to start the war right now! We have to warn the government! The reprisals will bring a full-scale attack on us!" His fierce outburst couldn't disguise the worry in his voice. "Preparing to go to light drive. We have to follow him! The world has to know so it can prepare for war!"

"Stop! He's not on his way there yet," Sandra said. The information poured into her screens, along with her study of the maintenance logs. Her mind spun as she tried to absorb it all. Underneath her flight suit, she felt sweat pooling in her armpits, even in the constantly controlled climate of the ship's bridge. Lionel never did anything without a purpose; that's why the brass loved him. To be so obvious about a major theft meant he didn't want you looking away from him. So, what else was going on? What were they missing? She studied the surveillance video from the refit facility and from the airfield. Sure, drones came and went, but nothing *big*. Nothing with sufficient firepower to make a difference.

"What are you thinking, Norstrom?" Vickers asked.

"It's an FTL ship, but under the circumstances, I don't think he's on his way to Sulawid. Not yet, anyhow."

"Why?"

Sandra studied the contrails in her scope. The photons led in the right direction, but something struck her as wrong.

"He can't go yet. There's nothing in the *Ascendant*! He hasn't had time to load armaments onto that ship, or anything else he's stolen. It has been under surveillance for almost two weeks. The junk that he left on the landing pad was just that: junk. He's trying to distract us from his real launch point."

"And where is that?" Vickers demanded. "We don't have time to waste combing the entire sector for his hidey-holes!"

Sandra mused. With a sigh, she realized that no facet of her past life could be off limits if she was to catch her former lover before he caused a war that would imperil the entire world.

"We had a number of places where we. . . ." She stopped, as Lowell let out a juicy snicker. She glared at his round face, contorted with laughter. "Damn you, Ned, I know you did the same thing before you and Tracey got together."

"Stick to the facts," Anders snapped. He still looked frustrated and angry. "Locations?"

Sandra tried not to look into the video pickup where she could see her own face reflected back at her. Her cheeks matched her hair.

"There are a few derelicts in orbit. A couple of them have life support still turned on, for use in training missions."

"Right. They're mostly in L5 positions or maintain stabilizing orbits," Vickers put in. Her expression was smug. "Is it a better idea to ask you which ones you *didn't* use?"

"Space it, Vickers," Anders snarled. "And where else, Norstrom?"

Sandra's cheeks might have just spontaneously combusted with shame. "That big cargo ship in the graveyard out beyond the near asteroid belt. But mostly, we borrowed one of the flitters and found a secluded spot. There's plenty of room inside them." Her throat closed up as Lowell burst into laughter. She would never be able to face them in person ever again.

"That's good information, Norstrom," Anders said. He had calmed down enough to take on information and process it. "All right. Let's split up the leads and investigate. I'll inform Colonel O'Day what's up.

The other teams will have to cover any cases for the next few days, or however long it takes. Approach with extreme caution. If you spot him or other signs of unauthorized activity, do not engage. Do you hear me, Norstrom? *Do not engage with him.* We don't know what kind of firepower he's got. You're right that he couldn't have amassed anything on Orania, but shipments and components have gone missing for months, even years. Whatever he has in mind is likely to be big. Any disagreement there?"

"None." Sandra was grateful that Anders had taken over. They all had the same rank, but Anders had been a marshal for years longer than any of them. He sounded grumpy, but she could trust him to the end. "I'll take the derelict in orbit over the far continent."

"No!" Vickers said. "Excuse me for not trusting you, but this is your boyfriend we're trying to catch. You could be planning to join up with him. We don't know."

"Ex-fiancé," Sandra protested, then realized it was futile to argue. "I want to catch him as much as all of you. More than all of you put together! He ruined my life!"

"All right, everyone take a step back," Anders said, holding up his hands. "I'll choose where everyone is going. Vickers, you take the L5 ships. Norstrom, I want a list of those other makeout spots. Lowell and I will cover those. Norstrom will take the cargo ship."

Grateful that the decision was being taken out of her hands, Sandra typed in the coordinates for all the places where she and Lionel used to go: out of line of sight of Orania scanners, behind asteroids, hidden in the debris left behind by mining ships, in the space junkyard that floated just outside the range of orbiting satellites, and sent them. In truth, she never wanted to see them again. She sent the file to all of the others. Then, she set her course for the cargo ship at .06 *c*, where it hovered idly, a hundred thousand klicks from any of the other derelicts in the ship graveyard.

She logged in her flight plan and went through the full checklist of safety precautions and readiness, wanting to make certain that this approach was absolutely by the book. No more carelessness or allowing her emotions to interfere with a necessary takedown. Lionel had gone too far this time. At that distance, she couldn't tell if there were any signs of life on the hulking vessel, nor whether the failing engines had been powered up at all.

The blue disk of Orania receded behind the IG-487, but Sandra was never out of voice range of her colleagues. Colonel O'Day came on the secured circuit to harangue her about keeping back private information that might have been useful in locating Lionel. Sandra was still kicking herself for the omission. She had been questioned a number of times over the last few months, but in all honesty, she had never thought of those private times away as being even remotely relevant to the investigation. Of course, those were possibilities. But Lionel couldn't be thoughtless enough to make use of any of those locations. Could he?

Technically, she, Sandra, was a liability to him, too. Anything she knew or remembered was a potential threat to his plans. Under the circumstances, she was almost surprised that he had left her alive.

And she was realizing that too late. O'Day should have grounded her. Even put her in protective custody. Because her own ship had just betrayed her. What did she always tell people? *Machines talk to Lionel.* And they listened.

It had happened so gradually that she didn't notice it at first. Her scopes showed her target, the faint green blip that indicated the cargo ship, hovering alone in the black nothingness. As was true of everything in the artificial asteroid belt made up of unused vessels and ship skeletons that had been scavenged for parts, the mass revolved around Orania's sun. At a reasonable distance, she put the IG-487 behind the shadow of another uninhabited hulk, so she would not be visible from the cargo vessel on approach. She ordered the IG-487's navigational system to adjust for the shift in location.

Nav hesitated, just a little bit. Then, it obeyed. Sandra patted the control console, as if the ship was a beloved pet. The program had been updated not that long ago. Perhaps it was taking other obstructions into account. At the speed she was traveling, even a tiny object could cause significant damage to her hull. If it was a matter of safety based on telemetry, the artificial intelligence that occupied her ship's computer and took over the controls when human reaction time was too slow would note changes to the program. She rolled back the log to see what it had detected. Nothing. She hadn't done it. The AI wasn't doing it. . . .

"Damn him to the center of a black hole!"

She slammed her hands down onto the console and began to enter new coordinates. Lionel had overridden the security coding and taken over her ship!

Sandra nudged her communications pickup with the side of her jaw. "Mayday! I repeat, Mayday! Attention, Orania Marshal Force, this is Marshal Sandra Norstrom, IG-487. My ship has been taken under the control of a hostile force. I suspect Lionel LeSueur, ex-Marshal, is behind the intrusion. I am within range of a place he may be concealing himself. Consider him armed and dangerous. Here are the coordinates. I need your assistance. He is planning to leave the system and may intend harm upon the people of Sulawid Prime. Time is of the essence! Mayday, Mayday!"

No reply. Not one. She continued to hear chatter from the many channels of her audio response system. Didn't they hear her?

Sandra dragged a finger down the communications console, looking for a fault, when a light, chiding laugh came over the audio channel.

"No way, honey!" Lionel's voice burst from the speakers. "Nice job figuring out where I am!... Oh, wait, you didn't. You told the OMC all of them. You're here by chance."

Sandra gritted through her teeth, fighting her own navigational computer. "I'm here to bring you in, you traitor!"

"No, honey." Lionel sounded bored, but she knew him well enough to understand it was a pose. "You're going home. I don't want you to get hurt. And you will. Don't you know this is a one-way trip for me?"

The IG-487 looped leftward in a wide arc. The space graveyard veered to the right and dropped out of sight. In a moment, the bright blue-white button of Orania's sun slashed across her viewscreens, to be replaced by the faint crescent of the planet. Coordinates scrolled up both sides of the main screen, and acceleration increased from .06 to .1 *c*. She felt the engines of the small but powerful ship kick up underneath the bridge. Sandra grabbed for the controls, but none of them obeyed her.

"It's one way because you are going to prison!" Sandra began scrolling through every protocol that her computer system had, looking for any that he had not corrupted. When had he done it? During one of their last times together? Afterwards, when she had taken all of his possessions back to his then-empty quarters? "Why are you trying to kill everyone in Orania?"

He sighed. "You'll never understand. I wish you I could make you. Goodbye, Sandra."

Sandra let out a screech of frustration. He and her ship had betrayed her. She couldn't even tell anyone, because he had cut off all lines of communication. Within days, he would be in Sulawid. Whatever he was planning would cause an irreversible incident. Within weeks, that enemy force that was massing would be around her world, bombarding it until the few survivors had no chance except to surrender. How could he?

Sandra listened to the other ships of the OMS. The three she had left behind at the top of the contrail were searching all the other locations and sending updates to one another and to Base Command. Other marshals were joining the manhunt. They hailed Sandra, asking for her status.

She clawed at the controls until her fingertips were bloody, trying to get Nav or Comm to respond. What had Lionel done to it? She initiated every command that she knew, but the computer ignored them all. It wasn't as if this was the *Orania Ascendant*. The OMC patrol ships weren't easy to break into, nor were they left unattended or unguarded at any time. The programming in her central computer should be intact unless. . . .

Unless it was listening to him, like any piece of machinery.

She unbuckled her safety harness and felt her way out of her pilot's chair. Ship's gravity was less than 60% standard in space, just enough that she wouldn't suffer bone loss over a long mission. At least Lionel had left her life support alone. She didn't notice a drop in oxygen levels or artificial gravity. Perhaps cutting off those was the *coup de grace* waiting for her if she did not obediently head back toward Orania. She didn't know! She didn't know him anymore. But was there a chance to free her ship and head back to intercept him?

Sandra clanked back over the metal plating toward the communications console on her metal-soled boots. Any of the law enforcement ships could be run by a single pilot, or by a crew up to six beings on the compact, circular bridge. All activity was seconded through the main command console, but the guts of every station was at its individual emplacements. The arrangement acted as a fail-safe. It could be inconvenient, say, if Ordnance became inoperative at the captain's position. But then, one could put the ship on autopilot and run the weapons from the remote station. She was certain Lionel had not been inside her ship since they had broken up, and Colonel O'Day had absolutely called in an inspection of it afterwards, so she was equally certain any device he had planted would have been removed. But had they inspected its programming? If he was sending a constant stream of commands to her ship to control it, she had to cut it off at the source. It was worth a try.

She slid underneath the Communications console and pulled the hatch open. A wave of harsh metallic smell wafted out and made her eyes water. She had no time to run diagnostics. Instead, she jimmied the flat rectagonal master crystal out of its nest.

The entire ship fell silent and juddered as if skipping over rough pavement. For a moment, she felt as though she had gone deaf. Then, the ordinary, small noises reasserted themselves: the computers chuckling and peeping, the creaks of plates shifting against one another, and the distant sounds of plumbing and air recirculation. Not one voice. Not one single voice. She couldn't hear any of the marshals. And she couldn't hear or see Lionel. With another tug, she disconnected the other inputs, such as updates of computer software and message delivery. Lionel wouldn't be able to use his powers of persuasion through there, either. She and her ship were free.

A wave of loneliness washed over her as she made her way back to her command chair and snapped herself in. The fastenings on the shock harness sounded unnaturally loud. How weird it was not even to be able to hear the constant stream of news reports and updates from Orania Prime. She felt like a ghost inside a whispering house.

But with silence came focus. No longer able to use her ears, she had to use her eyes, and those of her ship.

Secrecy was no longer possible or necessary. Her sole aim was to capture Lionel and bring him back to the homeworld. She engaged Navigation and whipped the ship back toward the cargo vessel. At her engineering console, she brought the ship up to its full speed. Lionel wouldn't have time to load the *Orania Ascendant* with whatever he needed to cause trouble in Sulawid, or he wouldn't still be there. The brief feint he had made to pretend that he had already left the solar system had failed. If he tried to make a run for it now, she could blow him out of the heavens with her ship's armaments.

Oh, but could she? Her heart sank. Even if they had broken up, part of her still belonged to him, belonged with him. She was as drawn to him as her own ship had been. Their love was real—she believed that. She hoped he did. She couldn't hurt him or subject him to the humiliation of a public trial and punishment. But he wouldn't go without a fight. His cause was greater to him than one small relationship, however true. But they had been so good...

Common sense reasserted itself, making her eyes tear with shame. Damn him, she *had* to bring him down, whatever it took. He had left her no choice. Either he or she had to fail, and she was going to make certain it was him. The lives of everyone on Orania counted upon that.

The scopes showed a bright halo of warmth in what should have been an idled vessel. It read as far more than that needed to keep one or more human beings alive. There was no mistake. The *Ascendant* had made its false flight, and lay hidden inside their trysting point. He had counted on sending the marshals on a wild chase into the outer reaches until he could load up whatever armaments he needed and make his escape. Therefore, she didn't have much time to intercept him.

Sandra went through the logs to make certain all the other systems were running. For captures during very slow speeds, she had magnetic grappling pads and stun guns. For faster chases in which she wanted to bring in her quarry alive, she had a host of small missiles that pierced hull plating and exploded inside engines and power supplies. For ship-to-ship combat, the IG-487 was fully armed, surprisingly well for its size. She hoped she did not have to resort to the lattermost.

While Lionel was assigned to the FTL combat brigade, he knew all there was to know about her job. He had helped quiz her on all of the processes she had to memorize, up to and including hull tolerances and explosion radii to advance in the corps. With his quick mind, he'd be able to anticipate anything that she planned to do. Therefore, she had to think in ways that he wouldn't. But how could she?

She felt for the emergency rations underneath the console, and munched on a fragrant, sticky protein bar, keeping her eyes on the dark hulk ahead. The heat signature grew brighter and brighter, until it took up the whole of one of the two cargo bays on the big ship. He had to be close to bursting out of it. The old vessel had more than one hatch at the rear. Which one would he use? If she guessed wrong, she didn't stand a chance of catching him. The IG-487 didn't have light drive capabilities. Her one chance was to head him off.

Wait, there it was! The flare was moving to her right, toward the main hatch on the side of the cargo bay. She threw full power to the engines, and prepared the missiles. Sandra threw the wrapper aside and licked her fingers clean.

She followed the infrared image rather than spotlights, and was rewarded with a brilliant sunrise emerging at the right side of the vessel. The *Ascendant* shot out into space, and she followed it. According to the telemetry files, the broad triangular warship could hold a crew of thirty, with room for over a hundred infantry in power suits or a dozen flying tanks. It also had five vulnerable spots, two of which were aft engines. She had the computer lock onto them, preparing to fire.

Just as she did, the leading ship began evasive maneuvers. Its rear began fishtailing and spinning, breaking the hold just before she could fire.

A blare of sound distracted her. A single monitor, at the bottom of the array in front of the Communications station, sprang to life. It was an emergency alert screen, intended for broadcast from Orania's central government only. Lionel, of course, had hijacked it for his own purposes. His face looked out at her, his expression bearing none of the playfulness or warmth that it normally wore.

"People of Orania, you have had long enough to act out against the tyrants that rule our fellow star's system. I have warned you again and again that Sulawid is assembling a fleet that our forces can't withstand."

His face was replaced by an overhead image of what looked like a gray cloud of pollinating insects, flying in and out from a central point. She zoomed in on the image, and discovered that each "insect" was a huge armor-plated warship. The engines were made for interstellar travel, with numerous hatches indicating dozens, if not hundreds, of gun emplacements along each side, the belly and the back of these beasts. Sandra shuddered.

"We can wait no longer to attack this infestation in its own hive! Orania must prepare for war, right now! I will make the first strike. They will retaliate. You must be ready to defend our homeworld and its colonies. For the honor and safety of our beloved world, you must follow me now! Orania Eternal! Orania Ascendant!"

The screen went blank.

Curse him. Curse him! She had seen plenty of reports about Sulawid's burgeoning fleet. Orania wasn't ready to attack that! All he was going to do was make the enemy angry enough that no quarter would be shown when they *did* invade.

But, something else he said stuck in her mind. "Follow me now."

She had cut off all other means of him communicating with her. Did that wretched bastard mean that message specifically for her? How dare he try to control her again, this time through her curiosity? She would find out anyhow. His conceit of weaving to avoid her rockets was slowing him down. Her speed just about equaled his.

Sandra nudged the coordinates until she was paralleling Lionel at a distance of mere meters. Now the Ascendant started to jerk back and forth, as if anticipating her next move. Could he guess? She hoped not.

Setting the computer to match his movement, she edged the IG-487 until the crescent touched the flank of the triangular ship. Grappling magnets shot out of the port side of her craft and sealed it tightly over a hatch. The *Ascendant* bucked as if trying to unseat a stinging fly. The marshal's ship clung on. She had caught him!

Sandra reenabled the Communications station long enough to send a message out to the other marshals and Base Command with details of the capture. Even if Lionel spoke to her ship then, she had enough time to board his before he could cause the IG-487 to detach. She was going to get him now.

She flung herself out of her seat and grabbed an atmosphere suit out of the nearest compartment and slid it on, pressing the seals closed. The solid helmet closed around her ears, and her ship's AI said "Working." An oxygen mix smelling of peanuts whooshed into her nostrils. She grabbed weapons from the wall and threw the straps over her shoulders. Her favorite riot gun slapped into her palms, and she activated the disable setting.

By the time she reached the hatch, the automatic servos had taken hold of the freezing door and pried it open and to one side. It was dark beyond the opening. Sandra knew that Lionel would be waiting. He had reach and strength, but her weapons handling was far better than his.

She slipped into the ship. Not one light burned anywhere in sight. She was going to have to rely upon the searchlight attached to the top of her riot gun. All marshals had memorized the original layout of every one of Orania's warships. There was a lot of real estate to cover here. Lionel could be anywhere. Her primary goal was to take control of the ship and prevent it from leaving the star system. The second was to capture Lionel, alive if possible, and bring him back to Orania Prime.

The Ascendant was still bucking furiously. Her knees dipped with every movement. She kept them bent to absorb the motion, but as she tried to round a corner, the ship lunged furiously to the left. She was thrown into the right-hand wall. Her hand slipped off the barrel of her riot gun. The searchlight's beam slipped downward.

Suddenly, she felt a hand clamp around her wrist and yank her forward into the darkness. Lionel! Instinct kicked in. Sandra spun into him and pulled him against her back. She jerked her hand downward, out of his grasp. While he flailed in the dark, she stamped her magnetic boot on his foot. Although he was certainly wearing the same kind of footgear, the top of the foot wasn't armored in the same way. She couldn't hear a grunt through her helmet, but it had to hurt. A fist struck her in the kidney. The punch made her gasp. She pushed against him to free herself and threw a backwards kick into his thigh. Suddenly, she felt a rush of cold air hit her in the throat. He had cut into the neck of her suit. The emergency response set off a tiny siren in her ear as microbots rushed to seal the breach.

Sandra put both elbows into his gut and spun on her heel, aiming the riot gun at where his belly ought to be. It was too late. Something hard hit her in the chin, and the smell of peanuts was overpowered by a sweet, sickly aroma. Even half a breath was too much. Her limbs went loose, and she dropped unconscious.

Sandra woke up with a terrible headache. When she could pry her eyes open, she found that she was zip-tied to a seat on the bridge of the *Ascendant.* Lionel sat in the captain's chair, watching her. One of the scopes displayed an image of the nose of her ship against the flank of his. His left upper leg was in a pressure cast. At least she had done some damage.

"Do you want a drink of water?" he asked.

He might as well have offered her poison. She yanked at the bonds. A sharp tug should have broken the nylon strands, so he must have turned some of them in the opposite direction.

"What is the matter with you?" she demanded, all the fury she had been feeling erupting in her voice. "How could you have turned into such a traitor?"

"I'm not a traitor," he said. He rose to his feet, favoring the wounded limb. "I'll even let you go free to prove it."

"If you do, I will blast you into tomorrow," Sandra said. "You have gone too far."

Lionel sat down, shaking his head. He didn't have the same air of conceit that had been evident in all the news videos she had seen. Instead, he looked . . . vulnerable. Even the color in his curly hair had faded. "I haven't gone far enough yet. Why did you come after me? I've tried not to involve anyone else. Of all people, I didn't want you interfering in my mission."

That was not what Sandra expected to hear.

"Mission? What is your mission?"

He glanced at the control console. Communications showed an open transmission, but only a graphic instead of a face. The image wasn't one that she recognized. He stretched out a hand and turned it off.

"It won't matter in an hour or two. In fact, I'm . . . I'm glad to tell you. I want someone to know, but I can't trust anyone else. War is coming. Premier Beckley has been dragging his feet to the point where we are going to fall. It's going to be bad. We . . ."

"*We?* Who else is involved here? We've been investigating you for months, since that manifesto of yours, but we have never been able to locate your cell, or whatever you call your co-conspirators."

A faint smile appeared on Lionel's face. "That's because you weren't looking high enough up."

The feeling of alarm in her belly was enough to make her want to throw up. She swallowed down bitter bile. "Lionel, what is going on? Who are you working with?"

He dropped his gaze. "A very small but determined minority that wants to buy us more time. They recruited me because I could pretend to be the ultimate shadow warrior, working against the government's stated interests. In fact, in this very minute, they are frightened to death that you have caught up with me and might slow me down. If your colleagues manage to make it here before I leave, everything we have been working toward is gone."

Now she was really frightened. "What are you going to do?"

The sardonic smile spread. "Just what you thought. I'm heading to Sulawid to destroy their fleet, or as much of it as I can."

"In this?" Sandra asked, looking around. "You might take out a few ships, but their fighters will stop you."

"No, they won't. They are flying in a mass above the capital city, like in the video I sent you. The hold of this ship contains a planetkiller bomb. My colleagues, as you call them, put it on board even before I launched off Orania. I'm going to set it off in the midst of the fleet. The destruction will set them back years. By then, our diplomats might be able to make some headway in peace talks."

She fell silent, digesting everything he had said. She wanted to believe him. The roiling sensation in her belly returned with reinforcements as an unavoidable, lonely truth blared in her mind.

"This is . . . a one-way trip. Isn't it?" Tears pricked at her eyes.

Lionel nodded.

"Damn you, why do *you* have to be a martyr?"

"So the rest of the government doesn't have to take the blame for my actions. One well-known terrorist, setting out on a fool's errand. He's no loss, right? If he sets the Sulawid war effort back a few years, that's unavoidable, but nothing they can pin on Orania." He raised his eyes and met hers. "Unless you blow my cover. If you report that I'm part of a government conspiracy to destroy the Sulawid fleet, they will come down on our planet with everything they have. Everything that you love—everything that we love—will be ashes floating in space."

He had always been a terrific actor. His ability to tell a lie and make it sound plausible had been a lot of fun in the past. She could remember so many parties where he had led on a gullible friend, as the rest of them had laughed themselves silly. He'd even done it to her. He could be doing it right that moment. But, was he? He looked as sincere as he ever had, and the stakes were never higher. What if she guessed wrong, and this was an elaborate lie to let him do what he wanted? She'd be a fool, and he would cause all hell to rain down on their home, when she could have stopped him.

The two opposing ideas circled around and around in her mind like angry cats. Was there really an organization that had recruited Lionel and had provided him with means and opportunity to commit a daring act like that, one that they could disavow with straight faces? Or was the man she knew just a pretense, and he had wormed his way into the bosom of the brass so he could commit terrorism that would destroy the lives of people on two worlds?

"We don't have much time," Lionel reminded her. He moved to kneel beside her and clipped the ties holding her arms to the chair. "Your colleagues will be on their way already. What's your decision?"

She jerked her head up, swallowing the tears in her throat. She rose to her feet.

"I'm coming with you."

"Oh, no, honey, no." Lionel smiled up at her. "There is no way I am taking you on a suicide misson. I'm putting you back on your ship right now. You're going home with the story of how you tried to capture me and I overpowered you. They'll believe you because there's still knockout gas in your lungs."

"No." She put out a hand to help him to his feet. "You're going to blast my ship out of space after I send one more desperate message. Won't that reassure your co-conspirators on Orania?"

He was now looking down on her. It had been so long since they had been together that she forgot how tall he was, and how those green eyes of his seemed to glow with their own light.

"But why?" he whispered.

Her heart melted. "Because I would rather spend one last flight with you, for the best cause in the world, than the rest of a long life wishing I had." It was true, but being true didn't make her any less frightened at what lay ahead. "Besides, I *have* to go with you. Because I know now what you are doing. People will know I know if I come back. No way they won't be able to interrogate me. I'll be subjected to every mind-reading technique they have, and as a marshal, I know them all. It'll be ugly. At least, if I'm with you, I won't be answering a million questions."

He wrapped her in his arms and held her tightly. "It's not going to be a very long flight."

"It will be long enough." She raised her face, and he kissed her. "Let me send my message, and let's go."

Communiques, both verbal and text, had been pouring out of the Communications station on her bridge. They must have been coming in since she had sent the message that she had caught up with Lionel. Since she had not replied to any, the tone of each, from marshals and senior officers back on Orania, sounded more and more desperate. She fought the instinct to tell them what was about to happen, to tell them that Lionel was no traitor but a martyr, that she was about to become one herself.

By the time she returned from setting IG-487 on its doomed flight, he had strapped himself into the captain's chair. She took the Weapons station. He gave her an odd look, but she shook her head.

"I'm part of your team. You say you weren't working with anyone, but you are now. You get us there. I'll set off the bomb."

She couldn't look as Lionel sent a rearward blast into the heart of her faithful little ship. Nothing held her back in Orania now, not even her heart. That was on the *Ascendant* now.

As she had thought, the three marshals in the area, as well as every other vessel that could lift, were in pursuit as Lionel kicked the warship into light drive.

Of course, the useless Premier Beckley would be forced to send an apology to his counterpart in Sulawid, vowing that he had sent his best officers to apprehend the terrorist Lionel LeSueur. Unfortunately, LeSueur had ended the life of the marshal who had caught up with him. Both worlds would mourn her.

In the meanwhile, the terrorist and the heroine made up for lost time with one another, in between discussing the way to make best use of the one opportunity they had to decimate the enemy's fleet. Sandra was certain that with the warning it had, Sulawid would move its fleets away from the point of defense over the capital city. Lionel was just as certain that they would leave it in place, assuming that the Potentate was the target of the coming attack, not his military might. She was terrified of what was to come, but just as convinced as Lionel that this was Orania's only chance to even the odds.

The only way they would know which one of them was right was the moment they came out of light drive, right into the center of the target, too late for the Sulawid Space Force or anyone else to stop them blowing up most of the fleet.

That moment came all too soon for Sandra. For the first and last time, sunlight came flooding into the cabin of the *Orania Ascendant*. According to their calculations, this was where the fleet ought to be assembled, and it was: an infinity of ships swirling around one another like insects in a nest.

"Hah! I knew I was right!" Lionel crowed.

Sandra just gave him an exasperated look as she set off the planetkiller.

# THE HUNTER BECOMES THE HUNTED BECOMES THE HUNTER

**Craig Martelle**

"One moves on the far side of the clearing," I whispered to my morbidly obese client. The short trees carried heavy vegetation, leaving small gaps through which to observe a furtive target.

The client was sweating while sitting and it wasn't even hot outside. His rifle shook in his hands as he tried to aim. I made sure it was on safe, then steadied it with a monopod. I gripped the support in one hand to keep the barrel from swinging.

"There!" I pointed, but he was looking through the scope and wouldn't see my direction. A bead of sweat ran into his shooting eye. He leaned away from the reticle and scrubbed at his eyeball with a dirty hand.

The figure hiding behind the bush bolted, running deeper into the woods.

I casually removed my monopod. "We'll get him next time," I lied.

"We'll wait here, and he'll come back?" the client wondered.

"No. We'll have to find a new OP—observation post—to watch for another scavenger. Don't worry. There's plenty of 'em out here."

"That's good. Sorry about spooking them."

"No one's supposed to be good at this stuff. It takes practice and a sharp eye. Maybe you can try a headband. Keep the sweat out of your eyeholes."

"Eyeholes. Is that cool military-speak? I'm going to use that," the client said. He wore the latest in camouflage fashion. It was powered and adjusted the external colors to match the environment surrounding it. The material was self-adjusting. And this swath must have cost a fortune since it was as big as a tent.

With a successful hunt, maybe I could convince him to give it to me as a tip. But first, we'd have to find another target. The easy one had spotted us and run. Humanity could be elusive when given no other choice. Deep down, I was happy he got away.

"Come on. Let's move to the second-best hunting spot in all the outside."

"What if they fight back?" the client asked.

"Then we kill them faster. If they're out here, they've been expelled from the city. If they've been expelled, what does that make them?"

"Criminals. Only criminals get expelled."

"And as such, they have no rights." I tapped the ten-millimeter high-powered pistol at my side. "They're not armed. It would be best for them to run. Fighting back isn't an option."

The fat man nodded. He struggled to stand. I offered my hand but only after he was most of the way upright. He pulled himself the last few inches. I had to lean back, way back, to keep from getting pulled over on top of him.

I led him along the widest trails to a hilltop that looked down on a lake and valley. The shot would be much longer, but the chances were high that he'd get a shot. At least the opportunity to take a shot. He paid me for the opportunity. There was never a guarantee that the client would make a kill. These guys tended to be terrible shots. It was a game to them.

It wasn't a game to the scavengers.

"Can we rest?" my client asked.

I didn't want to, but he was paying the bills. "Of course, Sky Marshal." The clients chose a name to go by to ensure confidentiality. I didn't care about their real names, and it was best that I didn't know them. I used to live exclusively on the other side of the wall, where I was one of the people who sent the criminals to the wasteland. Now I worked on both sides, and client anonymity was paramount.

The large man leaned against a tree, making it shake as he struggled to breathe. I wanted to feel sorry for him but couldn't. He shouldn't have chosen this diversion from whatever his problems were inside the city. He obviously had the credits to afford this trip but should have gone with something less strenuous.

"Let me carry your rifle and pack," I offered. It wasn't out of kindness. I wanted to get to the next OP. It was a small underground bunker where we could spend the night, although I was less than enamored of the thought. We had female clients on occasion, but they didn't want anything to do with the hired help. They usually brought their own man candy. This guy, though, would take up what limited space there was.

There was no sense fumbling around in the dark. I wanted to get a shot on a scavenger, blow his head off, and hand over a souvenir to the client, such as an ear or a finger. Each client wanted something different. It was up to them. Some were happy with a picture showing their dominance over their fellow man. This wasn't a hobby that was talked about openly. Hunting man for sport was a sadistic exercise of the rich. They'd show their trophies to their closest friends and no one else. If you knew, you knew. Otherwise, you knew nothing.

I'd take the credits they paid me and invest them. Maybe one day, I'd beat the market. Until then, I'd be carrying two packs and the client's rifle.

I put his pack over my shoulders to hang against my chest and hugged it to me with his rifle balanced across my hands. If we were ambushed, there would be a mad scramble, but I trusted my instincts and the firepower at my command. The scavengers had little to live for, but they usually didn't commit suicide by big game guide.

I hurried the client along, as much as I could. He wouldn't move fast on the best of days, but today was not his finest. I wanted to hate him, but I'd drop a surcharge on his invoice for carrying his equipment. I'd get mine and at the end of the day, that's all that mattered.

I stayed up front, stopping often to let the client catch up. While waiting and listening to him huff and puff, I heard another noise. Not far away, straight ahead. It sounded like footfalls, furtive and syncopated. I eased the client's pack to the ground and glanced to see where he was. Still too far, so I slung his rifle and pulled my pistol.

I stalked forward, staying close to the vegetation on my left, presenting as small a target as possible while leaving my shooting hand clear. I carried the pistol high, with two hands to keep it steady. I stopped. The sound was ahead. The client had also stopped, but not because of me. He stopped and bent over. He started to gag and, loud as a foghorn, puked.

A figure jumped out of the brush ahead and stepped forward, straightening with his spear in his trailing hand. He was going to throw it at my client, and he probably wouldn't miss at this close range.

I fired. It was a clear shot, and I had a steady hold with good sight alignment. The scav's head exploded. He dropped his spear and fell backward, dead before he hit the ground.

I scanned the area, looking for other threats. The entire area had gone silent. Not a bird on wing, nor a cricket chirp. It was a long minute before the sounds of the scrub returned along with renewed retching.

There wasn't much time before the darkness. If I wanted to get my client a shot today, then we had to get moving.

"Come on," I said, trying to sound as encouraging as I could.

"Can I claim that one?" the client asked.

"Of course. We'll get pictures." I handed the man's rifle to him. "Well done, Sky Marshal." I'm not sure I kept the condescension out of my tone. Some clients made it harder than others. We should have already had a kill in the books and been on the way back to the house, but no. Sky Marshal was afraid to aim and pull the trigger. "What's holding you back?"

I thought he'd say something about being out of shape, but he didn't. "I thought I'd be good with shooting a person, but I'm not. Let's get the picture and go home."

"They're not really human. They're scavengers, criminals scraping together a bad life. We're doing them a favor."

"Seriously? They look human to me," he whined.

"Take a knee behind him." I pointed. The client swept the barrel of his rifle past me. "Don't aim your rifle at me." I should have unloaded it. This clown was going to get me killed.

He mumbled an apology and pointed the barrel skyward. I took the official camera and snapped photos from two different angles before activating the three-dimensional capture mode and circumnavigating the client and the body. Some clients wanted to print a statue of their hunting prowess. I didn't expect the man who went by Sky Marshal would. He'd show the picture to friends and do his best to forget it.

"We better hurry. I'll carry your pack and rifle."

The man had renewed energy for the trip back to the wall, where a series of payments made sure that I had a way out of the city and, more importantly, a way back in.

I walked at a normal pace, which I found frustrating. I stopped looking back. If the client wanted to go home, then it was up to him to carry his bulk to the wall.

It was an hour after dark by the time we rolled up. I took off the client's pack and set it on the ground. I unloaded his rifle and opened the bolt. He walked up, sweat running down his head and staining his camouflage covering. In the light of the entrance, he looked flushed. It made me wonder if he had heat exhaustion.

"You'll want to get yourself checked by your doctor." I pulled a pouch of water from my pack and forced it into his hand. "Drink that."

He obliged me without argument and nodded once finished.

I gave him his pack and rifle. "Congratulations. Nice hunt," I told him and offered my hand. He shook it. I fought not to grimace at the clammy feel. "Go see your doc." I was sure it was heat exhaustion. He should choose something a little less strenuous next time he wanted to feel tough.

My guide company didn't need his testimonial. I had enough clients for me to live the life I wanted. I had a nice penthouse apartment. I had plenty of food. I didn't have a girlfriend, but that was probably for the best.

The gatekeeper looked at me. "Don't ask," I told him.

I unloaded my ten-millimeter, checked the chamber, and gave it to the gatekeeper. He placed it into an open slot in a lockbox. The client turned in his rifle. That went into a different slot. There were two other rifles and one pistol in that box. The gatekeeper secured it. I used my key on a secondary lock. I slipped him a hundred credits on a spare chip. He gave me a tight-lipped smile.

My client lumbered through the short passage and through another door. Without looking back, he disappeared into the darkness of the city's back streets.

I could only shake my head.

Three days later, I found myself waiting by the access gate for my next gig. This client had to be better than the last one. That guy hadn't almost gotten me killed, but he did the next worst thing. He was a liability the entire time we were in the waste.

I needed to do a better job vetting these people, but money talked. They had the credits. I knew I wouldn't vet them. They paid, and I took them into the waste to give them a shot at killing their fellow man. That was more food for the other scavengers. No mercy. No remorse. I had sent my share out there, but they were all criminals. I didn't second-guess what I was doing.

A well-built young man strolled toward me. He wore loose-fitting clothing. Nothing audacious or ostentatious. It was appropriate for the wasteland. With what he was wearing, he could go for a jog or a hunt or drink whisky over a game of billiards.

"Mister Smith," the man said by way of greeting.

That's the name I went by for this business. It was as unimaginative as it was anonymous. If the clients could use aliases, so could I. It was better for both of us.

"I'm Smythe, with a y and an e. Long aye in the middle."

We shook hands. His grip was strong and warm. He wasn't nervous about what his future held. He was supremely confident but not overconfident. I liked it. He wouldn't put me at risk unnecessarily. I was comfortable that my first impression was going to turn out right.

"Smythe, glad to meet you. You have a choice of three rifles. A .338 Lapua, a .30-06, or a .45-70. Old-school weapons with some serious punch. Do you know your rifles?"

"I know the first two can be good sniper rifles. I don't want to take shots at a thousand yards. I'm thinking more like fifty yards, so the cannon, the .45-70, will work best. Do you have any heavy loads, like a 510-grain bullet?"

"That's exactly the loads I have. 45-70 it is and angling for a close shot. See the whites of their eyes and all that?"

"It seems more appropriate. Give them a shot at us. Reaching out from a thousand yards isn't very sporting. They don't have high-powered rifles, do they?"

"No. Maybe spears. I carry a pistol for close-in defense."

"If I do my job, we won't need that," the man replied.

"It's refreshing to hear you're looking at it as a job. Take it seriously, and you'll have fun and bag your prize."

"That's the plan, Mister Smith."

"Let's go, Mister Smythe." I had the feeling that we'd have a good time on this run.

I delivered the secret handshake to the gatekeeper with a palmed hundred-credit chip. He laughed and opened the lockbox. I gave Smythe his chosen weapon while taking the one I was the most comfortable with. It was a big pistol and heavy to carry, but it gave me peace of mind. It helped me to feel safe in an environment that was anything but.

"There's another pair of hunters out there. Take care," the gatekeeper reported and pointed left. That made it simple. We'd go to the right. Avoiding another group was good form, so neither of the clients saw each other outside the wall.

Smythe was happy to go first as long as I directed him on which trail to take. The paths leading away from the wall were well-defined and heavily used this close to the gate, but they'd lose integrity the farther we went. Scavs didn't stay close. They moved away to where the tree cover and vegetation were denser. Where they could hide, scavenge, and survive to see another day.

In my opinion, it wasn't a life worth living. We were going to help with that.

Smythe moved like he knew what was doing. He walked softly, toe first, then heel. He kept his head on a swivel, looking everywhere, low to high and left to right.

He motioned with his fingers together to the left.

I let him follow his nose. His familiarity made me think he was an officer of the law. I also felt like he'd been outside before. The waste intimidated those on their first trip. There was so much that a person couldn't see, and people were used to trusting their eyes instead of all their senses. *What was that smell? The sound of the waste was different when a person walked by. Was that a frightened bird or an angry bird?*

It wasn't for weak clients, like my last one. I should have turned him around after we walked the first hundred yards. Should have. Didn't.

Maybe it was time to retire, but then again, I liked the credits with each new client, and there was something refreshing when working outside the city. No regulatory agency breathing down my neck. No people in my way. I was the supreme authority outside. That carried a heady intoxication. I hated to admit that I liked it.

The man followed a trail that lessened in use until it was nothing more than a game trail. He kept choosing the left branch of each fork until I had to stop him.

He turned on me, a furious look in his eye, but only for an instant.

I blew out most of my breath and whispered, "If we keep going left, we risk coming across the other hunting party. We need to avoid that."

He whispered back, "I doubt the scavs are heading toward them, don't you? I'm following a pair of footprints, a man and a woman."

I scanned the ground but could see no trail. I wasn't new to this. There had been no fresh footprints. I couldn't believe a client could see what I could not. He carried enough confidence and familiarity in the waste that I started to doubt myself. That wasn't the best way to continue, but, like my previous client, he was a paying customer. In the end, the decisions were his.

"Carry on," I told him.

Smythe nodded tersely, his mouth tight. The happy-go-lucky but adept person from before was gone. The individual before me was cold, but on edge. Why was he hunting? I never asked the clients. I didn't want them to admit that it was to stroke their ego—that part was obvious—but Smythe seemed driven by something else.

He continued forward until the trail made a hard right toward a valley. He stopped, looked around, and dodged left into the heavy brush. He picked his way through, using the butt of his rifle to hold branches aside so he could pass. After a quarter-mile, he held his fist over his shoulder.

I stopped. I leaned left and right to look past him, see what he had seen, but he blocked my view. He slowly brought his rifle up.

I loosed the pistol in its holster and held the grip, ready to pull it the rest of the way, if needed.

The man was smooth. The rifle barrel was steady. I still couldn't see what he was aiming at.

The shot caught me by surprise, and I flinched.

"Did you get him?" I asked.

"Oh yeah," he replied over his shoulder, leaving no doubt. "Let's go."

I bumped into him when I walked forward, and he faced me.

He pointed back the way we'd come. "We're leaving. Come on," he said with a sense of urgency.

I turned around. If he didn't want a trophy, not even a picture, that was his business.

A shot rang out from a short distance away and ripped through the leaves too close to the side of my head. I dove face-first to the ground, and Smythe—with a y and an e—ran over me in his rush to get away. A second shot sounded.

"You bastard!" a familiar voice shouted. "You shot my client."

I pushed up and ran after Smythe. He had some explaining to do, but it would have to wait until after we left the free-fire zone. I didn't like people shooting at me.

I almost caught up with him by the time he reached the game trail. Once on that, he ran at a full sprint. I couldn't catch him, but he didn't pull too far ahead. I could see him, and disturbingly, I could see that he no longer had the rifle. Some scav would find it, and then coming out here would get more dangerous than it already was. Too dangerous. The .45-70 was a cannon. I'd go back and look for it as soon as I caught up with Smythe.

Redoubling my efforts, I was able to close the distance. We were far enough from the engagement site that I was free to shout. "You stop!" It was the best I could come up with. I was breathing hard, almost gasping. I was in shape for hiking, not running.

He slowed and eventually stepped to the side of the trail where he leaned against a tree, keeping it between him and the path behind us.

"Your whole purpose was to kill that other client. That's murder," I managed between gasps for air.

"Not as far as you know. Did you see who was shot?" Smythe asked calmly. Evidently he was a lot fitter than I was.

I shook my head, opting not to speak any further because he had thought this through while I was reacting. One of us was emotionally prepared for this, and that person wasn't me.

"Some things have to be as they are," he said to no one in particular. "This opportunity could not have been squandered, and you'll not speak of it, lest the world come crashing down around your head."

He had all the cards. I studied his features so I could get someone to draw his face. I would find out who this guy was. I still had contacts on the force. He came out here and punked me. I may have accepted any and all clients, then carried their water, but I was no one's lackey.

"What'd you do with my rifle?"

"It's gone. I clearly panicked when we were being shot at by some derelicts from the human race."

"The last thing you did was panic. You were never out of control, were you, Mister Smythe?"

"Panic. Clearly," he deadpanned. "In any case, there were people shooting at us. It would be best if we not be here when they arrive."

He ran off, but at a slower pace. He recognized how much I was struggling, and he needed me to get through the gate.

The familiar voice that I'd heard? That was Aaron Shoemaker. He'd retired from the force before me and helped usher me into this business. He was a straight shooter. Literally and figuratively. I wouldn't run into him again because I decided, this very instant, that this was my last gig. There was no way I was going back out there.

We headed through the open area in front of the wall. We jogged toward the gate. I stopped him just outside of it. "This conversation doesn't need to happen inside," I started. "You paid me to guide you to hunt scavs. You didn't do that. You used me to get outside the city so you could shoot that other *tourist*. I don't want to know who it was or what your problem was with him. I only want to know that this is the end of it. I'm not going to say anything about this from here forward. I don't like being used. I'll take a one hundred percent kicker to my fee, and we'll call it equal."

He smiled. "You've been paid enough. There will be no more credits for you. I can destroy you more quickly than you can cause me any problems. To get credibility, you'd have to out yourself. You and I both know you're not going to do that. Get me back inside and we'll call it square."

He had as much leverage on me as I did on him. It cost me a rifle. I'd have to be good with that. Well, whoever I sold the business to would have to be good with that. I hung my head and walked past him without making eye contact.

He snorted in derision. I was another toady who succumbed to his brow-beating. I wanted to be angry, but I only felt hollow. I was helping people to kill other people for their entertainment. And I'd been used by someone who wanted to commit murder, kill a citizen. I needed a shower.

I waved to the gatekeeper. He watched me unload my pistol and hand it over. He tucked it into the lockbox and waited to fill the empty slot. Smythe waved as he walked past. "Lost it in a muck pool and weren't about to go swimming after it," I explained.

He gave me a single nod and locked the box. I looked behind me at the waste. It was better off without the likes of me ruining the day of those I'd sent there.

I don't know how long I was in the shower, but the incessant pounding on my door suggested I'd been in there long enough. I shouted, "Coming!"

The pounding stopped. "Open up."

"As soon as I get there," I called back. I wrapped in a bathrobe and hurried to the door. When I opened it, I found the police. "Can I help you?"

"We're looking for Vice Chairman Clive Carstairs," the first man said. A detective by his attire. His ident card hung prominently where the citizenry could see it, complete with current picture. He gestured at me, and I placed my thumb on his card to confirm who he was while confirming who I was.

I gestured toward the inside of my apartment. "He's not here, and I'm not sure I've ever met him in person. Why would you think he's here?"

"We don't. We think you're one of the last people to see him alive. We have it on good authority that you escort people into the waste outside. Ostensibly to shoot their fellow man."

I rubbed my chin and looked at the ceiling while frowning. "I'm pretty sure that I don't do any of that. That would be illegal. As you know, I'm a servant of the people, a former badge. I'm enjoying my retirement doing consulting spots for high-value clients. That's different than what you claim I'm doing. But please, look around and see what there is to see."

He stared at me as if trying to determine my truthfulness. Suspects were always incentivized to lie. Telling the truth got them put away or worse, expelled—that was, sent outside. Innocent until proven guilty was still a concept, albeit more fluid than the average citizen understood. I didn't have to prove myself innocent. They needed to prove I was guilty, but they could make implications and suppositions to support their case. It didn't take hard facts. Enough circumstantial evidence and one was guilty by default.

There wouldn't be any evidence. No one who knew wanted to be labeled as an accomplice. It was the way of the business. It also made me sorry that I had ever gone into it.

The police browsed through my apartment, looking casually around. The only one who seemed like he wanted to be there was the detective. "Dig deeper!" he snarled at his team. A new copper, judging by his fresh face, disconnected my computer and put it under his arm. He looked apologetic.

"It's okay, young man. You didn't have anything to do with this. And for the record, neither did I."

"We'll see about that," the detective said. "Put this on." He handed me a tracking bracelet.

I was being put on restriction. It was one step below being arrested. In a city of this size, it would be easy to get lost, but not while wearing a government tracker.

Everything we needed to live was produced in the city or the vast hydroponics chambers below. Greenery marked every other floor of a building and ended with a forest on the roof. The city looked like it had been overcome by nature, but it was the opposite. Mankind was living in conjunction with nature, but within the confines of a wall that circled the entire city supporting a dome overtop. The environment was controlled to every degree.

It was how society had decided to save itself.

Security came at a cost. We all answered to the authorities. My brief time as a guide was where rich people flaunted the authority that they themselves enjoyed. Average people, which accounted for the majority of the population, had everything they needed without excess.

So, some turned to crime. That gave me a job until I retired.

"Explain to me what consulting you do?" The detective was closer than I was comfortable with. He was in my face, a standard intimidation tactic.

"No." I wasn't obligated to give up private clients. Consulting was legal work. The authorities still respected fiduciary relationships. At least, that would be my defense. I'd seen it work when I had the day job. The problem was, I hadn't been on this side of the law. I maintained my façade. But it was growing tiresome. They removed personal files and every picture that I had printed and displayed, including my retirement photo from the force. They weren't going to charge me. They only wanted to crush my soul, so I'd be more pliable later when I was brought in for interrogation.

I hung my head. That was part of the game, but I was angry. My target was the man who went by the name Smythe. He had given me up in some way. I needed to find Aaron and make peace, but I suspected he was under observation, too.

My first order of business was to get rid of the tracking bracelet, but that was impossible. I only needed to spoof the device and mislead the signal. I had what I needed to make that happen... At least, I had before the authorities showed up and started helping themselves. I wouldn't get anything back in working order, so it was best to write it all off.

It was the way of things, no matter how wrong it was.

I would like to think I'd done nothing wrong, but I had. The challenge now was to avoid the consequences of what I'd done. Although the waste was off-limits, it wasn't a life sentence for going out there. It was only a fine, and that was the loophole we exploited. The guns were for our protection. That was the cover story in case we were ever questioned, which we hadn't been to that point. The people in charge were the ones who benefitted.

A fine? That meant it was legal if you had enough credits.

I had a stash but probably not enough. Best to deny everything. And find Aaron so we could provide mutual support. He wasn't going to be happy to learn that he was shooting at me, that I had helped my client murder his client. It was ugly, but burying my head in the sand was no longer going to work.

I had to get this thing off my wrist. For as complex as the tracker was, it was also simplistic. It operated through body temperature and the presumption that a perp couldn't get it off his wrist. But I had big wrists and flexed while the detective attached the device. He waited and then retightened it. It was a standard technique to defeat people who tried that ploy.

After they left, I turned on my stove and improvised a rack over top of an electric burner. I adjusted the height by adding dishes to the pans holding a baking sheet. I moved it higher and higher until the temperature was a consistent ninety-eight degrees. I soaped my wrist and pulled it over my hand to drop on a washcloth on the baking sheet balanced on two pans and a stack of dishes. The temperature would fluctuate. I hoped it wouldn't be too much to trigger an alarm at the police station.

If it did, then I'd be permanently on the run. It was a greater crime to remove the band than it was to be outside the walls. The irony wasn't lost on me, but the authorities had no reason to know where I was going.

A place we used to hide out and wait for informants to come to us. I bet that Aaron had gone underground.

It was Prime City. Everything was well lit, but not everything was under observation. That's what we knew that others did not. A downstairs apartment that was maintained for illicit liaisons came at a high rent, but it was free for cops who were willing to look the other way. That was us. We never bothered to tell the proprietor that we had both retired.

I knocked twice and slapped my hand on the access pad. The door obediently opened. Inside, I found Aaron, but he was tense. I could tell by the knife in his hand, pointed in my direction.

"Bad things happen to bad people," I said, reciting what we said about perps who were on the "wrong" end of excessive violence.

"All kinds of bad things," he muttered. "Come look at this."

He had a small pocket computer that he turned my way. It showed a man waving to a big crowd. I always considered those events to be staged, so I didn't think much about it.

"This is Clive Carstairs. He was the vice chairman of Barritrix."

Barritrix. The biggest corporation in Prime City. That made Clive the most powerful man in town because they didn't have a chairman. It was a name shuffle to hide the real power. It fooled no one. And there were no other cities that we knew of, so it made Clive the most powerful man in the world, even our small bit of it.

"I was running him outside and some sniper shot him dead."

I held up my hand. "That was my client. I'm sorry, Aaron. I had no idea what this guy had planned. He played me, but he was a pro. Nothing outside bothered him, and he seemed to know right where to go to ambush him." Aaron's mouth fell open, and he glared at me. "If it's any consolation, you almost hit me in the head with one of your shots. Missed by two inches."

Aaron managed to speak. "That's no consolation. You got my client killed."

"You could look at it that way. I took the money, like we do. I thought he wanted to be like the others. Kill a fellow human for sport. It's embarrassing, and for what it's worth, I'm out of the business. I'm not guiding people outside anymore."

The video looped. I tapped the screen to freeze an image. He was right there grinning.

"Do you know who that is standing next to your client? Because that's the guy who shot him."

Aaron sighed. "He's the deputy who moves into the vice chair position with the demise of his boss. A coup of sorts. That explains why the police have been looking for us. He's tying up loose ends."

"I'm not any scumbag's loose end," I blurted. It wasn't true. I was a lackey the second I accepted money to guide high-powered people outside the city and feed their sadism. "What do we do?"

"We might have to join those we sent outside," Aaron replied. "We can't hide forever in here. They'll find us."

"They gave me a wristband. It's currently over my stove enjoying being me."

He chuckled. "Just like I taught you. They gave me one, too. I tore it off and tossed it out of a people-mover window. I'm a criminal now. You may not want to consort with me."

We both laughed at that before settling into a long, uncomfortable silence. There wasn't much to say. We could have lamented our poor fortune, or we could do something about it.

"Can you search pictures on that thing?" I wondered.

Aaron nodded.

"Big dude. I mean, really big with a baby face, brown hair, brown eyes."

"Do I look like a sketch artist?" He waved the small screen at me.

"Can we check pictures of those in leadership positions at Barritrix?"

"Sure." He tapped away until he found what I wanted to see. He gave me the computer.

I scrolled through short bios with headshots until I found what I suspected. The big man's name was Thermotron, a single name like those the high-tech crowd adopted when they came of age. Thermotron was the director of computer systems. He didn't have a great number of employees beneath him because a lot of what they did was done by artificial intelligence. Enough of the work, however, wasn't automated and therefore required some staff.

"He was my client just before the one who killed Clive. I had a hunch there would be a link."

Aaron focused intently on Thermotron's picture. "Are you thinking we can leverage him?"

"I know we can. He was traumatized by the whole experience. I took the shot that he claimed. He never managed to pull the trigger. If we can get to him, what then?"

"Then we get access to the big man himself, and we kill him. Our lives are ruined. Might as well go out with a big bang."

"I'd like to think our lives are not ruined, but we'll be paying a fine. We need our boy Thermotron to testify that those two went outside and only one came back. We get fined, but the deputy—one Martin Dyke—gets charged with murder." I thought for a moment and then added, "I'll pay my fine to testify."

"Me, too. I saw the shooter, a glimpse of him, anyway, so it's more than just your word."

"The question is, will it go to trial? Once we take our shot, there won't be a second chance. Whether we try to take him out or take him down. We need to decide now."

Aaron scowled. He didn't like either choice, but status quo was no longer an option. "Get a hold of Thermotron and see if he can get us in. We'll confront the new vice chair and bring him down."

"That doesn't sound like a fleshed-out plan. Just confronting him gains us nothing."

"Then we kill him." Aaron sounded like he didn't care if that was the alternative.

"How about we arrest him and drag him out of the building in cuffs." The idea had just come to me. Publicity of the negative kind, even if he managed to extricate himself from the charges. The damage would be done when the allegations were made public.

"Look at us! We're going to be vigilante cops," Aaron quipped. "Contact Thermotron and let's get this party started. We'll need his schedule, and we can access the building when he's there. He only has to get us close, and we'll do the rest."

I used Aaron's small computer to send a message, trusting that it wasn't traceable because Aaron was the cautious type. He would maintain such a device. I did not, and the authorities had confiscated all of my electronics anyway. I had been unprepared for the fallout from the murder.

What happened outside definitely did not stay outside. The adage we used to swear by had failed me.

Barritrix Corporation's headquarters stood as the city's centerpiece. The corporation ran everything that mattered—food, water, waste processing, and the rest of the infrastructure. Once the government got overwhelmed, they had contracted down the slippery slope until the corporation was bigger than the government. Then came the question of who answered to whom.

The place was a fortress, even though it was supposed to be a bastion of public service.

That's why Aaron and I needed help from Thermotron to get into the building through the employee entrance versus the front door.

We waited outside the employee entrance, but Thermotron didn't show. We waited fifteen minutes past the designated time. I used Aaron's hand computer to call him.

He didn't answer. So I called again and again. On the third try, he answered but was out of breath.

"I'm almost there. Stop calling me."

I waggled my eyebrows at Aaron. He kept his head down so he wasn't so obvious to the cameras. I held my head high. I refused to act like a criminal.

The door opened, and a guard waved us in. Beyond a barricade, Thermotron waited. We went straight to him. "Aaron Shoemaker," my friend introduced himself. Thermotron nodded, opting not to shake hands.

"Elevator is this way." The big man turned and moved down the corridor.

It was an oversized elevator so easily fit the three of us. It stopped on the thirty-fifth floor. Thermatron walked out without a word. We followed him. He continued down a short corridor and stepped into the bathroom.

"Cameras, you see," he said. "And despite the law, they also have audio pickups."

We nodded. It wasn't a surprise.

"Go left in the corridor, then the first right. There's a bank of elevators down there. Take the farthest left one. That is the only lift to the top floor. What are you going to do?" he asked, pushing a key card into my hand.

I showed my tight-fitting clothes, turning left and right to show that I wasn't packing. Nothing except a set of handcuffs that Aaron had found in the apartment. They were for more exotic pleasures, except when we slapped them on Mr. Dyke. I expected that he wouldn't revel in the experience.

"We're going to arrest him for the murder of the vice chairman," Aaron explained. "That's it. No falling down stairs or unofficial tune-ups. We'll secure him and turn him in at the station."

"Martin Dyke did that?"

We both nodded once more.

"Please resolve this or he'll see me with you and kill me next. I should have never gone outside," the big man whined.

"No, and I'm not going outside again, either. It's a terrible place," I agreed.

He looked down as he walked out. We waited two minutes before heading for the elevators that would take us to the top floor.

"Do you have a badge?" I asked.

"Nope," Aaron replied. "You?"

"Turned it in when I retired, but I have an ID card. It'll be good enough. Retired officers can still enforce the law."

"I'm counting on his people to understand that when we march him out." Aaron nodded toward the door. It was time to go.

We walked out like we were supposed to be there. We strode boldly past an employee in the corridor, not bothering to greet them. We kept our eyes focused on the goal. The elevator on the far left had its own call button. We pressed it and waited. Inside, we saw a slot for the key card that Thermotron had given me. His office was undoubtedly the one that programmed the cards, and he kept spares just because he could.

After the key card, the floors showed up on the bank. They started at thirty-five and ended at forty-seven. I pressed the highest number, and we started ascending.

The elevator moved quickly. We had no idea what to expect, which had happened often enough when we served that it wasn't that big of a deal. The doors opened, and we stepped out into an oversized antechamber of glass and monuments to the great works of Barritrix.

Through double-doors that shone with expensive glass where the Barritrix logo was etched to leave no doubt about the hallowed spaces beyond.

It opened as we approached, the sensors oblivious to the intentions of those walking through.

We turned toward the area with a sign over it that read "The Vice Chairman." We looked for his office, but it wasn't obvious. The entire area was filled with cubicles surrounding open desks.

"He has to have an office, doesn't he?" I whispered.

"Door is built into the wall. This floor is bigger than what we see," Aaron explained.

It was obvious once I changed my mindset from looking for a standard entry. Fancy and smooth. It fit Dyke's personality. I didn't know anything about Carstairs, but it must have suited him, too.

We walked past the desks to the wall beyond, where we found an embedded handle. I reached for it.

"Hey!" someone shouted. I was surprised we made it this far without anyone challenging us.

"Yes?" I turned and pulled my identification card. The police emblem was big enough that she could see it from where she sat ten feet away. "We're here to arrest your boss for murder. Martin shot Clive. We have all the proof we need to send him away. Anyone interferes with us and you'll become an accomplice after the fact. Do you really want to be sent outside? You'll stay in your seats and do your jobs. Do not interfere with us." I said the last part with enough force to make them think twice about getting in our way.

Aaron opened the door, and we walked in. I closed it behind me as we found Martin in the middle of a tele-call.

He stared at me. "I'll call you back."

"You won't, Mister Smythe with a y and an e. We're here to arrest you for the murder of the vice chairman. You're done, Marty."

He stood, threw his hands up, and shrugged. "You only think you're going to arrest me." He smiled and with well-practiced and seemingly unnatural speed, he bolted toward what looked like a closet. The doors snapped shut behind him. Aaron vaulted over the massive desk, and I ran around it, but the private elevator was already gone.

"Dammit!"

"Front door?" Aaron asked, but he was already moving. We ran out of the office, having to slow for the automatic door. Once clear, we sprinted to the elevator, which would only take us halfway, and then we'd have to switch elevators. No matter what, he was going to beat us to the bottom.

The wait as the elevator descended grated on our nerves. We rushed from the elevator and almost mowed down two people who were waiting, but the doors were open on another. We forced our way in and punched the button for the ground floor.

Our lift-mates stared at us, trying to back away, but there was no room. We were wedged in there together. "We're here to arrest the new vice chair for murdering the old vice chair. Ugly business. Of course he's running, but we'll catch him," I said with a smile and a nod.

Might as well start our negative publicity campaign as soon as possible. We'd already primed those outside the vice chair's office, but these were average employees.

We reached the bottom and ran for the front door. No one monitored those leaving, but you had to pass through security to get into the building. We made it outside without getting molested by Barritrix security.

Once out there, we were left wanting to know where he'd gone. A school group stood near the pickup point for public transportation. Prime City didn't allow any private conveyance, no matter who you were. It evened the playing field for police and limited chases.

We ran to the group. Aaron asked the chaperone, "Have you seen this man?" He showed her Martin Dyke's picture.

"Yes. He took that small bus." She pointed at a vehicle just disappearing around the corner.

The next bus was already at the stop. Aaron and I jumped on board. He flashed his ID. "Under authority of Prime City Police in pursuit of a murder suspect, I'm taking control of this vehicle. Follow the previous bus, please. You are authorized to exceed normal operating limits."

"This is my day!" the operator said. "SEATS!" he shouted over his shoulder and put the vehicle in gear. It accelerated slowly, as electric buses were wont to do. It rolled silently forward before bumping past the next stop, around the corner, and continuing to accelerate after the other bus.

It took three stops before we spotted our target. "Did he get off already?" I asked, knowing that we wouldn't find out until we stopped the other bus and boarded it. Good thing there were two of us. We could enter using both the front and back doors.

We had our answer without getting off. The bus ahead of us skipped past its next stop and accelerated. The thing with the public transport was that it was regular and efficient. It didn't even need drivers, but that was part of the 100% employment goals for Prime City. Everyone had a job even if automation could replace the humans.

Erratic driving was something that never happened.

"Our bad guy has coopted the diver," I guessed.

"Undoubtedly."

Our driver matched the speed of the other bus, grinning as they went. This might have been the happiest day of his life, which didn't say a whole lot about the exciting role bus drivers played in Prime City.

The buses held straight lines down the main thoroughfare. They avoided the pullouts where they were to pick up passengers who now stared at the intransigent public transport that refused to pick them up.

The bus ahead turned toward the wall, the area where we departed on our guided hunts.

"This is a ridiculous chase," I blurted. Two public transport buses racing through the streets at speeds barely above a sprinting man.

Aaron looked up at me from under his brows. "You were always an upstart. This is exciting. Makes you want to go back to full-time, doesn't it?"

I laughed. "No, it doesn't." I was still trying to figure out how I was going to stay out of jail or keep from getting banished to the waste. "He's heading outside."

"You said he seemed comfortable out there."

"He never missed a step, and you know what? That .45-70 is out there. Not only will he be out there, he'll be armed with a cannon."

"You never told me about a rifle. He shouldn't be able to get through the gate, though." He didn't say it with conviction. All it would take was a bundle of credits.

The bus stopped near the gate, and Dyke jumped off and sprinted away.

Our bus stopped and once the door opened, we ran after our target. He was through the gate a hundred feet in front of us. As fast as we could run, he was already through and running into the waste by the time we got there, making a beeline down the track we'd used to return.

"We need our weapons. Open my lockbox, please."

The gatekeeper nodded and slid my box from its slot. The two of us opened it, and I pulled my ten-millimeter high-powered pistol. I also took the Lapua. Aaron grabbed a .45 caliber pistol and the only other rifle in the box, a .30-06. He cycled the bolt to send a round into the chamber. I did the same.

We stepped into the waste and were instantly rewarded with a view of our perp. I brought my rifle up. He was well within range, but within a second, he'd disappeared into a wooded area and then behind a hill.

That meant we had to chase him some more.

"Set a trap or run into his trap?" Aaron asked.

We ran for the wood. "You're going to get me killed," I managed while panting. This was far more running than I was prepared for.

"You're going to get *me* killed!" Aaron countered, but he was struggling to breathe, too. Dyke was younger and in better shape than us older guys. We could hike all day long, but running was for the young.

"Spread out. Don't give him targets close together," I said. I slowed down and ran crouched as I approached the trees. I was still in the open and didn't like it. I never saw where Dyke dropped the rifle, but this had all been planned. It wouldn't be far from the gate because the scavs didn't come this close. That's something Dyke seemed to know when he shouldn't have had that knowledge.

How many times had he been outside?

Aaron went left, and we slowed to a walk once we reached the trees. We were now fighting both the scavengers and Martin Dyke. Then again, we'd been out there enough times and tromped through endless miles of the place. We had returned safely every time, no matter what baggage we were hauling, like when I brought Thermotron out here.

I moved from tree to tree. I was the hunter. Dyke was the prey. I had been ready to never return outside, but this was different. I didn't have a choice. To clear my name. To clear Aaron's name.

A bush moved opposite the light breeze. I raised my pistol. It would be a long shot, but I could make it. I had to.

The bush stopped moving. I waited. Another bush farther back rustled and stopped. Then another. He was moving away.

I moved forward in short dashes, tree to tree, staying upright so I could see.

A shot rang out. Loud. The .45-70. I couldn't tell if he was shooting at me. I saw and heard no impacts or the bullet passing.

Where was Aaron?

A heavy shot sounded. That was Aaron's rifle barking in response. The bushes moved toward me. A head popped out, looking toward where the .30-06 shot came from.

I raised my pistol glacially slowly so I wouldn't trigger his peripheral vision. He ducked down but didn't move. It was hard to judge where his head was, but I could guess where his body was, giving me the biggest target possible.

Aaron fired the .30-06 again. It ripped through the bush beside the one where Dyke hid.

The .45-70 rifle barrel came up and pushed the top of the bushes down so Dyke could return fire but with a well-aimed shot.

I could see the top of his head. I aimed three inches below that and squeezed the trigger. The ten-millimeter roared. The barrel jumped up from the round going downrange. I started pulling the trigger before the pistol dropped, returning to my natural aim point. I fired again and again, hoping for body shots with a double- and triple-tap.

I stalked forward, watching with both eyes open over the top of my weapon, ready to fire again if there was any movement.

When I reached the bush, I stopped and eased sideways, looking for an opening where I might confirm if Dyke was still there.

A bullet passed my head and embedded in the tree before I heard the sound of the shot.

"Stop shooting!" I yelled at Aaron while ducking. When I hit the ground, I discovered Dyke had died with my first shot, as evidenced by the damage to his head. "He's dead, Aaron. You got him."

I crawled to the far side of the tree and slammed a round into the chamber of the .338 Lapua. If this was going to be a rifle battle, I wasn't going to fight it with my pistol.

"Coming in," Aaron called. He walked loudly to announce his approach.

I slid my back up the tree until I was standing. I ducked my head around the trunk and back as quickly as I had put it out there. There was no sense in giving him a target, but he had his rifle slung over his shoulder.

"Dammit, Aaron. That's twice now you almost brained me with your shot," I said when I stepped out.

Aaron laughed. He looked behind the bush. "Hey," he grumbled. "There's no way I shot him in the side of the head. That was you."

"Might have been." I moved to the body to recover my rifle. I wiped the blood off on Dyke's expensive clothing.

"Time to go home?" I asked.

"What home are we going to?" He held his arms wide to take in the expanse of the waste. He offered his hand. "I'll be seeing you."

We shook. "I'm not coming back outside. I've had enough of this."

"I'm going to see what it's like out here, as far from Prime City as I can get. We put them out here. Was it as inhumane as the authorities want us to believe? I'm not so sure, especially if people like you and I stop guiding the sadists in charge of us."

We locked eyes for a few seconds and then he was gone, disappeared into the trees with my rifle and pistol.

He could have them. I didn't need them.

I walked slowly back to the gate, expecting to be arrested the second I arrived. No surprise when the police detective and three uniformed officers were waiting with the gatekeeper. I nodded to them, and we unlocked my box. I put the two rifles and one pistol inside before locking it up.

"Is that it?" the gatekeeper asked.

"Got the .45-70 back but lost the .30-06 and the .45. It was a bad day out there. My partner is gone, too."

"And what about Mr. Dyke?" the detective asked.

"He was shooting at us, just like he shot Clive Carstairs yesterday. It was self-defense. He's quite dead."

"Why were you out there?" the detective asked.

"I'm a police officer and I was chasing a murder suspect. I was not going to let him get away."

"That's good enough for me, Officer. You have a nice day. This case is closed." He walked away.

# WHEN IT COUNTS

Marisa Wolf

*It's only treason if you lose.*

Norina had a number of mantras to regulate herself when out on orders. This one rose to the top more often than the others.

Perhaps that should have worried her, but to be fair she applied it to her targets as often as herself. As she did in this case. The idea of treason—and those who might be guilty of it—had surfaced repeatedly in her thoughts since her last conversation on Prima Seignur.

"This is highest priority. War is coming." Len had been her reporting agent for nearly three full cycles—a record in Norina's thirteen-cycle career—and usually maintained a steady, affectless demeanor. Whatever he actually thought remained locked behind blank eyes and stiff facial expressions, which was ideal in their line of work. It added to Len's ability to blend—sometimes when he stopped speaking and even Norina could forget he was in the room.

"War is always coming," she'd replied, smoothing the scuff on one fingernail that threatened to become a tear. "Isn't that the point of us?"

"Not unrest." Len's featureless office had not dropped in temperature, but her eyes locked on his in response to the sudden chill. "The Ninth System has gone dark, and we've sent three assets to the frontier to learn more."

"Who?"

"No one you know."

Possible. Unlikely, but possible. Len, or someone higher up the chain than him, didn't want her read in. Which meant... she corrected her consideration. *Could* mean several things. She didn't have near enough information to lock into a theory.

"So I'm going back out to the edge."

"Not alone."

"I don't—" the words snapped out, habit, and he lifted two fingers off his empty desk.

"Not someone assigned to work with you." Sometimes it was nice, maybe, having the same reporting agent for three cycles. He knew her preferences by heart and even obliged them, from time to time. "Fleet Intelligence. I'm not sure which of four possible candidates, but you'll know what to look for."

Fleet.

The Empire, eight systems strong for several hundred years, had many levers to keep its disparate parts in sync. The two main avenues to keep the Empire together were to make an economic split too much effort, and violent revolution purchased at far too high a cost. The bureaucracy that kept Empire states profitable, anchored in the empiric center of Mishthatar, wound its moneyed tentacles to do the former. As for the latter, the Empire had an overpoweringly well-supplied Space Fleet that handled conflicts with decisive force.

Each system had their own smattering of intelligence agencies, which deployed operatives for various specific goals under the heading of profit and prosperity for all the Empire's people. Norina's work in Prime had overlapped across a number of planets with individuals from many such offices. Mostly they were fine.

Except for Fleet.

She made a face—not her most professional response, but as her handler for a few cycles, Len had seen worse from her. "Fleet only ever has one move on the frontier."

"Kaskata isn't the frontier." Len shifted and pressed a section of his empty desk. A small drawer *shushed* open, he reached inside, then emerged with a tiny data circle on the tip of his index finger.

"Kaskata's close enough. Half the galactic center still calls it the ragged edge." Norina frowned at the databite and didn't immediately reach for it. "Is that the Fleet agent possibilities or my orders?"

Len did not roll his eyes, which left a sour taste in her mouth. He should have—of course her orders wouldn't be recorded, not even on the most encoded, decomposable bite ever made. Instead he extended his arm further and she tilted her own to position her wristlet.

A flicker of motion between them, and the databite vanished. Her wristlet pulsed once against her skin, indicating it was digesting the information—decrypting, to be technical, but Norina preferred the more descriptive term—and she sat back against the metal chair.

"So I go see if Ninth System is applying pressure to Kaskata—"

"If Kaskata is *in league* with Ninth System," Len said, his thin-lipped mouth curved faintly downward at the slight emphasis. "It wouldn't be the first time they've been on the wrong side."

"Technically they weren't a part of the Empire in the last war," Norina corrected, her voice as prim as any scholar.

"They are now. And Ninth System has operated in their orbit more than once."

"Ninth System has operated everywhere—including here." Norina didn't roll her eyes either, but she shrugged her shoulders nearly as dismissively. "Isn't that how you got promoted?"

"You should be downsystem bound within the day." He folded his hands on his desk and regarded her with a professional's dismissal of her attempted dig.

"I've got a student visa ready to go, and it comes with an open ticket on the Dessux Line. Expect my initial report on a..." She pressed her toes down inside her boots and called up her mental web of transport companies. "Probably a Stivven. I'll confirm in a message drop between Ree and her Uncle Lennox once I'm on site and have something."

His focus faded and his fingers twitched, likely tweaking something through his own wristlet to ensure the innocuous accounts were still burbling away with their semi-automated messages.

They were. She checked in on them periodically, enough to be sure the manufactured responses didn't start hallucinating and tip themselves into the kind of nonsense that might flag someone's notice. There were few easier ways to send information than in plain sight. The more innocent noise on a semi-active family update chain, the less notice anyone's data crawlers would take. Not a suitable avenue for reports, of course, but to signal her handler where to look for the actual information to follow? Nothing simpler.

"I have the Lennox drop open." If Len approved of her thoroughness, he didn't bother to share with her.

"Well, send your niece a birthday present, so she'll have something to thank you for." Norina made her voice excessively perky, and that time he did roll his eyes.

She rode that victory right out of the Empire's heart.

Kaskata had changed relatively little in the three cycles since she'd last seen its bubbled surface. The system had been claimed for the Empire because of its mineral rich orbiting bodies, and it had far more space stations and enormous company-sponsored living cargo ships than habitable planets. Kaskata the planet was only generously described as habitable. Seismically active, prone to belching poisonous gasses at its inhabitants, host to ever-hungry native life, it had only one continent stable enough for permanent settlement. The single sprawling city, also named Kaskata—not a lot of creativity in names—housed the headquarters of several inter-system corporations and a legion of people working hard just to survive.

Rich picking grounds for both Empire loyalists and Ninth System's agitators, all in one shining, deadly, neon-lit place. The loyalists pushed the path to success, right here in Kaskata's own wildly successful companies! Meanwhile the malcontents claimed the Empire wants to keep people poor and desperate, when they could be independent and free again!

Despite the single city, the population was more than large and shifting enough for Norina to create two helpful identities without risking a hint of suspicion.

Her daytime alias, "Rina," a long-suffering graduate student conducting research on the variety of aquatic vertebrates that populated the Empire's disparate waters, spent as much time in counter-shop eateries as the three city libraries. Rina had a trip disbursement that she had to spend or risk losing renewal for her next spot, and students all over the Empire were a soft touch for food.

Students always knew what counterculture messiness was available to them, or knew someone who knew someone. She only had about five cycles left with this particular guise—bright eyed curious cute little unthreatening grad student. She made the most of the approach while she could—little else was as perfect for asking awkward questions, going dark unexpectedly, and being a bit scattered.

Nighttime Nora, on the other hand, was an entirely different creature. The stripes of glitter and paint changed the angles of her face, rounded her angled eyes, and drew attention to her mouth. The current party scene trend in Kaskata worked in her favor—layers of accessories, all meant to echo the feel of the city. Oil-sheened jewelry that wound up her arms like the city's deep water canals, flashing pins studded through her hair, thick-soled shoes, and, best of all—long false eyelashes made of individual light-up filaments.

Food wasn't her entry point here. Instead it was a matter of finding the right group, timing a trip to the washroom, and making a point to blink rapidly and dry her eyes while staring into the mirror. On her first attempt she was surrounded by a cloud of beautiful, sympathetic young things, who adopted her into their circle and invited her out nearly every following night.

No threat could possibly be posed by a sweet student or a reckless party girl.

During a visit to the Sivastian Consulate—important for any visiting student from Bedovar University—she paused at the flashing holo board of various providers determined to be useful to planetary visitors. When she scanned the list of tech-adjusters with her wristlet, two names highlighted themselves in her display, and she strolled away without incident.

Of the two, she'd worked with Yelven before. New arrivals from upper systems more often than not needed to tweak frequencies and channels in their wristlets and comms upon connecting with a new city's framework. Her devices didn't need that, self-adapting as they were, but likely a student would require it, making an easy excuse for a visit. Though she did not hand over any of her materials, in days she had replacement strands for several of her false eyelashes, and several other intriguing tools. Thanks to her day and night guises both, Norina knew exactly where they'd best be used.

Foreign Shores, a bar and fun house that catered to well-paid corporate types with disposable credits, took up the first seven stories of a twisted tower made of a translucent gray stone. Blue and purple lights raced through the veins of the building's façade, and connected on a loop to flash the bar's name.

Nora circumvented the line and approached the rectangular machine by the front door. She scanned the wristlet on her right hand, the display lit up with a flash of deep purple, and a small door in the middle of the giant gleaming red archway swung open.

The wristlet on her left arm, buried under layers of slick beads, pulsed against her skin. Success. She got a drink—something luridly pink with a flashing ice cube—and danced for a few songs before she slipped into the bathroom to scroll through her gains. The claw program on her wristlet had lifted the list of people who'd been allowed admittance so far that evening, and she unfocused her eyes slightly as she swiped through the names.

After dozens of swipes, her pattern recognition locked in and she paused to match the name to one of the faces she'd studied. Austus Drellim, a team lead at KasCorps. After another minute, and a pause to join in on a spontaneous sing-along outside her stall, she found two more. Dougal Camitas, project manager for a new system at Stivven Industries, and Turia Mel, an executive for Central Mining, had apparently arrived at Foreign Shores directly after the other. Or together.

She hadn't turned up anything in her research to indicate they knew each other well enough to drink together, but in the grand scale of human civilization, Kaskata wasn't so big, and the group of people with easy credit even smaller.

First order of business, Nora found her group of new friends on the third floor. Two rounds of drinks and several bass heavy songs later, she'd invested enough time to go wandering with a few of them. Though possible any of her three targets might have left Foreign Shores before she could find them, she'd noted the average visitor spent at least three hours in the place. Something to justify the effort—monetary or time—it took to get inside in the first place.

She cheated, but not everyone had her resources.

Austus had a weakness for tall blondes, and Nora had found herself a friend group full of options. Carine towered in her heeled boots, and her light hair glowed under the swooping lights. Selvie, not quite as willowy but equally bright-haired, favored bold dance moves guaranteed to pull attention.

It didn't even take a full song for their gyrations to bring them into Austus's orbit, and for the mid-level executive to give in to their gravity.

"Can I buy you three a drink?" Smart man to make the offer to the trio, though his slightly blurred gaze remained fixed on Carine.

Nora nudged her and giggled to the side, and Carine straightened her shoulders. "I guess you could."

They followed him to the nearest bar—on this level it was made with the husks of fossilized sea creatures that Rina would have had a series of raptures over—and introductions were made with a fair amount of accuracy over the thumping music.

With drinks secured, Austus invited them to his quiet booth against the wall. Carine took a considering sip of her drink and exchanged glances with Nora and Selvie. The latter nodded, and they made a loose line to follow him through the press of bodies.

A slight buzz shivered over Nora's skin as she slid from bar to cubby—the sound screens made in Kaskata were excellent. While the technology couldn't do anything with the smells of half-dried liquor and enthusiastic crowds, the weight of music lessened into a gentle burr. Nora made a note to see what company made the sonic barrier in case they had a mobile version, and hung back as though examining the space.

Foreign Shores had a vague theme—floors based on various systems of the Empire, walls decorated with souvenirs or detritus from other planets—and the theme of this small, semi-private room appeared to be . . . yellow. If there was a settlement that favored the color so singularly, Norina had yet to visit it, but that could hardly matter to Nora. Instead she pointed at something bright and rectangular, which allowed enough pause for Carine, then Austus, then Selvie to slide into the curved, cushioned booth against the wall. Nora took up the end, propped her elbows on the non-sticky round table between them, and took a healthy sip from her new mug.

Two virulently green drinks later, Carine excused herself for the washroom, and Nora put on her best concerned-friend-face. "So you come to Foreign Shores a lot?" Her tone hovered between slightly judgmental and genuinely curious, and Selvie turned intent eyes toward the man.

"I have a membership pass from work," Austus replied, sitting up a little straighter like he knew the game.

Nora smiled briefly—a hint of approval to keep him focused on what he thought was happening. One of her first lessons—it was so much easier to hide one's real aim when it was couched in other people's expectations. Austus bragged without gloating, about his position and his influential clients. Selvie laughed in all the right places, and Nora widened eyes as though impressed.

"It can't be all fun-easy though, right? I mean, *every* customer can't be satisfied." The tease in her tone made him laugh, and Carine's reappearance upped his excitement and potentially lowered his inner editor. The next round of drinks appeared on the round table between them, a bonus of good timing.

"Got a new client from upsystem who might as well be plank in the canal." Austus snorted, and continued in a surprisingly good impression of galactic center clipped accent, "'I didn't expect to find such loose process outlines in such a key office.' I've heard him say it at least three times, and he just got here start of the quarter."

Nora noted the arrival time and the accent as likely for her Fleet compatriot, but let the conversation wander away from business as Carine and their other friend started teasing Austus about whatever loose processes might mean.

With the well temporarily tapped, Nora stood, steadied herself with a hand on Selvie's shoulder, and leaned across the table toward Carine.

"I think I'm going to go see where the rest of the girls are," she whispered—or at least hushed her voice in a drunk young thing's attempt at such—and glanced significantly at Austus.

"Oh we can go with—" Carine began, at least partially genuine.

Nora let go of Selvie to wave off the offer, paused to rub the corner of her eye, then repositioned to dip further across the table. Her hand rested on the table next to Austus's, which was wrapped around his drink. Selvie reached over to support Nora's arm, as though her friend might topple over at any moment.

With both women focused on her and Austus's intent interest on their conversation, there was little chance of anyone noticing that the non-glowing false eyelash on the tip of Nora's finger tapped against Austus's wristlet and briefly fused against the metal before falling disregarded to the table.

"Nah. It's good for me to move. You all have fun." Nora winked somewhere between Carine and Austus, and paused to hug Selvie around the shoulders before sliding out of the booth.

Music crashed against her and she did a little twirl and wave to assure the trio left behind that she was fine. Selvie waved, Carine laughed, and Austus had already forgotten she'd existed.

Perfect.

She found her second and third targets together on the sixth floor. Dougal leaned his back against the bar—this one made out of what might be genuine Kisnovian marblewood—and spoke repeatedly to Turia. Turia replied about half the time, but her body swayed with the music and her attention visibly tracked toward the crowd in the dance floor.

Nora timed her approach with a shower of glittering bubbles from the ceiling. She stumbled out of the crowd, laughing and waving pearlescent orbs out of her way, and nearly collided with Turia.

"Oh sorry there, pretty. It's a mess in there."

Turia smiled absently, her attention floating back toward the floor. "G'yon with ya," she murmured, a common Kaskata-ism good for acknowledging sneezes and accepting apologies.

"Picking up friends again?" Dougal shouted, leaning around Turia to ogle Nora.

Turia rolled her eyes and Nora straightened with a grin, because this was a clear opening. With a shimmy in time to the music, Nora stepped back and extended her hand. Dougal shifted as though to take it, but she locked eyes with Turia.

"Want to dance?"

Turia shouldered Dougal away with a laugh and put her hand in Nora's.

For the next stretch of evening, Nora was exactly engaging enough to encourage the flirting between Dougal and Turia, without tipping the point into a true focus on her. Quick, glancing touches transplanted tracker programs from loose eyelashes to wristlets, but Nora's hopes weren't high. Though Dougal had a bit of charm, he had little of interest to say, and Turia only mentioned work once in passing—her new upsystem contact was cute, but boring. Were all the cute ones boring? Dougal took the invitation implied, and Nora patted both their arms and danced away into the crowd.

Two corporate assets potentially already tapped by Fleet, if she'd read the comments from Austus and Turia correctly. She'd know more once her programs had time to worm through the information and sent back a digest.

In the meantime she rejoined her group of friends on the seventh floor and danced the night away. Not the first time, and may it not yet be the last.

It took "Rina" two days and three spliced security systems to identify the Space Fleet Intelligence agent. Len had been correct—he was one of the four potential SFI assets Len had suggested she might find on Kaskata. The winner of the ticket to the Empire's edge turned out to be Callan, no identified last name. He had almost as long and as redacted a history as she had, and no wonder it took another three days to properly map his movements and tangle her path with his.

Callan, roughly her age, had bucked Fleet expectations slightly—she had to give him credit for his slightly shaggy hair and relaxed posture. Though the way he scanned the room twigged the back of her brain the moment they were in the same space, he didn't immediately scream Fleet. Some of his compatriots could stand to learn that talent.

Rina pulled her hair into a loose bun and stepped up to the counter to order her cheesy wrap chock full of indeterminate proteins and vegetables. Perfect grad student food.

"Just you today?" the boy behind the counter asked, and she smiled warmly. Lerid had a crush on Ziff, one of Rina's new student friends. He'd made a point to recognize the girl's compatriots, apparently as some sort of subtle courting approach. Rina couldn't fault his efforts, and certainly it made her seem a more settled part of the ecosystem, nothing to draw Callan's attention too soon.

"Schedules are such a beast, you know? I have to be out on Tevvin's Canal this afternoon to see how many katavils migrated back after the last storm." She sighed heavily and tapped her wristlet to pay.

He wrinkled his nose. "Eating early so's the food settles before the smell hits, huh?"

Callan had booked a room high up in Tevvin's Quarter. Great views, and well-removed from the sulphur and sludge that stuck to the quarter's main canal. Luckily the smell originated in large part from one of Kaskata's unique aquatic vertebrates, which gave Rina plenty of reason to be in the area.

"You really know your customers," Rina replied brightly, and slid out of the way when her transaction flashed complete. Young Lerid waved at her and gestured to the next person, and Rina lingered at the end of the counter for her order with her back to the small assortment of tables like any other clueless student who didn't keep her head on a swivel.

Granted, she'd been here often enough that the security feed burbled to her wristlet, which would vibrate if a body moved suspiciously enough to flag an alert. A little extra confidence to bolster her guise's ease and carelessness.

The autoserver slid her cheesy wrap through a tube and she juggled the warm wrapping with a final wave toward Lerid. Scanned the tables, picked one against the half-wall of windows, and took a seat that kept Callan out of her line of sight but the door in it. Uneventful minutes passed as she ate, and the Fleet agent walked out the door as she folded her wrapping to throw it away. Only took another few moments for her to swipe a napkin over the surface and amble out after him.

She knew where he slept, so she didn't try and keep him in sight. In the end, her caution and distance didn't matter.

As Rina tucked her chin deeper into her scarf and passed the next alley, a hand wrapped around her arm and yanked her off the walkway.

The moment her momentum shifted, she reached for her weapon. Something hard pressed against the side of her rib cage, so she didn't hesitate in returning the favor against the body that had grabbed her.

"I haven't signed anything with KasCorps," a hoarse voice said, with a level of strain that hit her ears as a tinge forced. Certainly the hand at her side didn't shake like some corporate spy in over his head. "So if you're here on Stivven Industries's behalf—"

"I'm not!" Norina skewed her tone higher, breathless, a student completely taken off guard. As though she didn't have a weapon shoved into his lower gut. They weren't putting on a show for each other, she decided. Cameras in the alley? She hadn't looked, but probably. Even if they only existed to guide the delivery drones, few places in Kaskata were truly unseen. Alleys that intersected major walkways were hardly going to be the exception.

"Why are you following me?" Callan managed to sound reassured, but still tense. Excellent acting.

"I'm here for research!" Her voice still skewed wildly—"Rina" was a well-funded student from upsystem, and unaccustomed to confrontation. Nervous words spilled out of her, "The varied life-forms of Empire waterways, namely the kind with spines or other solid internal frameworks. I—" She dug her gun harder, angling lower, toward his groin. The drape of her sleeve would hide motion and weapon from anyone not so intimately acquainted as Callan happened to be. "I was on my way to Tevvin's Canal to take an updated count! It's smelly work, but critical for my report. Are you going there too?"

"I've seen you three times over the last two days," he replied, and his own weapon twisted between two of her ribs. Uncomfortable, but she kept her expression still.

Three times? She'd only been remotely in his view once, today... unless he'd managed to coopt the same feeds she had. Served her right, underestimating a fellow agent. Fleet or no.

"Oh. Have you? Well I've worked in the area. It's a small city. I mean, not for the system, I know, but compared to Centre—"

"You're from Centre?" Between one word and the next, his pressure on her side disappeared. She didn't even see the flick of motion that stowed whatever weapon he'd brought to bear. Callan stepped back and tilted his head at her. "Your accent—"

"I'm not *from* there," she murmured, crossing her arms and vanishing her own gun into her sleeve until she could readjust. "But my graduate program is there, and my uncle's lived there for practically his whole life so I've been visiting since I was little." Norina widened her eyes and scrubbed her empty fingers through the loose hair trailing out of her bun. "Are you from Centre?"

"Prima Seignur, yes." He ducked his head as if embarrassed, but his flat eyes never left hers. "Couldn't you tell from *my* accent?"

"I... don't really have an ear for them. Still getting used to Kaskata's drawl, and mostly I was scared that you grabbed me." Norina quirked a single eyebrow, and rubbed her arms as if cold.

"I'm sorry. Let me walk you to your appointment, make sure no one else accosts you?" Callan pitched it as a question, but she didn't have to be a trained asset to know there was only one answer.

Shaggy hair and slouched walk aside, he was Fleet enough to try and make her squirm.

Three hours he sat canal-side, and watched as Rina waded canal-water and painstakingly recorded waste levels and population numbers. Their wristlets's virtual handshake should have navigated the encryption fields and established her bonafides much sooner, but the joke was on him.

She liked the research.

Besides, by halfway through the second hour, she'd patched into the security system of his apartment, so his hot water would be cold for the next full rotation. The canal smell would stick, and he'd know to thank her for the discomfort of his shower.

Petty, maybe, but he'd earned it with his "encouraging" calls as she worked and he sat.

And he'd earned it by getting the drop on her. Couldn't let that go unanswered.

Had SFI told him there was a Prime asset being sent to Kaskata? Had Callan's handler been able to share more specificity on who he'd see, or had he just been faster to find her?

Didn't matter now—would, once the mission was done, because if she didn't learn, she didn't get better. Agents who didn't get better when provided the opportunity were the ones with short careers, and Norina had too much to do. No good in getting knocked out of the game early.

But a little pettiness now simply showed she was paying attention. They were on the same side.

*It's only treason if you lose.*

Felt a little like she'd lost when he invited her up to his rented apartment and offered her a shower after hours of work in the canal muck.

She sprawled across his couch and got comfortable while he scanned the room for any new devices that might have appeared while he was out. Their form of espionage wasn't the type that kept Kaskata turning, but the corporate types had tricks enough, and it did no good to be cocky.

For good measure, she scanned the area too, though her wristlet program turned up nothing of concern. Still, she didn't hide her envy when he set up a sound screen as subtle as the one she'd seen in Foreign Shores. The faintest buzz, more felt at the base of her skull than perceived with her ears, was the only sign of sonic interference that would keep any distance device from listening in.

*Gotta love a handy tool.*

Norina stretched her arms along the back of the couch and plastered on her most reckless grin. Lean right into any preconceived notions he might have about Primes.

He didn't react visibly, so she kicked her be-socked feet onto the table in front of her—he'd quite smartly made her leave her muck-encrusted boots by the door—and said, "Well? You didn't invite me up here for your water pressure."

"You're pretty and unassuming enough. I'm a businessman on a work trip. Why not?"

"Oh, are we still playing games?" She rolled her eyes and drummed her fingers. The cushioned frame muffled the noise, but his gaze flicked toward the motion on either side of her.

"Waiting on confirmation." Callan paced on the other side of the table, but she didn't believe he was actually worried about her authorizations. He had enough information to make the call.

"That'll be a day at least, unless you've got a remote station in orbit." When the man didn't react, Norina sat forward, interested. "*Do* you have a remote station in orbit? Warship? Courier? Maybe a clever little repeater drone, all geared up too—"

"We don't have repeater drones in service," he said, then snapped his mouth shut with an audible click.

"But you do have a handler in range, holding your . . . hand?" She let the tech slide, though a corner of her mind resolved to add a few more satellites to her scanning protocol. No satellite she could get into from the ground would have the capabilities to find Fleet's latest magnifier-effect bombship, more likely than not. But the more information she could gather, the more she could send back to Len. Make the streams of data his problem to parse, once he had the confirmation the hull was real.

"Yes. My company is in the habit of unnecessarily doubling resources sent to the cracked end of the Empire." While he didn't roll his eyes, his short shrug gave a similar dismissive response.

"So we're going to sit here until you get confirmation from upsystem? I mean, I can just list the other options my handler told me to watch out for until y—"

"They *knew* SFI sent someone and still sent you?"

"Looks like our company *is* in the habit of doubling resources, huh?" She held her idle pose until he stopped pacing and turned fully toward her, then dropped her feet to the ground and sat up straight. "You're dropping 'company' for SFI, so did you get orbital acknowledgment or are we done pretending? Because word on the waves was how three assets already went dark out here, and I imagine teamwork will suit us better than circling."

"Why would—" Callan clearly decided against answering her questions, much as she had his, but there were some things she wouldn't hide.

"I'm here for Ninth System. You?" Norina had no loyalty to the group of rebels determined to undermine the Empire's grasp on its systems. Their ends justified their means, and she had little respect for either.

The pause held for three seconds longer than she'd expected, but finally he replied, "Same," without a hint of disdain.

"And your handler didn't tell you we'd lost assets out here already?"

"It's not relevant."

"How?"

"They weren't Fleet."

"Stars and skies of all the systems, I hope you're good enough to back up the cocky."

The next three weeks settled quickly into a routine.

Rina traveled the city to do research. Nora traced meetings and backdoor connections through nightclubs. Callan moved in and out of boardrooms and corporate-funded luncheons.

Two breezy updates to Uncle Lennox.

One data package clipped to the cargo pod of a Stivven hauler.

Norina hadn't quite figured out Callan's reporting methods, but he'd only caught six of the ten tracers she'd gotten into his comms, so odds were in her favor she'd narrow it down before long.

Of course, she'd found eight of his, which meant he might have some programs winding their meandering, hard-to-pin-down paths through her own business.

Thankfully she didn't keep the most important parts in either wristlet.

The fact that he might have similar airgaps occurred to her, of course, but there was only so much she could do about it.

They met once a week—at the biggest library, at a small restaurant, along the windiest canal. Callan set their first meeting before she left his apartment. Norina made him access a dead drop and decipher a code for their second meeting. For the third, he scheduled her a fake meeting with a real asset, and the pattern of the building's alarm translated into directions to their third meet. Fun.

But for the fourth week she triggered one of her programs in his data, scrawling a message across his comm.

*Sankova Café, Tehelet District.* Once he confirmed receipt, the message would flash a timestamp and then burn itself out. She couldn't afford games—their pressing work had come into focus.

Tehelet was Kaskata's oldest surviving district. The buildings were squatter and thicker than the spun stone and glass concoctions in rebuilt portions of the city, and the bridges over the deep canal were smaller and more numerous. In fact, Tehelet's canal was the only one Rina had bothered to study, because the currents were deadly and the lifeforms ravenous.

The bare trees glowed under the muted purple and blue lights that outlined every structure, false motion that caught her gaze and threatened to make her jumpy.

Tension coiled in her gut and threatened to make her gait stiff, bring too much attention. She channeled it into Rina's over-caffeinated and unthreateningly excited posture—swinging arms and raised shoulders, physical notes in her hand, the occasional mutter into her wristlet about vertebrae similarities across mid-sized water planets.

The performance might have been for no one at all, but it was far easier to stay ready than get ready, and Norina kept her guises as easy to shrug on as the screamingly orange scarf wrapped around her neck and the lower half of her face.

Callan had already taken a seat in the back of the café, and apparently ordered as well. Several small plates and two freshly steaming mugs decorated his table, and she didn't think she had to worry about poison but it slowed her step all the same.

As she slid into the chair across from him her wristlet *brzzd* against her skin. She studied each piece of glazed dishware, but wherever his jammer was, it wasn't visible. Under the table? Her alert program could only tell her she was in the field of an active disruption. Finding the device itself was up to her—no matter how shiny the toys, they always needed a person on the end to make it worth it.

Still, the toys were fun, and she didn't intend on recording anything said in the meeting, so a signal-blocker was of no concern to her. Probably.

"We have a problem. Three of them, technically," she said when he held silent.

"More than three, I think. Ninth System is active in Kaskata. The city—and so the system—are in rebellion."

Norina blew out her breath, hard, to cover the reflex to pull back. The forcible exhalation kept her heart from hammering in protest, and she had long practice in keeping the adrenaline dump from making her fingers tremble.

"No, not the city, but there are collaborators." Norina reordered her plan to lay everything out. "You first, though. Sounds pressing."

Callan delivered a succinct report with such brisk efficiency Norina could feel Len drooling in jealousy from light-years away. Ninth System had a cell operating out of the caverns north of Kaskata. Allegedly tunnels led back to the city, though they were unreliable—sinkholes, flooding, rockfalls, burps of poisonous gas.

"I'm not against stalking their channels, rooting them out, and drowning them in the stenchy canal." Norina hoped the truth in her voice would read as genuine to him. She couldn't afford for him to get the wrong idea, not on this. "But that's not *Kaskata* in rebellion."

"You said you found collaborators, and where there are three there are bound to be more."

"No." She tapped her fingers next to the mug he'd ordered, ostensibly for her. "These three are pretty wrapped up in their own plans. There aren't—"

"Ninth System wouldn't stop at recruiting *three*—"

"The student groups are clear—some anti-Empire sympathizers, sure, but no real evidence of radicals dragging their friends into idealized violence. The last war *wrecked* Kaskata—system, planet, and city. It hasn't been long enough for the young to risk more."

"Still—"

"Local military toppers drink top floor at Foreign Shores, and half a dozen other bars I've visited and watched. Seem pretty comfortable with the status quo—but I'd imagine Fleet would have an idea of dissension in the ranks better than some party girl cozying up to the medals." She raised an eyebrow, and after a moment Callan grunted assent.

"My suggestion is we take out both the Ninth System cell, and the three corporate mucks who are pulling with the ninthers to pad their accounts."

"Tell me," Callan replied after a longer pause.

So she did.

Perasi Corrett, an executive over the fast-innovation wing of Stivven Industries, the local premier transport and weapons producer. Fourth generation Kaskata—frontier settler stock, well before the last war. Mother was from Centre, and Perasi claimed loyalty so loudly she was one of the first places Norina had looked.

Jor Shivel, high level decision maker for Dessux. Shipping logistics and cargo programming. Not likely to make as much if fighting goes hot, but likely angling to take out a competitor in the virtual and actual bloodbath that would follow.

Hyoke Tinash, internal co-president of Central Mining. Major stockholder in the mid-system ship manufacturies. Poised for a major boom if the fighting went active anywhere in the frontier—unlike his peers, Hyoke didn't seem to want to tip Kaskata alongside anti-Empire rebels, but he was very interested in setting them up with what they needed to make some ragged edge planet an actual player. He'd get rich either way.

Norina let the disgust bleed into her tone. She was not brisk, nor efficient, but low-voiced, intent. These were active threats to the Empire, no matter how the three twisted themselves into knots to pretend that wasn't what they were doing at all.

"Kaskata is the size of the landing fields on a Mishthatar moon. One of the small ones. They're not trying to topple the Empire. It's a city of glass and water and paper-thin stone. Three repeater bombs and they're done." Norina stabbed a finger against the table, between her still-steaming mug and one of his plates. "A whole planet never wants the same thing, but I guarantee you this whole city doesn't want war with the Empire."

"It's easiest to call in a preemptive Fleet strike. Like you said, three repeaters and we're done. No long, drawn out conflict, no spreading tension, no issues."

"Because we're sent out to do the easy things." Norina rolled her eyes, drawled the words so the sarcasm had time to linger. "And how does that wipe out Ninth System? They'll just try again somewhere else. Diurval has been getting stroppy about trade deficits lately, they're probably as ripe or more than a handful of corporate types eager to be war profiteers."

"A dramatic blow—"

"Has never stopped the Ninthers before. Hear me out—we take out the shadow alliance Perasi, Jor, and Hyoke think they have. Shuts out Ninth System's main local contacts. We flush out the tunnels, make it hard for the cell to operate in the dark. Tag 'em. Track 'em. Follow 'em back to the root cluster and crack their spines. Between the two of us, we can topple three suits and a fragile tunnel system in, what, a week or two?"

"Days," he replied absently, and so she knew he was thinking about it. She almost had him.

"Between Fleet and Prime we have the resources to follow Ninth out of Kaskata and to their next op. Cut off the heads and watch the necks writhe—imagine rooting out the loudest of the anti-Empirists." Norina paused until he shifted. A slight movement, shoulders back, chin lifted, there and gone again. Enough that she gambled, and continued, "Probably get a big shiny medal that you can never show anyone, for getting it done."

His grunt had the edge of a chuckle, that time, and she'd won. Better not to act like she knew it, though, so she finally picked up the mug and cradled it between her hands.

"So what do you say, Fleet? Isn't target hunting a helluva lot more fun than calling in orbital runs?"

For the first time in their acquaintance, Callan smiled what appeared to be a genuine, actual, real smile.

It wasn't the first time she'd invited a colleague on a killing spree—just a little one—but maybe this one would be her favorite.

Rina had access to so many maps.

Underground mapping was updated by drones weekly, and still

suspect given the reality of the planet's internal movements. Not as helpful as they could be. But thanks to her Rina guise, Norina had decades of historical maps to compare to the most recent, and pattern recognition skills honed by the Empire's highest expectations.

She'd hoped that getting to strategically collapse tunnels and flush out a nest of Ninth System agitators would fill Callan's drive for bombing.

Unfounded hope.

He kept some of the explosive materials—or had plenty more to start with—and the morning after tunnel diving she woke to find a residence tower had been swallowed by Kaskata's ever fragile surface.

A sad coincidence. An accidental byproduct, somehow, of the damage they'd dealt north of the city the day before.

But of course it wasn't.

The penthouse suite of the tower had hosted Perasi Corrett, and several other floors had been leased or sold to other higher ups of Stivven Industries.

Two hundred casualties, more displaced.

Collateral damage. Tragic, unfortunate, unavoidable, but ultimately underwhelming, in the grand scheme of what Callan could do to Kaskata—what Fleet *would* do—but…

Jor Shivel died in his sleep that night, the only people inconvenienced were the Dessux security members who were pulled out of bed to examine Jor's apartment when he missed an important meeting an hour after dawn. There'd be an investigation, to be sure, but no one would trace the death back to the smallest of eyelashes, emptied of an infinitesimal amount of poison. So little to interrupt a heart rhythm, when combined with the smallest surge at the wrong time from a wristlet, and so much preexisting heart damage to begin with.

Death was so easy. The fact that Callan had had to make a production of it kept the rest of the job from being fun.

Still, the satisfied smile on her face convinced Callan well enough when she appeared in his rented apartment.

"We didn't have a meeting," he said, but stepped back from the door to let her in.

"Thought we should compare notes on the scurrying of our former tunnel pests. Make sure none of them slipped their trackers."

"And?"

"And I thought you might want to help take out Hyoke. It took hours to confirm Perasi was dead, I figured you'd want something a little more up close and satisfying this time." She slipped off her boots without being asked and sauntered across the open space toward the couch.

"Perasi was dead before the building went down." Callan followed her, a step too close.

She didn't tense. He had no reason to come after her. They were progressing on their mission, as agreed. Maybe he was one of those who got turned on by competence. She couldn't blame him—if he'd been a little better, she'd be all for a brief interlude.

As it was, however…

She twisted mid-step and plopped to a seat on the nearer arm of the couch, tipped her chin up to meet his gaze. "Already dead, huh?"

"I don't leave things to chance." He hooked his thumbs into his pants pockets, came to a halt inches inside the personal space he'd left between them before. Not a demand. An invitation. A test.

She leaned back, made a show of crossing her legs. Neither acceptance nor rejection. The pleased smile remained on her face, and in a moment he had one that matched. And then he kept talking, clearly believing it was working for him.

"I killed her first. Blunt trauma, handful of minutes before the building went down, so there's no question about the order."

"You like to be sure." Norina tilted her head to the side, eyes locked on his. Her hair slid off her shoulder and he broke eye contact to follow the motion.

"I like to be thorough."

Cocky. Maybe his skills backed it up, but his mitigation efforts were for shit.

Not the sort of thing that mattered, to Fleet and to Empire.

But they mattered to *her*.

"So Hyoke. I was going to do it quiet. But it seems like you want to make a point." She shifted, ran a hand through her hair and pulled it all over the other shoulder. Again, his eyes tracked the movement, and his fingers flexed the slightest bit.

He wanted his hands in her hair. Her over the couch. Everything that followed.

It was nice, to want things.

Her smile broadened, and he cleared his throat and visibly refocused.

"It's not a public point. But I want Ninth System to see what happens to collaborators. I want them stressed while they run. Stressed runners make mistakes. Edge of desperation could be the difference between one trying to burrow and one going up the chain for advice and orders."

"Is that what you would do?" Genuine curiosity, with a layer of teasing to keep him talking.

"I only report when I have something to say."

"Mm." Norina considered twisting a strand of hair around her finger but dismissed it as overkill. "So you'll report when the job is done?"

"It's mostly composed. Just need to add in confirmation about Hyoke."

"Let's get on the same plan, then. After that... we can send in reports and take a beat to celebrate."

She didn't have to be well-trained in pattern recognition to know he liked the sound of that.

Because she hadn't hated working with him, not entirely, she made sure he never knew it was her.

Mid-afternoon the next day, a long-range micro-drone—a bleeding edge top of the line Stivven project that had been personally overseen by Perasi Corrett—broke wildly out of spec and drilled through Hyoke Tinash's eye in the middle of a demonstration meeting between Central Mining, Stivven Industries, and some of their new potential clients. Witnesses everywhere, confusion, chaos... but no extraneous casualties.

Or, rather, only one.

The drone, assumed inert, emerged from Hyoke's other eye after a passage best not to examine too deeply. It ricocheted around the room, and unfortunately the tracking program in Callan's wristlet triggered an attraction instead of repulsion signal.

The drone repeated its catastrophic failure, right through Callan's brainpan—through the ear canal, this time, but the sound screen field had also opened itself. The Fleet agent wouldn't even have had the high pitched whine of something small approaching at high speed to warn him.

Rina kicked a leg idly from a bench overlooking the canal outside the building. Ostensibly she was submitting the last of her Kaskata-dependent research to her advisor after making her goodbyes to her local friends. Truly she was winding a program through Callan's wristlet, ensuring she had everything she needed before it wiped itself.

Which it would do as soon as Callan's heart stopped beating. In five, four, three . . .

There.

Norina watched the eddies in the canal below her for a few quiet, contemplative moments. Ensured a pre-recorded message was sent to Carine, letting her know that Nora had been called upsystem for family matters.

She played a little longer with the message Callan had mostly finished, then sent it without completing it. Though she had the words in her head, an excellent approximation of his voice, better to let it go on to SFI without any lines back to her. Autosend upon cessation of asset life.

Because she was considerate, in her own report she requested that Len share confirmation of Hyoke's elimination to Fleet, so they knew the job was done.

At least as done as they'd ever know. One more thing she had to do before she secured her report out on the next transport and left Kaskata herself.

A section of the Tehelet canal had been rerouted after the war—something about a sinkhole draining a portion of the water flow, unending whirlpools, the stories conflicted. What mattered was that under the crumbled remains of an old bridge was a sewer gate that opened under a pre-determined pattern.

What mattered was the marks in the ever-shifting tunnels that guided very select people to a very particular place—or rather, a very particular person.

"Is it done?" the older woman asked without looking up. Despite the three cycles that had passed since Norina last saw her, she remained unchanged—long dark hair fastidiously pinned back, spine uncurved. Currently, her hand moved over paper—hand-writing something no doubt critical to the future of Kaskata—system, planet, and city all.

"The Fleet response is contained for now. Stivven, Central Mining, and Dessux might not be clean, but the main agitators are out of the game." Norina didn't bother to glance around the room—like everything around the head of Kaskata's underground, it was only temporary.

Tennie Sabiron had once managed to be a war hero to both Empire and Frontier. Once she'd decided to disappear, she'd known she could never stop moving.

Norina understood the inability to stay in one place too long. Already she itched to leave Kaskata behind, move on to the next set of problems.

"I've accounted for three of the Ninth System cell. I assume you have the rest?" Tennie put down her writing instrument but didn't look up until Norina dropped her second wristlet on the fold-up table.

"You can keep tracking them with this. The program on my comm will be delayed half a rotation. I can't do more than a few hours, but it should be enough for you."

"You have a great deal of faith in me." Fine lines around Tennie's eyes deepened as the corners of her mouth twitched. A hint of amusement, enough that Norina smiled briefly in reply.

"Have to have it in something. Might as well be you."

"Now." Tennie tsked and straightened in her chair. She did not reach for the wristlet, but poked it with whatever she'd been writing with. "You still believe in Empire. Profit and prosperity."

Norina lifted a shoulder. It did no good to argue with Tennie, who remained an idealist at heart. No matter how the Empire, rebellion, and corporations had wrapped their stinging tendrils around her, the older woman still believed in the good.

While Norina didn't... not believe in that, mostly she was sick of watching profits matter more than people. Nuance. Not bombing a city to sludge because a handful of suits wanted bigger and better penthouses.

"I'll be heading upsystem by dawn," Norina said instead of refuting the point. "Bought you some time, but I can't guarantee how much."

"Here." In a single smooth motion, Tennie vanished Norina's wristlet and dropped a near-identical one in its place. "I was able to confirm what happened to two of the Primes they sent here before you."

"The third?"

"That would be telling."

So Tennie had them, one way or the other. Flipped them, as Norina knew from experience she did quite well, or removed them in a way too revealing to report back to Prima Seignur. Idealist or not, Tennie handled her shit.

Norina quite liked that about her.

After a quick debrief, Norina and her replacement wristlet were on their way to untangle from Kaskata once more. She'd be back—the Empire would never let its eighth system go, no matter how troublesome such a thing became—but Kaskata was Tennie's love, not her own.

Norina didn't love her Empire, but knew very well how much worse the alternative was. So she'd walk her lines and balance her steps, until someone's pattern recognition eclipsed hers.

*It's only treason if you lose.*

# OFF DUTY

## A Blood and Armor Short Story

### Casey Moores

***Kaywan Military Base Annex***
***Kurdish Republic***
***11 December, Year 10***

*The concussive* thump *of the explosions. Three tendrils of smoke rising across the horizon. The muted, distant screams. The disgusting blend of acrid smoke and charred meat.*

Captain Jiwani Doski had enough time to shower and change before the debrief of the day's events, so he did so. As the Chief of Security for Timo Sheen, the president of the Kurdish Republic, it was important for him to appear professional and impeccable when he was by the president's side. Even if he had just barely survived one of the most vicious attempts on the president's life—which was saying a lot considering how often such attacks occurred.

However, Doski now felt practically naked in a simple military dress uniform compared to the General Ordnance Garment, or GOG, combat suit he'd been wearing for most of the day. The suit had been developed by Tang Industries for the Americans, but the project had been canceled, and Tang had offered them to then General Timo Sheen. They'd been primarily responsible for the Republic's survival across the Newroz War when Iranians had invaded, the No Fail missions to capture Iranian nukes before they were launched against the Republic, and the recent Syrian invasion.

He'd only finished training and gotten qualified on the suit a few days prior, but he was already addicted to its tremendous capabilities.

Still, those capabilities had done little to lessen the destruction caused this very day. A dozen other members of his security team had also qualified with him, and half of them were now dead as a result of the attacks.

*"How's the little one?" Doski asked the young, wiry Lieutenant Rivin Gursultur as they observed the primary target from a distance.*

*"Well, sir, she cries whenever she's awake, which is always, and she's a never-ending spigot of sewage, like this river. But she's also the most beautiful and incredible creature on this Earth."*

*"And the mother?"*

*"Doing well, sir. Blames me continuously for those first two points but agrees on the latter."*

Rivin would have made a good father, just as he had been a good husband. He had been a good man, a natural leader in need of seasoning only real world experience could bring. But now he would be none of those things.

"Captain, I presume you're here to escort me to the briefing?" President Sheen asked.

Doski honestly didn't remember walking to the president's office, nodding to the guards, and entering the room, but he clearly had. He couldn't let his mind wander like that now that he was once again directly responsible for the president's protection.

Timo Sheen had been young for a general and was even younger for a president, especially for such an ancient people. However, it was impossible to miss how much the man had aged in the past few months. It was clear he carried the full weight of the Kurdish Republic on his shoulders. He'd lost his wife and son in an Iranian raid shortly before the Newroz War. Now, Doski knew Sheen now considered the entirety of the Kurdish people his family, and he'd do anything to keep them safe.

"Captain, how are you?" Sheen asked.

It was this sort of quality which Doski admired the most. In all the attacks, of that day and all that had come before, it had been the president's life at stake. Doski had known and known of many politicians and generals who would've been more focused on their own lives and safety than that of those who protected them. But Sheen was the sort of man who cared more for the lives of others than his own. It was clear Sheen was troubled by those who'd lost their lives in his defense, and for the health of one Captain Doski, who'd commanded them.

"I'm fine, sir." Doski had perfected the stone face of professional stoicism, but Sheen didn't look convinced.

"Are you sure? You lost a good number of your security team. Men you'd worked with and handpicked to train with on the GOGs. It's not easy to lose so many so swiftly."

Doski stiffened. "But it is the job, sir. Better us than you."

The president opened his mouth to reply but didn't. Instead, he studied Doski with eyes full of sympathy. After a few long moments, he looked away. The president motioned for Doski to lead the way, so they proceeded down the hallway to the president's private conference room.

A collection of generals and civilian advisers were gathering around the long, oval conference table awaiting the briefing. A pair of sergeants fiddled with the computer at the podium, and the two large flat screens currently displayed the Kurdish flag.

The only man present who Doski didn't know was an unassuming man across the table with an aquiline nose, clean-shaven face, and thin trace of short, graying hair around the sides of his head. His dark brown eyes were sharp, calculating, and always scanning. *He's a spook,* Doski thought. *But for whom?*

"Under the circumstances, perhaps you should take some leave. Take some time to put this horrible day behind you."

"With all due respect, sir, I spent too much time away training on the GOG as it is." Doski clenched a fist at his side but fought to keep his offense off his face. "Besides, who would look after you, sir?"

"Major Khan oversaw my security while you were gone. She can resume the detail for another week or two if need be."

"Sir, shouldn't the great savior of the Republic be off, well, saving the Republic?" Doski asked. He meant the question honestly, but realized after the fact how sarcastic it sounded.

"Unless another neighbor invades, I don't need her until—" Sheen ended the sentence when the wiry, clean-shaven Major Celal Duhoki hurried into the room.

"Apologies, President Sheen," the intel officer said. "I was waiting on one last report in order to give you the greatest possible picture of recent events."

A satellite view of Kirkuk appeared on the screen, then zoomed in on an area stretching from the Presidential Palace to the ramshackle residential area across the Khasa River. Numerous markers populated, indicating where Doski's teams had located the numerous threats.

They'd begun the day focused on a single location in the slums beside the Khasa River. Plans to clean the mountains of trash in the Khasa had been delayed in favor of rebuilding after the Syrian invasion. This had left an ideal location for conspirators to plot an attack on the president. Doski had been informed of a potential bombing attack before they moved in, so he'd split most of his GOGs into teams to search for it. He'd directed Lieutenant Gursultur to lead the original assault.

"With your permission, President Sheen, I'll get right to it," the major said. "It's my assessment the original objective was meant to degrade the President's security team." With a laser pointer, he drew a tight circle around the location. That was where Gursultur and the entire assault team had been incinerated in a fiery explosion. The tall, gaunt General Sadeghi grumbled and shifted in his chair. The aging General Gokalp remained still as a statue.

"The other attacks were meant to be the primary attacks on the Palace itself," Duhoki continued. The screen scrolled to where Doski had intercepted and neutralized an explosive-laden Hilux. Then, the screen panned to craters where two of his other GOG teams had also intercepted trucks but failed to prevent their detonation. "They were meant to be in place immediately after the detonation of that first objective."

"Then why weren't they?" Doski asked, half a second before realizing the intel officer was probably just about to tell him. General Gokalp gave him a quick, curious glance.

*Your blood's up, but you must remain patient.*

"Because I intercepted their relay," the spook said.

"Yes," Duhoki said. "President Sheen, in my haste, I failed to introduce one of my Israeli counterparts. Mr. Naka, from the Mossad, was the source of our intelligence on the second target. Or rather, target *set.*"

Naka sighed and solemnly bowed his head in embarrassment. "Yes, my source indicated there was only one secondary threat, not several."

"By which you mean the *primary* threat," President Sheen grumbled. "And would you please explain how you came by this information, as well as what you were doing in my country in the first place?"

"Of course, President Sheen." Naka stood and nodded to Major Duhoki. "I apprehended an individual supplying explosives in my own country. In hopes of cutting a deal, he revealed he had also delivered explosives to a group here. In coordination with your nation's intelligence agency—specifically Major Duhoki and his associate here to my left—I located and, ahem, *detained* an individual connected to the plots here. He offered up the first target a little too willingly, so . . ." Naka pursed his lips and narrowed his eyes. "He was questioned more enthusiastically until he revealed the rest."

Sheen shifted his attention back to Duhoki.

"Have we obtained the source of the attempt? As in, who ordered it?"

"We have, sir," Duhoki said.

The screen switched over to a TRT World news report of a Turkish general giving a speech. Doski immediately recognized the balding forehead and thick eyebrows of the perpetually angry General Yusuf Çakmak. The Turkish general repeatedly thrust a pointed finger into the air and pounded his fist into his podium as he spoke.

*"And we will not have peace within our country until we have eradicated the legions of terrorists here within our very own borders! They flood the lands of our Syrian neighbors, not to mention the lawless region of thugs masquerading as a state, living in the ruins of yet another failed nation-building experiment by the Americans! It is our duty. Not only to our people that we end this tremendous threat, but to the world as a whole in the name of global peace and stability!"*

The Turkish general had become a staple of intel briefings over the weeks since the failed Syrian invasion. He'd led the Turkish "peacekeeping" forces into what remained of Syria and effectively taken control of the Syrian coastline—primarily to deprive the Kurdish Republic access to the sea. He'd directed the indiscriminate bombing of cities and towns in Rojava—Eastern Syria—before the Kurdish Army could get defenses in place. He was also arming militias in the Rojava area to destabilize the region and terrorize its people.

He was doing far worse to the Kurdish population of southeastern Turkey.

*And now he's responsible for the endless attempts on President Sheen's life and the deaths of my comrades.*

General Sadeghi grunted and shifted once again. "General Çakmak. I met him once, a long time ago in a US-sponsored exercise. Even then, his vicious ambition and pure hatred for our people was clear. I hoped he would be discarded as too much of a firebrand, but it seems that's precisely the quality the Turkish government seeks these days. This was even before he ordered the massacre in "Şırnak." As I've said before, his malevolence is exceeded only by his intelligence."

Sheen sighed, straightened, and waited until all eyes were on him. "While I'm honored they find me so threatening that I warrant near continuous assassination attempts, I'm perturbed by his other initiatives. There's nothing I dislike more in my enemy generals than competence. We've been thus far blessed in this regard. While our adversaries have had superior numbers and—aside from the GOG suits—better equipment by both quality and quantity, they've been lacking in leadership. But, as it's increasingly obvious that conflict with Turkey is inevitable, we'll face this man on the battlefield soon enough."

"Just a suggestion, sir," Gokalp said, straightening and leaning forward. "Maybe we respond in kind?"

"A part of me does wish to ask with dramatic flourish, 'Will no one remove this man from my ire?'" Possibly by coincidence, Sheen met Doski's gaze for several quiet seconds. Then, the president shook his head. "But the answer is no. During the Battle of Waterloo, one of General Wellesley's aides located Napoleon Bonaparte and suggested having a marksman shoot him, but Wellesley replied, 'Generals have much more important things to do than to take potshots at each other.' This might have been virtue... or perhaps he wanted the chance to prove himself the better general. Perhaps they might've ended the battle right there and saved the lives of countless soldiers. But I will adhere to the spirit of that decision. Besides, I cannot imagine we would have any more success killing him than he has me. And successful or no, they would blame us. If that is all on this matter, I thank you, Mr. Naka, for your assistance both with the event itself as well as your continued partnership in intelligence matters. Major, please continue the brief."

There were further updates in the political situations of their other neighbors, as well as global events. When concluded, everyone in the room shot to their feet and assumed attention.

Doski followed as Sheen rose and headed for the door.

"President Sheen," he said softly, right after the two exited the room.

Sheen paused and turned.

"Yes, Captain?"

"I've reconsidered, sir. With your permission, I would like to take a couple weeks of leave."

"Granted."

With a nod, Sheen departed.

Doski spun and found his next target. The Mossad agent was conversing with Major Duhoki, so Doski waited patiently.

"Captain Doski," the intel major said when he saw Doski waiting. "I would like to personally introduce you to Mr. Naka."

"Ah, yes, the Chief of Security," Naka said. "My great sympathies for the loss of your men. I apologize that my information was not more complete . . . or more timely."

"You did what you could with what you had," Doski said and then shook his head. "But you are not responsible for the deaths of my men. That lies with the men who delivered the explosives, the men who made them, and mostly with the man who gave the orders. Without you, they may well have gotten to our president. For preventing that, you have my great thanks."

As Doski shook hands with Naka, Duhoki stepped back and smiled. "Well, I've got much more to attend to. Gentlemen, if you'll excuse me."

Doski caught his arm, leaned in, and spoke quietly. "Mr. Naka, in the interest of improving response time, could we establish a more direct line of communication?"

Naka froze and studied Doski with narrowed eyes for a moment. "Of course."

Doski drew even closer and spoke in a near whisper. "And might I ask a favor? Is there a possibility you could help me with some travel arrangements?"

***Seven Hills Cafe, Istanbul***
***Turkey***
***18 December, Year 10***

Doski shifted his phone to minimize the glare since he was sitting in a rooftop café on a sunny day. On his screen, a raven-haired young woman smiled on a weeks-old Metagram post and gyrated with her girlfriends in a shallow pool along the gleaming white, calcified hillside of Pamukkale. She had deep, gold-brown eyes and wore a black bikini which was modest by American standards, but scandalous by current Turkish standards.

"This is one of the most beautiful places in all of Turkey, and one of the best places to party!" she said and then pointed to the cliff behind her. "And up there, back from the edge, there's a resort where you can swim in a pool with ancient ruins. Where else in the world can you do that?"

Doski set his phone down as the server approached. He sat by himself with an excellent view of both the Hagia Sofia and the Blue Mosque. It was a better juxtaposition of famous historical landmarks than any he could think of in the Kurdish Republic—a land equally as rich with historical monuments from countless empires past.

Parts of the Hagia Sophia dated back nearly seventeen hundred years and its construction had lasted centuries. It had been a Christian church for almost a millennia before its conversion to a mosque. Despite its conversion, a nineteen-year-old Sultan had still decided he needed to erect a larger and more impressive landmark to claim his own place in history.

In Doski's opinion, the Blue Mosque was a highly impressive structure but lessened by its purpose. If the young sultan had built the Blue Mosque anywhere else, it would have been a tremendous construction in its own right. It was the very fact that he'd built it to diminish the other which decreased its value.

"Your meal, sir," the server said as he set down a plate before Doski with a skewer of swordfish and vegetables.

Doski nodded and dug in.

The Kurdish president's chief bodyguard had departed Kirkuk as himself. Upon arrival in Doha, Naka had provided Doski with the means to continue his travels masquerading as a Saudi Arabian tourist, complete with a passport and burner phone. This explained Doski's green shirt with the white falcon of the Arabian Falcons, the Saudi Arabian national football team.

The bodyguard *could* have made arrangements through Roger Tang. Tang was, after all, the billionaire who'd supplied the Kurdish military with the GOG suits in the first place. He'd even spent his own money to help whole teams of GOG-equipped troops into Iran. But Tang was known, and watched, and a link would inevitably be made if Doski had used the billionaire's equipment. And that simply wouldn't do.

A flurry of activity erupted along the road in front of the Blue Mosque. Both people and vehicle traffic flooded away from the building. Somewhere amid the great delegation departing the mosque was one General Çakmak and his entourage.

He'd considered the moral question of murdering this man hundreds of times in the preceding days, but he'd always arrived at the same conclusion. Given the chance to assassinate the general who'd led the Iranian columns in the Newroz War before the invasion, he would have. Given the chance to execute the mastermind of the Syrian invasion, with their legions of combat-suited mercenaries, he most certainly would have. In point of fact, he *had* killed that man, but only after the invasion and only when the man had directly threatened President Sheen's life in front of the Iraqi Parliament.

Doski was beyond tired of watching the Kurdish people butchered, their military devastated, and their cities shelled to rubble. If killing one man could prevent that—and maybe reduce the number of attempts on President Sheen's life—then that's what Doski would do.

After all, Doski had personally shot the previous Kurdish president—for whom he'd also been the bodyguard—to ensure the survival of Timo Sheen. He'd done so because he'd finally realized who was fighting for the Kurdish Republic's survival and who was working to betray it for their own personal gain. If Doski could kill his own president, he was well beyond the philosophical implications of killing an enemy general.

Doski washed down a bite of overcooked, rubbery swordfish with the last drops of rose red tea as he stood and dropped a stack of lire on the table.

The server tried to catch his attention, but Doski ignored him and rushed away. He hurried down the steps, threw on his black helmet, hopped onto a motorcycle Naka had rented through third parties, and followed the general's convoy.

Tailing a convoy was difficult to do alone. A motorcycle in the city wouldn't be horribly noticeable, but if he repeatedly came too close to the motorcade, someone on the general's security detail was sure to take notice.

They were easy to follow from a comfortable distance for several blocks, and easier still when they forced their way onto a busy highway. Odds of his detection diminished greatly in thick traffic.

Doski expected they would exit toward the Turkish Army Staff Headquarters. However, they continued toward the outskirts of Istanbul. He now feared they might be traveling to the airport. This would spoil his plans entirely. Thankfully, they continued past the airport as well.

When they crossed the "İzmit" Bay Bridge, it became clear they were leaving the city. It was also unlikely they were headed to Ankara. Unfortunately, traffic also evaporated like a dissipating storm. He caught a uniformed man in a nearby car staring at him and speaking into a radio. It was clearly a tail car Doski hadn't identified. Doski was certain he hadn't done anything suspicious, but now he was at least on their radar.

The highway split a dozen or so kilometers ahead. He decided to speed past the convoy and observe them at the intersection. Doski flew through, around, and past the traffic until he arrived at the major intersection. Taking the exit just prior, he rushed around the surrounding streets in search of a higher vantage point where he could observe the highway.

There were no good observation points to be found.

In desperation, he got back onto the highway in hopes of at least relocating them. He looped through traffic in a blur for over an hour without seeing any sign of the convoy.

Frustrated, he eventually gave up and pulled over.

He cursed himself. It could days to track the general down again. The opportunity might be gone completely.

Doski envisioned Turkish bombers overhead Kurdish cities, tanks rolling into Mosul for the millionth time across several decades, and legions of Turkish soldiers flooding their border and gunning down civilians with reckless abandon. All because he'd failed.

Absentmindedly, he pulled out his phone to check his only other lead. The woman who's Metagram feed he'd been watching at the café just so happened to be Aysel Çakmak, daughter of one General Yusuf Çakmak.

And she'd just posted a new video.

The wild-eyed beauty was in a cramped bar with a live band playing in the background. "Sad news, friends, we couldn't go back to the villa this weekend because Daddy's using it for some big meeting. So instead, the girls and I are out here in "İzmir," at the Club Blue. Now who remembers this classic by Teoman? Paramparça!"

He flipped back through her photos to search for pictures from the villa. She—or, more likely, her father or one of her father's security people—had wisely ensured her posts didn't have geotags. Instead, he'd have to triangulate the spot using prominent terrain features in the backgrounds of the photos, check the weather in various areas against the dates and times of the posts, track the Metagram posts of friends she'd tagged in any photos, reverse images to better identify the source of photos, dig through real estate websites for property photos, etc., ad nauseum. There were dozens of tricks to determining where she'd been, and all of them would take time, but he didn't have anything better to do. Knowing it was in the vicinity of Pamukkale narrowed the search tremendously.

He drove several hours south to the ancient Roman spa city. On arrival, he wasted no time identifying prominent terrain features in the backgrounds of the general's daughter's photos. It didn't take him long to find.

General Çakmak was, by all evidence, spending a weekend on holiday in the Turkish countryside.

Doski stared at the site in frustration. He'd planned to identify the general's habits, routes, schedules, and the like to determine a time and location to set up a sniper rifle.

Try as he might, he couldn't find access to any vantage points around the villa to make that dream a reality. It was almost as if the general was a professional paranoid and thought about these sorts of tactical considerations in advance.

Reluctantly, he pulled out his burner phone and typed in a code phrase which translated to, "Request further support."

***Open field north of Pamukkale***
***Turkey***
***18 December, Year 10***

It was a cold, dark, overcast night. Doski stood beside a tall boulder, tried not to choke on the chalky air, and stared into the void overhead. There was no sign of stars, satellites, aircraft, birds, or even insects. It was peaceful, but perhaps too peaceful. It was the sky equivalent of treading water in the deep ocean. There was no telling what might be flying somewhere above. An entire squad of Turkish Bordo Bereliler might be parachuting in to kill him, and he'd be none the wiser.

Across a wide area to the north and east was an ancient necropolis with crypts from no fewer than three different ancient civilizations. Empires had come and gone through here for millennia.

Lost in time and thought, he wondered what he was waiting for. Would a team of Israeli spooks show up to lead an assault? Was he meeting a contact with guidance or equipment? All he had received were coordinates.

A dull, muffled crack echoed from somewhere in the valley. He braced, but it wasn't a gunshot. He moved toward the source of the sound, carefully padding through the underbrush, scanning, listening, moving. Scanning, listening, moving. It was painstaking, but such was the cost of staying alive.

Doski expected to find people and probably a vehicle of some kind. But he found neither. A little less than a hundred meters away, a large, black plastic container lay on the ground atop a plywood board and a few layers of compressed cardboard. It was all tied up in olive green cord, with a large black fabric panel tied to the top.

A parachute.

This box had just fallen out of the darkness. Apparently, something *had* been flying high above him.

He swept the rigging out of the way, popped the clips around the sides, and lifted the lid.

Inside were neatly arranged stacks of recognizable armored panels of varying shapes. Below those were gloves, boots, a bulky helmet, and two vicious, partially serrated blades.

It was a GOG suit.

Except, it wasn't the GOG he knew. The pieces and connections were unusual. The boots were a make he didn't recognize, and the helmet was significantly different. Was this some new model?

The answer become clear when he turned the helmet on and it started spouting gibberish.

Hebrew, to be more precise. While fluent in Turkish, Doski didn't know Hebrew very well, but he thought he recognized a few words. It was an Israeli suit. He rolled his eyes and wondered why he'd expected any different? They'd first made an appearance during the Syrian invasion, when Kurdish GOGs had met their Israeli counterparts on the outskirts of Damascus.

"Kurmanji?" he said in desperation.

"Welcome, user," the helmet replied in Kurmanji, though with a heavy Israeli accent.

The helmet walked him through assembling the suit, step by step. The blades attached to the forearms, like some feral American superhero.

The Kurdish GOG suit had no such attachment. During the Syrian invasion, GOG soldiers had jury-rigged and acquired their own blades, which prompted inquiries as to why their suits were not designed with blades. Roger Tang had very simply responded, "I figured if you guys wanted swords, you'd find some."

The grenade dispenser was similar, but empty. There was also no rifle or any other sort of primary weaponry. He already knew the Israeli suits didn't have rail guns or built in .338 rifles like the Kurdish GOGs, but he'd hoped this suit would be equipped with an IWI Tavor 7 rifle. It didn't seem too useful to have a combat suit without a rifle.

Pieces assembled, he finally put the helmet on and powered the suit. It carried the sterile, "new suit" smell that he remembered from the first time he'd put a GOG on. That hadn't lasted an hour.

Naka's voice came on, speaking much better Kurmanji than the automated voice.

*"As you've guessed by now, this is not the suit you're used to, but I imagine you can adapt. You've also noticed I haven't given you a rifle nor any grenades. Apologies, but there are two reasons. The first is to avoid leaving evidence of Israeli weaponry, the other is due to the somewhat brutal method of delivery the suit just experienced. It was a big enough risk with just the suit's explosive charges for what you would call 'cratering.' It was determined that every additional ounce of hazardous material increased the risk of the suit destroying itself on impact. You do have a blade on each arm, and I feel confident you'll find the means to locally source weaponry in some manner or another. Once you do, the targeting system will take some time to adapt to any weapon you find, but it'll be as accurate as you're used to after a few rounds. In the meantime, familiarize yourself with the suit and particularly its sanitization protocols. Even if you succeed, I would greatly appreciate it if you would detonate the suit to dispose of it. That's all I have for you. Good hunting."*

***Villa northeast of Pamukkale***
***Turkey***
***19 December, Year 10***

The villa was far enough from the town or any other dwellings that there were no sounds of traffic or even animals. The air wasn't as dusty as the field where he'd gotten his suit—it was almost as sweet as it had been in the Zagros Mountains of his homeland.

Finally, on the hunt, he felt a surreal sense of calm and focus, although his suit warned him of an elevated heart rate. His suit was set to a full black camouflage pattern. The Israeli suit lacked the adaptive camouflage the Kurdish suits had, so being able to quickly switch between preloaded patterns would have to do. As he stalked closer, his starlight/IR blended optics let him keep an eye on the driver and passenger.

The razor-wire-topped wall into the villa's grounds was too expansive to be well-manned, so he jumped it with ease, quickly moved a few meters to better cover behind some bushes, and paused to examine the interior. On his approach to the villa, he almost missed a pair of Turkish BMC Kirpi MRAPs parked beside a makeshift tarp wall, cleverly hidden among the trees on the western wall. They were shut down, but the Israeli suit had the same capability to view the world through a wide range of spectrums as the Kurdish GOG. When he scanned the area in a pure IR spectrum, he spotted the cooling engines of the two trucks. On closer inspection, he identified the heat signatures of a driver and passenger inside both and could only guess there were more soldiers in the passenger compartment.

He stalked in a low crouch through a thin grove of manicured cypress trees, moving head on towards the lead truck. Crouching in the Israeli suit wasn't quite as painful or awkward as it was in a GOG, but it was close.

When he judged he was close enough for a single leap, he paused.

He couldn't guess *why* they were there, except as a rapid reaction reserve force. Their presence suggested they might be *expecting* such an attack, which was concerning.

Even in an Israeli suit without a rifle or rail gun, Doski felt supremely confident he could take down a simple bodyguard detail, especially as it was unlikely the general would have too large a detail this deep into the "safe" part of the country. The reserve force was a complication, but still manageable. It was also the greatest threat, so he'd eliminate it first.

The only remaining problem was how to make the attack look like anything other than a Kurdish assassination. He could easily disappear and dispose of the Israeli suit afterward, but odds were the Kurdish Republic would be the prime suspect. Though the Turks would be losing their genocidal, firebrand general this evening, they'd be gaining more impetus to attack the Kurds.

It was a big problem, and he didn't have an answer. For the immediate future, he'd have to settle for killing their best general.

At the top of the hour, the MRAP passenger's radio crackled for a check in. The passenger responded all was clear, and all went silent again.

Doski flew into the air and came down in a deep crouch on the hood. As the front of the car crunched down, he drove both blades through the windshield and into both soldiers. He twisted his arms and withdrew blades slick with blood. One of the soldiers further back cried out in shock, but the squad seemed frozen in confusion. Fortune smiled on him in the form of grenades attached to the front passenger's harness. He punched a fist through the windshield, snatched one, pinched the pin out, and tossed it back. One of the soldiers finally fired his rifle, but it simply stiffened a single panel of reactive armor.

He launched himself onto the hood of the second truck and repeated the maneuver. He narrowly missed the passenger this time, so Doski shifted and sliced the man's neck instead as the *boom* of the hand grenade dealt with the first truck's passengers.

The squad in this new truck reacted faster, and more coherently. The two closest soldiers brought their MPT-76 rifles to bear between the front seats' headrests. Reacting fast, he punched through, grabbed the barrel of the one on the right, and tore it from the wielder's hands. He stabbed the butt of the rifle into the other soldier face and spun it around. He fought for a second to find the trigger. The gloves made operating a regular rifle a little awkward, which was why Kurdish GOGs had their rifles attached to the right forearm and operated by the suit—but beggars could not be choosers.

He fired just as the butt-stroked soldier recovered and fired as well. Though the stolen weapon had been set to semi-auto, he won the exchange as the return fire did nothing more than solidify a few more responsive armor sections. With the primary threat down, Doski raked the rear compartment with what remained of the magazine until the rifle went *click* instead of *bang*. The back doors opened, and two soldiers, maybe more, fled out the back.

Doski leaped over the Kirpi, twisting as he went, and landed at the back. He'd landed amid the fleeing survivors, and stabbed them both—one in the neck, and the other in the side. A mist of red sprayed over his arm. Over time, a coat of blood would degrade his suit's camouflage and eventually gum up the joints. He'd have to be careful with that.

The stench of emptied bowels wafted out from the Kirpi as he checked for survivors. He was thankful the helmet filtered the air at least a little bit.

The radio in front crackled to life with a request to report in. The soldier at the other end said they'd heard "something" and mentioned an explosion but not gunfire. Searchlights swept all around the compound, but none could effectively illuminate the two vehicles Doski had assaulted. They knew they were under attack, but sounded horribly confused over the nature of the attack. Which was perfectly fine by Doski. Calls went out for two patrols to investigate the Kirpis and the others to slowly withdraw to the villa while continuing to scan for threats. All the patrols were instructed to immediately report anything they encountered.

He charged through the woods toward a pair of soldiers who'd stopped beside the main road leading to the villa. One had his radio in front of his face, and both scanned nervously in every direction. Neither saw him approaching, but the one without the radio must have heard his heavy steps in the last second before he reached them. The soldier spun but was too shocked to bring his rifle to bear. Doski beheaded them both in two quick slashes and continued on.

One of the soldiers in the next patrol team got a few wild shots off before he took them down. A soldier in the third patrol team shouted "Demon" into the radio before Doski dispatched him. The rest of the patrol teams were ordered to "withraw with all haste to the compound" and Doski took down another pair of soldiers as they sprinted for the perceived safety of the villa. He grabbed their rifles and hurried to the nearest scant cover behind some low flower bushes.

The massive spotlights of the villa continued to pan in every direction, illuminating every inch of ground within a hundred meters of the building, but now Doski was at the edge of the trees and bushes and close enough to cast a noticeable shadow. This highlighted his next problem. Because they'd been alerted, his approach options were more complicated. The only approach with any sort of cover was among the manicured trees and bushes in front of the villa. The sides and rear had a fairly steep drop-off to nothing but flat, rocky fields. And the "rocky" was pebbles, not boulders.

Frontal assault it was. But charging in with blades alone no longer seemed optimal.

The villa had two low-roofed towers at the corners. An impressively wide staircase led to the building, and it was flanked by two high terraces on either side, each with their own stone railing. The driveway ran along the base of the stairs, with a courtyard in front of the driveway and a low, stone railing in front of the courtyard. As a big, black target would be highly visible with all that light, he switched to a mottled tan, light green, and gray camouflage.

He scanned it on a zoomed in IR blend and identified two

marksmen perched atop each of the towers. More peered out from second story windows, but Doski decided the ones on turrets would work best to sight in his rifles.

It was simple to place his targeting reticle onto the left tower sniper, but his rifle arm did not automatically track it as a GOG's would have. Instead, a tall, narrow oval floated into his HUD when he attempted to aim his rifle manually. The suit was giving him a circular error probability. It would've been just as simple if the rifle had a laser sight, but it didn't, and the suit was ergonomically *very* awkward with the iron sights.

He put his target in the center of the oval and hoped for the best. The suit highlighted the bullet's flight path, which went well high and slightly left. The slightly left was probably due to his large, gloved finger pushing sideways against the trigger as he fired. If he'd been shooting unaided, he would have adjusted his finger position. However, the suit's rushed training program had emphasized that one must attempt to fire the same way every time and NOT to compensate on your own. In short, the targeting system was smarter than you were if you'd just let it work.

However, the training had also said it took several shots to zero in the targeting. Case in point, the oval was much narrower and about half as tall, but still an oval. Doski decided it probably adjusted its fire in increments and, therefore, probably hadn't lowered as far as it should. He targeted the shot slightly below the sniper's thin IR signature and fired again. The shot pocked stone from the turret a few centimeters below the figure.

The sniper shifted and disappeared from view. Meanwhile, the targeting oval was now so tiny it was more like a short, vertical line.

A small hammer tapped against his helmet. The right tower sniper had found him. He'd foolishly fired several shots from the same position. He'd spent too long as a bodyguard and away from proper combat.

Doski hurriedly put the right sniper's signature in the center of the line and fired. The figure jerked and slumped. Doski scuttled a few steps to the left and spotted the left sniper re-emerging atop the tower in another position. Now, the suit locked onto the target directly. Doski fired with confidence and moved again. Nice and steady, he put two rounds each into the heads of the four shooters in the windows.

Frantic, erratic gunfire raked across the field in response, but none came anywhere close to him.

Next, he knocked out the spotlights in rapid succession until the field was lit only by rifle-mounted flashlights.

He raced diagonally across the rocky field and targeted the IR signatures behind the flashlights. In no time, the survivors dropped behind their cover and only popped up sporadically for quick, uncontrolled bursts. More than a few weren't quick enough.

Doski's rifle clicked empty, but he'd advanced toward another pair of dead guards. He swapped rifles and grabbed a spare. The targeting window was a proper oval again, but smaller than before. After his first couple shots, the bright bursts of machine guns lit up at each end of the low courtyard wall. Without the searchlights, the machine guns were firing blindly and wildly, but it was still a lot of bullets across not too wide an area.

In his GOG training, he'd learned how to use that suit's targeting system to identify enemy weapons and vehicles. However, Doski hadn't taken the time to dig that deep into the Israeli suit's capabilities. Even if he had, it would have been highly difficult to focus his targeting reticle on the machine guns while in a dead sprint perpendicular to them.

That said, from his side view, the bursts from the left machine gun were larger and he guessed roughly 12.7 mm or 14.5 mm. Assuming the Israeli armor was the equivalent of the GOG, 12.7 mm would quickly degrade his protection, and anything higher would punch through and splatter the flesh and bone inside. The other machine gun had smaller, steadier flash, so he guessed that one was 7.62 mm.

A round clipped his right calf's armor and he skipped a few steps to avoid tumbling. Once recovered, he launched himself the remaining distance to the left end of the low wall before the courtyard. He moved past the wall in one more quick hop and emptied his second rifle, taking out the machine gunners and the handful of other defenders along the wall. He emptied the third rifle, clearing out the courtyard and the steps leading to the entrance. He snatched another newly available rifle while bounding to a tall wall beside the main steps.

He crouched and hopped up and onto the terrace above. Two soldiers were crouched and hiding behind the stone railing, and both looked panic-stricken and ineffective. Still, he couldn't leave them at his back. He put two rounds into each one, which worked well to sight in his lastest weapon. Which was fortunate, as he had a serious threat to deal with up ahead.

Momentarily stationary, he easily identified a .50 cal M2 machine gun perched at the back of the terrace. It was set up to be hidden from the base of the stairs but had a good field of fire across half of the stairs. Logically, there would be another such weapon at the other side of the staircase.

The operator had just noticed him and was swinging the machine gun around to bear when Doski put several rounds through the man's neck. The soldier slumped against the weapon. Doski leaped to the weapon, shouldered the dead man aside, knelt behind it, and fumbled to grasp the butterfly trigger. As he'd guessed, there was another machine gun at the opposite end of the staircase. This one was a Belgian FN MAG 7.62 mm, a lower caliber, sure, but a lot of bullets at close range could do some damage. Its operator, having seen the fate of his counterpart, was fired up and screaming with rage when Doski came into view. The man fired a fraction of a second before Doski.

The idea this might be the end of his suicidal charge gave Doski a strange sense of peace.

Several rounds cracked responsive armor panels like hammer blows up his legs and torso, and a single round bounced off the side of his helmet, but none punched through. Those panels would be near useless against further hits, but he was fine.

At the other end, his opponent was torn to shreds and collapsed in a broken heap.

He drew in a long breath and tried to slow his pounding heart.

Doski lifted the weapon—a feat the suit accomplished with ease—and ran to the other terrace in expectation there would be another pair of soldiers there. He was correct, and he quickly dispatched one before his machine gun jammed. The sole survivor was kneeling and trembling but still raised his rifle.

Doski sprinted forward, taking a few minor hits on the way. He grabbed the M2 by the barrel with one hand, then the other as he went, and clubbed the last soldier hard on the nose. He dropped it, spun, and ran back to grab the FN MAG. Despite a couple dings, it looked operable. He picked it up and headed for the door.

He'd noticed when he first leaped atop the terrace, but was only now fully processing, that the entire front of the building was walled with sandbags.

Paired with the reserve force in the grove, the snipers, and the machine guns, he revisited how well prepared for an attack they had been.

*Very* prepared—not that it had saved them.

He met physical resistance when he tried to kick in the front doors, so he backed up and charged into it instead. He rammed it with his right shoulder to keep hold of the machine gun. The hinges on both sides separated and the double doors folded onto the floor together. It slammed down hard in a great cloud of dust. The enemy had braced the entry with a metal bar, but he'd broken its mounts free from the walls.

A quartet of guards inside riddled him with mostly ineffective fire before he raked them with his FN MAG. He spent the next several minutes stalking through the building, putting bursts of 7.62 mm into anyone he spotted. He'd feared coming across some servants or house guests, but everyone appeared to be soldiers. The machine gun ran out of ammunition after he killed a few soldiers in the dining room, so he grabbed their rifles and continued.

He caught sight of himself in a mirror, and a sight it was—painted with blood, cracked helmet, banged up patches of armor, two great, serrated blades dripping with crimson, and rifle in each hand. He looked like a demon straight out of a nightmare.

Someone shouted orders down a hallway to his right. Heading toward it, he was met with bursts of gunfire from a pair of soldiers in front of a door. He dispatched them both, dropped a newly emptied rifle, picked up speed, and rammed through the door. This one gave easily.

Another soldier was half a meter back when he crashed through, so he stabbed them in the neck. A long spurt of blood washed across him, but it was no matter. Camouflage was no longer a priority.

He was in a wide, high-ceilinged garage full of both military vehicles and expensive civilian cars. The nearest garage door was opening over a Humvee.

A turreted machine gun atop the Humvee swung toward him, so he heaved the dead soldier in the way. As the machine gun opened up, he dropped low and sprang forward as low to the ground as he could manage. The nearly decapitated soldier fell off his blade, and

Doski landed flat on his chest beside the vehicle. He hopped back into a crouch and jumped upwards.

None other than General Çakmak himself was manning the turreted machine gun. Doski's elation soared.

The general attempted to swing the gun toward him, but Doski pushed the barrel aside with one hand and lightly smacked the man with the other. Doski quickly caught the general's shoulder before he slumped into the Humvee.

The driver's side door opened and a sergeant tumbled out. He staggered to his feet, nervously raised a pistol toward Doski, and fired. The round bounced harmlessly off his helmet. Doski swept his blade across the man's neck and turned his head away from the red spray.

General Çakmak had a trickle of blood down his cheek from where Doski had struck him. He feebly rolled his head and glared at Doski in defiance.

"And here I thought it was my own government coming here to kill me. But it's the Jewish dogs in their shiny new murder machines."

He pushed the blade through the man's chest, through his heart, and continued to push until the blade punched out the man's back.

Doski flipped his faceplate open. "Not Israeli. Kurd."

There was one last flash of hatred in the man's eyes before his wretched soul departed.

With a twist and wrench, he withdrew the blade. The corpse dropped.

It was over.

Doski lifted his chin, closed his eyes, and released a long, calming breath. The visions of Turkish columns sweeping through the Kurdish Republic evaporated from his mind.

Perhaps, with this man dead, none of that would happen.

Perhaps.

He hopped down and strolled out the open garage door.

The bright beams of headlights cut across the landscape in the distance, stretching across the road from the entry gate. A reaction force was arriving.

Doski switched back to a total black, albeit blood-splattered, camouflage, edged behind the bushes beside the garage, and became one with the stone.

✧✧✧

One angular-armored, four-wheeled Otokar Cobra and two unarmored jeeps with mounted machine guns rolled in along the road. The jeeps fanned out to the sides as they approached. The machine guns were manned, and their operators searched hungrily for targets.

They raced around the road into the courtyard and screeched to a halt in front of the stairs.

Two squads of soldiers poured from the three vehicles and stormed up the steps with NCOs barking orders, heedless of the destruction. An officer wearing the two stars of an *Üsteğmen* stepped out from the Cobra and stared at the carnage in wonder. A more junior *Teğmen* joined him.

"What happened here, sir?" the junior man asked.

"Another team must have arrived before us," the senior one said. "And praise be to God they did. Do you see how many soldiers were here protecting General Çakmak? The machine guns, the sandbags? We would've been slaughtered. It looks very much like he expected us, like he knew we were coming to arrest him. Can you imagine? He would've massacred us, and would've proclaimed it an assassination attempt, instead of our carrying out lawful orders. He may very well have gained even more power as a result."

"Well someone else got here first. Perhaps we were meant to be a backup? In case this first team failed?"

"Without telling us? Something is very wrong here. Either way, let's proceed with caution, and make sure the general is indeed here."

***Kaywan Military Base Annex***
***Kurdish Republic***
***22 December, Year 10***

The president's chief bodyguard examined his face for any missed hairs. Kurdish military grooming standards were nowhere near those of, say, the US military, but he was not a common soldier. The president's bodyguard needed to be immaculate, to set the standard.

He took his leave shortly after the arresting force found Çakmak dead, leaving them with more questions than answers. He'd cratered the suit in the middle of a reservoir, and ridden his motorcycle back to Istanbul. He'd had another day and a half to enjoy the city before his trip home. The change in tone was like something of a dream.

It was as if he'd stepped outside of himself and imagined the entire endeavor. Everything felt surreal as he walked into the briefing room and stood at his position by the door. Everyone shot to attention as President Sheen entered a few minutes later. The leader of the Kurdish Republic went straight for Doski and put a hand to his shoulder.

"Captain Doski, my guardian angel. It is wonderful to see you again. I trust your holiday was relaxing?"

"It was exactly what I needed, honored president."

*And what you and the country needed as well.*

"Excellent to hear, Captain. And Major Khan here, I imagine, is glad to hear it as well. At the very least, she's ecstatic that you've returned."

The oval-faced female major with intense brown eyes smiled and greeted him as well. She examined him with a hint of sympathy, much the way Sheen had after the recent bombings.

"It was an honor to protect our nation's president," she said. "Even for an *extended* period of time. I understood the necessity, better than some might. Still, I am greatly pleased by your return. I relinquish command of the president's protective detail back to you, its rightful commander."

"I am honored and eager to resume command of it, Major."

"I thought you might be."

The president's staff took their seats.

Major Duhoki, as usual, stood at the forefront of the conference room to give the daily intelligence brief. A picture of a scowling General Çakmak appeared on the screen. He looked far more dignified and confident than when Doski had last seen him.

"President, my first report is an update on the death of one General Yusuf Çakmak. As I mentioned yesterday, the official report was that he died from 'medical complications' with no details offered. However, in the last twenty-four hours we've received intel from numerous sources—though none are verified—that the general was actually removed by his own government under suspicion of plotting a military coup. Theories range from a Turkish military assault on the compound in which he was planning the coup to a theory that a simple arrest attempt turned violent and he died in the exchange. There are even wilder theories, but I'll spare you those."

President Sheen looked back at Doski. "No matter his cause of death, let's hope this means your job will be somewhat easier in the future."

The bodyguard straightened and lifted his chin. "Honored President, while I will agree it is fortuitous this man is no longer capable of threatening your life or the security of this nation, I do not believe my job, or any of our jobs, will be any easier. The Kurdish people never lack for enemies, and so I will remain faithfully vigilant."

# NO EXTRADITION

Kacey Ezell & Nick Steverson

Olivia Hastings rounded the corner and backed up against the cinder block building. In the distance, she could hear the roar of the engine as the truck sped off in the other direction. For the moment, they were off her trail, but it wouldn't be long before they figured out they were chasing a ghost. She had to keep moving and find somewhere to lay low. Everything had gone to shit in the worst way possible. Now she was stuck in Venezuela, no local contacts, no safe house, and no jurisdiction.

"And no ammo," she grumbled through gritted teeth as she checked her ammo count. Only three rounds left—and those from her spare magazine. "Fuck."

She tucked her weapon into her waistband and pulled the jacket of her business suit tight around her. With her tongue, she depressed the switch in her back right molar to send out an encrypted emergency signal from the neural link embedded in her skull. Ahead, a group of kids played soccer in the street with a filthy ball as she hurried down the street.

"Operator," a monotone voice answered, echoing in her ears as if he were standing next to her. Only years of training and practice kept her from an outward reaction. The neural link made it so that only she could hear the words, but that wouldn't matter if she telegraphed the conversation with her body language.

"White Sparrow compromised and hamstrung," she muttered under her breath, knowing that the link would catch the sound and transmit it. "My team is . . . I'm isolated."

"Pulling up location. Wait one."

Olivia turned east down another street, her eyes continuously moving, searching for threats.

"No assets in your location. Additionally, extraction is currently unavailable."

"Yeah, no shit, Operator. I know that. I need options."

"There's a dock about sixty miles north of your current position. You could obtain a boat and make for Puerto Rico. A team can be there in approximately seventy-two hours for extraction."

She stopped and pressed a hand to her forehead. Pain shot through the gash above her eyebrow and made her wince. "There has to be something better than that. I'm on foot."

Something crashed in the alley as she passed and her hand shot to her firearm. A calico cat ran out of a toppled trash can, a rat, weakly struggling, clutched in its mouth.

"Besides, I don't want an extraction. I want to complete my goddamn mission. Send options to my personal link before you enact compromise protocols for the team."

"You are advised to abandon the mission and make for the nearest extraction point. Any further actions towards your former objective will be disavowed."

"Unless I'm successful," Olivia muttered.

"You are advised—"

"I don't want your fucking advice, Operator," Olivia snapped. "Give me *something*."

There was a long silence before the operator spoke again. "Incoming infodump. Again, any further actions towards the former objective will be disavowed. Standby for compromise protocol."

Olivia continued down the street until she came to a small intersection. Rather than stay out in the open, she turned north and ducked into an alleyway. She knew she was running out of time before her friends—not that they were her friends really, not anymore—came back for her.

The way clear for the moment, she scanned her memory for the downloaded intel packet. Background knowledge filled her brain, as if she'd read the file and memorized the contents.

The file contained the dossier for a man named Matteo "Matty" LaMorte. Her eyes narrowed as she absorbed the information. He was a known mob enforcer and hit man and had established an alias in

Caracas as Brian Smith. To all appearances, he'd lived a quiet life since evading capture by the FBI about eight years ago. With the advancement of facial recognition, he'd been located and tagged. Since Venezuela was a non-extradition country, no agency had pursued him further. The file—and now her memory—contained photos, a few addresses, including the last known, and a single known place of employment.

*A fucking mobster? Really?* She sighed and pinched the bridge of her nose.

She wanted to complete her mission rather than go home with her tail tucked between her legs, but she couldn't do that alone with only three bullets and a tattered suit. She needed help and her options were less than limited. Approaching a gangster in hiding would be a gamble, but it was better than giving up. Plus, she had one thing that might work in her favor. She just hoped it would be enough.

"Got it," she whispered, squaring her shoulders and bracing against what she knew was coming next. "Go ahead, enact compromise protocols."

Searing pain stabbed through her skull, burning out the neural link and making her eyes water. She stumbled forward as nausea burned up the inside of her throat. She turned and threw her hands against a nearby brick wall mere seconds before the vomit exploded from within, splattering against the filthy, cracked pavement below.

She swallowed hard and pushed off the wall. "Hope you enjoyed that as much as I did, you fuckers," she whispered, glancing toward the mouth of the alleyway and relishing the thought of her former teammates being surprised by the pain of having their neural links burnt with no warning.

Screams, shattering glass, and the sound of a racing engine in the distance drew her attention back to the present. She was out of time and out of options. Olivia took a deep breath, wiped the back of her wrist over her mouth and turned toward LaMorte's last known address.

There was more than one truck after her now, as well as men on foot. She was two streets from LaMorte's address. Two more streets and she'd theoretically be safe. She hoped, anyway. It was more likely

LaMorte would just tell her to go fuck herself and she'd just have to keep running until her luck finally ran out.

Just as she turned the corner, weight slammed into her and shoved her against a brick wall. Pain shot through her shoulder and the cut above her eye.

"Got you now, bitch," a heavily accented male voice said close to her ear.

Air whooshed from her lungs as the asshole drove a fist into her gut, dropping her to her knees, her arms wrapped around her midsection. He grabbed a handful of hair and forced her to look up at him. He had dark skin, black hair, and light brown eyes and wore a dirty flannel shirt.

His teeth were bright yellow against his complexion as he grinned down at her. "I'm gonna have a little fun with you before I give you to the boss."

One hand went to his zipper, the other still grasping her hair, but both her hands were still free and wrapped around her waist. She gripped her Glock, drew, and shot the man right through his hand, zipper, and presumably unimpressive manhood. The henchman dropped to his knees, pained and panicked eyes level with Olivia's. He groaned and clutched his wounded hand and crotch, blood pooling on the ground beneath him.

She stood and, without another word or preamble, put another round in his forehead, spraying blood and brains along the ground and wall behind him. His body crumpled to the stone. No time to lose, she checked him for weapons. All she came up with was a bowie knife in a leather sheath.

"Fuck. You could at least have had a gun, you piece of shit." Someone in the distance shouted again but it was indistinct, with her ears ringing from the shots and her pulse hammering in her eardrums. With only one bullet left, there was no way she could make any kind of stand. Her ribs screamed as she bolted in the direction of LaMorte's house.

Olivia slowed her pace to a brisk walk and approached the blue front door. There was a small peep hole, but no window and the windows to either side had the shades drawn.

"I think she went this way!" someone shouted in Spanish.

She knocked on the door three times. A few seconds passed. She knocked again. A few heartbeats later she heard chains rattling from the other side and the distinctive sound of bolts being slid aside. The door opened partially to reveal a man in his late thirties or early forties with light brown hair silver streaked on each side. He wore a white tank top, jeans, and leather workboots.

He was handsome, she realized with a jolt. Not in a pretty kind of way, but in that rough, distinguished old school kind of way. Like he had no problem getting his hands dirty, roughing up the guy who just slapped your ass, and then slipping on a tux to take you dancing at the fanciest night club in town.

*God damn it. Why'd he have to be a silver fox?*

She looked down and noticed the snub-nosed .357 Magnum aimed at her gut from his waist. She had one bullet, her weapon was holstered, and he had the drop on her.

"Mr. La Mor— I mean, Mr. Smith?"

LaMorte's intelligent eyes narrowed as he looked her up and down, taking in her bedraggled appearance. Her suit was torn and tattered and she had blood spattered on her from the douchebag in the alley. She also had dried blood running down the side of her head from the gash above her eye. That would probably require stitches.

"The fuck you want, Fed?" he asked, his voice deep, rough, and New York accent thick.

"To survive and to do my job."

*Shit. I called him by the wrong name and told him the truth? I should have led with the offer.*

LaMorte snorted. "Fuck off..." He went to shut the door.

"Wait! I can make it worth your while."

He sneered down at her. "I doubt it. All you feds are good for is—" there was a shout down the street a loud crash. His eyes narrowed again. "Who the fuck are you running from? And why the *fuck* did you lead them here?"

Olivia saw her chance to press the advantage. "The *wrong* people. They'll be here any minute. I killed one of them in the alley two streets over that way." She pointed in the direction she'd come.

He nodded. "Yeah, I heard the gunshot. Fuck." He pulled the door open wide enough for her to squeeze though. "Get your ass in here before someone sees you and I get labeled a narc."

She shoved through the door and into his house before he had the chance to change his mind. The door slammed behind her and multiple locks slid home. Her hand was on the butt of her pistol when he turned around. He held the .357 in his hand, the hammer locked back.

He grinned at her. "You got spunk, Fed Girl." Slowly, he released the hammer and stuffed the gun in his waistband. "Better?"

"Slightly," she replied.

He pointed at her face. "You know you're bleeding?"

"Observant of you."

LaMorte shrugged. "Okay, be a bitch about it, then. Ain't my ugly mug leaking blood all over the place and probably hurting like hell."

Olivia sighed and let go of her weapon. "I got butt-stroked in the face with a rifle about an hour ago."

He nodded. "Sounds about right." He pointed down a hallway. "Two doors down on the right is the bathroom. Go wash up and clean that out. There's a first aid kit on the counter. Should be some butterfly band-aid stitch things in there."

When she didn't move, he added, "Look, sweetheart, if I was gonna kill you, I wouldn't send you to my nice clean bathroom to do it. I'd drag you out in the back yard and do it there. Blood don't hurt dirt none, but it plays hell on my décor and white towels." He gave a dismissive wave. "Go. You're fine. We'll talk after."

Olivia pivoted slowly, wary of giving her back to him, but he simply turned and walked into the kitchen. She let out a sigh and turned for the bathroom.

Once inside, she leaned on the sink and grimaced at her reflection. The long, jagged gash above her eye was worse than she'd first thought. Dried blood streaked most of the right side of her face and her eye was swollen.

She turned the tap on full hot and used her wet fingertips to scrub as much of the blood away as possible. Next, she pulled a Spanish-labeled bottle of isopropyl alcohol from the medicine cabinet behind the mirror. She grabbed a cotton ball, too, and used them both to clean the cut, hissing and cursing the whole time. She also found some butterfly band aids that turned out to be Clozex, the ones with the little zip-ties in them.

*Matty LaMorte knows what he's doing,* she reminded herself as she closed the gash. *Let's hope he can perform an op as well as he stocks a medicine cabinet.*

Matty opened the liquor cabinet and pulled out two tumblers and the decanter full of whiskey. He heard the bathroom sink start running as he poured himself a drink and downed it in a single gulp. What the hell was a fed doing at his house? More importantly, how did she know he was even here? *And* his real name? His eyes darted to his cell phone on the counter. It was a cheap burner and not in his name, but the technology was really what he considered. Times were changing and so was tech. It wouldn't be all that hard for certain agencies to track him down using street cameras and such. He'd seen it on TV shows. Either that or they'd known where he was all along and never moved because they had no jurisdiction and Venezuela didn't extradite. He supposed it didn't really matter.

*Make it worth my while, huh?*

The water shut off and the bathroom door opened.

*Speak of the devil.*

When Olivia entered the kitchen, LaMorte was leaning up against the stove, a glass tumbler in his hand and a second sitting on the counter.

"Drink?" he asked as casually as if they were two friends hanging out. He poured two fingers worth of an amber liquid from a decanter into the tumbler next to him and held it out. When she didn't take it he said, "Come on, Fed Girl, it'll help with the pain."

Despite the professional agent in Olivia's head screaming at her not to take the drink, the throbbing pain drowned that little bitch right out. She took the glass and tossed the alcohol back in a single gulp. Her eyes widened.

A shit-eating grin split LaMorte's face. "Good, huh? Pappy 23 year." He sat his glass down and crossed his arms over his chest. He pointed to a glass pan sitting on the stove. It was filled with something that looked like a mix of pasta and pizza. "You hungry? You look hungry. I got some leftover stromboli. My grandmother's recipe. Made it myself. You know how hard it is to find fresh Italian ingredients here? Fucking animals, I tell ya."

This was not the same guy who'd held her at gunpoint less than twenty minutes ago. At least it didn't seem like it.

"You're awfully nice for a mob enforcer."

He rolled his eyes and shook his head. "Alleged mob enforcer, Fed Girl."

"I have a name."

His eyebrows rose and a teasing smile appeared. "Oh yeah? Well, I ain't heard it yet, so until I know what your name is, I'm gonna keep calling you 'Fed Girl.' Though, seeing as you already seem to know *exactly* who I am, it would only be proper etiquette for you to formally introduce yourself. Ya know, so we're on even playing fields here."

Olivia scowled, looked at the stromboli, then back to him. "My name is Case Officer Olivia Hastings, Central Intelligence Agency."

"See?" LaMorte said, his hands splayed open. "Wasn't that hard, was it? Since we're getting to know each other and becoming such good friends, you can just call me Matty. Tell you the truth, I miss being called by my real name. Anyway, to answer your question, I ain't some kind of monster. You ain't done nothing to me, aside from nearly leading a bunch of Venezuelan thugs to my front door, so I got no reason to treat you like a dog." He grabbed a plate and dished out a helping of stromboli then stuck a fork in it and slid it over to her. "After all that running, I know your skinny ass is hungry."

She couldn't deny she was starving. It had been over twenty-four hours since she'd last eaten anything more than a protein bar.

"I can see you thinking it, Olivia. Eat. You can explain this offer of yours while you enjoy my grandmother's stromboli." He waved for her to follow. "Come on."

Matty led her to the kitchen table where he sat down at the head and picked up a cigar from an ash tray and held it up. "You mind if I smoke?"

Olivia sat at the other end of the table. "It's your house. Why are you asking me?"

"Because it's polite. Smoke used to bother my mother, so I never smoked around her. Contrary to popular opinion, I'm not really an asshole."

It pissed her off that she felt like she had to agree with him. While she hadn't actually seen his files, she was pretty sure this guy had murdered people on behalf of the Ambrosi family. What else would an enforcer do? The mob tended to deal rather decisively with anyone caught selling secrets, whether that was to rivals or the law.

"If you say so." She shoved a bite of the stromboli in her mouth and nearly moaned in pleasure. It was next to heavenly.

"I do," Matty said with a smile.

"You're enjoying this, aren't you."

His smile turned into a grin. "I am. Not often you get to deal with feds in a situation where they got no power. Here, you're just like me. Like I said before, even playing field." He lit the cigar and took a couple puffs before leaning back in his chair and rubbing the end of his nose with his thumb. "So, tell me why you're being chased, who's chasing you, and why and how you ended up at my table, eating my grandmother's stromboli. How is it, by the way? Good? Sometimes I go too heavy on the garlic."

She looked down and was shocked to see she'd already eaten more than half her helping. Part of her wanted to lie and say it was overcooked and that it tasted like an entire garlic clove. But there was something in the way he asked, a sincerity that made it seem like it really mattered to him that she enjoyed the food.

"It's perfect. Your grandmother knew what she was doing. Thank you."

"Hey, forget about it. Now, give me the details."

"Have you ever heard of a man by the name of William Hebert?" Olivia leaned back in her chair, eyeing Matty's face closely for a reaction. The aging mobster took a slow drag from his cigar and let the smoke curl around his head for a long moment before he shook his head.

"How about Guillermo Arrenque?"

*That* got Matty's attention. He looked sharply up at her, his eyes narrowing.

"Arrenque as in—"

"The Lago del Norte cartel. Yes. He is—was—one of ours."

Matty's eyebrows went up. "A spook?"

"A contact. An incredibly *valuable* contact with ties to organizations in Pakistan, North Africa, and Southeast Asia. His activities here were the source of a lot of frustration over at DEA, but no one could provide what he could … and then he got taken out."

"Last year," Matty said, nodding. "His wife's son. Came up through the ranks of Arrenque's *soldatos* and convinced them the old man was losing his edge. Happens all the time."

"Yes, well, as I said, Arrenque had certain data that the Agency needed to recover—"

"Documents?"

Olivia sighed. She shouldn't go into it, but so far, the more forthcoming she was, the more sympathetic Matty seemed to be. She wondered if that was a mobster thing or a Matty thing. "Dossiers... and full genetic profile information for his contacts around the world. The kind of stuff that enable biocloning and things like that. Things the Agency would prefer *not* fall into the hands of his stepson."

"Ares Salvaje," Matty supplied. "Crazy fucker. *Not* someone you want hunting you down, Fed Girl. Law enforcement sent a token force up into the Lago del Norte district about nine months ago. Only thing that came back were their severed hands." He took another drag and vaguely pointed at her with the ember. "It's a message, ya know. To feds and rivals alike. Hands off."

Olivia pressed her lips together as old anger tangled with new frustration in her chest. "We know," she said. "One of those CICPC men was ours, too. That's why the Agency sent my team in. We infiltrated the cartel headquarters over a period of *months* to try and get a status update, and to get our hands on that data."

"Bold move, considering." He waved her on. "And?"

"And what?"

"Did you get it?"

"Yeah." Weariness crashed over her like a wave, drowning all her fire and leaving her feeling limp and exhausted. "We had it, we were headed for extract. Then everything went to shit. I'm still not 100% clear on what happened. All I know is that half my team is dead, and the other half is fucking complicit. I'm dead too, if they find me."

"Probably," Matty agreed. "So, what? You want me to help you get out of the country?"

"Eventually," Olivia said. "But not right away. What I really want is for you to help me complete my mission. *I need that data.* It could mean the difference between life and death for dozens of American operatives around the world."

"Hmph," Matty grunted and stood to grab the Pappy. He poured a glass, downed it, then poured himself another before setting the decanter on the table with heavy thunk. Using the hand holding the glass he pointed at her. "So, you, already having failed, half your team compromised, the other half dead, and you nearly iced in the street, still want to run face-first into this shit, knowing they know who you are and what you look like?"

Olivia straightened in her seat and raised her chin. "Yes."

A chuckle, deep and dark, rolled from Matty's depths. "Like I said, Fed Girl, you got spunk." He shook his head. "But you're crazy. How the hell do you expect to even get close now? They know who the fuck you are. You won't get within a mile of Ares before someone plants a bullet in the back of your head." He sat back down and picked up his cigar, rolling it between his fingers. "You'd be smart to just get the hell out of here and go home."

"That's what the Operator said, too," Olivia said.

While she knew both the Operator and Matty weren't wrong, neither was she. She had to finish the mission. There were literally lives on the line if the information fell into Salvaje's hands. If she didn't get her hands on it and get it back to the States, Arrenque would have done all that work and died for nothing. As would the contacts he'd curated. She couldn't let that happen. Besides, the half of her team that turned needed to face justice as well. She was pretty sure she could fit treason into the charges somewhere.

"Who?" Matty asked.

She shook her head. "Not important. What *is* important is that I get my hands on that intel. I need your help."

"And you think because you show up on my doorstep like a wounded little puppy that I'm just gonna go all soft and give you what you want just because you look so pathetically cute?"

Olivia cocked her head to the side and gave him a crooked smile. "You think I'm cute?"

Matty blushed a bit and cleared his throat. "You know what I mean, smartass. You said you could make it worth my while when you were a minute away from becoming another statistic in the street. What's the offer?" He waved a hand in the air to forestall anything she might say. "And don't give me any of that reduced sentence or charges or plea offers or any of that bullshit. You better make it good. Because if not, well, you know where the door is."

*Asshole.*

She didn't say it out loud and actually had to bite her tongue to not do so. It would seem that her initial thought of what to offer would be the only way forward. She just hoped her mother could come through for her on it.

"How about complete immunity on any and all past cases and your record wiped clean?"

His eyes narrowed again as he scrutinized her.

"And, uh, exactly how is it you can make such lofty offer, Case Officer Olivia Hastings of the Central Intelligence Agency? You got a fancy title that makes most people's buttholes pucker up, but that don't mean dick when it comes to a court room and the judge's final decision."

"My mother is an important woman, and DOJ owes her a favor or two. She used to work there."

His eyebrows rose and his head tilted to the side.

*That's right, bitch. I got connections, too.*

She took another bite of her stromboli and gave him a thin smile as she chewed. Matty just sat there, silent and watching her. After she swallowed, she gently set her fork down and took a dainty sip of her Pappy.

"Does that sound like a fair offer?"

After a moment he nodded. "Sounds fair. But I still don't know what you expect to do. Like you said, and I already reminded you of once, they know who you are."

This time she smiled like a shark. "But they don't know who *you* are."

"Ah, fuck me."

"Our original plan was to download the data from Arrenque's servers onto a secure physical drive, then remote wipe the server. Not too hard with modern tech. Arrenque was smart, but to a certain degree, he had to work within the local infrastructure, which is . . . dated, at best.

"Unfortunately, the shooting started before Benson, our IT guy, could finish the wipe. He was the first hit, and the only one of my team I know wasn't complicit." Olivia swallowed and pressed her lips together, keeping her face blank and professional. It had been a little over an hour since they'd talked over Matty's grandmother's stromboli. She'd had some calls to make on her low-tech encrypted cellphone, and had taken Matty up on his offer to shower and change clothes.

Olivia wore a pair of his sweatpants with the waistband rolled down to fit, and one of his white t-shirts she'd tied at the waist so she didn't swim in it. She was certain she looked ridiculous, but to Matty's credit, he didn't give her shit about it as they reconvened over his little table.

Or not much shit, anyway.

"Benson was a friend of yours?" Matty asked, his voice low and sympathetic. He slowly puffed on his cigar as she looked down at the glass of his very excellent booze she held.

Olivia nodded. "We came up through training together. He deserved better."

"Don't we all, Fed Girl?"

"Anyway, Arrenque's encryption was substantial, so there's a good chance that Salvaje hasn't been able to access the data yet, but it's just a matter of time. Especially now that he's got Green and Thomas working with him. They'll hire a black hat to hack the encryption. They've probably already done so, honestly."

"What happened to Benson's key?"

"It was stored on his rig, which was in the van when it blew. The physical drive was there too, thank fuck. Like I said, Salvaje's men jumped the gun when they started shooting. I wasn't even in the van yet."

"Where were you?"

Olivia smiled sadly. "My cover was part of the cleaning staff. I was saying goodbye to the Abuela who ran the outfit. She was sweet and wanted to give me a gift for my supposed upcoming wedding—that was my reason for leaving when the op was done."

Matty nodded. "Not a bad story. Girls leave all the time to get married and move to their husband's town."

"Yeah, but just another reason I can't go back there. So that's what I need you for. In the end, it's a simple op. Get in, get my backup transmitter within a hundred meters of the server room, get out—"

"Where you gonna get a backup transmitter?"

"Already have it. I was carrying it on me, in case Benson's plant had an issue. Same with the localized EMP. I'll use that to remote wipe the servers as soon as the download is complete." She snapped her fingers. "Data's gone, and so is any trace we were there. And then..."

"And then?"

Olivia blew out a breath. "Green and Thomas. I can't leave them as loose ends. Either they're apprehended or... eliminated."

The man across from her, whose name literally meant "death" stared into her with dark, emotionless eyes.

"Grabbing and transporting them ain't gonna be an option," he said. "No extradition, remember?" Again, his voice was soft, even as it made her skin pebble up with dread.

"I know," she whispered. "But this is a matter of national security."

"Am I gonna get immunity for them, too?"

Olivia straightened up and laid down the papers she'd printed from her phone to Matty's ancient inkjet printer.

"Yes," she said. "This is the full offer. Go ahead and read through it and make sure you don't have any questions before you sign." She slid the papers across the table.

When she'd called Operator earlier to arrange the deal via her mother, Olivia hadn't been at all sure it would work, but she shouldn't have doubted. Becoming a supreme court justice had changed many things in Carla Hastings's life, but her love for her kids was a constant. Olivia didn't know what strings she'd had to pull, or what favors she'd called in, but Operator had the requested offer back to her within an hour.

"So," Matty said. "This says that immunity is contingent upon me assisting with your mission to a satisfactory degree and getting you safely back to US sovereign territory." He raised his eyes to hers again. "'Satisfactory degree'? You gonna use that loophole to try and fuck me here, Fed Girl?"

Olivia's eyes narrowed. "What? No! Matty, I wouldn't do that."

"So, what the fuck does 'satisfactory degree' mean?"

"It means..." she let out a sigh. "It means that we have the data, Salvaje doesn't, and Green and Thomas are no longer a factor. One way or another."

"So, dead."

"Probably."

"Okay. I got a guy I can call for some intel. We need an in and if anyone knows one, it's this guy. Storming the castle isn't gonna do the trick with just the two of us. We'd be better off suck-starting a shotgun."

"Well that's colorful."

"Just sayin'."

Matty picked up his phone and dialed a number. "Yeah, Enrique, I'm calling in that favor. Yeah, *that* one. Uh huh. We'll be square—mostly. Exactly what I just said, *mostly*. Mother fucker, not only did I pull *your* ass out of the fire, but I got your brother off the goddamn hook, too. Do I need to come over to that shithole and beat the fucking memory back into your thick skull? Didn't think so. You're gonna cooperate. Awesome. Huh? No, I don't think I'll be at the card game next week. Because I got shit to do, that's why. So you gonna help me or not? Good. Now, listen, I need everything you can get on how to get into the Salvaje Compound. Do I sound like I'm fucking joking? I need it yesterday. Okay."

He put the phone on the table and took another puff from his cigar. Olivia just stared at him in disbelief at the conversation she'd just listened to.

"Well?"

Matty raised an eyebrow. "Well what?"

"What'd he say?"

"That I'm an asshole and he'll call me in the morning with what he has and that if I get caught I never spoke with him. Pretty basic stuff."

Olivia put her face in her hands and plunked her forehead on the table. "We're gonna die, aren't we?"

"Probably."

"Who the hell uses this much starch on a work shirt?" Matty grumbled as he adjusted the stiff collar of the AracniTech uniform. While uncomfortable, he had to admit the Venezuelan spider logo on the chest was pretty funny. It was basically a tarantula wearing black-framed glasses and working on eight different computers at once. Olivia hadn't known about the tech company. That would have been something Green and Thomas would have discovered and reported. Being as they'd gone native, it was no surprise they'd never made the report to Olivia.

He turned the black and red AracniTech van into the driveway of the Salvaje compound and came to a stop at the main gate. An armed guard in jeans and a t-shirt approached as he rolled the window down. Two men with long-handled mirrors rounded his van, using the mirrors to scan the undercarriage. The back door opened and a third scanned the inside, rummaging around in a bin or two and even opened a couple of tackle boxes full of fuses and circuit boards. After an annoyed grunt he slammed the door shut.

"Clear, Carlos," the third one announced.

Carlos gave them a nod and they stepped to the side. Another man appeared in the doorway of the guard shack, a pistol tucked into his waistband.

"Here for the monthly updates," Matty said in perfect Spanish.

Carlos's head cocked to the side and he raised his rifle to point at Matty's face. "You're not the normal guy."

"Juan's in the hospital," Matty replied cooly. He tugged on the laminated identification card clipped to his shirt. "I'm Todd."

The best lies held a bit of truth. In this case, it was completely true. It had taken some percussive persuasion to get Juan to lend Matty and Olivia the van and uniform necessary to complete the mission. Said persuasion caused a fracture to appear in Juan's skull, hence his current stay in the hospital. The fact that it was an abandoned veterinary clinic and not an actual operating or even human hospital was beside the point. He'd make a phone call in a day or two and report the bound and gagged man to the local authorities. Anonymously, of course.

Assuming he and Olivia survived this harebrained scheme.

Suspicion shined bright in the guard's brown eyes as he studied Matty. "How come nobody called ahead to let us know it would be someone different, *Todd*?" He pushed the muzzle of his rifle into Matty's cheek. "Huh, gringo?"

Matty didn't flinch or pull back. This punk thought he was intimidating, but Matty had dealt with real gangsters back in New York that would have made this cafone piss his pants. Instead, he pushed into the barrel and locked stone-hard eyes on Carlos's. "Because Juan got his skull cracked by some thug in the street only a few hours ago and we had to scramble to keep Señor Salvaje's appointment and get here on time. We were lucky Juan was even lucid enough to give me proper instructions." It was a risky move considering he was supposed to be a nerdy tech guy and not a fearless mob enforcer.

Fortunately, Carlos didn't seem to be all that astute, so he pushed his luck and doubled down. "You wanna be the one to call him and let him know his servers won't be updated and backed up this month because you didn't know a different tech was coming to do the work? I'm sure he won't take any offense to *you* making the call and putting his entire system at risk. Home security system, personal information, banking info, business records, your payroll, and whatever else Señor Salvaje might have on there. You have that sort of authority and pull with him, right?"

The man swallowed and his eyes shifted from Matty to the house.

A dark, humorless smile split Matty's face. "Thought as much. So, you wanna let me in so I can do my job and keep both of our ballsacks intact, or do you want to make that call?"

A long moment passed before Carlos turned to the other man who hadn't moved from his place in the guardhouse doorway. "Open the gate." He turned back to Matty. "Stay on the driveway and park next to the second garage. Follow the footpath to the fourth building. You know the passcode to get in?"

Matty held up a small notepad with a ten-digit code written on it. "Got it." To Juan's credit, it had actually taken some effort to get that bit of info out of him. He'd been surprisingly tough. But Matty always got what he needed in the end. Olivia knew where the server house was on the property, from her time before the op had gone completely to shit.

"Don't go anywhere but the server house, gringo. You hear me?" He stepped closer and again used his rifle to point at Matty's face. "Or I'll put a bullet in your head, your mother's head, your father's head, and I'll sell your children to the lowest bidder. You understand?"

Matty raised his hands placatingly. "Understood. Server house only. Get in, do my job and get out. Simple. I'll be out of here in no time."

Carlos narrowed his eyes again before stepping back and waving him forward. Matty watched through the side-view mirror and saw Carlos speak into a radio. There was a good chance he would have an audience as he worked.

"Save the stupid Fed Girl," he muttered under his breath as he put the van in park. He grabbed the laptop bag in the seat next to him. "Help her take down a fucking crime boss she said. Take a deal from her judge mommy she said. It'll be easy she said." His lip curled in disgust as he shoved the van door open and walked to the back. "The fuck is wrong with me."

*"I can hear you, you know,"* Olivia said in his ear. In addition to the commercial earbud in his right ear, he had his phone tucked into his shirt pocket with the camera side poking out the top. It wasn't ideal, but it allowed her to watch as the mission progressed. *"Good job at the gate, though I thought you'd blown your cover for a moment there when you went all mob guy on him."*

He grunted in amusement as he opened the back door, grabbed a black plastic toolbox, and used his elbow to slam the door closed again. Actually responding to her with words would raise suspicion if he was being watched, and he most likely was.

*"I'm in position at the rendezvous point. Once you have the device activated, report and I'll resume the data download."*

He could see the server house in the distance. It looked about a hundred yards away from the parking area. If he'd been a real technician, he'd have been pissed about the walk. Having to go back and forth for tools or replacement parts would have been a real pain in the ass. He suddenly felt a bit sorry for Juan. Kind of.

"I hate this janky shit," Olivia muttered, squinting at her phone. She couldn't see much, but from what she could tell, Matty was in motion, moving quietly and confidently through the compound. She'd heard him exchanging a few words and chuckles in Spanish earlier in what she assumed was him leaning into his cover story as the technician.

Suddenly, the bumping, rolling motion stopped and the video on Olivia's phone steadied to show a cluster of buildings.

"That's it," Olivia said softly, knowing Matty would hear her voice in his earbuds. "That middle building there. The smallest one."

Matty said nothing, but the video started moving again, and Olivia pushed back the edge of motion sickness that threatened.

"Keep your eyes out for Green. He might be with the *soldatos* there," Olivia murmured. "He was our backup to Benson, and I guarantee his ass is on the line until they break the encryption. Remember, you don't have to have the transmitter inside the building. You just have to get it close by. Even against an exterior wall is good enough."

Matty grunted something that she took as an affirmative acknowledgement, but said nothing. On the screen the picture pixelated and froze.

"Fuck!" Olivia spat. The signal indicator at the top of her phone screen showed only one bar. With a sigh, she opened the driver door of Matty's pickup truck and stepped out onto the rutted dirt road she'd used to get close to the cartel's compound. For obvious reasons, she hadn't driven right up to the perimeter, but she'd needed to be nearby to pick up Matty after his egress.

And she'd wanted to follow along on her phone. If the fucking shitty-ass cell service in this place had been worth a damn, that should have been no problem. But this was Venezuela, and it seemed Murphy had brought the full force of his law to bear upon her.

She huffed another sigh and started walking along the road, half of her attention on the trees and undergrowth that pressed close to the narrow dirt track, and the other half on her phone screen. The bone-grating hum of insects buzzed through the air, and the wet, thick scent of the jungle wrapped around her. A bead of sweat rolled down her back between her shoulder blades.

*"Vid—hiss pop!—loop running."*

Matty's fragmented voice came through her earbud, accompanied by the sizzle of static. Olivia stopped moving and looked down at her screen. The image was pixelated all to hell, but she could make out the shape of Matty's hands opening a toolbox and removing the false bottom. The movement on her phone screen froze, but the secure receiver in the breast pocket of her vest buzzed twice, indicating it was receiving data.

"Download in progress," she said, lifting the phone to her mouth and speaking slowly but quietly into the microphone. She reached into her pocket and checked the simple digital readout on the receiver.

"Seventy-two percent," she said, and slipped it back into her pocket. "I'm going to try and get closer. My signal is terrible."

Matty didn't acknowledge her, and another glance at her phone screen told Olivia that the brief increase in signal strength had dissipated. Her phone was now showing no service at all . . . but at least the download was working.

She hiked up the road for a few more minutes, taking care to step quietly on the dried mud tire tracks baked into the dirt surface. Here and there, tropical birds called out in sudden bursts of sound that punctuated the buzzing drone of the ever-present insects. Olivia slapped at one particular mosquito that landed on her neck, and thanked all that was good her malaria shots were up to date.

She'd gone no more than fifty meters from the truck when a voice materialized in her earbud again. Once more, Olivia halted and checked the download progress on her receiver and then focused on what was happening on her phone screen.

A familiar man with dark red hair and a beard stared at the camera for a second before speaking into a shoulder mic. Olivia couldn't quite catch the words, but then he turned back and spoke directly to Matty and she knew.

"Matty," she said quietly. "That's fucking Green. *Do not* let your guard down around him. If he's there, he likely suspects something."

"Mmhmm," he hummed. Having Olivia in his ear was both comforting and annoying at the same time.

The code Juan had provided proved accurate and the panel turned green with a high-pitched beep followed by the metallic clank of the door unlocking. It smelled like a stale corporate office and the cool air was filled with the low hum of about a dozen servers.

In the far back of the building was a single terminal with three screens and keyboard. Using his peripheral vision, Matty spotted at least two cameras watching him. There were likely more, but searching around for them would look suspicious to whoever was monitoring the security system. Instead, he made straight for the terminal and set the toolbox on the floor next to him and the laptop bag on the desk next to the keyboard.

From within the bag he pulled out a laptop and a USB cord that he used to connect it to the mainframe. First, he began running the systems check in the same sequence Juan had instructed, once he'd been good and motivated to do so. Luckily, Matty had written it all down on the pad of paper. Once that was running, he opened a tab at the bottom of the screen and began running another program that Olivia had installed. As they were hardwired into the main system, they could access the security footage. The new program, courtesy of the CIA, would loop a three-minute video of Matty running the system check. The loop would end once the connection was cut.

"Video and audio loop running," he said when it was safe to speak openly.

He knelt, opened the toolbox, removed the false bottom, and activated Olivia's transmitter. That done, he locked the box lid, stood, and nervously watched the laptop work. His hand slid down to his waistband where his non-existent gun rested. Fear of being searched had forced him to come in completely unarmed. Feeling helpless wasn't an emotion he particularly cared for.

*"Downlo— in —ogress,"* Olivia reported. Her voice was crackled and broken, but he could make out her words. The building was likely causing interference. He wasn't sure if that would have caused issues with her device EMP bomb thing, but he was glad he'd been able to get inside. Besides, it wouldn't have made much sense for the tech guy to not go into the server house. It was kind of the whole point of the visit.

*"72 —ercent."*

There was a loud click and a flooding of light into the dim building as the door opened. Matty turned to see a man enter. He was dark complected with dark red hair and a beard. The way he moved was smooth and his eyes were hard and focused as he looked Matty up and down. As soon as the door shut, he reached up to the mic clipped to his shoulder and activated the radio. "Thomas, do a quick perimeter check."

*"Roger."*

"You must be Todd, Juan's replacement." He spoke English and stopped just out of arm's reach, his legs shoulder width apart, hands loose, and knees slightly bent. Clearly a trained man.

*"Matty, that's —ucking Green.* Do not *—et your guard down— him. If he's there, then he ——spects something.*

"I am," Matty said in Spanish with a professional smile. He tried to keep the worry that Olivia might be discovered hidden off his face. Their meeting point wasn't far from the compound. He hoped Thomas wasn't part of a large party. If so, her chances of getting away would be slim. He doubted she'd have the same luck as she'd had days ago. Regardless, there wasn't much he could do for her at the moment. She'd have to take care of herself until he could get back to her.

"You can speak in English," Green said. "Your accent, though good, still has a hint of Brooklyn."

This time Matty genuinely smiled and answered in English. "You can take the boy out of the city, but . . ." he shrugged, "New York never really leaves *you*."

Green nodded and smiled, but it didn't reach his eyes. "Indeed. Georgia boy, myself."

The laptop chimed. Matty held up a finger. "One second, I gotta get the next scan going."

Green stepped closer and peered over his shoulder as he worked. "A bit odd that a trained technician needs written instructions step-by-step to do a routine scan, isn't it?"

Matty typed in the proper instructions and clicked start before straightening and turning back around. Again, Green kept himself out of arm's reach and his posture ready.

"Juan said Señor Salvaje is very particular about the procedure in which his system is maintained. I want to do things in the exact same order as Juan so that none of us end up on his bad side."

"Riiight," Green said, nodding slowly.

"I don't think I caught your name," Matty said, extending his hand.

Green ignored it. "That's because I didn't say." He put a finger to his lips as if in thought. "It's funny, because, last time I checked, Juan hadn't hired any help. He likes to handle all his own work. It was part of the reason we hired him. And, no offense, that shirt looks a little tight on you."

"Just got hired the other day," Matty answered. "Ordered the wrong size shirts." He shrugged and smiled again. "Fucking new guys, right?"

"Uh huh." Green clearly wasn't buying it. He pointed at the toolbox and then the laptop. "So, you won't mind me giving your equipment a quick once over then, will you?"

*"Fuck. He knows."*

He moved toward the box, but Matty stepped in his path and looked him square in the eye. "Actually, I don't particularly care for people touching my tools."

Green smiled brightly. "I thought as much."

*"Download complete. Matty, handle him and get the fuck out of there. Once you're clear, I'll blow it."*

"Only one person I know that would be trying to get in here," Green said. His voice turned sing-song. "Oh, Oliviaaa. Is that you on the other side?" Quickly, he reached behind his back, but before he could remove whatever it was, a gun most likely, Matty rushed him.

Matty's hand caught Green's wrist mid-draw, a black semiauto pistol in his grip. Green's other hand shot up to the radio but Matty caught that wrist too. Before the turncoat could react, Matty smashed his forehead into his nose, once, twice, crushing the bone. The gun clattered to the floor and Matty kicked it across the room. Releasing Green's radio hand, Matty snatched the mic off his shoulder, ripping the cord from the main device and tossed it behind him. An unexpected knee to the groin knocked the wind out of him.

Pain and nausea shot up through gut. "You dirty bitch," he managed to groan.

Green, blood running down his face, looked up to the cameras and shouted. "Get someone down here, you fucking idiots!"

The traitor turned to run for the gun, but Matty composed himself and tackled Green to the floor from behind. He looped his arm around and tried to get into position to lock in a choke hold, but Green sank his teeth into Matty's forearm.

"Gaaahhh! You motherfucker!"

Matty slammed his other fist into Green's temple, but the man was tough. And strong. He bucked his hip back and twisted with enough force and speed that he was able to swing back an elbow that connected with Matty's eye and knocked him to the floor.

Both men stood and faced each other, bloodied and breathing hard.

"Whatever that bitch is paying you . . ." Green huffed, "Salvaje can triple. All you gotta do is give her up."

"Like you did, you rat bastard?" Matty snapped. "Go fuck yourself."

"Don't say I didn't give you the chance."

Green charged like a raging linebacker and slammed into Matty, lifting him off the ground and driving him backwards. His lower back exploded in pain as he was slammed into the steel desk. The laptop fell to the side, but luckily it remained connected to the mainframe. Green rose up over him and swung with a wild right hook that Matty blocked with his left forearm. He looped his arm around the other man's and slammed a right uppercut to Green's ribs. Without giving Green time to recover, Matty spun left, shoving Green into the desk and continued landing shots to the man's ribs. There was a pained scream when Matty both felt and heard bone snap under his fist.

A lifetime enforcing mob law had taught Matty that when you had an enemy up against the ropes—or a desk—you didn't let up. You pushed harder. Green's guard was getting weaker and his breathing became ragged as Matty landed punch after punch to the face and body. Matty lost his grip and Green collapsed to the floor.

Breathing hard himself, Matty knelt next to him. "Just give up and come back with us."

Green spit blood in his face. "Fuck you," he gurgled through shattered teeth and shredded lips. "And that cunt."

Matty wiped the blood and spit from his eyes. It had been a long time since he'd felt the kind of rage that flooded his body and ignited his blood like molten lava.

"Fuck me, huh," he ground out through gritted teeth. He slammed a blood-coated fist into Green's already shattered nose. The steel chair under the desk caught his attention and he pulled it out. "I'll show you fuck me, cocksucker."

He rolled Green over onto his stomach, grabbed the back of his shirt and snatched him up off the floor. Next, he grabbed the steel chair and slid it in front of Green. Before he could protest or fight back, Matty slammed Green's face into the edge of the steel seat. His hands came up to brace himself, before Green could push himself off and onto the floor again, Matty stomped down on the back of Green's neck as hard as he could, caving in his skull and snapping his neck all at once.

He stumbled back, breathing hard. "Now who's the fucking cunt?"

There wasn't time to process. It had been a long time since he'd done anything quite so... ruthless, so he shoved whatever it was he was feeling aside and headed for the door. Matty retrieved the gun and exited the building. He kept his head down as he made a beeline for the work van. As luck would have it, he managed to make it into the van without being accosted. He took a look in the rearview mirror and winced. His face was splattered with blood and his eye was beginning to swell.

He noticed a roll of paper towels and grabbed them. Using a bottled water, he cleaned his face off as best he could and slid on his Ray-Ban Aviators. A thin jacket hung on the back of the passenger seat with a spare shirt. He changed into both to hide the blood and the bite on his arm. It was the best he could do. A twist of the key and he backed the van out of the parking spot and headed towards the gate.

*"Fuck you!"* came Olivia's angry voice through his earpiece. He hadn't heard anything from her in several minutes.

"What's going on out there?" he demanded as he steered the van as calmly as possible. Gun shots rang out over the connection.

*"You always were a shit shot, Thomas!"* There was the sound of a scuffle followed by resounding silence.

"Fuck. Fuck. Fuck," he chanted. "I'm comin', Fed Girl. Almost back to the gate. Hang in there."

Silently, he prayed to God to let him make it. It had been far too long since he'd attended mass or gone to confession, but he hoped the big man was still listening to even the most wicked of men.

Carlos was there waiting, an impatient look on his face. He expected to be stopped but the gate master just waved him on. Matty was more than willing to keep going and leave him in the rearview.

"I'm out, Olivia. Blow it."

Nothing.

He floored it.

Olivia picked up the pace, walking further down the road, her eyes flicking up to scan the tree line and the road in front of her and then back down to her phone. At first, the pixelation got worse, and the dialogue faded entirely under static pops and hisses. But then, suddenly, she must have crossed some invisible line, because the static in her earbud disappeared, replaced by Matty's crystal clear voice.

"Just got hired the other day," Matty was saying. "Ordered the wrong size shirts. Fucking new guys, right?"

"Uh huh," Green's voice answered. "So, you won't mind me giving your equipment a quick once over then, will you?"

"Fuck," Olivia ground the word out as certainty soaked through her mind. "He knows."

She would have said more, but the receiver in her vest buzzed twice. She reached in and checked the readout: 100% of data received.

*Thank fuck.*

"Download complete," she said into the phone, turning to face back to the truck. "Matty, handle him and get the fuck out of there. Once you're clear, I'll blow it."

Olivia tucked her phone into her pocket and began heading back toward the truck. Within moments, the static took over in her ears again, and she grimaced. For a hot second, she thought about pulling her earbud out, but she didn't want to risk missing something crucial. Better to get back to the truck and wait for Matty to arrive at the rendezvous site.

She had zero doubts he could handle Green. At the end of the day, Matty was a stone killer for a reason. He'd agreed to help her, but Olivia refused to forget that. He'd take care of the traitorous Green, find Thomas—who was no doubt nearby. The two of them were buddies going way back—and drive out the gate to meet up with her.

As she rounded the last curve in the jungle road before the truck, Olivia was contemplating the wisdom of driving the truck up to the place where her phone reception had improved. It was closer to the compound, and therefore more of a risk, but at least she could count on solid comms.

She'd do it, she decided, and looked up just in time to see Thomas fire his pistol at her from behind the tailgate of the truck.

Instinct took over, and Olivia dove for cover behind one of the giant softwood trunks that loomed near the road. Adrenaline sang along her nerves, making her hands tremble as she unholstered her weapon.

"Come on, babe, I know you'd like it if I chased you down, but we're on a bit of a time schedule."

Thomas's voice, smooth and wheedling, made Olivia grit her teeth. Once, many, many years ago, a series of alcohol-fueled bad decisions had led to a one-night stand with Thomas back at her apartment. He'd seen her stack of dark romance novels and never ceased giving her shit about them. It had become something of a fun in-joke they shared.

Until he betrayed their team and killed Benson . . . and tried to kill her.

"Seriously, babe, I just want to talk."

"Fuck you!" she called back, trying to buy time. Maybe Matty would hear her? "You always were a shit shot, Thomas."

She checked her magazine, then began moving as quickly as

possible through the foliage while remaining quiet. She worked her way back around toward the tailgate of the truck. She stayed low, using the vegetation as concealment as she followed the sound of her onetime friend's voice.

"You know I shot wide on purpose, right? I don't actually want to hurt you. Green thinks we should. He says you're too much of a Company girl to come in with us. But he doesn't know you like I do, babe. He has no idea how dark and dirty that mind of yours can actually get."

*Neither do you,* Olivia thought, but kept her mouth shut as she got closer. The problem with hiding behind the foliage was that concealment worked two ways. Thomas couldn't see her, but she was having a hard time getting a clear shot on him without giving herself away. Still, this was going to be her best chance.

She crouched behind a flowering shrub and lined up her sights. Thomas pulled his phone out of his pocket and lifted it to his ear. Olivia squeezed the trigger . . .

*Pop! Poppoppop!*

Her first shot hit low center mass, staggering him backwards, but not dropping him. Realization flowed through her: he was wearing body armor. She kept firing, but he turned and ran at her, making her stumble backwards. The heel of her foot caught on something and she went down hard, feeling the sharp sting of myriad scratches from the thorny vines draped over the undergrowth.

Olivia struggled to her feet, panic beating in her chest, bringing her breath in quick little gasps. She couldn't see her weapon. It had fallen beneath the vines somewhere. She reached down into the thicket, wincing as wicked, inch-long thorns scraped red lines up her arm, but she didn't pay much attention. She had to find her gun! If Thomas found her—

—the hard, hot muzzle of a weapon pressed against the back of her head.

"Gotcha, babe," Thomas said, a bit of breathless laughter lingering in his tone. "That was fun! What d'ya think of my plates, huh? Pretty kickass composite. Light as fuck, too. Arrenque had one of his pet scientists working on it before his kid popped him. CPCD is going to lose their shit once Del Lago starts deploying these bad boys. The Agency *wishes* they had anything this good." He shifted slightly, and the muzzle of his weapon pushed harder into her skull. "Hands up slowly, then stand."

Out of options, Olivia complied. She continued complying as he instructed her to turn to face him. He smiled, his Ivy-League pretty boy looks only slightly disheveled.

"Good girl," he said. "I knew you'd be reasonable. Let's go back to the truck and you can tell me what you think you're doing out here."

Olivia swallowed and nodded. Her eyes flicked down to Thomas's belt, where the clip of a folding knife sat next to the belt loop of his usual black cargo pants. She looked back up to see Thomas's smile growing.

"Well, well, Livvy," he said, his voice taking on a low, intimate note. "I know we said we'd forget about that one time back in DC, but it looks like I'm not the only one who remembers. That was a good night, wasn't it?"

Olivia swallowed, her hands trembling as she held them up at her shoulder height. Then she slowly nodded.

Thomas chuckled and took her right fingers in his free left hand. He kept his gun pointed right at her face, but he tugged her toward him. She took a tentative step and didn't flinch as he leaned down to breathe in her ear.

"Don't think you're going to honeypot me, babe," he whispered, his lips brushing against the shell of her ear. "Remember I have just as much training as you do. But I like you, Livvy. I always have. This doesn't have to go badly for you. I can keep you safe from Salvaje, from Green. From everyone. You just have to trust me and do what I say, all right?"

He caught her earlobe between his teeth and nipped lightly. "Can you do that for me, babe? I really don't want to kill you. I *like* you, Livvy. Always have. Ever since DC."

Olivia nodded, and slowly put her left hand down. Thomas straightened up and looked down at her with eyes gone dark and intense. "Good," he said. "Good girl. You just keep being reasonable and you'll stay alive."

He tightened his grip on her right hand and led her back to the road. They emerged from the jungle a few meters behind the pickup truck, and he kept walking, kept pulling her behind him until they reached the tailgate. Then he spun, slammed her up against the rear of the vehicle and leaned in with a moan to devour her mouth with his.

Olivia kissed him back, letting her tongue tangle with his while her free hand pressed against his pectoral—or rather, the body armor covering his pectoral muscles. She shifted her hips to press closer to his and let her fingers trail down over his stomach until they reached his belt...

And the clip of the folding knife.

"Fuck," Thomas murmured into her mouth. "Goddamn, Livvy. I've wanted you so bad for so long. You have no idea. I dream about that night all the time... you'll see, baby. I'm gonna be so good to you. You're gonna be so glad you stayed with me. I'll make you forget every other man you've ever met. Ever."

Olivia let a soft, needy sound out on a breath, and Thomas took the bait. He plunged his left hand into her hair, cupping the back of her head. His right hand, unfortunately, still held the gun on her, but it was no longer pointed at her face.

She let her right hand join her left on his belt and began tugging at the fastening. A low, masculine chuckle rumbled up from his chest as she pulled the tail end through the buckle.

"Fuck, yeah. I knew you still wanted me. That's it, baby, take what you want."

*I will*, she thought as she let the folding knife slip off the belt into her right hand. With her left, she reached inside his fly and let her fingers trail across the waistband of his boxers while she carefully thumbed the knife open by her side. Then, as Thomas leaned in to ravage her mouth again, she let her left hand grip lower long enough to distract him as she whipped her right hand out and up to bury the knife in the side of Thomas's neck.

The lousy four-cylinder engine of the work van whined, tools shook loose from their hooks, and spools of wire tumbled across the cargo area as Matty tore down the dirt jungle road. He winced as the shocks bottomed out in a particularly deep rut that nearly caused him to hit his head on the roof.

"What's going on, Fed Girl?" he asked. "Can you hear me?"

After the shouting and gunfire died off a loud scuffle had come through the connection and then there was a new sound. It made him wince for a whole new reason.

"Are you *kissing* that guy? The fuck kind of tactic is that?"

He turned the van hard as the road curved and immediately slammed down on the brakes. Olivia was supposed to be positioned another quarter mile up the road, but he saw his truck less than fifty feet away. His seat belt locked up as the van slid to a stop mere feet from Olivia and a man he assumed was Thomas.

She wasn't kissing him anymore.

There was nothing intimate about the knife she had buried hilt-deep in his neck. The sneer on her face held nothing of lust and nothing of desire shined in her eyes. Instead, her expression screamed pain, betrayal, sorrow, and loss all at once. Thomas stared at her, his face inches from hers, mouth agape. He coughed and blood spattered across Olivia's face and shirt.

Matty tore at his seat belt and bolted through the door. He was barely upright when Olivia ripped the blade through the rest of Thomas's throat. Arterial blood sprayed, covering her in a thick coat of red. Eyes pleading, Thomas dropped to his knees, hands clutching at his ravaged throat. Blood poured between his fingers as he stared up at her, choking and unable to breathe. His mouth moved as if to speak, but only managed gurgled gags.

Olivia remained still as a statue as she watched her one-time friend, and apparent lover, collapse to the dirt and fall still. Her wild, wide eyes never left Thomas and she still held the blade in the air. Blood ran down her hand, covered her face, soaked her hair, and stained her shirt.

Slowly, Matty walked up to her, his hands up in a comforting manner.

"Hey, Fed Girl, you with me?"

She didn't move. Didn't answer.

"We gotta get moving. The rest of those guards will be hot on our asses in no time."

Still nothing. She just continued to stare down at Thomas.

Matty's jaw tightened with the mental flash of a young man's pleading face. Plastic on the floor. Memories of twisted emotions of loyalty, friendship, and betrayal. The flash of gunfire. Instant remorse. A clap on the shoulder. Crumpling plastic. A bright red drop of blood running down the side of a gold ring identical to his own.

"You gotta let him go, Fed Girl," Matty finally said, shoving the memory back into the depths of his mind where it belonged.

Again, she didn't respond.

She looked so young in that moment. Like a child, really. One that needed help finding their way back. CIA or not, no training on the planet could have prepared Olivia for what she'd just had to do. Matty knew all too well. He stepped up and gently took her knife hand in his, pulling the blade from her grip. He closed it and tossed it in the bed of his truck.

"Fed Girl," he tried again.

Nothing.

"Olivia!" he finally shouted.

She jerked as if she'd been shocked and her eyes met his, still wild and unfocused. He gripped up upper arms and kneaded them. Her face crumpled and tears welled up in her eyes.

Matty ripped the jacket off and began using the cotton lining to wipe the blood from her face. "I gotchya, I gotchya. Shake it off, Fed Girl. Don't waste your tears on a fuckstick like that guy. You did what you had to do. It was him or you."

The tears never fell but her eyes darted back to the dead turncoat.

Matty took a deep breath.

"We have to go." He looked down at Thomas and back to her. "Look, I get it. Trust me, if there's anyone on this fucking planet that gets it, it's me. He was your friend. You two had history. A relationship. It's fucked up and it's hard, but you can't have a mental breakdown over that right now. He's dead and you're not. If you hadn't acted, he'd have killed you. Kill or be killed. That's just how it is." He gave her a gentle shake. "You gotta snap out of it. The mission ain't over yet. *Your* mission, Olivia. You dragged my ass into this shit and I'll be god-fucking-damned if we get this far only to fuck it up now." He lifted her chin with a gentle finger and looked right into her eyes. "You promised to take me home, remember?"

There was movement behind her eyes. Something snapped back in place and she stood straighter and her shoulders squared. She sucked in a deep breath through her nose and pushed a blood-soaked lock of hair behind her ear.

"Took you long enough to get here."

"Excuse me, your highness," Matty said, his lips curving in a smile.

"I was a little busy doing all the hard stuff while you hung out in the truck." He raised his eyebrow. "Did you blow it yet?"

Olivia smiled. And if it didn't quite reach her eyes, he gave her credit for trying. "That's an awfully personal question, Matty."

His cheeks burned and they must have turned red because she actually laughed. Olivia reached into her pocket and pulled out a small device that looked like a lighter. She depressed a black button on the end and smiled.

"Consider it blown."

A confused look crossed her face and she reached into her other pocket and pulled out her phone. "I've got full service now. Salvaje must have had something jamming commercial cell signals. Good sign that the EMP worked."

"Good," Matty grunted and tossed the bloody jacket to the ground as he made for his truck. "Now let's get the fuck out of here."

He jumped into the driver's seat and brought the engine to life. Olivia climbed in and they took off, slinging dirt and rocks onto Thomas's body. Matty pulled out his own phone and dialed.

"Enrique. Yeah. Time for you to go from *mostly* even to even. I need a boat."

A salty ocean breeze fluttered Olivia's hair as she stood from the sedan. The warm Florida sun shone brightly overhead and seagulls squawked in the air. Matty stood from the other side and adjusted his sunglasses. She spared a thought of thanks for her own shades as she took a moment to appreciate the sight of Matty in his tailored Italian suit with a brown leather duffle in his hand. He wore a white dress shirt with no tie and the triangle of tanned skin at his throat acted like a beacon for her eyes.

Olivia pulled her mind back to business and walked around the front of the car to join him on the sidewalk. They stood in front of a pastel pink two story home on the water in the Florida Keys. Matty hadn't been messing around when he'd set his mother up while he slummed it in Venezuela. It made her wonder just how much cash he'd managed to squirrel away in his days as an enforcer.

For just a moment, jealousy spiked through her. There was no way she'd ever be able to afford anything half that nice on her salary. And she was the good guy.

Olivia paused at that thought. It wasn't right of her to think of Matty as the bad guy. Not anymore, anyway. Dirty past or not, he was definitely a good guy. She was happy she'd been able to get him a fresh start with a clean slate. He even had a new name and everything.

They reached the front door and Matty sat his bag down and removed his sunglasses to look at her properly.

"Well, Fed Girl, it's been real." He shrugged. "Not real fun, but real all the same." He grinned down at her.

"Oh, come on," she said, forcing her lips to smile and her tone to sound light and teasing. "Admit it. You're gonna miss me."

He snorted and knocked on the door. "I'm gonna miss you like I'm gonna miss that shit hole." Nobody answered the door, and he frowned. "I told her I was coming." He knocked again.

"Please . . . you know I was the answer to all of your prayers."

"You're more like a curse that won't quit no matter how much holy water I dump on it. Where the hell is she?"

On impulse, Olivia reached out and took his hand. "Matty," she said, her voice low and suddenly serious. "I just . . . Thank you. Not just for the mission but for the other thing. After Thomas . . ."

Matty swallowed and nodded, his eyes dark on hers. "You're welcome," he said.

"I just need," she squeezed his hand once before letting it go. "I just need you to know that I'm grateful. And I need to know that you'll take this second chance seriously. Please don't go looking for—"

"Trouble?" he asked, the ghost of his smile returning. "You don't have to worry about me, Olivia."

Matty tried the handle. It turned and the door opened right up. He rolled his eyes and rubbed his temple with his free hand.

"You gotta be kiddin'me." His Brooklyn accent was thick as his irritation came through in his words. "*Ma!* Why you leavin' the door unlocked for everybody in the neighborhood to come in? Any mook could just waltz in here and do whateva they wanna. What are ya thinkin', ma? Ya gotta use ya head!"

A loud, high-pitched feminine voice from deep in the house answered, the accent even thicker than Matty's. "This is my house and if I wanna leave the door unlocked, I will. Don't show up here after all these years tellin' me how to run my house like you own the place!"

"I *do* own the place, ma! Who the hell do you think paid for it?"

A thin woman with thick salt and pepper hair in a braid down her back wearing black tights, black heels, and a pink silk button down shirt rounded the corner. She froze for a long second, eyes wide with emotion. Then the corners of her mouth turned down and she leveled Matty with a scolding look. "Don't talk to me with that attitude, young man. I am your motha!" Her eyes landed on Olivia and they doubled in size. "Oh my gawd, Matty she's *gorgeous*!" Her eyes, bright and intelligent, took her in in a second, landing on her left hand. "And she's not wearing a ring, eitha'."

"Come on, ma..."

She gave him a dismissive wave and reached for Olivia's hands. "Hey, darlin', how are ya? Come on in! Matty, why are you makin' her wait outside and why haven't you introduced us yet? I'm Stella, Matty's motha."

"I'm Olivia," she answered, pressing her lips together to keep the laughter from spilling out as she allowed herself to be pulled into the house.

Stella grinned, her teeth bright against vibrant red lipstick. "It's so nice to meet you, Olivia. Are ya hungry? You look hungry." Stella smacked Matty on the shoulder. "Why does she look so hungry? How come you didn't feed her? Gawd, what is wrong with you?" She gave Olivia an apologetic look. "I'm sorry, sweetheart. I don't know what happened to this one. His fatha was a gentleman. A real class act, ya know? We did our best, but I guess you can only do so much. Matty! Close the door! You're letting all the air conditioning out! Come on, Olivia, I've got a lasagna in the oven. We can get to know each other while we wait. So, are ya Catholic?"

Olivia lost control and laughed out loud at Matty's sigh of utter defeat. The enticing aroma of homemade lasagna filled her nose, and she could have sworn she heard Matty chuckle close behind her.

# SUPPLIES PARTY

## Michael Z. Williamson & Jessica Schlenker

***Somewhere in Redactistan, during the War***

The truck-sized generator coughed and spat black smoke, but finally settled into a discontented thrudding not-hum. Anyone with a shred of mechanical inclination knew the machine was on its last legs, if not last stubs. Sergeant First Class Thompson growled and nodded at Natasha's multitool.

"I follow the manual, give up, threaten it with percussive maintenance and it just fucks off harder. *You* show up, and it turns over. And you're not even a 52D, you're an EM whatsathingy."

SSG Natasha Cassidy detailed, "Electromagnetic Spectrum Intrusion Security Specialist. But my dad runs a generator shop in Tucson. It did watch me get angry last week, and tear the clinic's unit apart." Natasha shrugged. "I have to make up the foot of missing leverage somehow." She looked up at him from barely over five foot tall.

The Hesco berm blocked what little breeze there was. The layers of mesh above didn't provide credible shade. Sun, desert heat, generator emissions. It was *hot*. Sweat disappeared as fast as it formed and didn't feel cooler. The air stank of diesel.

She scowled at the generator. "But I don't trust it. These were old when Daddy brought one in to rebuild for a local ranch, and this data plate says it's even older than that one. All of my UPS batteries are burning out from the line surges this thing keeps shoving out, even with power conditioning. If my computers get fried . . ." She didn't finish the thought. Everyone knew what real risks that involved.

She added, "I could adapt some of the laser designator batteries with a crossover connection, but it's not like the grunts will let me have those."

Thompson said, "We were supposed to get a replacement for Number Three, two months ago. Supply keeps promising it's supposed to be on the next lift. I don't even know if a replacement for *this* has made it on the list yet."

"Just like my damn batteries," she grumbled.

"At least it's not the ones for your vibrator," he joked.

She locked eyes and said, "Plug-in is superior. But if you need some for *your* vibrator, I know who has a stash of AAs."

Martinez, the Engineer officer walked up. He was reedy and tanned and looked relieved.

He nodded and spoke loudly enough to be heard. "Thompson, Cassidy. Got it running I see."

Thompson said, "Mostly her, Major. But yes, still running. I told you about the valvetrain wear. And the engine management module."

Natasha said, "I bypassed the thermal safety with a jumper."

Martinez winced. "So the sensor is shot."

She shook her head. "No, sir, the sensor is fine. It's just so goddamned hot it thinks it's melting."

He pointed up at the sun and said, "It's not wrong."

"But if it does get much hotter it will crap out. Assuming the dust doesn't do the mechanicals in first."

Martinez shook his head. "Yeah. These have a ten-year operating span. Here, it's eighteen months."

She shrugged. "It's all I can do, sir. I'll email an article on shunts and bypasses, but we'll probably be flipping the battle shorts if it gets much worse."

Martinez winced. Bypassing all the safeties was an extreme measure, and there'd be a ton of paperwork from the failure that would follow shortly thereafter.

"I appreciate the update. I'll ask for more gear. Again."

When the Major left, Thompson gestured towards the admin block. "Back to the data mines, then, nerd."

Natasha replied, "Back to the tower of air conditioning and fresh coffee, you mean."

She added, "Air Defense's main generator is still down, too."

Thompson looked tense. "What about the backup?"

She shrugged. "Supposed to have two. One is a split unit. It's in the same shape as the power gen. The sand is killing it. Their separate backup is on order."

"Delivery when?"

"It's also been three months."

Right then a buzzing noise overcame the thrum of the generator. They both looked up.

Natasha mouthed, "Get bent, Leroy," and made a gesture at the device's camera.

The quadcopter joggled as if nodding. It lowered, orbited, hovered right in front of her chest, maneuvered out of the barrier, lifted back into the air, and back into patrol formation outside the camp perimeter, with occasional passovers for security scans.

She left the generator revetment and trudged past the double-barriered Air Defense position on this side—the battery had one at approximately each cardinal point. Reassuring, and they worked. The barely protruding quad launcher with an empty tube and scorch marks was proof of that. Several of the decoy drone buckets were empty, too. From there, she crunched across the gravel, over power conduits, back to the HQ bunker. "Bunker" wasn't really the right word. Between Hesco, impact mesh, camouflage and diffusion screens, it was an amorphous blob that looked like a rock outcrop until one was quite close, and secure against most threats. She entered through the dogleg, gave her eyes a moment to adapt from scorching sun to inside, and stepped over to the EM lab, nicknamed the Coffee Shack, though half of the denizens operated on Red Bull.

She stowed her civvy phone in a slot, coded the door and entered. Body armor off and ready at hand with sidearm, helmet next to it. This place had to be kept air conditioned if they wanted to have any kind of technical defense, and stay alive. It was relatively frigid. They kept it at 68° F. It was 117° F outside. She felt the sweat here as it evaporated. Her skin chilled against her uniform fabric. It was just bright enough for footing, dim enough for dozens of monitors with glare-free screens to illuminate everyone like ghosts. Cable runs with color-coded ties ran neatly around and behind everything.

"Having fun, Leroy?" she asked SPC Adam Jenkins. He was sitting at the monitor bank with the shifting drone views and the fixed cameras, a can of Red Bull far enough aside to not damage anything if it spilled. He was tall, lanky, with arms like a spider. She checked the other screen that had all the commo waveforms running as they should.

It wasn't just concern on her part. Until they got a new Electronic Warfare officer, she was covering that slot. Or rather, faking it as well as she could. They were even short of personnel here.

Jenkins spoke while staring at his screens. "Yeah, it's all cool. I very professionally did not try to get a drone view of Shraybman, despite her tauntingly having the shower trailer door open while toweling herself off."

The female showers opened toward the perimeter barrier, but she still should have closed the door. There was a difference between banter, teasing, and risking an altercation.

"Sigh. I'll talk to her."

Her military phone pinged. She pulled it and glanced. It was the reminder about the commander's meeting.

"I have to pretend to be in charge. If you need backup, call Brach."

Jenkins nodded. "He's supposed to be back soon."

At least the recent transients hadn't looted their jammer units yet. Brach was doing a manual count, just to be sure they hadn't. His shift overlapped hers by only a few hours, but today's priority was tracking the ever-failing equipment and ensuring they had *some* of their necessary tools available. The last unit had been particularly greedy.

Modern war ran on power and technology more than anything. Forward Provisioning Base Vernon had only two hundred and fifty odd troops, but tons of equipment and ongoing replenishment. Aircraft brought in gear. Drones moved it. Drones guarded it. Computers tracked it. They sucked water from an aquifer that was no longer an oasis despite the name, and used the terrain as the basis for their construction and defense.

Movie audiences liked the glamour of men fighting, but the reality was far less visual. The enemy tried to hack, Natasha and two people successfully stopped them, with a variety of software. Jenkins' element created shifting algorithms for the drones that defended the physical position, against incoming weapons. Air defense stood by to actually shoot down threats that made it within that perimeter. That was a mix of drones, missiles, and saturation charges on close-range rockets that would fill a volume with frag as a last resort. After that, they'd rely on sandbags and concrete.

All the while, logistics leapfrogged forward from base to base, staged for whichever ground element needed it. High overhead, aircraft and their drones meshed with the networks below, and that of satellite imagery from above. In theory, it all created an impenetrable shield. In practice, it was non-stop skull sweat, understanding that a single miscalculation could mean death. The tech teams did not have the tolerance for slots filled with deadweights. The people had to mesh as well as their tools.

Colonel Silvestri's door was open, with several officers and senior NCOs already seated. He nodded as she stepped in and took the nearest empty in the cluster.

His phone chirped for attention just as he waved her in. He hit the speaker. "Silvestri. Secure but in conference."

Admin SFC Cedric Prescott's voice, curt even for him, crackled over the line. "Sir, advisory and FRAGO. Infantry unit coming through, 2-239. Redirected due to enemy hot spot. We're bedding them down for three days and they're expecting resupply, plus extending them support as needed. They're supposed to move further inland after that."

Silvestri swore and his jaw clenched. "Jesus Christ, we can't get a break. They'll take everything not nailed down."

Major Daniels, the Logistics commander added, "And what they don't take is failing as we speak."

Prescott sounded as frustrated as Natasha felt. "It's boggling how much leeway they still get in the modern era."

Silvestri continued, "Without us they die in three days, but we're 'support.' Only the way nurses in the ICU 'support' a patient on machines. Alright, clear B Block shelters, everyone consolidate. There goes our privacy." He paused. "I wonder if we can get them to help order the shit we need?"

"We can ask," Prescott replied.

"Silvestri out."

He looked at the Engineer. "Major Martinez, any good news on generators?"

"I had Sergeant Cassidy assist, with her background. It's improved for now."

"But still failing," Natasha noted. "It is jury rigged to hell at this point. We're asking miracles."

Martinez continued, "Sergeant Jenkins was able to source some solar panels on the civilian market. We have them installed. They're supplemental only, but do add power to the grid and help charge batteries. They need to be swept off daily and will have a finite lifespan even if they don't get damaged in an attack. The ROWPUs are working, but we do need filters. We can only backwash so many times. That pungent taste is safe, but increasingly unpleasant."

Silvestri pinched the bridge of his nose and nodded. He looked at Natasha. "Thank you. I was afraid of that, when Jenkins said you were out assisting, just after Power rang me. And your section?"

She advised him, "Software is up to date. Our hardware is mostly up to date. We have solid control of EM signals. We have barely enough drones for the defensive grid. We could use one or two more personnel, but we've got it all working."

"That's one bit of good news. Air Defense?"

Master Sergeant Domingo had that, with Major Keaton apparently dealing with stuff in person. She said, "Everything function tests as good to go. Obviously we did burn an igniter for test yesterday. Intercept drone tracking tests ready. They're good. The Close Operation Kinetic Cannon always works. But as I said previously, we've got barely enough of any of it. We stopped that incursion three weeks ago. We can do one more like that with no concerns. After that, we'll have holes in defense and potential strikes. We're running on a single primary generator and one backup. We should have two and three."

Support was actually being run by Sergeant Major Roulet. The base wasn't deemed big enough for a Personnel Support Officer.

"The engineers assure me the water supply is adequate, and we have plenty of pallets of bottles for a short term fill. Assuming Region would actually respond at that point. I've got it secured because as Major Martinez noted, the pumped water's a little bitter. Food is coming in reliably. Recreational stuff is short, but enough—caffeine, magazines, candy."

Silvestri half-shrugged, half-nodded. "Good. We'll hang in there. Major Daniels?"

The Logistics officer rattled off, "On the support and provisioning side, transient units tell us what they want, we order, they take. Simple. When it doesn't arrive, they either take from us if they can or do without. I understand why other bases have 'inventory errors.' At the same time, that's considered harmful to warfighting and bad for career advancement. I prefer actually doing my job to the best of my abilities. On our side, we have everything we are supposed to, on paper, but a bunch of it is 'in process' and has been for months. The Golden Conex ain't coming. What we have is what there is."

Silvestri agreed, "I don't want to lie about capabilities and inventory. Besides the career hits and personal integrity, our job is to keep those maneuver elements alive. They're less of a problem than the massive backlog that just can't get things delivered."

Daniels said what they all knew. "It's cost, contracting, environmental statements and restrictions, transportation regulations, it never ends."

Natasha knew that wasn't entirely correct. Leroy's side hustle and civilian training let him run a second set of books. Several items had been combat- and environment-lossed, reported as stripped or disposed of. He'd even done the HAZMAT paperwork, swearing up a storm in three languages as he did so. It didn't get them additional gear, but it might save some of what they had.

Daniels noted, "We need bigger elements. They sized the base around the supply line, then massively increased the supply line."

Silvestri nodded. "I know. We even had the Engineers write us an approval and recommendation. We're supposed to get all that stuff Real Soon Now."

SGM Roulet said, "Stress to them again that if we get a couple of failures, we become indefensible and a huge, juicy target."

Silvestri agreed. "I'll be taking that up with Brigade again. They say they're aware. They keep promising. Then they get shorted higher up, who's being shorted by Congress, and they can't endanger their precious boots on the ground."

Daniels commented, "If we die, they die."

Silvestri sighed. "Everyone knows that, but it's politically impossible to say it. Okay, I've held a meeting, I can report I have done so. Everyone released back to your duties, thank you very much."

At that moment, fireworks sounded and the attack alarm blared.

Natasha beat feet, punched code for the Shack, and slipped in. She grabbed headset as she sat at her station. The earpads were sticky with sweat. She'd need to wipe them down again. Brach was on duty, but she was NCOIC.

She reported, "Electromag on net. Staff Sergeant Cassidy."

She heard Leroy echo live and through audio, "Drone Net on net. Sergeant Jenkins."

Next was, "Air Defense on net. SFC Whitworth."

It was only seconds before, "Command on net. LTC Silvestri. How's it look?"

She replied, "Echo Whiskey Section. Command, all elements are networked and engaged."

"Air Defense. Command, we are active and engaged."

Two of Leroy's element arrived and thumped into chairs, brought up their screens and got to work.

Leroy's voice was clipped and professional. "Drone Net, establishing interdiction."

Through feedback, the Guard Array Network Grid drones sounded like an angry swarm of steroid-enhanced hornets, weaving into a complicated web. Outside, they'd be a dissonant mix of howls. There were firework explosions to the north. Incoming ground-hugging attack RPVs, delta-winged and jet powered, ran into swooping swarms of explosive stings. One got lucky for just a moment, dodged through a gap left by its predecessor and an empty spot in the pattern. Then a 60mm air defense missile shrieked from its pod and ended it in a cloud filled with sparkles.

Whitworth spoke, "Air Defense. Bogey destroyed."

"Sounds like quite the unwelcome party, doesn't it?" Natasha said, idly, to no one in particular.

Brach reported, "Sergeant Cassidy, we've got jamming signals, but they're uncoordinated, just noise to fill primary frequencies."

She pulled up a screen and saw the waveforms. Just noise. Technically not white noise, but that's what most people would call it.

"I see it. Nothing coded, all manageable. I do see sequenced intrusion."

Brach replied, "I think they're trying to hack through. The attack was to get our signals active for analysis at their end."

"How's coding?"

The man used keyboard and pointer to pull an insert view. "Secure. If they find a freq I'll rotate to our next cryp as precaution."

"Understood. Once this is over switch anyway. Burn the existing encryption."

"Will do."

Another voice said, "Signals on net. Staff Sergeant Troub. USAF control is in contact, assets loitering."

Right then a second inbound got GANGbanged in an orgy of fire. The video was glorious.

"Air Defense. Command, intercepts successful. We should be secure momentarily."

Jenkins grumbled. "They could have held off another ten minutes. I'd be in my bunk asleep by now." He was busy watching a geometric blur of drones. Three did their jobs and vanished, he launched a half dozen more to keep the levels up.

"Is that what we're calling it now?" Leroy's assistant commented.

"Fine, Watson," Jenkins replied, rolling his eyes. "I'm really just after the medicinal round of *World of Warcraft*."

"*Medicinal* Warcrack? I need that prescription," Watson replied.

Natasha shrugged again as the boys discussed their favorite mods. She preferred books out here, since the only lag was how long it took to turn a page. The attack was under control, only costing them money and shorting them on munitions.

Outside, it sounded like the would-be partiers got the hint delivered by the missiles . . . mostly. She tagged their updates to Command.

Ten minutes later, *All Clear* sounded.

"Command. Secure from Alarm Red. Exterior perimeter remains Red until cleared by EOD and MPs."

The debris could be toxic, unexploded, and a slim chance of useful intel. Not that most troops normally got outside the wall at all. There was nothing to see or do, and risk of eating a munition drone.

Leroy sighed, "Gah. So now we're down fifteen more GANG. At least Air Defense was able to launch."

"What's the margin now?" She leaned back and looked at his screens.

"We're at one hundred fourteen percent of baseline."

"Damn." Assuming ten percent down for repair or replacement, that was under 4% safety margin over what was considered the minimum necessary. They wanted 50%, but they were still waiting for resupply on those, too.

After shift, Natasha trudged to the chow hall, grabbed a bowl of glop and some uninteresting bread. She took a seat next to a couple of MPs.

Oteroy was a big SFC out of New York, Army Reserve, apparently a security guard in the civilian world. He almost never cracked an expression. Whitney Shriver was 19, fresh from AIT, and stuck close to her mentor. She bunked in the hooch next to Natasha.

"Hey," Natasha offered minimally.

Shriver replied, "Hey. Heard the excitement."

Natasha dipped bread and took a bite before replying, "Yeah, we stopped it. They're not very sophisticated but they're getting better."

This was supposed to be chili. She grabbed Tabasco sauce and added a dollop.

She didn't say it, but Oteroy said it for her.

"We're getting short on munitions."

"Yes. It won't be technical skill that kills us."

He said, "They're sorting debris now. You'll hear if there's anything of use."

She shrugged. "It would mostly be software, minimal intel. The hardware is all Chinese off the shelf."

She was too tired to talk. She ate, nodded and mumbled, cleared tray and left. She carried her battle rattle rather than the effort of donning it. Even this late it was oven-hot. The air smelled of some sort of rot from the drainage sump. The same breeze blasted sand at her.

At her billet, she banged her feet on the pallet in the vestibule to clear off some of the sand, and stepped in.

Her hoochmate was there, down to bra and panties. Shraybman had to get custom bras, which were very much not Army issue strapping, but definitely provided support. Natasha had two good civvie bras she kept on hand for the hottest, longest days. They were supposed to wear PT uniform here, but even with AC it was barely tolerable.

"Hey, Iris."

"Hey."

Sergeant Iris Shraybman glanced up, reached and pulled a curtain across to contain light. With that and the door closed, it was gloomy enough Natasha could sleep comfortably. Not that she ever had an issue in the Army—when you had a chance, you slept. But a bunk in a dark can with AC was more than adequate, especially with a roommate who had basic manners.

"Leroy said you left the shower trailer door open."

Shraybman audibly shrugged. "Why was he looking?"

"He didn't."

"It's so fucking hot in there. Open the door and woof, evaporation."

"I know." All the females had to share five showers. In a Six Sigma rush to minimize space, personnel, and materials, the Army had gone from trimming fat to cutting muscle and bone. Everything was short.

Though they did bunk two females per expandable, instead of six. For now.

She offered, "I'll see if we can get a couple of draw-through fans."

"I can install them if you do." Shraybman was in Mechanical-Electrical Section.

"Those may not be super high demand. We'll see. Sleep ops."

"Night."

Jokes aside, Natasha did not try to enjoy mechanical devices in her hooch. She probably could. Shraybman was rather blunt about a lot of things. The woman had been a stripper at one point. Natasha didn't want anyone hearing a breath of her doing anything. The dichotomy of being able to sleep anywhere and wanting to be alone at the same time.

She peeled down to bra and panties herself, and racked out.

The arriving convoy was visible on GPS and visually by billowing dust before it crested the low hills south of the oasis. Four Remote Operated Air Suppression Trackers defensive RPVs in high ground effect patrolled each flank. Front and rear were Mobile Air Defense Drone Opposing Gun Systems ready to stop incoming. Inside that nest were other support vehicles and several IFVs. Despite being called an "infantry" unit, three quarters of the element were other MOSes in a modern war. The Persian al Bayt might be socially backward savages, though one never said that in public against charges of racism, but they did have an effective technological base.

Natasha watched scrolling info on RF signals against possible intrusions. Both Jenkins and Brach monitored their screens as well. The other troops of each team were asleep.

Silvestri stood behind and watched their monitors as the stretched-out line approached. The MPs and drone network operators confirmed IFF, itinerary, and direct contact with the unit commander. Then the angry swarm of GANG wove a defensive screen overhead as the gates opened to allow passage.

He observed many of the inbound elements, and it seemed to be curiosity and awareness. He never interrupted or stuck his nose in it. They worked, he watched.

Nodding, Silvestri commented, "Thanks, soldiers. Going out to meet our guests."

The maneuver troops bedded down in the prepped section of Tent City and immediately set about looting the PX of every energy drink, soda, candy bar, much of the coffee, all the women's fitness magazines, batteries, and a bunch of lotion and sunblock. Within two hours the utility section was repairing the laundry trailer, and unclogging latrines.

Then the chow hall was hit like a three-legged gazelle on the savannah. Within minutes the cooks were frantically slapping sandwiches together, having run out of hot food and reluctant to get ahead of the planned menus.

Natasha, Jenkins, and the rest of their section were swamped with requests for more bandwidth on official phones, and complaints that civilian phones couldn't connect.

"*Of course not,*" Brach grumbled as he double checked his scrambling units were still working. He was far crustier than his 22 years, with a bushy moustache and shaven head.

"Just like they're not getting any more bandwidth," agreed Natasha. "That'd be more obvious than a line of pizza deliveries."

The man grumbled, "That, and they were pissing against the berm rather than walk ten meters to the latrine. I had Watson buzz them with a couple of recon drones, used illumination. They got the hint."

She nodded. "Good. No need to log that this time."

Thus limited, the grunts settled for being boisterous, loud, and committing random but careless destruction. None of them deliberately broke anything. However, they considered it the height of humor to throw each other against the shelter sides to bounce off.

Eventually, panels popped free or bent, and then Engineers's Structural Section had to effect repairs. Jenkins came on shift, bitching up a storm, as it was his shelter they'd chosen for horizontal trampolining.

"They're supposed to break enemy shit, not ours. They stopped when the MPs came by."

Natasha commented, "I hit the PX early. They cleaned it out of everything snack-related including jerky and even diet sodas. Everything is gone. And I heard the walls bouncing from our end of C Block."

That evening, the other four bunks in her can were occupied by women from the engagement unit, who stayed up late watching movies and talking loudly.

Surprisingly, supplies did arrive the next morning. A Skyhook twin-rotor with a fleet of quads pinged IFF, called on voice, was cleared through Jenkins' network, and hovered in to drop on the painted circles of the LZ, blasting grit in all directions. Available troops would always watch. It broke up the monotony, and there might be cool stuff to loot quickly. Possibly candy or snack food. The pallets were placed and even stacked properly. Those drones were largely automated, but there was a controller aboard the bird as backup. Either way, the wrapped bundles were staged and waiting.

None of the subordinate craft were big enough for a generator, or a kit for one.

Nastasha tagged along with LTC Silvestri to the LZ, hoping that some of the smaller batteries for her backup units had arrived.

Martinez said, "So we have a tank of fuel, good, but no generator."

Daniels sounded mild but frustrated. "They commoed that it exceeded assigned mass allowance."

The infantry officer, a Lieutenant Colonel Hampton, shrugged. "I asked. They said it was in your supply chain, not mine, and mentioned excessive mass."

Martinez groused, "Of course it's massive. It's a generator. I'll take parts and do a rebuild on site if we have to."

Silvestri growled quietly, meeting Natasha's glower. It was well and good to supply the pointy end, but without a shaft, the spear didn't work. So they got the shaft.

There was nothing to do but keep on.

"They did get us the fuel, replacement water filters, and an additional cube of bottled water."

"Useful, but not what we needed most."

Hampton added, "I'll note again the urgency. I owe you for giving my boys and girls a little leeway on stress relief."

Duty shifts could be chaotic, especially in 24/7 taskings. Natasha clumped into the Coffee Shack, slid into her seat, logged in, and checked ephemeris and schedule.

"Sergeant Cassidy, want a beer?" Brach asked, setting a can on the desk beside her.

She picked it up and stared at the label. "Holy shit. Yes. And make sure these cans get melted afterward. Where did those come from?"

"The Infantry got them in the supply drop." He sounded almost amused. Almost.

"How much?"

He shook his head. "No charge."

"No, I mean how much did they get?"

"Oh, a couple each. Though some horse-traded and got extra. Don't worry, they're not sick or violent, just loopy. And yes, they donated us a few. They were listed as sodas."

She calculated and groused, "That could have been a crate of batteries or some drones."

"Yeah. And they'll justify it as 'warfighter morale.'"

"And blame us if caught. Enjoy it quick and destroy the evidence."

She popped the tab and took a swig. It was low-grade commercial beer, but damn, it was cold and refreshing. Well, cooler than outside, possibly cooler than room temp. Whatever.

"I'm going to get buzzed tonight."

"What, you got more alcohol?"

"No. Batteries."

"Teasing bitch." He glanced at her side-eyed. "Wait, you said one twenty volt."

She smirked. The joke was all the pleasure she was going to derive right now.

The infantry platoon and four "support" platoons moved out the next day. They took one of the GANG drone launchers, leaving the base with two. They took one of the counterfire batteries, and a chunk of the available ammo. They'd have taken more, but Jenkins' and Daniels' database "errors" only admitted to a smaller loadout number.

LTC Hampton did leave some batteries the techs could adapt for backup in the Shack, and one deadlined ADA vehicle with a partial complement of 60mm missiles. It was far less effective than the unit he took.

Jenkins muttered. "So now we're even lower on critical gear. Divesting ourselves is supposed to be an emergency evacuation item, not routine operation."

Natasha wondered aloud, "What now?"

Jenkins quietly offered, "I have sources... but I don't think the Commander would like them."

"Leroy... at this point, I think he would."

"Okay, if you want to tell him..."

Natasha stirred as the door rattled. "Unh?"

Shraybman muttered, "Sorry. We were still fixing shit the grunts broke." She held up a bandaged finger in the crack of light from outside. "It takes effort to break a touchpad lock."

"Goddamn."

"I'll change in the dark. Didn't mean to wake you."

"It's cool," she replied as she laid her sweaty head back into the pillow. That despite the AC.

The morning briefing wasn't good.

Martinez started with, "Generator One, nicknamed Brutor, is having intake and mix issues from the sand. We don't have spare injectors. Back-ordered since last month. It's running, but I don't know how long. Gen Two is struggling with the heat, after Staff Sergeant Cassidy helped us duct tape it along. Three is running, but if it starts having issues, we'll have no backup at all, and if any of them fail completely we'll be overloading the other two. There's a list of other parts and tools we need, but those are critical. Water filtration is still an issue. The ROWPU has a finite output. Climate control is working for command, comm, intel, security, the clinic. Everyone else will have to be patient. That's a manpower issue."

Yeah. Iris was running 16–18 hours daily doing not only her section repairs, but any others.

Silvestri said, "We're told there's an additional supply run today. We'll see."

After the briefing, there was in fact another acrial supply drop, that included a rather sizeable cargo lifter, human piloted. He brought it in, dropped down, and idled the engines.

The ramp dropped, and a heavy, wheeled box with a stubby exhaust pipe appeared. In the meantime, drones homed on their tags, dropped their bundles and pallets, and idled awaiting signal. The pilot got clearance, flipped a notional salute, and lifted.

Daniels looked at the boxy generator. "Oh, good, that covers air defense."

Major Keaton growled up at the sky.

"That's the wrong type!"

Daniels held up his tablet.

"It's the right power. One fifty kW."

Natasha replied, "That's a standard power generator. Sixty Hertz. Air Defense uses four hundred Hertz. That's why we specified that one."

"Depot supply said this was a suitable substitute."

Keaton swore. "Well, it fucking isn't. There's an adapter set we can use, but I doubt we can get that either. That's been on order since previous rotation."

Daniels sighed. "Meanwhile, some contract office weenie just put themselves in for a bonus for saving the Army money with a substitute."

Natasha said, "At least we can use that as backup for our others."

Daniels shrugged. "I will try to get another order through."

Power Section gratefully took the generator, even if undersized. In an hour they had it set, staged, grounded, connected to distribution, and belching diesel smoke. The military requirement for "environmental" controls had lasted two weeks in the desert extremes, before failing equipment caused a general to risk his public relations by authorizing uncapped exhaust.

Meetings didn't improve operations, but until the base could get what it needed, discussion would continue.

Daniels sighed that, yes, everything was still on order. Some was arriving in piecemeal fashion, but nothing significant.

Nastasha broached it carefully.

"We have personnel with connections. They can source non-munitions, but it's going to take money and finesse."

Silvestri rubbed the bridge of his nose and his eyes.

"I know about Sergeant Jenkins. There is so much questionable acquisition going on, usually stolen from other units, I don't see a problem with just buying stuff outright. Get what we need, keep quiet, and if there are any questions we'll either shrug and blame last rotation, or I'll write a 'needs of the operation' exemption SOP. Let's talk to Jenkins and see what he can do."

Jenkins got called in, and sat down. He projected an odd mix of confident, but shy. *Cagey*?

"Good afternoon, sir."

Silvestri acknowledged, "Well, it's an afternoon. In the closest to hell Earth gets. I appreciate your offer of support."

The tall man nodded. "No problem. I'm here to support my unit and nation. I'll still transfer everything by proxy. My name isn't on anything."

Silvestri half-smiled. "I wish mine wasn't. Have you seen the list?"

Jenkins admitted, "I have a pretty good summary. There's routine supplies that just take money, and might be slightly below milspec, but better than nothing. There's the specialized stuff that can't be sourced outside easily. Then there's munitions. Those are tough."

Daniels asked, "Anything on top of the list you can help with?" as he handed over a sheet.

Jenkins glanced down the handwritten tally.

"I already called the Air Force for a flightline generator for Air Defense. They're the correct freq."

Daniels asked, "Trade?"

"Gift. I told them the problem. There was cussing in horror and 'sure, I'll manifest it now.' Inter-service loan. We have to return it eventually."

Silvestri closed his eyes and sighed. "It must be nice to be flush with gear."

Jenkins said, "I need to take this list with me. I'll shred and burn once I make some coded notes."

"Thank you."

When Natasha entered the Shack, Jenkins had a laptop. It wasn't connected to anything and had no modem contact. So that was his personal and very unofficial system. She let him work.

Eventually he rubbed his eyes, stretched, stood up. He grabbed a Red Bull from the mini fridge, popped it and chugged. Then he sat back down.

He looked at her and said, "I went through the list. I can get all the non-armament gear on account. They offered some discount out of patriotic duty. I won't have to blow anyone for the favor."

"Epic."

"Silvestri is going to shit when he sees the cost."

"Exceeds discretionary limits?"

He shrugged. "I don't know. It's the best I can do."

He turned the screen around.

Natasha felt her spine freeze.

"Jesus."

Jenkins ticked off, "Items, priority transport, avoiding Host Nation Customs who'd tie it up for weeks. Delivery is half the cost."

"Yeah, but…"

He continued, "I've sourced some drones. One of the oil rigs is willing to sell some explosives. Is our EOD section any good?"

"They still have all their fingers," she noted.

"If they can make it work, these won't be as good as purpose-built defensive drones, but they should thicken the defense net. Sergeant Brach says they'll require near-direct hits but should work."

"I guess you pitch it, then."

Leroy nodded. "Yup, going to see him in thirty minutes."

Jenkins came back after a half hour conference. He was tight-lipped.

"What's up, Leroy?"

"CENTCOM and Regional apparently struck all discretionary funds except as approved through them. Apparently we aren't the only ones struggling to source stuff."

Natasha boiled inside. "Can you get one missile, maybe, and drop it on them? I'm joking of course, don't court martial me."

"I thought about it. Silvestri said to hold onto the list. He'll try to find funding. *He* might have to blow someone."

"It's not that we have an effective enemy. We have four. The official enemy, Army leadership, Congress, and the fucking sand people."

Leroy grimaced.

"Okay, I can pull funds from one of the game hacks I sell. I've got other funds, too."

Natasha was curious and asked, "Do you make more money on your side gigs than the Army?"

He grinned and blushed. "A lot more."

"Why are you even here?"

"To serve my country. Doesn't mean I have to be poor in the process. I'm going to make the ultimate sacrifice and donate some other funds."

"Uh . . . which?"

Jenkins sighed, turned, and gave an almost-embarrassed smile. "I sell porn, very specifically sanitized files, malware free. No, I don't use any military computers for this. I download via an uplink bypass around the proxy protocols. I also sell that app so others can do it, along with a file cleaner that isn't as good as what I use but skims out the obvious stuff. And an anonymizer up to run inline so people like us can't track them. And yes, there's a backdoor in it just in case we need to go digging for OPSEC issues."

She was impressed. "Damn, Leroy, that's a hell of a sacrifice."

He shrugged. "We need to win the war."

"Against the enemy or the Army?"

"Yes. Do keep in mind that since I'm paying for this crap, it's mine when we're done. I'll be re-selling."

The routine supply drop three days later was positive. In it were some of the Shack's batteries. There were more filters for the ROWPUs. A precious pallet of GANG to reload one of the systems. Routine food and materials. Fuel injectors to repair Generator 1.

Natasha commented, "Well, we get to eat this week and maybe defend ourselves."

Leroy said, "There's another inbound."

"Whose?"

"Air Force. For us. Generator."

"The right type?"

Jenkins said, "It should be. They specifically referred me to Aerospace Ground Support shop, power section."

There it was, fast and low, then slowing.

The delivery was all drone—one lifter, three escorts with defensive gear. Those cleared IFF with Brach, then loitered. The cargo quad had a strapped and boarded payload half-protruding below. It eased in and down amid a maelstrom of roaring dust, made contact. The latches clacked free, the payload settled, the craft rose in a howl, blowing dust like a sandblaster, and departed with its side-bots.

Majors Keaton and Daniels jogged forward. Keaton snapped a restraining band, and used a bar to pry plywood free.

"Holy shit, that's it. One fifty kW, four hundred Hertz."

Daniels looked up at the sky. "Hallefuckinglujah." Then he made eye contact around. "Get this over where it belongs. No one say a goddamned word to anyone. We don't know where we got it or how we got it and it doesn't get logged anywhere. I can take one admin hit if necessary. Since most units are taking hundreds."

Later that day, another cargo drone pinged for attention.

Brach was at his console, and said, "Sergeant Cassidy, this is an unmarked drone. It claims to be delivery."

"Stand by." She stepped out for her civilian phone. "Call Leroy."

It buzzed, and he replied, "Yo." She could hear his game in the background, the soothing sounds of a warlock casting Rain of Fire on mobs. She felt a twinge of nostalgia for her own destro-warlock.

"We have what claims to be a supply drop. Is it yours?"

"Wow, that was quick. What's the transponder code?"

"Here." She turned her phone around to the screen, violating a ton of OPSEC and COMSEC procedures, but it was the fastest way to do it.

He glanced and nodded. "Yeah, that's it. Alibaba. Ironic name given we're right here."

She cut video instantly. "Noted. Brach, let it in."

She turned to the shift drone herder. "Watson, keep it in defensive control."

He replied, "'Insecure RPV In Airspace Threat Readiness Protocol.' Am doing."

In the morning, a fixed wing flew nearby and dropped a lander with Mesopotamian Oil markings. That settled very carefully, very exactly. HAZMAT transponder codes noted EXPLOSIVES, STABILIZED.

EOD quickly fitted the drones with fuses and charges. Air Defense took control and prepped them. The officially ordered gear was still due as well, on paper.

It all helped, and for a few minutes, the base could relax just slightly. Leroy's Commendation Medal for "above and beyond" made no mention of exactly what he did to earn it, but "promoting warfighter readiness" would get approved.

Silvestri continued to squeeze funds to pay back *some* of the items, but it became clear from his tone during the daily meetings that he was being completely stonewalled by higher up. The transient groups were *supposed* to be funding what they took, even if it was only account shifting. Commands for the last three groups through, though, had balked at admitting what was taken by their grunts, which explained some of the shortages. Even with secured video documentation of what was removed, higher up insisted that the "authoritative" count was whatever the "warfighters" claimed it was.

Daniels called it the Finance Spiral of Death, while he and Silvestri tried to prioritize what next to acquire. In the relative privacy of the Coffee Shack, lit by monitors, Natasha called it the Great Circle Jerk. Brach had cruder designations. But even with Leroy's unofficial influx of support, the base still barely kept abreast of necessities, while the time between incoming locust units decreased.

After lunch, Natasha checked network ops, scanned commo for anything funky—the enemy had actually tried to piggyback signal through standard commo, using an AI implementation to predict signal, create a parallel sound or code that presented as an echo. So far, their standard software stopped those, and confirmed the attempts. Eventually that might be a threat.

She stepped out for a latrine and fresh air break. She pulled her civilian phone from its stowage slot and glanced at it. Silvestri had texted, "Informal query when you have time."

She could take a minute, she walked through.

His door was open, she stepped in and saluted.

"You wanted to see me, sir?"

He saluted back, enough to be official but casual. "Close the door please."

She did. That was interesting. The man never had his door closed with a female present. Liability concerns.

He said, "Natasha, this isn't official, have a seat."

She slid into the nearest. "Okay, sir. What's up?"

"So, you know about the supply issue and finance."

"Yeah."

"You seem pretty down to earth and flexible."

She gave him a guarded look and raised an eyebrow. "What's up?"

"We need a fundraiser we can get all those grunts to kick in on to cover the shortage."

"Like a dance or something? Posters of hot Army chicks?"

He said the word. "Wrestling."

She raised her eyebrows and pursed her lips for a second. "Ah. *Girls* wrestling."

"In pudding."

*So it was down to that.*

She looked off to the side, took a deep breath, and replied, "Well, sure. I'll do it. I think if I ask Shraybman she'd be agreeable."

It was clear he thought he'd have to backpedal, or ask if she knew some available sluts of the three dozen odd women on site.

He almost stuttered, "Really? *You'll* do it?"

She locked eyes and said, "As long as I get a commendation medal and a glowing enlisted report, yes. Both of us. I excel at my MOS, and several others."

"That actually seems reasonable. Thank you so much. . . . It's important that we give those idiots a good show."

She rolled her eyes. "Yes, the bras might accidentally come off. That's what you're not asking, right?"

"Uh, yes." He looked horribly embarrassed.

"I'm eligible for Sergeant First Class in August."

He gave a single brisk nod. "I'll make it happen."

She reiterated, "I am really, really good at my MOS."

He nodded again. "You are. We're going to combine it with a 'martial arts competition' as cover."

She nodded. "Good. That's my next concern. I'll see that we set up interdiction on phones."

"That was the part I was originally going to ask about. The thing itself..."

She shrugged. "Compared to some other units' shenanigans, we're tame."

"Disturbingly true."

"But you're still angling for a show."

He sighed. "I don't know what else we can do at this point. We've got little to barter. What we had has been looted. Jenkins donated personal funds exceeding half my annual salary, for God's sake."

"Right after, you will have to stress to everyone here that I'm not the camp bicycle everyone gets a ride on. And I want SFC Oteroy to escort us back to our hooch. I'll have Shraybman beef up our door. It will be non-milspec. This is strictly a duty-related favor."

Silvestri looked really uncomfortable and drummed his fingers on the desk.

"Absolutely... I was planning to bow out before then for both deniability and so I don't... well..."

She halfshrugged and stared at him. "Sir, if I'm going to show my tits you may as well enjoy a look. But I don't want to hear a word about it afterward. Ever."

He might still not look... and who was she kidding? He was male. She had a rack.

He agreed with, "Fair enough."

"Is that it, sir? I'll plan for it, would rather not go into detail."

"Yes, by all means, dismissed."

She left his office, turned right, and headed for the Coffee Shack. This was rapidly getting out of hand.

She stepped in, took a deep breath.

"Leroy," she said to get his attention.

He glanced over his shoulder. "Yeah?"

"Did you discuss other fundraising with Silvestri?"

He looked puzzled. "No, just my stuff, why?"

"Okay. That's what I needed. More later."

It was bit shy of her shift end, but Brach arrived and she logged out.

✧✧✧

The vent fans *did* make the shower trailer a lot cooler. The damp evaporated off her in seconds, and her hair started drying at once. She still had dust and sand in her ears, even after swabbing them several times a day. It never ended.

Back in the hooch, she leaned past the divider to Shraybman.

"Iris, you said you were a stripper, yes?"

The woman looked up. "Yeah, for about six months before I said fuck it and joined the Army, why?"

"How did you feel about doing it?"

Iris leaned back, sat up, and said, "The first night was sheer adrenaline. After that I got used to just running through a routine and losing clothes, gathering up the cash tips and running backstage to scan the balance and get dressed."

"Would you do it again?"

The woman shrugged. "I might as long as it was a safe venue and I knew I'd get paid enough."

"Your nation needs your service."

"Do what now?"

Shraybman was in, and had experience. That would make it easier for Natasha. And they both definitely deserved promotion and decorations out of this. *Goddamn.*

Back in the Shack, she demanded, "Leroy, I need another favor. Professional."

"What's up?"

She summarized the planned activity. Concluding, she noted, "They need phones to send funds. We'll need to jam any upload attempts with the tower. I don't know what to do about recording."

He looked thoughtful. "I can set up a suspended pod with gimbaled lights to glare out any attempt at recording. They might get a couple of blurry low shots that can't really be placed. I'll sit here and monitor personally."

"We'll want to have the network set to counter-hack and alter the timestamp and geolocation." Most phones auto-updated their stored date-time from the nearest tower, which happened to be in control of the Coffee Shack, obviously. *Adjusting* that, which would also severely screw with alternative connection methods, was fairly easy. Intermittent GPS jamming was already in place for OpSec; they would just need to ensure there were no inbound flights.

"You're better at that than I am."

She nodded. "I'll write the code."

"Okay. I'll run a standard scramble as well, just because."

"Thanks. I don't mind doing the job to help us. But I don't want my career fucked over it."

He tossed his head. "Got you covered."

"And because you didn't ask, I'll make sure we get you a couple of choice images, no faces."

Jenkins half blushed, half grinned. "I can't say I haven't thought about it."

She shrugged. "You're male. You're programmed to think about it."

He shrugged back. "Try explaining that to the Army. They're still in complete denial."

"Oh, and some way to funnel donations through a clearance site."

"Sure. Any crypto and most cards, I already know where."

"I assumed you would, you urban entrepreneur."

Leroy smirked and said, "Never drugs. We mostly dealt in car parts."

Leroy had taken control of all the unofficial acquisitions as cutout for the others. Hand-written notes came to him, leaving no trace to be recovered on any network. He had his sterile laptop, the notes, and still managed his headset and station.

Out of the blue, he asked, "Pudding. Vanilla or chocolate?"

Natasha winced. "Oh, god, chocolate would look like poop. Vanilla."

"Okay, though that looks a bit like—"

"Yes, their filthy minds will go there. That's the plan, right?"

Jenkins squinted, "I think I can actually get this into a support order for the chow hall. Food is easiest to approve for any unit."

She replied, "Good. I want Thompson as referee, but I can't ask him directly."

Jenkins nodded in understanding. "I'll do it."

✧✧✧

LTC Hampton's unit rolled back in close to estimated itinerary. They arrived exhausted and filthy, swamped the shower trailers again, leaving actual puddles outside, frothy with soap residue. That added another piquant stench. It was silent for an entire six hours after that. They'd had a couple of WIA and were reserved until they had updates. Then boredom and hormones kicked in and shenanigans resumed, though at a lower level than previously.

The signs advertising MARTIAL ARTS TOURNAMENT with CASH PRIZE got attention. Immediately, they were busy gauging each other and deciding who to bet on. A QR code for donations to the base support fund did generate some needed income. The medics treated some minor contusions of troops prepping themselves for the ordeal with fists and beer.

The next night was Fight Night. The gym filled, the noise began.

Natasha hung around the Shack past start time, while Leroy confirmed, "Yes, outgoing signals blocked. Watson took his phone in. I was able to glare it out. If your coding works, we're good."

She replied with a mix of prickly reassurance. "Showtime."

She grabbed her electronics duffle, walked to the rear of the gym, through the fire exit into a vestibule, which Shriver opened and locked again behind her. Silvestri and Shraybman were both present.

Natasha demanded, "Are those EPRs written?"

"Yes."

"Great. We can sign them now. And I want to hold onto the originals."

He nodded, pulled out printouts and scrawled. She'd scan and re-file later. She didn't trust anyone on this. And of course, any kind of investigation would promptly kill those promotion chances, even in the current Army. No explanation would make it better. In fact, it might tank his career, too. She held them up, Shraybman nodded, she filed them in her duffle.

But dammit, there was no legitimate way to get the gear they needed.

She could just peek through a service window. The ground pounders had just enough smuggled beer to loosen them up, but not dangerously so. A martial arts contest was live entertainment, and they were in.

The modular gym was packed, with the cordoned and walled

area for competition, and a chute back into the latrines and changing rooms.

The first two guys came jogging out. They were young, buff, and just bright enough to not clobber each other, but tumbled around trying to get a grip, as it were. The larger one head-butted the other, clutched his opponent's knee and threw. He went for a pin.

The next pair were a bit more even, and one yelped as his knee flexed too far sideways. He tapped out. Referee Thompson called a hold. There was a pause while the medics took a quick look and feel, thumbed up, and helped him hobble out. Held breath turned to cheers. This was supposed to be friendly.

Donations trickled in, as did bets on their faves. Not enough, but it was a start.

A couple of the base MPs were in the mix. First, to give the home team someone to cheer for. Second, they were ringers. Tetao was a massive Guamanian, five foot tall and five foot across the shoulders. He simply waded in, grabbed his opponent, raised him overhead, then lowered him gently halfway before body-slamming him to the mat. Done.

Quirino was from Indonesia, a former Marine turned Army Reserve. He knew several martial arts plus Marine Corps Semper Fu. He was a blur of limbs and striking hands. His opponent was busy shouting, "Ow! OW!" while backing up to the wall, then got rolled into a tangle. He had a delightful noseful of Quirino's armpit until he was pressed to the ground and pinned.

The other bouts let the transients cheer their friends as they grappled and grunted. Some of them were quite skilled and imposingly strong.

The crowd was impressed. Jenkins arrived, caught Natasha's eye and gave a slow nod and a thumb wiggling level. They were getting there.

She took a deep breath and headed to the female shower.

Shraybman was there waiting. Her only obvious garment was a PT jacket. Her legs were bare. Natasha had tried not to think about the undress.

The woman half-grinned and asked, "Ready?"

*No.*

Natasha replied, "Yeah. I guess." She stripped down to the prepared costume.

Shraybman handed her a glass.

"A single shot of rum. Don't do more, but that should dull your nerves a tad."

"I fucking hope so." She took it and knocked it back. It burned down her throat.

She winced and said, "That's vile."

"AAFES issue."

They turned and walked to the center doors, and paused there. Oteroy and Shriver were on guard.

Overhead she heard the PA, "Now we'll have a demonstration of female martial arts."

Natasha muttered, "Here goes."

This wasn't anything like dance clubs where she'd occasionally risked flashing a date. This was brightly lit and full of very focused observers. Starting with the fact she and Shraybman were female.

Iris was a half-step ahead as they cleared the chute into the ring. That itself got the men hooting and hollering. They were hopped up on caffeine and guarana, some on smuggled vape juice, all on isolation, deprivation, and stress, supplemented with a beer or two. This just dialed them into the red. The handful of women in the unit had expressions ranging from amused to raised-eyebrows.

She glanced at Iris. They stepped forward, unzipped their oversized PT jackets, and dropped them.

They were already in lingerie. Snug, no-frills, but minimally-cut not-quite thongs, and bras that were engineering masterpieces. Iris had spray bandage over a tattoo on her calf. They were *stacked*. They were wearing superhero eye masks secured with surgical tape as backup to the electronic blurring. The crowd went wild.

Whatever she felt was a weird combination of excitement, calm awareness, and the sense of being very, very exposed.

Then two engineers dragged the tub out; a PVC pipe frame with a mylar liner.

There were sounds of, "WWWWOAH!" and such. It was obvious where this was going.

Thompson loudly announced, "On my left, The Wrench Wench. She uses Snap-on Tools! On my right, the Number Cruncher. Her favorite number is 34D!"

The crowd vibrated like heated molecules, and she saw thumbs busy with phones. *Good.* That was the point. And God, that was embarrassing. She flushed, while Iris grinned.

He continued, "So we'd like some donations for encouragement. You can place your bets. And we need to fill this tub with pudding." He indicated the pallet of jugs as someone pulled the tarp off.

The resultant roar and cheering was impressive, and scary. She was very glad they had an armed escort.

A different login code appeared projected on the gym walls. Leroy had set that up. It had no connection to DoD whatsoever. It could take any credit card, most crypto, and major bank transfers. The processor would take twenty percent. The rest would be in a sanitized crypto account he could access. Not a government monitored "crypto" either. Complete blackweb.

Gallons of pudding glopped from jugs into the pool, and some troops licked the lids and spouts. On the one hand, field conditions and you took what snacks you could get. On the other hand, generic, shelf-stable pudding was rather bland, especially compared to watching chicks wrestle.

Of course, anything they ate meant less pudding and more naked chick.

Thompson took her hand and Shraybman's, they turned and shook, meeting eyes.

She tried to indicate "ready" and Shraybman nodded with a bare smile. *Here goes.*

Natasha stepped into the creamy goo and felt it ooze between her toes. *Yuck.*

There was no point in waiting. She stepped forward, Shraybman tried for an arm bar, but not very hard. Twist, kick, and Iris went down into the pudding. Natasha stepped back fractionally. Then she felt a kick to her calf, and controlled a fall.

Pudding in panties and buttcrack was *much* worse than between toes.

Then they were on their feet again, swapping a couple of grapples, fell, back up. Pudding in hair, bra and . . . everywhere.

Well, that was enough lead up. She grabbed Iris' strap and pulled. The pre-stressed clips failed as they should, and she made a point of dramatically falling backward, waving the trophy. There was a momentary flash of bare nipple and the crowd went wild.

Then Iris collapsed across her, getting a fresh glaze of pudding. It was a staged fall, not enough to hurt, but Natasha certainly felt a whuff from the impact, and sticky goo all over.

They half-slipped back to their feet, got into the pre-planned wrist lock, and Natasha took a breath.

*The things I do in service to America*, she muttered inside.

Then leaned forward, wrapped her mouth around boob, slurped off a mouthful of overly-sweet pudding, and leaned back so Iris' bare nipple was visible again.

The noise was insane, and she even heard, "OH. MY. GOD!" Some of the women were howling in support and mild shock.

She heard a woman shout, "Damn, girl!"

At least there weren't any angry feminists. Yet.

*There better be donations pouring in. A deluge.*

In short order, she was topless too, Iris' tongue tickled and that felt weird. Then her arms were pinned, and Iris had a disturbing glint in her eyes. A moment later a vanilla-flavored tongue was against hers, and that hadn't been discussed, but, *what the hell, make the show work.* She clutched and kissed back, gave it a few seconds, then pulled away and heaved Iris down with deliberate malice.

Because that kiss had not been discussed.

The crowd of well-repressed troops liked that one. The cacophony could probably be heard in Tehran.

It became a real wrestling match, just augmented with pudding. The grunts could imagine what they wanted from there. Though she did slap her breasts across Iris' face, to much applause, even though it strained her flesh a little. Then an arm lock and takedown.

Iris came back with a clutch around her collarbones and under her crotch, fingers very visible from the front. So she spread her legs a bit to give them a good show, and then shoved back, as Iris broke their fall with armslaps and splashed pudding.

*Any time, ref,* she thought loudly. Nipples and a surprise kiss was as far as she was going.

It only felt like a half century before Thompson shouted, "We'll call it a draw!"

Natasha hopped out of the pool, turned, and PFC Shriver tossed her a towel. She made a dramatic, arms up turn for the audience, wrapped up on the second turn, and jogged back out the passage. Iris was right behind her. Oteroy was waiting. Behind was a mix of cheers of approval, and disappointment at it ending.

She spoke clearly as she strode past, "I'm going straight to the shower. Wait for Shraybman."

Oteroy nodded, "Absolutely." His face was a mask of professionalism. He had said he'd been a bouncer.

She ran in, turned the water on, stripped the thong, and started flushing pudding away from hair, ears, behind the mask as she peeled it free, pulling hair, crack of her ass, everywhere else, and wondered what *that* would do to the drain pumps. Shraybman came in to do the same behind her, and Natasha did not say a word. It seemed the woman had enjoyed that a bit much for Natasha's taste.

Facing the wall, she said clearly, "We're not dating."

Behind her, Shraybman replied, "Oh, fuck no. I got into the act but that's not me. We won't mention this again."

That was a relief.

"Agreed. We do need those pics for Leroy and Oteroy."

Shraybman agreed. "As soon as we're done here. Then we never mention it again."

Next morning, she entered the Shack feeling completely naked, despite uniform and body armor. She'd worn eyewear and gaiter while walking outside, in case she was recognized.

Jenkins glanced up and didn't undress her with his eyes. Just a glance of recognition and acknowledgement.

"Hey, Nat."

"Hey, Leroy. Here's a flash drive. Don't stick it in any military computer."

He nodded, slipped it in a pocket. His eyes were still on his screens. Without looking, he commented, "I may check it out at some point. Honestly, it's easier to not think about certain things here in the ass end of Camelstan."

She was grateful for that attitude, whether he looked or not. "Either way, thanks. The things we do for our country."

Jenkins said, "We actually got three times as much as we needed. Silvestri told me to go ahead and scrounge stuff on the market, have it delivered. I suggested a cash-out for you and Iris, but he said no."

She nodded. "Yeah, that would be a bad idea. Putting on a show can be argued as bored troops in the desert being silly. Getting paid for it . . . that would be bad."

Leroy had sacrificed cash.

She and Shraybman their dignity.

All including Silvestri were risking court martial, just to keep operating and alive.

The reward: the promotion she was due anyway.

Without facing her, he slid a drive back across the desk. "There's a crypto wallet with an access code I sent via a friend, to your Seekrit dot com account. You should wait until you're stateside. I have one for Shraybman, too. She'll need to create an account."

"Oh. That works. Thank you."

Though getting paid felt rather icky.

The afternoon brief was much more positive than previous ones. The improvised defensive drones were second tier, but plentiful, and one of the ordered lots actually was manifested for arrival. They had working generators. There was a pallet of private purchase tacticrap they could horse-trade. The departing unit had "expended" one of the missile pods per records. It was now tied back into Air Defense.

Silvestri commented, "Thanks to Colonel Hampton for that. As to the rest, I'm not going to dwell on details. I did submit decorations for several of our personnel for going above and beyond."

Under her breath, she muttered, "Beneath, between, behind."

Silvestri concluded, "We do still have some unofficial discretionary funds, which we'll manage carefully."

Major Daniels almost whistled and said, "Good, because there's one last item."

Silvestri looked over, seeming shocked. "Huh? What?"

Daniels replied, "That pudding and express delivery wasn't cheap." He handed over a bill of charges.

# BUFF ORPINGTON CROSSES THE FINISH LINE

## Buff Orpington

Hey, so, the name's Orpington. Buff Orpington. For the last while, I've been working with two of the most talented editors I've ever met, Jamie Ibson and Casey Moores, chronicling my team's misadventures through space and time after an op in Classifiedia went completely sideways. Very long story. But before the League of Conspicuous Evil's quantum handwavium bullshit portal device threw me and my team a thousand years into the future, I had a moderately successful career with one of those TLA agencies where we went places and had meetings, got into high energy trouble-shooting sessions, engaged in some ballistic problem solving, and probably broke some traffic laws.

Of course, all of those ops, the ones that didn't happen, definitely didn't happen to me. *Who, me? In El Denialador? Absurd.* I was an analyst, like everyone else who's ever worked at the Puzzle Palace. Regardless, my buddy Jamie was banging his literal face against his metaphorical keyboard, wrangling cats for this anthology—no really, he's got like, three cats at home and they love to chase his mouse cursor across the TVs he uses for monitors—and I was like, "My dude. If you need material for this shiny new anthology of yours, you know I am a source of all kinds of fictitious BS that never happened, not even that one time in Belgrade. So let's talk turkey. Well, actually, come to think of it, Casey's story is set in Turkey, so, let's talk… Finland."

So there I wasn't in St. Petersberg, not negotiating with a guy named Igor over some fuel filters that just so happened to be threaded so they'd screw onto any standard AR-15, when my phone rang. "*Zdravstvuyte,*" I said. "*Que pasa?*"

"Dammit Buff, quit with the language switching, and you *know* how I feel about Spanish right now. What are you doing?" Shawn asked. Shawn was supposed to be my backup for this op, in case the Russian mobsters making "clandestine deliveries" (running guns) proved less than trustworthy. (Weird, I know.) He'd been my oldest friend in the Agency and had only just recently come out of a mandatory mental wellness break, on account of having his entire team killed out from under him. Russian mobsters, Mexican cartels, sometimes it seemed the only difference between them was the quality of the food.

"You mean you don't know?" I asked. So much for "covering me." I held up a finger to my shipper. "*Odnu minutu, Igor.* I'm finalizing the sale on these, ahem, 'bulk fuel filters,' and you're harshing my vibe. What gives?"

"That thing, with the stuff? The one that had Liz's boy shorts in a bunch? It's on. Hurry up."

"Liz wears boy shorts? How the hell do you even know that? You know what, never mind. She's probably listening in. I'll wrap up."

*(I was, for the record, listening. Also for the record, I do* not *wear boy shorts. —Liz)*

I concluded my business with Igor, slipped the tracker into place when he turned to get the pallet jack, and passed him a valise of cash. I got back in my SUV—a UAZ Patriot, one of the better Russian SUVs, for values of "better"—put it in gear, popped the clutch, and rolled out.

The tracker in question was the key to the whole op. It was based on a new kind of tech that wouldn't get blocked by the usual problems that interfered with tracking devices. When crates get loaded into metal sea cans or into the backs of semi trucks, the metal messes with any normal tracking device's signal. Faraday cages are built to deliberately take advantage of the same principle, and Igor's people were known for how cagey they could be about their shipping pipeline. This pipeline had been causing no end of shit all over Europe and thus far, it had been impossible to trace.

Whether it was fuel filters that could easily be converted into rifle suppressors, replacement parts that would switch a standard, semi-automatic rifle into a fully automatic assault rifle, Czech, Hungarian, or Polish women looking to "make it big" in sex work, Afghan opium, Mexican coke, or Canadian maple syrup—the real stuff—the League of Conspicuous Evil had its mitts into everything. The tracker—and a dozen more like it, would broadcast its location using some new kind of highly accurate 6G cell tower signal tech that didn't matter to me. Liz, back in Operational HQ, was slowly and steadily building a map of stops, transfer points, warehouses, whorehouses, outhouses, henhouses . . . you get the point. I'd been seeding those trackers into their ports for points east, while another Agency team was seeding them in from the far side, westbound. It would be interesting to see at what point they'd cross each other on the map.

But none of that mattered now. I called Liz.

"Hey, Shawn says the thing with the stuff is a go. Where do I need to be?"

"You're going to collect Shawn, cross into Finland at Torfyanovka, common spelling. I pulled Shawn off covering you because he needed to collect your new passports. The rest of your team will meet in Helsinki at the airport."

"Rest of the team? Who?"

"Gina, for one."

For those of you who don't know Gina Torrano (pronounced like the big city in Canada), she's my Gun Girl. When I'm out, uh, not doing my job, her normal gig is definitely not covering me with some kind of "reach out and touch someone" support weapon that probably has a calibre that starts with 3 or 7. When my ass is in someone else's crosshairs, Gina's the cavalry who'll clear a corridor or plow the metaphorical road.

"Excellent. Who else?"

"Local assets from FiSIS, our local equivalent agency. Technically they're called SUPO but I am not going to be calling anyone a SUPOman and the acronym translates to the Finnish Security and Intelligence Service, so I'm going with FiSIS."

"'Local assets,' hmm? There's something you're not telling me. Are they Vikings? Are they hot?"

"Dammit Buff . . ." Liz grumbled. "You know, technically, most

Vikings were actually Danish, Swedish, or Norwegian." I could practically hear her arguing with herself over how best to say it. There's a reason I'm the faceman of the team—I'm not one of those guys who need a clue-by-four and a map to know when someone's dancing around an inconvenient truth.

I laughed. "So, they're both?"

"They're both," she admitted. "Anja and Anjelika Laukkanen. They're twins, and—"

"They're *twins?* I echoed. "Liz, you *shouldn't* have..."

"Oh, for fuck's sakes, Buff, not every girl on every op is going to fall for your charm."

"No, clearly not. But you have to admit, I'm batting six for nine right now. Wait one, I'm about to pick up Shawn."

I pulled down a side alley, unlocked the doors to the UAZ, and shifted into neutral. Shawn emerged from an alcove, I slowed to a stop, and pulled the parking brake. He threw a heavy duffel into the trunk, and slipped in up front. He gave me two bogus passports and a fist bump, and I put it back in gear. We got back on the main drag and I drove us north out of town.

"Sorry, Liz. You were saying. Viking *twins*?" I grinned at Shawn, and Shawn shook his head in exasperation, but grinned right back.

"Right. You're going to an invitation-only auction north of Kuopio. You'll get there by helicopter, which is why you're meeting the team in Helsinki. One for you and Anja, one for Shawn and Anjelika. The timing on this is tight and they need to come in as a liquor caterer so they need to go almost as soon as they get here because they need to sneak in before the event starts. Gina's here at the airport, she'll be overwatch. You and Anja will walk in the front door with the invitations I've secured for you."

"With you so far."

"The target is a MacGuffin codenamed Mirrorfox. It's a package the size and shape of a paperback book and is the prize item being auctioned at the end of the evening. Mirrorfox is—you know what, I'm not even going to give you the technical specs."

"Thank you," I replied with a grin. It was good to work with someone who understood my lack of patience when it came to technobabble. I had people for that. People like Liz.

"Basically, if it's installed in a comms system, it can deepfake real-time voice and video communications with a lag measured in microseconds. The capacity for intelligence disruption is *incredible*. The League wants it. We want to make sure they don't get it."

I shivered. The ability to edit audio and video in real time would be devastating. If one of these boxes got installed in the wrong place, communications, news, journalism, reels, tweets (or whatever the hell they're calling them these days), everything everywhere would immediately be suspect. Any world leader could get up in front of a camera and start spouting the kind of garbage that starts wars—more than they already do, I mean—and there'd be no way to know if the supposedly live broadcast was legitimate or bogus. Apps like Snapchat that apply select filters at the user's direction would be like banging rocks together to make fire, compared to what Liz was describing.

"More specifically, Anja will be securing MirrorFox. She and Anjelika will be using their identical appearance and dress to carry out a swap without anyone realizing there are *two* statuesque blondes in expensive glittery dresses. Buff, you're their public cover and close protection. Shawn does covert entry, gets Anjelika into position, and helps hack the security system. You and Anja have to steal a retinal scan and a palm print to defeat the vault's locks, and then Anja needs to do the entry without anyone noticing the statuesque blonde Viking babe has gone missing. Once you've got what you need, she and Anjelika trade roles in the ladies' room and Anja commits her bit of technothievery. She and Shawn extract to the west, while you and Anjelika walk out the front door."

"So I'm the obnoxious distraction, am I? Playing to stereotype much?" I asked. I looked at Shawn for a moment. "Questions?"

"Liz, I've got an M7 for up close and an M250 for support in the trunk. We've both got our sidearms as well. Do we need to stash those before we cross the border or has the route been cleared?"

"Route's cleared. Those passports will tell the Finnish border guards to clear you without any questions, so long as Buff drives your wheels like he stole it."

"Not a problem," I replied. "Full stops at all stop signs, signal at all turns, keep up with the flow of traffic."

Shawn snorted and buried his face in his phone. Liz let the joke slide, as she normally did. "Good. See you at the airport."

✧✧✧

As promised, the passports Shawn provided got us over the Finnish border without trouble, and then it was a steady cruise down the E18. Something had him interested though, because he spent most of the multi-hour trip swiping and typing and generally acting very distracted.

"You alright?" I asked. "We didn't get a chance to talk after Mexico."

Shawn let out a bitter chuckle. "No, we didn't. It was just 'Right, Shawn, shit happened, get your head right with the shrink and we'll get you back into the game once you're given the all clear.' I got the all clear, and next thing I know, I'm on a Lufthansa flight to Riga by way of Prague and given an address to meet you at in St Petersburg."

"And just like that, you're back at it."

"And just like that, I'm back at it," he echoed. "I don't know. What would you do if you could walk away from it all and just not look back? I'm feeling pretty mortal these days, Buff."

"Ain't nobody gotten outta life alive yet, amigo. Just gotta keep on keepin' on. I've got a whole case full of medals locked up at the Agency I've got to book an appointment to go see if I ever wonder if what I've done matters. In the meantime, I've got you, Liz, Gina, a couple others, people I trust to have my back when the shit hits the fan. Maybe one day I settle down. Have a few kids. Tell lies and stories about all the shit I didn't ever get into while supposedly working as an analyst. Who knows, maybe one of these Finnish twins is into thirty-somethings who can deadpan snark with the best of them." Shawn rolled his eyes, and I protested. "What? It could happen."

"Kids," he mused. "Yeah. I've got three dead teammates who had four kids between them, and now they're gonna grow up without their mom or their dads."

"Shit happens, Shawn. Seriously. No one on your team didn't know the risks, no one on your team didn't know they were spies fucking with one of the most savage criminal organizations to have ever existed. Anyone could trip in front of a bus, or go down with cancer, or choke on a poorly chewed piece of steak. Or get ambushed by the fucking Sinaloa cartel, mid-op. We are all on a finite timeline, amigo. We do what we can with the time we have, make the differences where you can, and don't worry about the rest. If it's really bothering you that much, then maybe it's one last op and time to pull the rip cord. Pop chute. No one would blame you."

"Oh yes they would," he grumbled, and that was the end of it. He kept his eyes on the wintry snows out the window that flanked us the whole way to Helsinki.

I was worried for him. I was right to worry.

The airport was in the north end of town, and we drove to the private chartered terminal. Once we'd parked, Shawn threw his go bag over his shoulder and a parking pass on the dash. Inside, Liz wore her typical field gear—black t-shirt, jacket, and grey cargoes with boots. She had her ballcap pulled down low, to better hide the HUD visor she wore whenever she was surfing the darkweb. Gina lounged next to her, a similarly lumpy kit bag of weaponry by her feet. Gina was a stunning woman, with exotic features I understood to be a blend of Cuban and Italian, with long black hair and a perpetual olive tan. That said, she was part of my core team, and therefore off limits.

*(You know, no matter how many times you tell people that, they're always shocked that you've got, like, your own self-imposed rules on the subject. Makes me laugh every time. —Gina)*

*(Right? The looks I get from people who just assume that we're like, inner circle Buff Babes or something, it's absurd. —Liz)*

"We can't just call an air strike and paste the area?" she was asking. "I know, I know, no can do, it just seems to me there are some problems that ought to be solved with a sufficiently ignorant gatling barrage."

I strolled up to them and pounded fists with Gina. "Somebody say gatling barrage?"

She let out a huff and rolled her eyes. "Liz was just shutting down my plan to nuke the site from orbit."

"Oh come on, Liz, it's the only way to be sure," Shawn chimed in.

Beside Liz, picture . . . well. I know this is going to sound cliche, but honestly it's true: Anja looked like she and ScarJo could have been sisters. Johansson's father is from Denmark, so it is what it is, and that's who she looked like. She was wearing Jessica Rabbit's preferred red, sparkly gown, over closed toe heels. The only . . . imperfection, I won't call it a flaw, was a red barbell eyebrow stud she wore.

"I'd try to remember whether you're Anja or Anjelika, but I've just been overcome by a sudden severe case of lightheadedness," I flirted.

"Because the blood feeding your primary brain suddenly felt the need to be elsewhere?" Liz snarked with an eye roll so harsh it was audible.

*(Why is it again that they're viable . . . partners? You just got finished saying you don't sleep with your teammates. —Liz)*

*(They're not Agency, they're not part of our core team. They're allies, but I'm not their boss and I don't write their assessments. —Buff)*

*(You write our assessments? Really? Press X to doubt. —Gina)*

*(Okay, you got me there. It doesn't have to make a lot of sense. —Buff)*

"Correct. Which is the point," I agreed, offering my hand to shake. "Very nice to meet you, Ms. Laukkanen."

"I'm Anja," she said. She dimpled when she took my hand and I kissed the back of hers. "You're cute, but Liz warned me about you already, so you can dial the charm down three or four notches until we have to play act the married couple."

"Ouch, Liz, you're supposed to be on Team Orpington, aren't you? Fine. Since this is already a snap kick, what can you two tell me about the target building? Try not to use words that would show up on a Mensa test."

Liz shot me a, "I know you better than that" eyebrow lift and relaxed her haptic gloves, swiping away her invisible keyboard. "Big obnoxious dome. Triple pane glass arranged on the outside like golf ball dimples. Think Epcot Center in Disney World, but transparent."

From the nearby ladies' room came Anja's twin, Anjelika. She was dressed for the op, wearing a caterer's tuxedo, unbuttoned, over a black "ninja suit," a snug Kevlar-and-rayon two-piece suit that fitted her like bulletproof lululemons. She joined us without comment, and Anja continued.

"It's called AuroraLux because the northern lights are highly visible and the dome is designed with that in mind. Exterior has thermal and motion sensors, private guards who aren't *officially* armed, but will be. Inside, there are six distinct public levels, two sublevels, all connected by a central vertical core of elevators, washrooms, offices, and access points. Outside the core, it's divided up like someone ran an apple through a mandoline."

"Mandoline?" I interrupted. "What did I just say about Mensa words?"

Gina smirked. "Didn't you have to pretend you were a chef one time? A mandoline is one of those slicer thingies that cuts tomatoes and onions and cucumbers real thin."

"Oh. I just called it the slicer thingie. No wonder they pinged me as bogus that op. Huh. I presume given the . . . clientele, we'll be on the top floor?"

"Correct. The whole floor is reserved, with one section isolated for the auction itself. Anja will have to acquire the device after it has been demonstrated to work, but before the payment arrives and the device is handed over. Between those two time ticks, it will be in the vault in the second sublevel. So naturally since that's the most secure location in the facility, that's where we have to steal it from." Liz looked up from beneath her baseball cap. "Your optic link is synced, Anja. Give me a spot test?"

I looked between the two women, clueless, and Anja focused her eyes on me for a moment.

"Good. Sending the update." Liz tapped on some invisible keys only she could see, and then Anja's eyes . . . *changed*. One moment they were an ice blue, then her irises went brown with little green flecks. It was uncanny, like watching an octopus change its colors. They looked . . . familiar.

Liz brought up a device that looked like *Star Trek* binoculars and had me look in one end. One light blinked green. Then she passed it to Anja, and she looked in as well. A second light blinked green as well.

"Perfect," Liz said. "You're good to go. Reverting to your natural blue, instead of Buff's shit brown."

I could have sworn the corner of her lips tried *extra* hard not to curl into a smirk. Then I thought about what I'd just witnessed. "You just mimicked my retinal pattern?" I asked.

"And here everyone says you're just a pretty face," Liz replied deadpan. "Correct. Chameleon contact lenses. In your mission kit, you're going to find a one-shot puddle of bioflex palm print memory goop. Technical term. As you just demonstrated, any guy who gets a chance at Anja isn't going to go for a boring-ass handshake, they're gonna want to kiss her hand all charming and shit. So it's up to *you* to get the security chief's palm print via handshake. There's a corresponding 'wedding band' that has the trigger to lock the palm print into the memory goop. Chief is Arvo Virtanen. Once you make him, shake with your right, lock it in with your left, then pass the imprint off to Anja so she and Anjelika can do their swap. Anjelika replaces Anja on your arm, Anja cracks the vault with Shawn's help. I'm on cyber-overwatch. Once they've taken the device from the vault and substituted a nonfunctional forgery, Shawn and Anja exfil with MirrorFox aboard the catering truck while you and Anjelika walk out the door, arm in arm."

"How did she take the retinal-" I started, then I looked back at Anja again. Her necklace was a plain white gold figaro chain with what looked like a heraldic lion on it with two tails. That couldn't have been it. I scanned her over again. "The piercing?" I asked.

"Not bad." Anja dimpled again and tapped her brow. "Latest in micro-optics. Battery only lasts for a couple hours, but this is, as you Americans say, the New Hotness in covert image collection. I think you know Ocean Tyde from previous work? She designed it."

"I do know Ocean, yeah, she's good people. Unfortunately, she came away from that 'pretend you're a chef' op swearing it would be her last with me. She's not a fan of two-way ranges, and when I got made, it got rather more kinetic than she likes and felt I may have been responsible. She's a sweetheart, gets along with anyone and MacGuyver is her spirit animal. When *I* talk about hearts and minds, I usually mean a Mozambique drill. She does not."

> *(You absolutely WERE responsible, and don't pretend you don't know why! —Ocean)*
>
> *(Ocean, you're not even in this story, why are you commentating? —Gina)*
>
> *(Anja tipped me off. If I'm getting mentioned, I'm going to see what foolishness Buff is going on about. And in this case, it's a good thing too. He was completely unprepared for that op. He thought grilling and barbecuing were the same thing! His*

*solution to making meals taste better is to just add more garlic and more bacon! It was appalling! —Ocean)*

*(I mean, he's not wrong. You measure garlic with your heart, and never have I ever said "Ew, no, too much bacon." —Liz)*

*(STOP HELPING. —Ocean)*

"If it's all the same to you, I'd rather this op didn't become a, as you say, two-way range," Anja said. "This dress covers little enough as it is, and it's not exactly spectra."

"I will endeavor to please," I promised. Shawn and Anjelika headed out to their helicopter, and it quickly departed. We spent another hour or so on mission prep, Anja and I getting to know each other in particular, going through some personas she could adopt as my "wife," until it was showtime. Gina threw her bag and a pair of cross country skis into the passenger compartment of our helicopter and led the way in. In a few short minutes, we were off the ground and northbound.

My kit bag contained a tuxedo lined with soft armor, and I winced internally at Anja's comment about the vulnerability of her gown. It was testament to her courage that she'd go into an op in a dress with a slit so high it barely concealed her thong, never mind Kevlar or a sidearm. I tied, retied, and tried to tie the fucking bow tie three times before Gina snorted at my total incompetence and beckoned me close. In my defense, there wasn't exactly a mirror on board. She also yanked it tight enough she made it clear it was a vulnerability in any fisticuffs we'd get into.

I would endeavor not to wind up in fisticuffs, either.

*(And how did that work out? —Liz)*

*(It would have been fine! —Buff)*

*(Would have? —Liz)*

*(How was I to know? It was fine. Mostly. It's not like I could have snuck a gun in, even if I'd wanted to. We handled it. —Buff)*

"Two minutes to first LZ," the pilot warned, and Gina began pulling on her winter whites to cover her gear. By the time she was ready to debark she looked like a very lethal version of the Stay Puft

Marshmallow Woman, and her winter camo extended to white hockey tape she'd applied to the frame of her C-14 Timberwolf. The helicopter flared, dropped to the deck like a stone, and I threw the door open for her. She tossed her bag, jumped the last five feet, and was already strapping into her skis by the time we were climbing for altitude again.

It wasn't all that far to the AuroraLux facility that was hosting the auction, but there was just the one helipad and there were more birds than you'd find on a power line. We circled the facility several times, and on the third pass I thought I was able to pick out the tree line Gina would be using as her sniper hide once she skied into position. The facility itself was all glass and chrome, designed to give the occupants a fair shake at spotting the aurora borealis any time it made itself visible.

We finally got clearance, and as the pilot brought us in, Anja got a faraway look in her eye. "All, this is Anja. We're about to land. Game on."

I frowned. I hadn't gotten a radio, and she wasn't wearing one either. Anja's eyes glinted when she caught me looking puzzled.

"What's wrong, Mister 'Buffington'? Didn't know about the latest in bionetics? Anjelika and I operate as twins, often doubling for each other as we will be today. We each have a subdermal bone conduction implant with a mic so we can keep each other up to date in real time. Liz linked the two of us to her and Gina as well, since putting an earpiece in your ear would be too obvious."

"Nope, that detail escaped me too. Any other cool upgrades? Adamantium claws? Captain America super serum? Tragic vulnerability to kryptonite or charming, ruggedly handsome spies?"

She smiled at me, one that actually appeared to be genuine. "You Americans and your superheroes. No, no other superpowers. Not even Batgirl underwear. If I meet any charming ruggedly handsome spies, I'll be sure to let you know. Now. You and I are supposed to be married. So kiss me, and let's get the awkwardness out of the way, shall we?"

My eyebrows went up of their own accord, and I couldn't help but wonder if the underwear comment meant just *regular, barely-there underoos* or if it meant *none at all*, but we were about to land. She was right though, if we were to be playing a couple, we needed to get our act on in a hurry. I leaned in and kissed her.

She was a hell of an actress.

I love my job.

*(And the Academy Award for best fake kiss goes to . . . —Liz)*

*(Hurtful. You and Gina both. Savage and hurtful. —Buff)*

I retrieved the palm print imprinting goop from its case and slipped it on like a sticky, very thin, virtually undetectable latex glove. I might feel a bit clammy, but that was all. On my other hand, I fitted the plain gold band on my ring finger with its button on the inside. The goop warmed to my skin temperature quickly and was invisible against my palm. The helicopter landed, the rotors slowed, stopped, and then it was showtime.

Security was quick and professional. Men in one line, women in the other line. Everyone patted down and wanded. Once we'd been cleared, we went forward to reception, who controlled the gate access. They took our photo, which wasn't great for a couple of professional spooks, but it is what it is. They explained it was for their active facial recognition software and would be scrubbed once the auction had concluded.

Our credentials identified us as Cocoa and Orphille Buffington, which matched the invitations Liz had forged and inserted into the guest list.

*(Orphille Buffington? Really? —Gina)*

*(Remember, this story never happened. If such a story had occurred in real life, any identifying details would have been . . . tweaked. —Buff)*

We strolled into the upper level of the AuroraLux snow globe, and I had to shield my eyes at first. The afternoon sky was that brilliant blue you only get in the higher latitudes, and the sunlight refracted through the glass windows to bathe the interior in little spots of rainbow everywhere. Where the rainbows touched Anja's dress, she sparkled like a crimson snowflake. Conversations stopped, jaws dropped, and a couple men earned well-earned finger-waggings from their dates. You know the distracted boyfriend meme? Like that, but eight times at once.

I won't bore you with the remaining details. Over the next few hours, we worked the crowd, made friends, pissed off a few people, and I generally got to play the obnoxious over-the-top American boor. It was great. One man in particular stood out, though.

"Mister . . . Orpington, is it?" a deep, South African-accented voice said. Dude sounded like he gargled whiskey and smoked half a pack before breakfast. I turned to come face to face with a bow tie tied even nicer than mine. I looked up.

"Buffington," I corrected evenly, to the man-mountain who was entirely within my personal space and positively *loomed* over me. "I get that a lot. Wow. They're growing them big in Cape Town these days, are they?"

"Pretoria, actually," he corrected. "Baron Damien Van Der Beer, of Weyland-Cyberdyne Systems. Your reputation precedes you, Mister Buffington." He turned to Anja. "And you are?"

"Cocoa Buffington, as of, like, three weeks ago? Orph and I just got married," she squealed, sounding very much like the beachiest beach bunny to have ever escaped California. "This is totally our first stop on our honeymoon tour of Europe! We're going to see, uh, Venice—the Italian one, not the beach in LA, and, um, Dublin, but the Irish one, and Palermo, oh, but that one's in Italy too . . ."

"Congratulations," Van Der Beer interrupted, before "Cocoa" recited our supposed itinerary. He leaned down to leer at her chest, and I was about to object when he reached out to touch the necklace she wore. He examined it closely. "The double-tailed lion of the Czech Republic. Very nice. *Kolik zaplatil za takovou děvku, jako jsi ty?*"

Anja just smiled airily and let a puzzled look cross her face. "I have no idea what you just said, but it sounded nice! Was that German?"

"No, sweetheart, that wasn't German," I replied, giving Van Der Beer a glare. "Have a good auction, Baron, may the best funded man win." I let Anja guide me away to the bar, where we loaded up new flutes of champagne.

"*It's fine, Anjelika,*" I heard her whisper without moving her mouth, like a ventriloquist. "*That's what we want him to think.*"

It *was* what we wanted him to think. Because what he'd asked, in Czech, was "how much I'd paid for a whore like her." It was to Anja's credit that she hadn't broken character in the slightest, despite speaking like, six languages without an accent. Including, it turned out, ditzy bimbo.

"He made you," Anja said quietly as she sipped something fizzy and fruity, draped over my arm. "Soon as we hit the bar, Liz intercepted a call from him calling someone named Gaetzerberg. They know you're here from the Agency."

"That's fine," I said. "Expected, even. Gaetzerberg would be either Will or Marc. That confirms Van Der Beer is working for the League of Conspicuous Evil, and assuming he's being honest about the Weyland-Cyberdyne line, it identifies that as a League asset, too. Couple more moles in need of whacking later. Today? We're just here for the MacGuffin."

Two expensive whiskys and another mimosa later, the Master of Ceremonies called for everyone's attention and had us file into the wedge of the snow globe that had been set aside for the purpose. Bidders were handed numbered paddles, and we found seats. There were a number of items up for auction, including something purported to be a third party sculpture of Anish Kapoor and Stuart Semple arguing, painted in Vantablack and Pinkest Pink, respectively. It sold for seven digits, and it occurred to me I was really in the wrong business.

Finally, the MacGuffin itself took the stage. It wasn't particularly noteworthy looking—a simple black box that could have been a Wi-Fi router or fiber optic modem, about the size of a mass market paperback. It had plug-ins on one end, and the auctioneer cleared his throat for attention.

"Now, the final item on the evening's list is this . . . device, known as MirrorFox. Its creator, an independent engineer who prefers to be known only as MikeTython68, has developed the means by which any livestream to which it has access can be remotely deepfaked, meaning one or more individuals in the stream can be, uh, it says here, 'reskinned,' to appear to be someone else. I'm sorry, ladies and gentlemen, I'm not quite sure what that means, I still use a Nokia—and it doesn't even have Snake. Regardless, the bidding will open at fifty thousand Euros."

"Fifty thousand," someone to my left bid.

"Fifty-five," someone else said in front of me.

"Sixty!" the first bidder declared. You've seen auctions, you know how they go. After letting the amateurs banter for a few minutes, Baron Van Der Beer raised his paddle. "One hundred million."

You could've heard a pin drop.

Until I laughed, that is. "Now *that's* what I'm talking about," I replied. "A hundred and ten!"

And so it went. There were two other high-end bidders in the room, and the four of us pushed it all the way to $175 million before the Baron locked eyes with me from across the room and raised his paddle. "Three hundred million Euros," he bid, eyebrow raised in a dare.

The other bidders' eyes went wide. They'd only *thought* they were in the game. But no, the Baron was the shark in this tank, and he knew he had us beat.

"Three hundred million," the auctioneer echoed. "Do I hear three-twenty? Do I hear three-twenty?"

I admit, I was tempted.

I mean, there was no fucking way I was actually going to end up paying a dime. Guaranteed, if Van Der Beer was here with League backing, he had shown up with an effectively unlimited line of credit.

But that wasn't the point.

The point was, I really wanted to get spiteful for that crack about me "buying" Anja, making him pay even more for the stupid box, which he wouldn't get anyways. Just the thought of him trying to wrangle back nine digits worth of currency from some dork with a handle like MikeTython68 made me giggle.

"Let it go," Anja whispered, using that ventriloquist trick of hers, and hearing a blonde Scandinavian princess quote Elsa just about made me break character. I bowed my resignation to the Baron and put my paddle away. The device was his.

Which, to be fair, was entirely the point. Everything up to this point had just been foreplay, and now it was time to fuck the League, good and hard.

After the auction broke up, Van Der Beer made his way up front to make arrangements for his funds transfer. Anja and I waited a respectful distance away as he talked to the banker and when they'd wrapped up, I went forward.

"Congratulations, Baron," I said, shaking his hand. The League factor eyed me warily, but returned the handshake.

"You gave me a run for my money, Mister Buffington," Van Der Beer said. "I had no idea you were so well funded."

"And I had no idea Weyland-Cyberdyne was so interested in this kind of tech," I replied smoothly. "I was hoping to get it for a song, and then you came in and just . . . boosh," I said mimicking him unzipping and laying his equipment out for everyone to see.

"Orph, don't be so crude," Anja frowned. "You know I don't like it when you're unnecessarily . . . vulgar."

"What? It's true. We hadn't even hit a million bucks before Mister Der Beer here announced playtime was over with all the subtlety of a Bloodhound Gang song. I think a couple of the wannabe players choked on his metaphorical—"

"Everything alright, Mister Van Der Beer?" a tall drink of water interrupted. He was wearing a paramilitary uniform with a name tag that read "Virtanen." Well. That was convenient.

"Ah. Chief Virtanen. Yes, all is well. Mister Buffington here was just being a gracious silver medalist in the MirrorFox Games. Have you met?"

"We have not," Virtanen said, and I offered him my hand to shake. As our hands connected, I touched the control stud on my left ring finger with my thumb, and stored his palm print in the bio flex goop.

"Very pleased to meet you, sir." I retracted my hand and placed my hand on Anja's far hip, pulling her in tight to my side. "May I introduce my wife, Cocoa?" I tried to transfer the palm print to her dress, but it simply refused to peel free.

"Your wife?" Virtanen said with the raised eyebrow of a man who was trying very hard not to say. *How the hell did you wed a smokeshow like her?* He bent to kiss the back of her hand, and "Cocoa" smiled widely at the gentlemanly gesture and returned the greeting with a California curtsey. "Very nice to meet you both. Though I confess, it is odd. I remember reviewing the guest list a week ago and there was nobody named Buffington on it."

"That *is* odd," I agreed. I refused to let my emotions show on my face, but I was having a hell of a time getting the goop on my hand to release and transfer to Anja's dress. "I'm quite sure I'm on the list. We had to provide our credentials just to get space on the helipad.

Regardless, we're here, vetted by your *exceptional* security precautions, and having a wonderful time. I've noticed your cameras everywhere. Subtly placed, but nicely done. I think I noticed a few of the catering staff were actually plainclothes security as well?"

"Proprietary," Virtanen replied with a grin. "But it's no secret that there's ongoing facial recognition software for every guest, to ensure no uninvited parties crash the proceedings. Speaking of precautions, I really must be going," Virtanen said. "Duties require my attention elsewhere, now that the auction has been concluded. Safe travels, gentlemen. Ma'am."

"Off to handle some Very Important Packages, no doubt," I said to Virtanen's back as the Chief headed for the central hub. I grinned at Van Der Beer. "Not *all* packages are created equal, of course. Some packages like things a little rough—especially with the right kind of cushioning." I slapped Anja's ass with an audible *crack*, eliciting a gasp from my "wife" and a furious blush coloring her cheeks.

"Orphille Buffington!" she snapped. "That's quite enough of that kind of misbehaving! Just because I like it when—" then she froze, as if realizing what she had been about to say. "Just because—*Ooh*! You are *insufferable* when you're being crude."

Anja turned to Van Der Beer, her cheeks flushed with embarrassment. "Do you, perchance, know the way to the ladies' room? I suddenly feel the need to powder my nose, before I wring my idiot husband's neck in high-def on eleventeen different cameras."

Van Der Beer grinned at my faux pas. "Follow Chief Virtanen, Mrs. Buffington. There are security staff posted at access points around the hub, they will escort you to the facilities and back out again."

"Thank you, Baron," she said, smiling at me with a dead-eyed glare that would have made a great white shark proud. "So good to know *some* men know how to behave in polite company."

With that, Anja departed in the same direction as the chief had—with the bioflex palm print goop stuck, invisibly, to her right butt cheek.

*"Anja" here.*

*Let me make something perfectly clear up front. "Anjelika" and I are still operational, so it was honestly the weirdest conversation I have* ever *had, when Buff tracked us down—well, when* Liz *tracked us down—and asked if he could tell our story, with the serial numbers filed off, as it were. We agreed, so long as we got to look over what nonsense he's telling, and much of it is, indeed, nonsense. Yes, he's taking liberties here. Yes, he's covering up actual tradecraft with tropetastic bull. It's fascinating, honestly, having been there, to see how much of the story has been massaged to be plausible, yet not at all accurate.*

> *(I have no idea what you're talking about. This entire tale is entirely fictional, and I have it on good legal authority I should say so. —Buff)*

*That said, I can't say I've ever had a fellow agent smack my ass, in front of our primary opposition, as tradecraft. Until then, that is. The outrage? I won't say it wasn't feigned. But I didn't have to act very hard, either.*

"She is a fiery one," Van Der Beer commented to her retreating form. "Wherever did you meet her?"

"Proprietary," I echoed Virtanen from before. Then I grinned. "If I tell you, then the secret would be out. But let me just say this: I strongly agree with that joke, that the reason Scandinavian women are all gorgeous is because the Vikings took the pretty girls home with them. It just makes too much sense."

Van Der Beer laughed. "There may be some truth there. I'm sure you know, the Boers—my ancestors—were primarily Dutch. There existed a state of casual warfare between our peoples for more than a century, and we lost plenty of women and plunder to the Danes."

"That may be true, but let's not pretend the Dutch are lacking for pretty women either," I said, giving the Baron a finger wave. "Though I did notice a distinct lack of companionship on your arm today?"

"It is summer in Pretoria, Mister Buffington. My lady is presently sunning herself on the patio at our villa. She is not so foolish as to want to travel to the land of ice and lutefisk in winter."

"Fair," I said. It was at that moment "Cocoa" returned from her trip to the ladies' room. She shot me a glare that would have melted I beams. "May I have a moment of your time, *husband*?" she fairly snarled. I rolled my eyes apologetically to the Baron and allowed myself to be pulled away. Once we'd gotten a good distance from everyone and were standing near the outer glass wall of the facility, where her face wouldn't be spotted by observing cameras.

"Before you start, please convey my apologies," I said. "The... thing was stuck. Your gown has all the viscosity of bacon grease and I needed to get it unstuck."

Anjelika grinned. "Don't be sorry. I think Anja was more startled than offended. Startled and... maybe something more."

> *(Anjelika... —Anja)*
>
> *(What? Tell me I lie. Especially given how... later went. —Anjelika)*
>
> *(ANJELIKA! —Anja)*

I raised my eyebrow. "Is that so? Duly noted."

"She's already into her stealth suit and doing her thing. Now let's shmooze some more. I'll be appropriately horngry if you'll pretend to be appropriately chastised."

"Horngry?" I asked.

"Like hangry, but horny."

"Ah. Horngry. Delightful."

We mingled, sipped champagne, and Anjelika kept me updated on Anja's progress. The HVAC ducts Anjelika had used to sneak into the ladies' room undetected led to a maintenance room, where Shawn had stashed coveralls stolen for the purpose. Anja pulled them on over her ninja suit and met up with Shawn to run the actual heist.

> *(It's not a heist when spies do it, Buff! It's covert asset seizure! —Liz)*
>
> *(Totally a heist. —Gina)*

Anjelika used the same ventriloquist act her sister had perfected to narrate.

"Liz is reprogramming her contact lenses," she whispered. "Shawn's clipping into the data line. Liz is remotely activating the scanner. Moment of truth. Green light. She's in."

Anjelika took a sip of her champagne, and a slight tremor in the fizzy wine betrayed just how nerve-wracking it was having to stand by and be cool. "She's making the switch. She's out. Into the corridor. Door shut. Shawn's removed his bypass. Tracking beacon is lit. Shawn's with her. They're heading for the truck."

She threw back the last of her champagne and I collected her flute. We made our way past the bar, deposited our glasses by the hot-wash station, where we waited until they'd been rinsed by an attentive busboy. Then we made our way to the door.

"Device is into the exterior compartment. Truck is moving. Clearing security. Security is taking their time," Anjelika narrated. "Full sweep. They have a dog, mirrors on sticks, the works."

"Mister and Missus Buffington," I told the valet, and the valet got on the radio to the distant pad where the helicopters were parked until their passengers required pickup.

Security did a thorough job of checking over the slightly battered catering truck Shawn and Anjelika had arrived in. We could see our helicopter in the air by the time Shawn was given the all-clear, and they rolled out.

As we waited for our bird to land, Van Der Beer approached one last time. "Have a good flight, Mister Buffington," he said. "I will admit, I am somewhat let down. My employers were *entirely* sure you'd get up to some manner of mischief. You have a rep, Orph Buffington, or whatever your name is. But I've kept my eye on you this whole evening. Never once did you leave my sight."

"I'm entirely sure I have no idea what you're talking about, Baron," I replied. "Give my regards to the Gaetzerbergs, would you?"

And with that, we strolled out onto the frigid landing pad and boarded our helicopter to fly home. Mission accomplished, right?

Wrong. While we were southbound towards Helsinki, Anjelika got a look of worry across her face. "Liz? Gina? Tell me you're hearing this."

I couldn't hear shit, and the helicopter's radio was tuned to internal mics only, so my headset wasn't any use other than to hear what Anjelika was saying.

"They're past you already? Hell. Pilot, new course, northwest, now, now now!"

The pilot froze for a second, but I had no choice but to trust

Anjelika would update me. "Do as the lady says," I snarled into my mic, and the pilot obeyed. The helicopter banked hard, and then we were heading back almost in the direction we'd just come. "What's going on?"

"Double-cross. Once Shawn was well clear of Gina's position, he pulled a gun on Anja. Ordered her out of the cab, bound her hands. Shot out the tires to the truck and took the device."

"He's *what*?"

"Anja's been subvocalizing with her implant. I don't think Shawn knows she has one. I never mentioned mine, so he may not know we're in contact. He cleared Gina's field of fire and now he's pulled over in. He's got . . . shit. Anja says there's a snowmobile, it was concealed under a snow covered tarp. He's pulling away, northbound."

"Hell. Pop chute indeed, you bastard," I snarled. "Does Liz have the device's beacon? Anja did tag it, right?"

"Liz? Do you have the beacon? You do. Okay. We're going to . . ." Anjelika looked to me for instructions on what to relay.

"We're going to pick up Anja, catch up to the snowmobile, and take down Shawn. Can Anja confirm there's no way Shawn swapped out the beacon?"

Anjelika relayed, then shook her head. "He took the device directly from the compartment where she'd hidden it and stuck it in his inside jacket pocket. Left side. There's literally no terrain whatsoever, he's been snowmobiling away for a good two minutes already and she can still see him. He hasn't ditched the beacon. What the fuck is he thinking?"

"He's thinking the League just paid 'Fuck You I Quit' money for that thing. He's thinking if he can get it back for them, he can retire to Cancun for a fraction of what they paid for it. Gods damn him. If he had a snowmobile prepositioned then, who knows how long he's known about the auction, and that we'd be attending?"

I thought back to all the time he'd spent on his phone, during the drive from St. Petersburg, wondering if he was setting up this whole subterfuge while riding shotgun with me. "In the end, it doesn't matter. Is that Anja up ahead?"

The helicopter flared hard and came down on the highway just ahead of the catering truck. I bailed out and ran for Anja. She'd just worked her hands free of the packing tape he'd used to secure them, and I checked the truck. Yes, he'd put a couple rounds into each tire, guaranteeing it wouldn't be moving anywhere not involving a flat deck truck. We'd abandon it.

Anja and I reboarded the helicopter, Anja getting up front next to the pilot so she could point out the snowmobile's trail. Once airborne, we were away northbound, following a distinct set of snowmobile tracks.

"Where's Gina?" I asked.

"She's on her skis, making her way to a roadway now," Anjelika relayed. "Oh. Oh my. She's not subtle, is she?"

"Who, Gina? Subtle as an orbital napalm barrage, why?"

"She's... acquired local transport. At gunpoint."

As the helicopter chased after Shawn's snowmobile, I perceived the flaw in my sketch of an outline of the beginnings of a plan. The terrain was flat as hell, with a forest well northeast, and it was towards this forest Shawn was heading. The helicopter had precisely zero ability to block or cut off or otherwise prevent Shawn from simply driving around us, the moment we put down. Because of the op's requirements, the only one of us with a gun had been Gina, and she had her gear with her.

It was time to get reckless.

"Bring us down off his left side," I asked the pilot. "Low as you can get and a little ahead of him."

"Buff? What are you doing?" Anjelika demanded as the pilot brought us into position.

"What needs doing. If this goes badly for me, stall him."

I threw the door to the helicopter open, and before I could think better of it, threw myself out the door.

I'd like to tell you it was heroic as fuck, that I shoulder tackled him cleanly, that we tumbled off the snowmobile into a heap, that I came out on top, started swinging, and thereby saved the day.

I'd like to say that.

However, there were witnesses.

What actually happened was, I led the way with my feet, and my fancy tuxedo-shoed size twelves hammered into Shawn's shoulder in an entirely awkward and ungainly way. Yes, I knocked his ass off the snowmobile, but said snowmobile was racing along at a solid fifty or sixty miles an hour. I'm told the rooster tail I kicked up when I tumbled into the snowbank was glorious.

I staggered to my feet, vision all messed up from having just faceplanted into all that snow at near freeway speeds. Off to my left, the helicopter found a place to set down. Shawn was a little bit more messed up than I was, on account of him not having expected the impact. His full-face helmet must have occluded his peripheral vision, because he'd gone flying like the snowiest tumbleweed that ever tumbled. I staggered my probably-concussed ass over to him and grabbed him by the helmet. I buried a punch into his gut and tried to wrangle him over onto his front to hold onto his arms.

It didn't take Shawn long to clue into what was going on. Plus, his helmet made for a distinct advantage in any bare-knuckle brawl. He rolled out of my attempt at an arm bar, and we exchanged a flurry of blows. I'm not going to pretend I'm any kind of super ninja—that is to say, I wasn't at the time—and Shawn and I had both gone to the same schools, learned the same styles, rolled on the same mats.

We were pretty evenly matched. In this biz, if you find yourself in the middle of a fair fight, something has gone terribly wrong. He figured that out just a moment before I did, the cheating cheater, and drove his knee into my junk.

"Dirty pool," I wheezed, bent in half, and it was at this time the second critical flaw in my non-plan revealed itself. Namely, it hadn't registered to me that Anjelika had told me he'd *shot* out the tires to the truck. He produced said handgun now.

Anja and Anjelika, bless them, had decided they'd assist and were trying to stay in his blind spot as they crept up on him. Anja wore her operational ninja suit and had proper footwear on. Anjelika had evidently sourced some mukluks from the helicopter—maybe the pilot's, I didn't know—and was tromping around in the snow with fur-lined boots that came up almost to her shins, below her smolderingly hot—and by hot, I mean freezing cold—cocktail dress.

"Gods damn you, Shawn," I cursed. He didn't shoot right away, which, under the circumstances, was pretty decent of him, so I raised my hands. Anja and Anjelika, who'd been trying to stay in his blind spot, froze when he whirled on them, as well. He peeled off the helmet.

"Gods damn *you*, Buff Orpington," he spat. "You weren't supposed to know. How the hell *did* you know? Was it that little heart to heart, tête-à-tête talk?"

"Nothing so insightful, Shawn. You had me fooled entirely. But the girls have subdermal microphones, and the moment you drew on Anja, Anjelika knew. Why are you doing this? Some kind of resentment towards me because your team got wiped and mine didn't? *Did* the League offer you Fuck You I Quit money?"

He rolled his eyes, sheepish. "They did, in fact, offer me Fuck You I Quit money, yes. It's not all about you, you conceited peacock. 'Why' is because of the Agency."

"Shawn, come on. Seriously. You're just going to walk away from everything you've built, your rep with the Agency, the good you've done?"

"You're goddamn right I am!" he bellowed. "When was the last time you had your entire team killed out from under you, Buff? They hung me out to *dry!* We were in Chihuahua, working against the Sinaloa, when some rat sold us out! One moment we had full field support, satellite comms, drone overwatch, and the next moment, we were in the cold. Our cell phones didn't even work, we couldn't even call 911. Completely cut off. Before we could rig a work-around, a kill team of cartel hitters rolled up and it was a running gun battle for an hour and a half. I'm the only one who escaped, Buff, and do you know what they told me when I made it back to Agency HQ?"

"I don't."

"'*Sorry Shawn. No idea what went wrong with our comms. Nothing to see here, move along.*' Their deaths were written off as an aviation accident since we weren't officially in Mexico. Since our ops had to remain off the books. We had to remain deniable."

"Yeah, well, that's part of the deal when you sign on the dotted line," I told him. "None of us signed up for glory or a place in Arlington."

"I don't give a fuck about glory, Buff, but three of my team had families. I told you that. They left behind two wives, one husband, four kids. None of them will see the kind of death benefits they'd get if the op had been sanctioned. So yeah. The League knew the auction was coming up. When they approached me, I took their offer. I took their Fuck You I Quit money, and I very quietly set up trust and education funds for the kids. The Agency sure as hell won't take care of them, but I will. It was my op, my responsibility, and good people died."

"So what are you monologuing for then?" I asked him. "Shouldn't you just be on your way?"

He smiled. "We were friends, Buff. I'd hoped to just disappear, but now? Maybe I need to assuage my guilt. Justify myself to you, before my face-heel turn is complete. Plus, Baron Van Der Beer and a handful of League assets are on their way here now in Sno-Cats, so they can collect the device they've rightfully paid for. If I get on my snowmobile right now, there's nothing stopping you from getting back into that heli and having another go at me and I'd rather not murder you, the girls, or your pilot. I didn't want to hurt anyone. Once they arrive, they'll have the hardware necessary to dissuade your bird from following until we can get the box into a proper Faraday bag and disappear."

Indeed, as I looked away to the east beyond Shawn, I saw a trio of bright orange boxes on wide snow-chewing tracks rumbling our way. They were still at a good distance, and we had a minute or so before they'd be in range for any competent rifleman.

"Ladies, how about you move over and stand next to Buff, where I can keep an eye on all three of you together?" Shawn ordered. "Nothing personal, but I do know that he was the distraction, and you two are vastly more competent than you let Van Der Beer think. Move. Now."

Anja and Anjelika did as he instructed, and they took up a position on either side of me. Anjelika's red gown flapped faintly in the breeze, and their mouths formed little wisps of condensation as they breathed. I realized they were talking under their breath.

"Wind is left to right, maybe ten kilometers," I heard Anja say. "Yes, use her gown as your flag."

Speaking of competent riflemen, I had only a moment to realize who she was talking to before Anja tackled me flat. Anjelika dove on top of the both of us. I heard the hypersonic snap of the round well before I heard the boom of the gunshot.

When I looked up, Shawn was down.

As delightful as it was being the meat in a Laukkenen Twins sandwich, we got to our feet in a hurry. I searched the horizon for Gina, and perhaps a kilometer back, I saw an SUV stopped by the side of the road and a familiar form leaning over the hood with her rifle on a bipod.

*(I don't often preen, but it was a helluva shot, if I may say so myself. —Gina)*

*(Preen away. Hitting a paperback book-sized target, first round, from what—nine hundred seventy meters you said? Badass. —Buff)*

My view returned to Shawn, down in the snow, twenty or thirty yards distant. I went to cross the distance to him, but the snow was deep, footing sketchy, and Anja caught my hand. She pointed to her ear. "Liz says she just lost the beacon's signal. Whether Shawn lives or dies, Gina must have hit the device itself."

"They're already dismounting, Buff," Anjelika warned me, pointing at the forms still two, maybe two hundred fifty yards away, but clearly armed with tactical gear including rifles. We were already in range. The helicopter's blades still spun, and I considered the distance between us and the bird. It was a big target, and if we went for it, the League's shooters could ground us, and we'd be no further ahead.

But the snowmobile…

"Onto the snowmobile then," I shouted, and we ran for it. Tromped for it. It was snowy as hell and made for slow going. I gestured for the helicopter pilot to take off and pointed at Gina, well distant. Hopefully he understood.

I mounted the snowmobile. It had seats for two. "Buff! I'm wearing a *cocktail gown!*" Anjelika protested.

"It's that or we take our chances with the nice Baron who just paid three hundred million dollars for so much shattered circuitry," I said. "Anja, you've got gear on, sit on my lap, facing me. You're going to be our windshield. Anjelika, you ride behind. Stay tight as you can so she and I can be your windbreak. It'll be cold, but it's better than being ventilated by those assholes with the rifles."

We peeled out. I didn't know where we were going, other than "away from the League, and the rapidly cooling body of the man I'd once considered my best friend at the Agency." We rode north, and Anjelika narrated into my ear. We couldn't go too fast, on account of her gown and my lack of helmet or goggles, but we could go faster than those orange Sno-Cats.

Gina, it turned out, engaged them at distance, to make sure they couldn't pursue us. She didn't kill anyone, but six magazines of match grade .338 convinced them to stay put for a good long while. They had very little by way of cover, aside from the machines, but at the same time she couldn't exactly hold position and wait for the Finnish federales to roll up on her and take the League's side.

The helicopter found a safe spot to pick her up and she boarded the bird. Fuel then became an issue, and the helicopter had to return to the airport or risk an unscheduled encounter with the edge of the air. I told Anjelika they should head back to Helsinki.

"Liz has found us a spot to lay low," Anjelika told me a few minutes later. "Five more klicks, we'll come across an active snowmobile trail. Turn left, and it'll take us to the E63 and there'll be a hunting cabin that's actually a FiSIS safehouse."

We made it to the safehouse without too much trouble, parked the snowmobile around back, and used a code Liz relayed to open a lockbox with the housekey in it.

By this time, Anjelika was turning damn near hypothermic, and I scooped her up into my arms to carry her inside. The cabin was sparse, made of thick wood with modern windows, and had a charming wood stove with a small pile of kindling and logs next to it. It had a queen sized bed, a kitchenette, and a workstation for cleaning... whatever Finns hunted. Elk? Reindeer? Russians?

I tucked Anjelika under the blanket, as Anja got the wood stove fired up.

"H-h-h-hey, Buff?" Anjelika chattered. "D-d-d-d-did what Shawn say make sense? About the Agency cutting out his team and leaving them for dead?"

"Hard to say," I told her. "I knew he was hurting. I don't know if the Agency screwed him or if it was someone from the cartels. Doesn't matter. Gina smashed that MirrorFox device with one shot and he was wearing armor, so it's possible the round didn't penetrate. Either he's alive or he's dead. Maybe we see him again, maybe we don't. Don't worry your gorgeous head about it right now. Right now, you need to warm up."

"I h-h-h-hear body heat is the best thing for that," she purred, and I felt Anja's arm slip around my waist.

"She's right, you know." Anja unzipped the neck of her stealth suit, and then unzipped more. "We Finns know all about how best to stay warm in the cold. Take one for the team, Buff, and help her warm up, won't you?"

For the record, I took *two* for the team.

*(BARF.—Liz)*

The next morning, I awoke when Anja stoked the woodstove back to life again. We were, in fact, warm and cozy. Anjelika was none the worse for wear, and in fact perhaps even a little rosy cheeked.

"Liz just checked in," Anja said. "The theft at the AuroraLux has been discovered, Baron Van Der Beer is flexing Weyland-Cyberdyne's political muscles as hard as he can, he canceled the funds transfer, and though the feds received reports of shots fired west of the AuroraLux, the police have no suspects. The League knows it was us, but since they can't say *how* they know, they can't say what they know. Since they don't know how we did the swap, they don't know where we got to, and they don't know who we actually are, the investigation is underway. The Agency needs all us out of the country, stat. So a ride out has been arranged."

"Back to Helsinki airport?" I asked. "I don't favor the odds of us getting there without someone from the League eyeballing us and calling in some hate."

"No. Not the airport," Anja smiled widely. "Or rather, not an official airport."

I heard the scream of a jet engine—no, *three* jet engines rip by overhead, and they must have been stupidly low because the windows on the cabin shook. I crawled out of bed and searched for the pieces of my tuxedo from where they'd landed the night before.

"Anja? What aren't you telling me?"

"Well you see, Buff, it's like this. Russia is *right there.* And it hasn't been all that long since they rolled over the border and picked a fight with us. So the Finnish Air Force practices . . . dispersing to safer places than air bases where any Russian cruise missile could crater a runway."

I found my errant sock, pulled it on, and pulled on my shoes. As I did up my belt, I went to the front of the cabin, I looked outside to see three F/A-18D Hornets taxiing down the highway we'd followed on the snowmobile.

"Since Finland joined NATO not all that long ago, it turns out there's a need for Finnish fighter pilots to cross-train with other cold-weather NATO pilots who fly similar airframes."

I frowned. "But the USAF switched over to Raptors and F-35s ages ago."

"That's right," Anja said sweetly. "But the Canadians haven't. They're a little slow, on the procurement side of things. It's a whole thing with them, and just because they said they wanted to buy F-35s in 2010 doesn't mean it's actually happened yet."

The three of us made our way out to the jets that had come to a stop on the barren freeway in front of the cabin. The lead pilot's hatch opened. "Good morning," he called down to us in accented English. "I'm told you three have a sudden pressing need to see CFB Cold Lake, Alberta?"

"Uh, yes? Yes. Yes we do, Captain," I replied. "I'm told Cold Lake is . . . Cold, this time of year."

"That it is, sir. We have three spare seats, and a long flight across the Atlantic and most of Canada before we're wheels down again. So if you'd kindly climb aboard and keep your tray tables in their upright and locked position, we'll be on our way."

And that, friends, is the totally made up and not even close to accurate story of "Buff Orpington Crosses the Finnish Line." Be sure to check out my memoirs, there's more Bufftastic nonsense where that came from.

Cheers,

Buff

# ABOUT THE AUTHORS

**Jacob Holo** has been a recreational geek since childhood, when he discovered Star Wars and Star Trek, and a professional geek since college, when he graduated from Youngstown State University with a degree in Electrical and Controls Engineering. He started writing when his parents bought that "new" IBM 286 desktop, and over the years, those powers combined to push him to the next level of nerddom: a sci-fi author who designs intricate worlds and tech systems... and promptly blows them up in a string of nonstop action. He is the author of over fifteen books, including the best-selling Gordian Division series (with David Weber), YA urban fantasy *Time Reavers* (a Kirkus Reviews Best Indie Book), and fantasy adventure *Monster Punk Horizon: Excess* (with H.P. Holo). Between novels, Jacob enjoys gaming of all sorts, whether video gaming, card gaming, miniature wargaming, or watching speed runs on YouTube. He is a former-Ohioan, former-Michigander who now lives in South Carolina with his wife/boss H.P., the ghost of his cat/boss Nova, and his new kitten/boss Dazzle, who is a very good boy even if he does try to lick light bulbs.

✧✧✧

**Edie Skye** wrote *Titan Mage* as a joke and, in doing so, discovered that while she really likes writing smart stuff, she also likes writing smut stuff. Pretty spicy smut stuff, too, 'cause if you're gonna do it, you might as well do it *hard*. Specifically, she likes to spin fun (and funny) adventure fantasies about badass women and the equally badass dudes who want to do them. *Vigorously*. There's action and monster-punching galore, sometimes with airships and mech upgrades, sometimes with monster girl gamers, but always with a substantial side of harem and fun-for-all-involved graphic *spice*. (Which is to say, it's super NSFW. Unless your workplace is, like, *really* cool.)

✧✧✧

**Jack Clemons** was a paladin and a master storyteller. A comic who possessed deep emotional intelligence and invented the "My Bad $20" and "Trap Hoodie" practices. An incredible son and a trusted big brother to his two sisters, Jack was also deeply devoted to his chosen family and loved his mother above all others. Jack knew more about firearms than many experts in the field. They trusted his recommendations. He worked at GAT Marketing in a variety of roles including head of social media. Jack Clemons passed away on May 4, 2024 and is even now in the halls of Valhalla.

✧✧✧

National best-selling author **Jason Córdova** is both a John W. Campbell Award and Dragon Award finalist (though not in the same year), and is the editor of the Baen Books anthologies *Chicks in Tank Tops* and *Dancing with Destruction*. He is also the coauthor of *Monster Hunter Memoirs: Fever* with Larry Correia, and author of the best-selling *Mountain of Fire*, a Black Tide Rising novel. Along the way, he has had his novels published in multiple languages around the world, been featured in over 40 anthologies, and has penned over two dozen other novels across multiple genres including YA, horror, science fiction, and urban fantasy. A history nerd, he is a Navy veteran, former teacher, and is currently working as an Associate Editor at Baen Books. He can be found on Twitter/X at @warpcordova, as well as his website, www.jasoncordova.com, where he updates irregularly.

✧✧✧

**Melissa Olthoff** is a science fiction and fantasy author who delights in sneaking in romance wherever she can. She is a lifelong geek and a veteran of the United States Air Force, both of which are incredibly useful when writing. Her degrees in meteorology and accounting are slightly less applicable to writing but absolutely useful when it comes to supporting her family. In 2023, she took second place in the annual Baen Fantasy Adventure Award Contest with her story "Fall from Grace" and won the Imadjinn Award Best Short Story in 2023 and 2024. She is published by Baen, Chris Kennedy Publishing, Hit World Press, and Three Ravens Publishing, and is best known for her novels in the Griffin Corps, Four Horsemen Universe, the Blood & Armor Series, the Salvage Title Universe, and Hit World Valkyries, as well as numerous short stories. She can be found at melissaolthoff.com, baen.com, chriskennedypublishing.com, Facebook, Twitter, Instagram, and on her Amazon Author Page.

✧✧✧

**Jody Lynn Nye** lists her main career activity as "spoiling cats." When not engaged upon this worthy occupation, she writes fantasy and science fiction, most of it in a humorous bent. Since 1987 she has published over 50 books and more than 200 short stories. She has also written with notables in the industry, including Anne McCaffrey and Robert Asprin. Jody teaches writing seminars at SF conventions, including the two-day intensive workshop at Dragon Con, and is Coordinating Judge for the Writers of the Future Contest.

✧✧✧

Million-selling author **Craig Martelle** specializes in science fiction and thrillers, bringing elements of both to the other. See his body of work here—craigmartelle.com.

✧✧✧

**Marisa Wolf** is a second-generation nerd who started writing genre stories at six. Over the years she taught middle school, was headbutted by an alligator, built a career in education, earned a black belt in Tae Kwon Do, and finally decided to finish all the half-started stories in her head. She writes SFF that ends with hope, regardless of the circumstances, as shown through her coauthored novels in shared universes, solo novels in her own worlds, and a plethora of short stories. All contain various levels of snark. After several years living on the road in an RV, Marisa, her husband, and their high-maintenance rescue dog are currently based in the woods of New England—but it's anyone's guess where in the country she is at any given moment. More at www.marisawolf.net.

✧✧✧

**Casey Moores** was an Air Force Academy graduate and rescue/special ops C-130 pilot for over 17 years—airdropping, air refueling, and flying into tiny blacked-out dirt airstrips in bad places using night vision goggles. He's been to those places and done those things with those people. Now he lives a quieter life, translating those experiences to military science fiction, fantasy, alternate history, and post-apocalyptic fiction. With seven novels and over twenty published short stories, his biggest challenge is focusing on any one genre. Or focusing on anything at all, really. He won the Imadjinn award for Best Historical Fiction for *Witch Hunt*, and was part of the Helicon-award-winning anthology JTF-13 Legends anthology. He is currently developing the Blood & Armor series, a near future military science fiction series with Bill Fawcett.

✧✧✧

**Kacey Ezell** writes emotionally charged adventure fantasy and science fiction. She is a two-time Dragon Award Finalist for Best Alternate History and won the 2018 Year's Best Military and Adventure Science Fiction Readers' Choice Award. She has written multiple best-selling novels published with Chris Kennedy Publishing, Baen Books, and Blackstone Publishing. Additionally, she is a retired helicopter pilot with 3000+ hours in the UH-1N Huey, Mi-171, and EC130 helicopters. She is married with two daughters. You can join her fan community and get free stories at kaceyezell.net/the-dragons-horde/.

✧✧✧

A blue-collar truck driver from the Panhandle of Florida, **Nick Steverson** is the winner of the 2023 Imadjinn award for Best Science Fiction Novel. He has 9 novels in the soon to be cinematic Salvage Title Universe as well as multiple short stories. More of his work can be found in the Four Horsemen Universe, This Fallen World, Starflight, Ashes of Entecea Universe, Last Brigade Universe, and he also coedited the *Thirteen Stories of Horror* anthology with Three Ravens Publishing.

✧✧✧

**Michael Z. Williamson** is an immigrant from the UK and Canada, and a retired veteran of the US Army and USAF. He definitely never ran short of supplies nor engaged in shenanigans during his time in uniform. He is thankful for the VA's 17 years of expert assurance that none of his health issues are service connected.

✧✧✧

After a nearly 30 year career in Information Technology in civilian but military affiliated roles, **Jessica Schlenker** can firmly reassure those looking forward to military retirement and better funded work environments that performing miracles with tattered rolls of duct tape and broken shoes laces is still a required skill set. But no worries... the upper echelons will still get their bonuses.

✧✧✧

**Buff Orpington** is the super secret covert cover name for a pair of authors who aren't quite sure they want to have their real names associated with his nonsense. Kayfabe requires that he say nothing further.

# ABOUT THE EDITOR

**Jamie Ibson** is from the frozen wastelands of Canuckistan, where moose, bears, and geese battle for domination north of the ice wall, among the hockey rinks, igloos, and Tim Hortons. After joining the Canadian army reserves in high school, he spent half of 2001 in Bosnia as a peacekeeper and came home shortly after 9/11 with a deep sense of foreboding. After graduating college, he became a redcoat and was posted to the left coast from 2007 to 2021.

He retired from law enforcement in early 2021 and moved clear across the country to write full time in the Maritimes. He's pretty much been making it up as he goes along, although he has numerous writer friends who serve as excellent role models, mentors, and occasionally, cautionary tales.

These days, he's turned into an amateur one-stop-shop for numerous author-related services such as cover design and typesetting, as well as editing anthologies and Buff Orpington-related mischief. *Plausibly Deniable* is Jamie's eighth edited anthology. You can find out more about him at www.ibsonwrites.ca.